"If anything will sell me besides my looks," said Angelica, "it will be my horsemanship. I am more exciting in the saddle than in the waltz." And sell herself she must, to rich, little Mr. Monk. It was the only way to save the plantation and her uncle's honor.

Then Beau Berrien came riding up and watched Angelica—dirty and disheveled—struggling with her beloved Teaser, the silver-white horse with the strange blue eyes.

Their romance began as gently as a waltz, and endured through all the horrors of the Civil War.

Don't miss these and other teeming sagas of women in love and the South at war by Elizabeth Boatwright Coker
DAUGHTER OF STRANGERS
INDIA ALLAN
LA BELLE
Available where Bantam Books are sold

Blood Red Roses

*A romantic novel of
Hilton Head Island, South Carolina,
during the War Between the States*

Elizabeth Boatwright Coker

BLOOD RED ROSES

*A Bantam Book / published by arrangement with
E. P. Dutton & Company, Inc.*

PRINTING HISTORY

*Dutton edition published September 1977
Bantam edition / June 1978*

*Bantam Books are published by Bantam Books, Inc. Its trade-
mark, consisting of the words "Bantam Books" and the por-
trayal of a bantam, is registered in the United States Patent
Office and in other countries. Marca Registrada. Bantam
Books, Inc., 666 Fifth Avenue, New York, New York 10019.*

*This book is dedicated to
Lucy and Jonathan Daniels with love*

*My special thanks, for maps,
family papers and letters lent, and courtesies
shown by Mrs. Carrie Lee Kalber, Ms. Beth Littlejohn,
Rev. R. E. H. Peeples, Everybody on Hilton Head, Misses
Edith and Charlotte Inglesby, my cousin, Louise Alexander,
Emily Badham Coxe; Jon Jicha, my mapmaker; finally
Aunt Ethel, for happy childhood summers in her
Bluffton cottage on the River May.*

Librarians and historians were helpful and patient.

*Cotton Hall and Cedar Grove, though fictional,
are prototypes of actual plantations. The principal story
characters, except the Elliotts, are fictional. The
military and island people were really there.*

Blow down, You Blood Red Roses, Blow Down

BOATMAN:	Out on the river in wind and rain
ROWERS:	Blow down, you Blood Red Roses, blow down
BOATMAN:	Your chest get cold and your back get strain
ROWERS:	Blow down, you Blood Red Roses, blow down
BOATMAN:	Oh, you pinks and poesies
ROWERS:	Blow down, you Blood Red Roses, blow down
BOATMAN:	I give you word: To sea must run
ROWERS:	Blow down, you Blood Red Roses, blow down
BOATMAN:	Chasing sharks in the midday sun
ROWERS:	Blow down, you Blood Red Roses, blow down
BOATMAN:	Master drink rum but your throat stay dry
ROWERS:	Blow down, you Blood Red Roses, blow down
BOATMAN:	Your head hurt so you wants to die
ROWERS:	Blow down, you Blood Red Roses, blow down
BOATMAN:	Last night that yellow girl call your name
ROWERS:	Blow down, you Blood Red Roses, blow down
BOATMAN:	Your heart do sing and your pulse do flame
ROWERS:	Blow down, you Blood Red Roses, blow down
BOATMAN:	You pull for home don't want no rest
ROWERS:	Blow down, you Blood Red Roses, blow down
BOATMAN:	And lie all night on her soft gold breast
ROWERS:	Blow down, you Blood Red Roses, blow down

Note: "Blood Red Roses" was a sea chantey from the early 1800s. Sometimes it was sung "blow down," sometimes "row down." It was used to pace the strokes of the rowers.

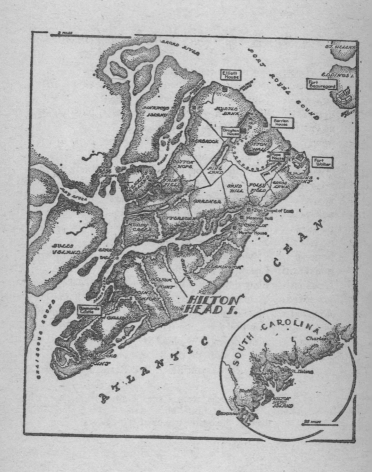

Part One

The Fox

*The Cedars, Albemarle County, Virginia,
October, 1860*

One

Everything was upside down at Cedar Grove Plantation in Albemarle County, Virginia, on the 13th day of October, 1860. My whole delightful, wonderful world was about to come to a bad end suddenly as Aunt Dell had constantly warned me it would when I was overexcited as a child. Ironically this was going to happen because of my noble gesture: agreeing to Aunt Dell's velvet-veiled suggestions that I immediately marry a rich man who will adore me enough to pay off Uncle Jim's tobacco and racing debts, saving his honor as well as the plantation.

It was my duty to do this awful thing. Papa put me in Aunt Dell's arms minutes after I was born. Barely hesitating to give the farewell kiss to her younger sister's corpse, Aunt Dell rushed out of the room, to show me to Uncle Jim, who was Papa's elder brother. I don't believe it ever occurred to them thereafter that they hadn't conceived me themselves.

Oh, how I will hate that rich husband. Aunt Dell insists that if he isn't a thoroughly bad hat I will learn to like him well enough after the children start coming. My precious little half-sister, Amun, who is frail, can be the one of us to marry for love.

Misfortune struck The Cedars this past May when Uncle Jim wagered a great part of the plantation on one of his racehorses. In the match the gallant animal broke his leg and had to be destroyed. In July the tobacco crop was shredded by hail. Then in August the cider house burned down and the apple harvest rotted on the ground. In September a heavy storm broke in the night. The James River roared like the ocean and went over its banks. Rain filled the outbuildings and barns and fields. The boats were all swimming in the boathouse. An enormous oak tree upended and crushed the whiskey still. Six skilled tobacco field slaves ran away.

To cap his bad luck Uncle Jim was so exhilarated by the way the "Chosen," wealthy Mr. Monk, of the Eastern Shore of Maryland, looked at me at supper last night that he drank so many bumpers of wine on top of brandy, hallooing and toasting first the hunt, then jolly Mr. Page, the Master, then Mr. Monk's racehorses, one after another, that on finally setting out to resume his chair at the head of the table, he misjudged the distance and fell hard on the floor.

After silently watching him make a few unsuccessful tries at rising, Aunt Dell languidly summoned Great Peter, our head house Negro, to carry him off. Great Peter laid him on his four poster bed from which in this October daydawn he was shouting orders.

I was dressed in my expensive new green velvet riding habit, determined to make the most of Mr. Monk's interest, even though he is a full head shorter than I and one of his eyes rolls around in its socket.

Mr. Page, Uncle Jim's best friend, aware of his financial difficulties, arranged this hunt today just so Mr. Monk could watch me take Parasol, my peppery mare, over the fences. If anything will sell me besides my looks it will be my horsemanship. I am more exciting in the saddle than in the waltz for, though fine-boned and graceful, I am almost six feet which is a trifle too tall for most gentlemen to be able to look down into my eyes.

As I finished adjusting my plumed hat and a sheer veil over my face I heard our horsekeeper, Jason Jenks, in Uncle Jim's room. I flew down. Jenks was saying it had to be today or never. Bonnie Bet had fooled him. This could be the end of her heat, not the beginning. He'd turned the teaser horse into the next run to get her frolicky and excited, ready for *her* chosen: the big bay stallion, which Uncle Jim had mortgaged the now-extinct tobacco crop to obtain to stand for a season. The bay was in the pen raring to go, said Jenks. A wonder we hadn't heard him neighing in the night.

"What's happening?" In my haste I stumbled over my long skirttrail.

"You're supposed to hook it over your wrist," Aunt Dell's voice came from somewhere in the dim room.

Uncle Jim shouted, "What's happening indeed! This clod, Jenks, has had the gall to suggest that if I can't walk, you give up hunting and cope with the teaser when Bonnie Bet is taken from him to the bay. My proud beauty! What villain would deprive the huntsmen of such a vision?"

Jenks stood staunchly on his thick young legs. "There'll be two hunts a week, Mr. Burwell, from now until late spring. Miss Angel's the only one the teaser won't harm at such a time as today, you excepting, of course, sir."

"Just give me a minute to take off this endless riding habit, Jenks."

"Do." Uncle Jim wrathfully lifted his bushy salt and pepper head from the pillow. "I've changed my mind. If we miss breeding Bonnie Bet we're out of the racing and the tobacco business."

"Don't fret, darling. I'll enjoy taking part." I was already unpinning my hat.

I could see Aunt Dell now, rocking in a cane chair by the woodfire, nightcapped and wrappered in flowered flannel. She said how could I, her own niece, think of taking part in a going-on like that. I said I didn't intend to take part in the actual going-on but what if our teaser got out of control and jumped the fence and got to Bonnie Bet as he was so capable of doing? Was Aunt Dell eager to go to the poorhouse?

Uncle Jim said, "Don't argue with that fool girl, Mrs. Burwell. She's well aware of what's expected of her. But the crazy way she is about the teaser she'll probably open the gate and slip him to Bet first. Her pity for the underdog will be the ruin of her yet. Help me up, Jenks. God damn you—my back's broken for sure." He fell back, groaning.

Great Peter tiptoed in with a silver mug of warm

rye whiskey and sugar water and supported Uncle Jim while he drank. "Be gentle now, Master. Miss Angel knows what's fitten for a lady. She won't go no further than the run; not Miss Angel."

Jenks, his yellow whiskers standing out from his rosy cherub cheeks, spoke to me across the bed. "He's slipped a joint, Miss Angel. This ain't the first time. Usually he manages to hide it from you all. We rub him with liniment at the stables and loosen him up. But today he's worse than I've ever seen him. You take off that pretty green skirt and put on something real old. The runs are a bog of mud."

Uncle Jim waved his hand. It was trembling. I took it and squeezed it hard, saying, "Mr. Monk wouldn't do for me, Uncle Jim. You might as well know that I saw him nodding when I played the Chopin waltzes after supper. I'll be very careful around dear Teaser."

"I don't trust you, Angelica. Not when your emotions are involved. You're too much like your father. He could always be counted on to behave rashly and grieve about it later."

"If you don't trust Angelica, Mr. Burwell, tell her to pin her hat back on and gallop to the Inn where the hunt is this minute assembling." Aunt Dell had risen and put her arm around my waist. She was a tall listless looking lady with marked remains of beauty. She was listless because she never took any exercise. Her green eyes glittered when lighted with interest, which was seldom. Most of the time she had a vague stare whether she was talking or not. Today was no exception.

Jenks was going out through the door into the hall. "I say, Mr. Burwell, I'll not let Miss Angel nowhere near the pen. The teaser needs her."

"And *I* say, Mr. Burwell," Aunt Dell's eyes were staring at nothing in the fringed bed canopy, "Mr. Monk and his money are more important to Angelica *and* us than the teaser."

Suaged by his hot toddy, Uncle Jim raised up on his elbow, "And *I* say, Mrs. Burwell, that unknown to you I've wagered everything on a successful crop of foals next year. A get of Bonnie Bet and the Sir Archy bay, unrun, will bring enough to pay off the wager on The Cedars. Once the colt runs, Angelica can be an old maid and spend her life with the teaser if she so chooses. Hurry, girl, they are waiting for you at the stables."

A light frost had fallen in the night. The ridge horizon was robed in a haze of dream-stuff blue. I heard the melody of the huntsman's sweet-toned copper horn and the belling of the hounds. As the hunt distanced I thought, well, there goes the best chance I'll probably ever have to pay the bills for my fine coming-out clothes and help Uncle Jim settle his debts. When Mr. Monk vanishes there's nobody around here rich enough for me to set my cap for. We'll be bankrupt by New Year's whether we breed Bonnie Bet or not.

A high-crouped, Roman-nosed white stallion with light blue eyes and long silver lashes, the teaser was a kind horse; big but light in his movement. His registered name in the stud book was Eclipse's Silver King but I called him Teaser because I loved him. Usually he ran up to greet me, but today it took over half an hour of his racing up and down and whickering after her who had been led away to the breeding pen before he realized she had truly disappeared. There remained only I, in a shabby, mud-spattered Balmoral skirt and wool sacque holding out handfuls of sweet feed and apples.

Teaser had impeccable bloodlines but Uncle Jim had a horror of a white colt with blue eyes. Teaser had been an accident that befell Silver Star, full sister to Kitty Fisher. Silver Star was one of Uncle Jim's most prolific grey brood mares. Five years ago, a grey hunter of Mr. Randolph's ran away and vaulted the six-foot fence surrounding the east pasture where Silver Star was trotting along with her two-week-old black filly. Jenks had found her and the hunter there grazing together but no one suspected what had gone on before until Silver Star began making nests in the hay in her stall a week before she dropped Teaser.

One look at the poor shivery little creature had

been enough for Uncle Jim. The two greys had made an albino! The best fate I was able to bargain for him doomed him to frustration whenever the breeding pen was active.

But every now and then I loaned him to Farmer Grundy, who considered himself lucky to get, free of charge, white colts descended from the great Eclipse. Teaser was the swiftest moving, boldest jumper in our entire stable.

There was a lot of commotion beyond the near barn where the breeding pen was set up. This was the nearest I'd ever come to the "going-on" as Aunt Dell called it. Hog killing and horse breeding were secret rites. Ladies and children stayed behind drawn curtains at such times. If Jenks saw me so near he'd order me back to the house. I picked my path through the mud and into the barn, staying close against the stalls.

Through the light at the end of the runway I saw Jenks and four black men coming with the big bay. The stallion was plunging and throwing his head, snorting clouds of steam through his dilated nostrils. His eyes were fiery, his breathing loud. He struck the soft earth with his hard hoofs. Bonnie Bet, held by two black stablehands, was kicking with her back feet and thrashing her well-set flaxen tail back and forth in the stallion's face; suddenly she threw her tail far to one side.

He was just about to——

"Angelica! Hurry!"

I could have killed the beloved caller. "Amun! What are you doing here? Don't you know what's taking place? Get back to the house."

"Aunt Dell and Uncle Jim want you at once. It's an emergency."

I caught the hand my tiny blonde half-sister held out and fled with her to the rambling old strawberry-colored brick house.

The spare chilly entrance hall had funny cane settees pushed back against the wainscoting. On one side of the hall was a gracious drawing room and a library; on the other, Uncle Jim's bedroom and the dining room.

In the dining room a dripping chandelier of blue Bohemian crystal hung over a Sheraton table that could seat twenty-four people. Aunt Dell never shortened it. The high-backed leather-covered chairs had come from Holland a hundred and fifty years ago. That the leather was worn and scuffed thin was no matter. They had accommodated so many important bottoms they would look superior so long as one tatter of leather was left.

Amun kept chattering about a letter as we ran through the weedy, formal garden hedged with unclipped cedars. I hadn't listened but was aware that great news had come when I saw Aunt Dell in a closebordered tarleton cap, seated at the head of the dining table. She was wearing her widest hoop under her least-shiny grey taffeta day gown. Her green eyes glittered as she waved some rumpled sheets of paper in my direction.

"We're saved!"

"Let's go into Uncle Jim's room. I'd rather hear about it when he does."

"He's savored every word already. Great Peter is shaving him now. He's going to make an heroic effort to put his trousers on and be brought out into the drawing room."

Two

The Meeting Street House
Charleston, S. C.
October 7, 1860

My dear Adelia,

There is only one subject discussed a days in Charleston, SECESSION! The resolution to quit these United States consumes everybody. Throughout South Carolina men of all stations in life sit together under spreading oaks talking about it. I doubt you could find more than a handful of Up Country souls who agree with Mr. Pettigrew and Mr. Calhoun that we should put up with Yankee meddling in our private affairs any longer. What impudence! In *their* sailing ships *they* fetched the blacks here from Africa. Now that they've pocketed *our* money their pious preachers demand that *we* set them free! To the devil with them, as dear Papa would have said.

There are no mosquitoes today. A cool wind is blowing in from the ocean. I wish you were here to enjoy it with me. Everything is exactly the same in Papa's house as when you and Isabella were rowed up from Beaufort to become the belles of the Ball twenty years ago and met those two outrageous Virginia boys. Pretty as you were why couldn't you have lit on richer catches? The red and white camellia you wore in your hair that night is already showing color in the garden. The mansion retreats of the rice planters are still the finest ornaments of our dear city; but you should see the splendid waterfront summer palaces the sea island cotton planters are now putting up. Which brings me to the point of this correspondence.

Aunt Dell turned to the second page, muttering, "She was always feather brained, was Aunt Beck. Secession! Who cares about that? And new houses!

Don't kick my chair, Amun. What ails you, Angelica?"

"I'm worried about the teaser. If he gets too nervous he'll break loose somehow and start a fight with
the other stallion. I'll hear the letter later."

"Sit still and listen. Aunt Beck says:

Baynard Elliott Berrien of Cotton Hall Plantation
on Hilton Head, S.C., sailed into town about a month
ago and took up residence at the Charleston Hotel. He
resembles his late father, our Cousin Hazzard, being
six and a half feet high and considering Hilton Head
Island more important than Charleston. Have you
ever known such gall?

But, lacking Hazzard's rude conceit, Beau, as he is
called, possesses an almost royal presence heightened
by the rufous coloring and the bold hooked nose that
have been in the Berrien family since the Crusades.
His fiery brown eyes give him alternately the look of
a sly fox or a swooping hawk. It's difficult to describe
him. He's different from anybody we ever had in the
family before.

The ladies flock after him, those from the uptown
back streets as well as ones of our kind. Tales of his
wildness where wine and women (including his
young stepmother) are concerned have been whispered behind fans ever since he returned from his
studies at Harvard College six years ago. He never
noticeably refuses the role gossiped about; if folks
choose to be shocked he generally obliges. But since
his father's death and his inheritance of the Berrien
fortune, his eccentricities are called quaint and amus-
ing. His friends say that under the dwindling bouts of
carryings-on he has improved, changed considerably,
except for being unpredictable.

Aged twenty-five, he plants cotton on Hilton Head
Island and St. Helena Island and Fripp Island and
along the River May. Lord knows the extent of the
Berrien holdings in blacks *and* cotton land in Mississippi.

He possesses parts as well. His peers speak him as
the finest deer and waterfowl shot in the Low Country, a magnificent horse rider, a careful father 'in

locus' to his three younger brothers, and properly proud of his Huguenot heritage.

Did Beau hold the reputation for being too often in his cups or for cruelty to his slaves as did his father I would not be writing you. As you know, our Cousin Julia, this boy's mother, broke her heart and health over it. They say the second Mrs. Berrien knew how to cope with Hazzard. She rarely, if ever, set foot on a sea island plantation, and let her husband lie wherever his drinking flung him. Beaufort keeps an aloof distance, she having managed to make enemies of every family connection. So far as I know Hazzard only brought her to one Ball in Charleston. I was serving the oyster stew that night so merely glimpsed her. Mainly I remember that she had too much hair and the way she kept fidgeting with her diamonds and her raspy Northern voice complaining that Southern ladies didn't appeal to her.

I mention this because it struck me as odd for Beau, on his first visit, to bluntly state his reason for calling: I must help him find a suitable bride! Have you ever? He is anxious to marry and settle down before war clouds darken the horizon.

"War?" I asked.

"Of course, Madame," he answered firmly. "You aren't under the illusion that the North will let South Carolina depart in peace, are you?"

Not caring to pursue unpleasant subjects I returned to his request. "Why me, rather than your stepmother?"

"Frankly because I don't want Elsa to know a damn thing about it."

He chose me as his mentor having often heard his mother speak of me as THE Grand Dame of Charleston!

Flattered, I arranged dinners and teas for him in the best houses and he went through all the motions of the proper courtier. Ten days ago he gave me his reaction to the Misses Ravenel, Middleton, Chisolm, Prioleau, Stoney, Heyward and Alston: though Miss R had gorgeous blue eyes she also had brown spots on her teeth; Miss M fell off her horse and cried; Miss C affronted him, reading aloud vulgar poems by a fellow named Whitman; Miss P pretended to faint when he bit the tip of her ear as they were waltzing; Miss S constantly fanned and giggled; Miss H had an offensive odor; and Miss A had thick ankles.

I was about to send him packing. After all I'd spent the better part of a month at his disposal and so far he'd only presented me with a silver rice spoon. But suddenly I thought of you. Angelica's heron-like beauty has been carefully reported in Charleston by several young gentlemen who have recently hunted in your area. Already I have received six requests for the pleasure of escorting her to my Oyster Roast at the Cooper River Plantation in February!

However, knowing that things have not gone well for you and Jim of late, I have given Beau Berrien directions about arriving at The Cedars and have been advised that he left on the cars for Richmond October 6, thinking to procure a mount from his Cousin Harrison there and ride on to you. Expect him on the 13th or 14th.

I would have alerted you earlier but have had a spell of quinsy which Dr. deSassaure has finally cured. Bid Angelica wash well and drench herself with attar of roses. If she has spots on her teeth, scrape them off or pull them out. Advise her to read aloud from the Bible, if she must confess to reading at all. She must not resort to tricks with her fan nor should she faint unless the occasion merits it. For the last, if she has fat legs, keep her pantalettes well down to her slippers until the wedding band is securely around her finger.

In return for presenting this *opportunity*, I will ask a favor of *you*. Mama's branched silver candlestick made by Ebenezer Coker in London in the last century has been much admired in my parlor. Would you send me the mate Papa gave *you* for a wedding gift? From your letters it appears you entertain few except horse people.

Write me at once what happens with the Chevalier Berrien. I am always at your service, dearest niece, with affection and appreciation of all you have done for me and my grandniece, Angelica, throughout the years. I remain

Fondly,
Rebecca Bacot

P.S. What of Landon's other daughter whom Jim has
made you bring up? I refer to the half-Jamaican with
the funny name that sounds like a nut."

"Why does Aunt Beck call me a nut?" asked Amun.
"She's talking about almonds, silly; and she isn't
your Aunt Beck." Aunt Dell put down the pages
and looked sharply at me. "I thought you'd be wild
with excitement."

I squeezed Amun's arm to say I loved her. "A fox—
A hawk? I'll take silly Mr. Monk."

"Your mother and I played with Beau's aunt in his
grand house in Beaufort when we were children. I
would love for you to be mistress there."

I could feel my hair slipping down from its net.
"I simply *must* put Teaser into his stall."

"Don't go back out there, darling, you look worn
out."

"I've been running ever since dawn. What time is
it now?"

"Ten o'clock. Do make haste. The South Carolina
Hamptons are stopping by for dinner on their way
from White Sulphur Springs after visiting the Prestons. Mr. Page has sent word that Mr. Monk was so disappointed at your not showing up for the hunt he's
going to stay over and hunt tomorrow. They will be
here for dinner, along with Azilee and Lizora Bizarre.
You'll have to watch out for that Lizora. She looks
stunning in riding dress and she's poor too. Oh, everything is working out perfectly. The Walkers are here
already, playing whist in the drawing room."

"Lizora Bizarre makes me feel awkward. She knows
it and always stands close to me to show off my tallness by her littleness."

"That makes thirteen people at table, Aunt Dell,"
Amun said.

"Then you'll eat in the kitchen, Miss Puss."

"If the rich fox gets here in time *he* will save me."
Amun nodded her round little head shining with
cropped flaxen hair, she having had typhoid fever last
summer.

Aunt Dell airily waved a silver teaspoon. "He'll get

here. I've got one of my hunches. If he isn't here by three I'll delay dinner till four then five then six o'clock. I've ordered Great Peter to fill the gentlemen up with grog and the ladies with a concoction of brandy and sugar water. Competition between Beau and Mr. Monk will turn the trick. You must wear Mrs. Meriweather's blue silk, Angelica. It makes your eyes glisten like morning glories."

I had never seen Aunt Dell so enthusiastic. Nor have I ever felt more wretchedly desolate. "He won't like Chopin and I don't like pompous asses."

"His mother played for Chopin in Paris when she was a girl. And Chopin listened! He rarely did, you know."

"I'll tell Dinah to fix you a bath in the big tub. You've got to smell good. You smell pukey now." Amun was jigging around excitedly on her skinny legs.

"You go on like a jackanapes." Aunt Dell tapped Amun's sharp little shoulder with the spoon. Her eyes took on the glittery look again. "Hepzibah is boiling our last three-year-old forty-pound ham. There's a white-faced sheep on the fire and all those wild geese and ducks you and Jenks shot day before yesterday; *and* a turkey gobbler and a dozen pullets and hominy and sweet potatoes and syllabub and lemon ice cream."

I couldn't stand any more. I rushed away through the kitchen, which was filled with chattering black women and quick little mulatto serving boys in white long-sleeved aprons, with red and white turbans on their heads. They were egg whipping, butter creaming, meat basting, raisin stoning, salad chopping, sugar pounding, biscuit beating, fowl picking, silver polishing, napkin folding, wine cooling and things like that.

There was no doubt about it, Aunt Dell had executive talent. She had put everybody, except me, to a task they could happily accomplish. In her book, today was one of life's great occasions to which, without appearing to do anything at all, she planned to rise superbly. It was maddening.

When I reached the lot it was obvious that Teaser was determined not to be put into his stall. His game of catch-me-if-you-can had a peculiar effect on me. Being on the edge of hysteria, I burst out laughing. Recklessly jumping up to catch his halter I stepped on my skirt and tore it half off. Still laughing I admired my shapely leg and didn't duck away from a clod of mud Teaser's forefoot kicked up. It smeared all over my forehead. This was the last straw.

"Come here, you damned demon!"

The unfamiliar, screaming tone of my voice arrested him. He quieted, nuzzling my shoulder with his long soft lips.

"You funny old horse." Exhausted, I leant my cheek against his lathered neck. "You poor funny old horse."

Three

"No funnier than you."

I recognized him immediately up there against the sky, looking like an over-life-sized equestrian statue in an exaggerated stovepipe hat. Did he go all the way up into the hat? Apparently he did for when he lifted it off he was still the tallest human I'd ever seen in a saddle.

Dismounting, he bowed smartly, "Baynard Berrien, at your service, dear lady."

Teaser tensed, pricked up his new-moon ears and neighed angrily. As the giant secured his mount to a post and, waving his hat, headed toward the gate, Teaser wheeled away from me and galloped along the rail, sending mud and stones flying right and left as he went.

"Climb through the fence quick, you idiot. I've panicked him."

The gate opened and Teaser made for the space to escape.

"Hoa, there. Hoa, you scoundrel," the newcomer roared, jamming his hat back on.

Teaser was on his way to freedom. I kept running and calling, "Mr. Berrien! Mr. Berrien!" knowing Teaser saw only the open gate and not the man blocking his escape.

The thought of those powerful hoofs and huge hard teeth crumbling that magnificent specimen into a muddy-bloody mess undid me. I kept on shrieking and screaming. Teaser was upon him. I froze, paralyzed. For a few seconds of hideous noises it was man against horse. Then a yell; then a squeal; a jerk; and it was all over.

Teaser snorted and kicked and snapped his teeth like castanets. Flecks of foam exploded from his nostrils.

The Chevalier Berrien, his whole powerful body turning flexibly, iron arms taut, Wellington boots planted ankle-deep in the mud, hung on to the halter as the stallion plunged and reared.

"You're killing him," I gasped, stumbling and slipping as I ran, "you're killing him."

"Better him than me," he shouted. His linen shirt frill was ruined; his cravat gone; his sleeves torn from the shoulder seams of his tight fitting fawn broadcloth coat.

As I reached up to snatch the rope away from him my hand came in contact with a hairy wrist above a sodden chamois glove. Flame from the bare reddish flesh darted into my fingers, ran up my arm, through my armpits, tightening and thrusting my breasts toward this wild man. He was the fox! I heard his rapid heartbeats; and mine.

"What in blazes were you doing fooling around with this crazy stallion. Do you work here?" he asked, breathing heavily.

He thought I was a stable hand! My weariness vanished. My audacity and courage returned. "My uncle works here. I was on a special assignment to lock up the teaser. They're breeding the finest Burwell mare over beyond the big barn. Teaser wouldn't hurt me. He loves me."

"Which goes to show you know nothing of the male sex when he is deprived of his rights. Where the hell are my cigars? In the mud, dammit. Come on, I'll lock him up. Lead the way to his stall. He won't make any more trouble. He's met his match and knows it."

Teaser did too. Capriciously he snapped at a mass of flying russet hair. My rich prospect was about to be scalped! But, not liking the taste, Teaser let go and whickering, head down, gave a playful hoist of his back feet and lightly picked his way behind us through the muck toward his stall.

As the bolt dropped into place the newcomer said, "Even in this disheveled state I must present my compliments to the Burwells. First, I'll stable my dull mount, then I'll look in on the breeding. See if the horses are as ill cared for as the land. Then I'll be

forced to endure an endless dinner full of conversation about Virginia people I never heard of. After that
I'll slip away and take tea with you."

"How will you find me?"

"Your uncle will direct me. I'll make friends with
him at the breeding pen. Don't worry; I'll not divulge
my wicked designs on you. I'll tell him I might drop
in on him later and talk horses."

"You can't miss him. He has yellow hair and bushy
yellow sideburns. His name is Jenks. The stall on the
end is empty. I'll see that your horse is fed."

After Mama died, Papa sailed away to the West
Indies and married a Miss Thorpe who owned a sugar
plantation. When word came that they had drowned
in the hurricane of 1847 but their little daughter was
alive, Uncle Jim made haste to Jamaica and fetched
Amun back to Virginia. Aunt Dell took one look at
the rickety five-year-old girl who had a fairy air about
her, and went into a decline, declaring I was her own
flesh and blood and the child of her heart, but she
was too delicate to take on this weakling who not
only was no kin to her at all but only held to this
earth by the thinnest thread.

So Uncle Jim bought a nurse from a family in
Charlottesville. She was an unamiable yellow woman
named Dinah Glass who claimed to be descended
from Thomas Jefferson and never let us forget it.
Dinah looked down her long sharp nose on all of us,
except Amun. She insisted that Amun was one of the
little people, blessed of the Lord.

I was luxuriating in the fragrant bath Amun had
arranged for me in the water closet when the noon
plantation bell rang. An oak fire was crackling cheerfully. In my bedroom, my maid, Nannie, and another maid were ironing and singing. Dinah, muttering, kept pouring hot water into the tin tub and
trying to make Amun go outside and play.

"No call for you to stand there staring at Miss
Angel, Missy, like as if she was a picture. She's
nothing but a plain naked female woman. Nothing."

Dinah had been jealous from the beginning of my

affection for Amun. She never pretended to like me nor I her.

"Angelica is a beautiful lady, Dinah. Say something nice to her for once. Please. Just for me." Amun dripped a few drops of cologne on my shoulder and rubbed it around my neck.

Dinah lifted her nose contemptuously and simpered, in her imitation of the way Aunt Dell talked, "Well, I must admit, that among all my fine friends and relations I never saw skin to equal Miss Angel's. It's like a round bowl I touched once at Monticello; alabaster it was made of. The Master would put a candle inside it and it glistened like Miss Angel's backsides do. Then there was an ivory Chinee lady on the mantle, lying on her side, buck naked too. There; don't ask no more favors of me today, Missy."

"You're just being truthful for a change." To annoy Dinah, I turned on my side; "Is this how the Chinese lady looked?"

Amun and I giggled.

"Hum. Hum. Hum. That ghost horse sure has got you fired up. Never saw a woman in love with a horse before. You oozing happy juice the same as common folks. A disgrace you are in front of this innocent child."

"I love to see her looking so happy." Amun bent down and kissed my lips.

I was tempted to throw the soapy wash rag in Dinah's mulatto face but I didn't dare. She might throw it back at me. All the Negroes on the place, even Great Peter, were afraid of her. They said she had the evil eye. Nannie and the other maid, listening, stopped singing as Dinah tried to put the evil eye on me; tried to shrivel me: "My grandmother used to say nothing is really beautiful but useless things."

"Angelica's not useless. She's been working hard all day."

"Then she's not beautiful. You proved it yourself." Dinah's mean laughter sounded like a cackling hen. Then, seeing Amun's pointy chin quivering, she said,

"I'm teasing, sugar pie. Look at her smooth white back stretching itself out like a velvety cat."

Dinah *was* a witch. *She* knew I was thinking voluptuous thoughts. But no one could know they were of a hard sinewy wrist dusted over with fox-colored hairs. The wild surprise of it. Or that, romantic and sentimental, I was secretly erecting a sanctuary, a temple within me in which the idol of my soul would dwell.

Amun sensed it. "You've got to tell me why you are so glowy. You hated the idea of the new beau in the letter and last night you hated Mr. Monk." Playfully she pinched my big toe with her dainty fingers.

Curling my toe around her middle finger I sat up straight: "Hark! Can't you hear? My destiny is at this very moment passing through the periwinkle patch. The question of my life is about to be decided."

Amun darted away to see if what I said was true.

Four

Last year, at a Hunt Breakfast, Aunt Dell invented a horrid game. She put all the guests' names on slips of paper and passed them around. We were told to anonymously write our opinion of the person whose name we had drawn. When mine came out of Uncle Jim's hard hunting hat it read: "Angelica uses too much physical charm."

Now I do but then I wasn't aware of having any. My tallness had made me consider myself an ugly duckling.

There was only one other lady who rode with the hunt so tall as I. She was very old and proud. Her name was Mrs. Meriweather. She had lived in all the great capitals of Europe. She fancied me and often invited me to tea. One winter afternoon, after we'd drunk our tea and I'd played a new Strauss waltz on her piano, she made me try on the costume she'd worn when she was presented to Napoleon and his Empress. It was blue silk watered with silver with a small train that she showed me how to flick up with my heel. Her French-trained maid undid my heavy chignon and piled my hair high on my head in an elegant, faintly disheveled way. That dress and coiffeur changed my whole outlook. She led me to a long mirror. I straightened up and believed her when she told me I was the most beautiful girl she'd ever seen in Virginia.

After my bath, Nannie and I concentrated on fixing my hair like that again. Nannie was securing the last pin when Amun came flying back in.

"He wasn't in the periwinkles; he was changing his clothes right down the hall. I saw him come out of the door and told him who I was. He asked me if I was eight years old. He said his little brother, who is eight, could skin the cat on his arm. I said I could too. He held his arm out straight. It felt like doing it on a tree limb. You should feel his muscles. When I told him I was fifteen he asked me if I was a dwarf. Oh I do hope he is your destiny."

Dinah reared her small head up on her long thin neck. "Be ashamed, Missy, to even think about men's muscles and you just begun being a woman. Miss Angel always has had a bad influence on you. Let's get out of here. I've finished ironing your new yellow hoop-skirted dress. At least *you* will look like a lady."

Ignoring Dinah, Amun ran her hands down the blue tissue silk of my dress. "Your bosoms are going to fall out if you aren't careful. Why aren't you wearing a hoop? Everybody else will be."

"I like being different. This is an Empire mode. Napoleon's Josephine made it fashionable. The train makes me feel like an empress."

"You look lovely." Amun blew me a kiss as I ran down the stairs.

Nobody was in the hall; murmurs came from the drawing room. I tried to make out Beau's voice but the doors were too thick. I opened one a tiny crack. The drawing room was filled with rickety Chippendale and Sheraton chairs and sofas scattered about on faded Turkey carpets. Flanking the ceiling-high mantelpiece were two tall cabinets made of cherry wood. These were full of silver cups and waiters and bowls won by Burwell horses. The cracked green plaster walls were barely discernible under myriad hunting scenes and horse paintings and dark portraits of bewigged ancestors and their powdered ladies.

The only modern portrait was one of me at the age of five in a white tarleton dress with a blue sash, holding a whip, sitting on a white pony. Uncle Jim had sold a prize filly to pay Mr. Sully for doing it.

The Walkers, more Hamptons and Prestons than were expected, Aunt Dell and Uncle Jim were collected in front of the fireplace, listening to the newcomer.

Beau had on a wasp-waisted, sky-blue swallow-tail coat, showing a white ruffled shirt with a pointed collar so high it pushed his chin forward. His cravat was cream colored and his tight cream-colored trousers were strapped under very pointed-toed black patent leather slippers. He was waving a lacy handkerchief, saying he'd been distressed at the poor condition of the land he'd travelled through from Richmond. Especially in this county.

Mrs. Walker said he should see her greenhouse. She had three fruiting orange trees in it.

He said he was talking about crops, not *folies*.

Uncle Jim said he was aware tobacco exhausted the soil. All Virginians were cognizant of that but tobacco brought in more money than anything else, enough more, in his opinion, for the wearing out of the land. He sounded very irritable.

Beau said why didn't Virginians look into the use of fish heads and bird droppings and things like that. He even made good use of rotted marsh canes to cover his land as well as guano.

It was time for me to interrupt. I gave my train a flick-up and, confidenced, glided in.

"Two gentlemen of South Carolina on the same day! How fortunate."

I had hunted with Mr. Wade Hampton and his son Preston at White Sulphur Springs last summer. He reminded me of it gallantly.

Uncle Jim pulled me down, whispering, "What kind of creation do you have on? How can you show so much and keep so much hidden? Take Mr. Monk. The big fellow fancies himself too highly."

Aunt Dell said, "This is your cousin, Baynard Berrien, Angelica. We call him Beau. He and the Hamptons are old friends and he shared quarters with the Walkers' nephew at Harvard. Isn't that exciting?"

Beau gave a snappy bow from his pinched-in waist. "Have I not had the honor of touching this dainty hand before? Or has it spent the morning in perfumed cream to reach such smooth perfection?"

Taken off guard I looked up (a novelty for me) into wickedly sharp eyes.

Before I could think of a clever reply the front door opened and the huntsmen were among us enthusing over three foxes found and the best run of the season. Lizora Bizarre's golden curls were fetchingly blown about under her tiny black velvet hat. Her round-hipped figure was obvious in her snugly draped black velvet skirt.

What if I tripped over something or said something silly? Mr. Page saved me, giving me a hug and saying can that really be my friend Wade Hampton over there?

Mr. Monk, his brown beard all rumpled and his unsteady blue eyes eager as a child's, disentangled himself from the yard-long plume dripping from Lizora's hat, and took both my hands in his.

"It's a sin, Miss Angelica, for anyone to grow this much more beautiful in a mere twenty-four hours."

Towering over him, Beau took out a gold watch, snapped it open and shut. "You err, sir; it has taken exactly four hours and twenty-seven minutes."

The party came alive. Or I did. It was off to a flying start.

Nobody had any pretense nor any parlor manners. For a while everybody stood around tracing each other back to the remotest generation, then began squealing with pleasure when they discovered mutual relations. Mr. Monk still held my hands and I let him because Lizora's eyes were so envious. Beau and Mr. Page and Wade Hampton huddled together happily. Round-nosed Mr. Page was fat and tall at the same time; Wade Hampton was almost as tall as Beau and a great deal more massive. He said, "I've missed being in South Carolina in autumn having been so much in Mississippi. How are the partridges this year, Beau?"

"Plentiful; so are ducks."

Mr. Page said, "Wade brags about being the best damn shot in your state. What's your record?"

"Oh—once I killed six out of ten flying but nobody

thinks much of that kind of shooting. Mr. Hampton's grandfather, the old General, once killed ninety-six out of one hundred shots flying!"

Uncle Jim said, "Two years ago Angelica——"

Aunt Dell said, "Goodness gracious, Mr. Burwell, don't tell *that* boring story."

"Very well, then, Mrs. Burwell," Uncle Jim said huffily, "we will continue our conversation in the hall. Summon Great Peter to carry me there. It's time for a sip of grog."

Great Peter was listening, just outside the door. He came at once but Beau had already picked Uncle Jim up like a baby. Uncle Jim was frowning and sticking out his tongue at me.

Lizora and her sturdy sister, Azilee, came to my room to freshen up. Lizora said she sure was glad I'd stayed home today and given her the chance to get to know that darling Mr. Monk. She *did* like him and was *sure* he was going to invite her to the Christmas Ball in Baltimore but she *did* hope Aunt Dell let her sit by that gorgeous rich gentleman from South Carolina. And she didn't mean Mr. Hampton either.

Azilee said, "You look divine in that dress, Angelica. Will you mind if I have it copied? Don't pay any attention to Lizora. She galloped after Mr. Monk all morning. He actually cried when you didn't show up."

At three o'clock a bell rang and at three-thirty Great Peter, in knee breeches and much-mended white stockings, announced dinner.

More flushed of face and louder of voice, the gentlemen came from the hall to fetch the ladies.

All except Beau, who remained under the hanging lamp talking to Mr. Page, his head touching the glass globe, having no intention of being shut up. He was giving reasons why the South must form itself into a confederacy of states, having mutual interests, shared goals, and similar customs and dialect. The Ordinance of Secession for South Carolina had already been drawn up. Delegates from the districts and parishes were being chosen to attend the Secession

Convention in Columbia and sign it within a few weeks.

"You are convinced South Carolina will so move?" Mr. Page was saying.

"As must we," Aunt Dell interrupted, beaming with satisfaction, as Lizora hurried to Beau's side, touched his elbow and looked coquettishly up into his surprised face.

I could have killed her, but I enjoyed Beau's obvious frustration as Mr. Monk held out his arm to me.

"You have the most bewitching smile I've ever seen. How kind of you to wait for me! If I'm not seated by you I swear I'll march away from the table. You were a bad girl to duck the hunt, but it only made me more eager to see you again. Now I forgive you."

Had I been a cat I would have clawed him.

Aunt Dell swept her fan in a circle gathering her guests around her. "Will you take me in, Billy?"

Mr. William Cabell Rives of Castle Hill had stopped by less than a half hour before and been persuaded to stay. We were now nineteen. Amun was safe. She and the little Preston girl were giggling and whispering on one of the cane settees.

Great Peter stood inside the doorway holding a silver tray with a white card on it which carried everybody's name (even Mr. Rives's. How did Aunt Dell do it?) and a number. A corresponding number, worked in marigolds, was at each place beginning with Aunt Dell as number one. After a gay untangling, I found myself on Mr. Monk's left; the gold Lizora, preening herself, was beside Beau across the table.

The ham was in front of Beau; the saddle of mutton in front of excited Mr. Monk.

"After the blessing, will you two gentlemen do me the honor of carving? Poor Mr. Burwell can't do it with his back, you know," Aunt Dell purred.

"I don't carve with my back," Uncle Jim muttered, slightly blurred of tongue. "You've put on one of your blamed games. I'm on to you."

While the turkey and the geese and ducks smoked fragrantly on silver platters, the two rivals stood and attacked. Beau's face got very red but he made ham slices so thin the sunlight shone rosy brown through them; courageous Mr. Monk skillfully cut the mutton into proper wedges. It ended in a draw, both finishing at exactly the same instant. Great Peter directing, the little serving boys and quick maids passed the food and never bumped into each other or spilt sauce on anybody's sleeve. They didn't dare. Aunt Dell's martinet gaze was on each and every one of them.

Mr. Rives was recent home from his second time around as United States Minister to France. Aunt Dell encouraged him to lead the conversation. "Say something about Paris, Billy. Tell us what they are talking about in the grand salons of all those wicked French women." Aunt Dell was pretending she was a lady-in-waiting at Louis XIV's Court. She often put on this air. Uncle Jim and I grinned at each other.

As Mr. Rives smiled politely and bowed his willingness to oblige, Aunt Dell motioned everybody to be quiet and listen.

"I hope it's not going to be a long story," Mr. Monk said, adjusting his linen stock as if unless it were just so under his chin he could not start on his wedge of mutton.

"Why no, sir." Amazed, Mr. Rives shrugged his shoulders and picked up his fork.

"Because I hate those wicked French women," Mr. Monk said so emphatically I couldn't tell whether he was being sarcastic or stupid.

Aunt Dell smiled indulgently at Mr. Monk and asked him whether he hadn't spent the past July in Paris?

Mr. Monk's face took on a leery look. "All they're after is your money, those French women. And one way or another they get it."

"Especially one way," Beau laughed.

"Oh, you and Mr. Monk are such terrible men!" Lizora wiggled around on her cute little bottom, trying to cuddle as close to Beau as she could without the Virginia ladies catching on to her.

"Paris, Billy!" Aunt Dell reminded.

"The French are curious as to whether America is headed for civil war. You South Carolinians should take steps to muzzle your United States Senator, Barnwell Rhett. He's leading you straight into Secession and that will inevitably lure other states to follow and that——"

"Will inevitably lead to war," Wade Hampton said cheerfully.

Uncle Jim rose from his chair at the far end of the table. "Then of course you'll expect Virginia to help and the battles will be fought in our Valley, not in your cotton patches."

Beau banged his fist enthusiastically on the table. "We're aware of that possibility."

"Why is he making so much noise?" Mr. Monk whispered in my ear.

"Sh-h." I didn't want to miss a word.

"But," went on Wade Hampton, "the cotton states —Alabama, Georgia, Mississippi and South Carolina —have no other choice than Secession. The present tariff is ruining us. I believe I'm the largest cotton grower in the country. I sent my entire cotton crop to England to be sold last year and will again this year. I bought all my manufactured goods there as well. I'm through trading with Yankees. When the North shakes a finger at me about slavery, I open my mouth and shout back about child labor in their New England mills."

"Splendid. Splendid," called Beau, once more banging the table, ignoring Aunt Dell's frown and disapproving little coughs.

Mr. Monk sputtered through a mouthful of oysters, "I swear Maryland won't secede. We're getting along first rate. My horses won every major race in the country last spring."

Beau put down a fork on which he'd speared a whole duck breast. "Maryland's problems are not the same as ours, Mr. Monk. Neither are Virginia's, Mr.

Rives. Mr. Hampton is correct. King Cotton makes different demands. It's a question of numbers. I walked through Mr. Burwell's slave quarters today and marvelled at the tidy cabins divided in half with a good chimney in the center and nice gardens and chicken yards. I counted twelve of them. You must have forty-odd blacks at the most to take care of, Mr. Burwell. Just the number you need for this place. I have two thousand to feed, house and clothe in sickness and in health on my various cotton plantations."

Aunt Dell broke in, "Your father used to say that the Negroes lived in holes in the ground in Africa and they could do the same in America."

"I am not like my father, mam." Beau answered with a wicked smile that warned: Don't tread on me.

Azilee Bizarre said, "I read somewhere that in this whole country not more than twenty-five hundred men own as many as a hundred slaves."

"And two of them are right here at this table. My friends, I give you the gentlemen from South Carolina!" As he sat down Uncle Jim almost missed his chair again but Great Peter got there in time to save him.

Glasses tinkled gaily.

Aunt Dell said, "Barnwell Rhett was a suitor of mine in Beaufort when I was a girl. Why are you so against him, Billy?"

"I was giving my report on the French situation before the Senate in Washington a couple of weeks ago and in puffed that jackass breathing fire and brimstone, forcing everybody to listen to him. He was determined to break up the Union before I could prove that neither France nor England was going to back a Southern confederacy. He behaved as if he were a clown in an act spoiling a dignified minuet."

"Ah, the minuet!" Aunt Dell rose, tall and queenly, wearing her little cap like a crown. Waving her damask napkin to take attention away from Mr. Rives she danced the stately steps around the table, bending down to this one and that one: will you have another pickled peach? a beat biscuit to put a teeny slice of ham in? the celery's from our garden; how pretty your hair is; etc. When she came to me she pinched my ear hard.

"Stop looking at Beau like a moony calf. Flirt with Mr. Monk. Say something witty and not about war. You're going to drop your candy in the sand if you aren't careful."

Eventually she sat down and gave a sign to Great Peter, who gave a sign to the little boys, who cleared the table quickly. Then he pompously removed the top table cloth and began serving the desserts.

I hoped Beau didn't notice all the darns in the table cloth. I put my fan over a particularly large one.

Uncle Jim said he rather liked that fellow Lincoln, who was running for President. Lincoln was witty as hell and had promised not to touch slavery with a bamboo pole. The newspaper accounts of the debates between him and Douglas proved he'd be able to squelch nuisances like Barnwell Rhett in a whipstitch.

"Lincoln's a scoundrel, defend him as you wish," muttered Mr. Monk to a spoonful of ambrosia. "Don't you agree, Miss Angelica?"

Aunt Dell gave me a commanding nod.

"Do you think it will rain tomorrow?" I commented desperately.

Everybody burst out laughing.

Mr. Rives said, "Dell, you won't do. This girl's no puppet. Speak up, Angelica—what do you think of Secession?"

Flaming, but dogged, I unclenched my fist that was pushing Mr. Monk's hand off my knee. "It is enough to make one dizzy. It is as if South Carolina has gone mad."

Mr. Rives was animated. "If they don't simmer down they may find themselves homesick for the rest of their lives. I've seen what civil war has done to our class in France and its beautiful estates. They simply don't exist any more. Dead and ravaged and burnt and pillaged."

Aunt Dell paled, horror struck, but when she realized that Mr. Rives's remarks had not outraged either

South Carolinian her color came back and she told about visiting a beautiful chateau once in the Loire Valley and seeing the very stump on which the original owners, the marquis and his marquise, and their seven children had been beheaded during the French trouble of 1792.

"I don't think the North will actually cut off heads. It's not fashionable any more," Mr. Rives said. "But—"

Mr. Monk jumped up and said he'd heard a funny riddle in Baltimore and would treat us to it.

Everybody turned politely to listen, relieved to be done with headsoffs.

He began to giggle. Aunt Dell smiled encouragement to him to go on.

Why was she coddling him and cutting Beau off whenever he spoke?

"Well, why do Miss Angelica and Miss Lizora want to go to Ceylon?"

He laughed so hard he almost choked on a chestnut, which flew out of his mouth, landing on my bare forearm. It sat there like a wet bug. I wanted to knock it off but dreaded touching it.

"Why, Monk?" his host, Mr. Page, tried to help him out.

"Because there are so many Cingalese there! Have you ever heard anything so funny?" He bent over laughing.

"Yes, yes, delightful," Aunt Dell chimed in, "go on."

"That's it. Don't you get it? Single *Hes*. Like that big fellow across the table and me!"

Instead of being amused, Beau had grown more and more agitated as Mr. Monk went through his performance. The instant Mr. Monk collapsed, still laughing, into his chair, Beau put his elbow on the table and, with every muscle in his face quivering with excitement, resumed the conversation where Mr. Rives had left off.

"You were talking about what happened to the landowners of France in the Revolution. At least the proletariat didn't disguise their envy and hatred under the pretense of piety. Where they used the guillotine to accomplish their ends the North plans to annihilate us by emptying our pocketbooks; legislating to make our most profitable investment worthless."

"You refer to slavery, Mr. Berrien?"

"I do indeed. It's the hypocrisy of the North that infuriates me. When I was at Harvard College I was always on the defensive, arguing human decency and social attitudes; in other words being told that I must free my slaves instantly whatever death blow it dealt to my way of life or however responsible I felt for their welfare. Yet one morning, after a club dinner during which I had admitted to having nursed at a black woman's breast and, as a child, slept in the bed with her, I was requested by one of my Cambridge friends not to call at his mother's house on his sister thereafter. He felt the black sustenance had tainted me."

This was too much for Aunt Dell. She snapped her fan angrily, "Here comes my best dessert. You must all open your mouths and concentrate on my trifle for a little while."

"You mean, Dell," Mr. Rives shook a beautifully manicured finger at her, "keep the talk trifling?"

The second cloth was removed. Raisins and figs and almonds in silver baskets were put on the table. Wine glasses were set in front of Uncle Jim, along with six bottles of his finest wine. Soft Malmsey for the soft ladies! He filled the glasses and spun them down the polished table to each of us. The gentlemen had their choice of Port or Madeira. Talk turned mellow and relaxed.

I couldn't help myself. I tried to catch Beau's eye. He was whispering something in Lizora's ear and her mouth was an O of astonishment. "Guess what this outrageous wretch just said to me?"

Mr. Monk's knee was pressed against mine. His hand, under the table, groped around my leg. "I know," he cried gaily. "He told you how pretty you are, Miss Lizora."

Everybody laughed except me. I tensed my thigh to make my muscles refuse the squeeze.

Beau put in quickly, "Wrong, Mr. Monk. Being

obvious that fact requires no saying. My remark was
this: whenever I am out of sight of my ocean and
smell of my marsh, I am homesick. That, however,
takes nothing from the pleasure of the present. Especially this excellent Port and, Mr. Rives, the whole
problem boils down to getting and keeping. If war
comes it won't be over slavery or principle, though
that book by Mrs. Stowe has fired a lot of misguided
pity. It will be over the distribution of wealth."

Mr. Rives clapped, "Harumph Harumph, fancy a
gentleman of South Carolina saying anything *that*
cool headed and sensible."

"It makes sense to me too, Mr. Rives," Mr. Monk
put in heartily.

I saw at once that this was a mistake.

"To you!" Glaring across the table at Mr. Monk,
Beau's powerful fingers clenched around Aunt Dell's
best crystal tumbler. It cracked—ping!—like a shot.

I held my breath. The dying crystal echo was the
only sound in the sudden silence. Uncle Jim looked
sternly at Aunt Dell, forbidding her to interfere with
one of her nonsenses. Mr. Monk dropped a bunch
of raisins and Amun began to hiccough. Or was she
giggling?

Slowly Beau undid his fingers from the tumbler
that somehow still held together. He wiped his mouth.
The sharp noise had shocked him too, but his eyes
were still wild.

"I merely spoke the top of my mind, Mr. Rives.
It counts for nothing. My soul and heart are fully
armed; ready to commit cold-blooded murder on any
Yankee who sets foot on my land to free my slaves
or touch my cotton. I care more for my island world
and my independent, free way of living than you
Virginians can imagine."

No one cared to dispute him, whatever they were
thinking. Mr. Rives, the experienced diplomat, relaxed.
There was a grain of amusement in his eyes.

"So long as you continue to give lip service to sense
and wait for somebody else to fire the first shot you'll
not get yourself or us in trouble."

Beau looked over at me.

I dared not speak a word to quiet him. It was the same face that had conquered the stallion, all bold angles and full of rigid pride. But there was more; something exalté, unsubstantial and infinitely quixotic. He said, as though to the wall, or to himself, "You must forgive my rough handling of this exquisite tumbler, Cousin Dell. Usually my manners protect me from such flights of fanciful indiscretion."

Everybody gave sighs of relief and began chattering at once. The battle was over.

"Fellow's mad in the head. I'll keep away from him from now on and advise you to do the same. I had a crazy uncle who used to fly off the handle that way. Beat his wife to death one night, he did, then threw her body in Chesapeake Bay," Mr. Monk whispered.

Aunt Dell, still euphoric, though I couldn't imagine why, directed Great Peter to put down the silver waiter of brandy and cigars in front of Uncle Jim and invited the ladies to accompany her to the drawing room.

The men hardly noticed our departure. They had gone back to war.

"How could you be so pleasant to that——that—— monkey and so mean to Beau?" My voice was trembling. Was I going to cry?

Aunt Dell tapped me on the shoulder with her fan and winked. "Oh, go along," she laughed, "I've known the Berrien men all my life. Nothing excites them like competition. Play the harpsichord or sing or do something attractive for a change. You were heavy as lead during dinner."

The sun was sending slanting rays through the bay window in the drawing room where my harpsichord stood. The sky was going all red and gold. It would be a fine day tomorrow. A hunter's day. I started toward the stool. Lizora beat me to it.

"Beau's absolutely precious. I can't wait to ride with him tomorrow. Have you all got a horse big enough for him? We have. I told him Papa would——"

"He can ride Teaser."

"Not that awful pink-skinned white stallion."

"Why not. Can't he ride?"

"I just don't want him killed until after——"

"After what?"

"Oh nothing. He says he loves music. What shall I play? Let's lure him away from all those old men."

She began with "Lorena" and went up and down Stephen Foster. Nobody came. Mrs. Walker and Aunt Dell and the Misses Preston were comparing mistakes they'd discovered in the new edition of *Mrs. Randolph's Cookery Book*; Azilee Bizarre was napping in her boots on the sofa; fragile Mrs. Hampton had gone into Aunt Dell's room to lie down; and Anna Preston and Amun sang along with us in their shrill voices. After "Camptown Races" and "Oh Susannah," Lizora banged a chord and said she was tired and curled up on the rug in front of the fire.

I sat down at the keyboard, twisting my fingers to tell them to prepare to play for their life.

Amun leaned on the harpsichord. "You look worried, Angelica. Don't be. He likes you. I saw his eyes brighten, then go soft whenever he looked over the table at you. Play a piece *you* enjoy. It will happy you."

I played my favorite air of Purcell's. Through the closed doors of the dining room a true, rich tenor accompanied me:

> I know a lady, sweet and kind,
> Fairer than she you ne'er will find;
> I did but see her passing by
> Yet I will love her till I die.

"Wade sings well," Caroline Preston said.

"That wasn't Uncle Wade," young Anna giggled. "He sounds like a hungry bear when he sings."

Aunt Dell put down the cookbook. "Play a waltz, honey. Everybody has had such a good time. A waltz will end the day so pleasantly."

Still ruled by my sad feeling, I played Chopin's haunting waltz in A Minor.

When I was halfway through, the door opened. Beau strode in.

"You! I would have sworn it was Miss Lizora."

Had he not looked so happy I would have burst into tears. But there was an attack about him, a devil, a challenge. He stood behind me, pressing himself against me, as I played four more waltzes, during which all of the gentlemen joined us, including Uncle Jim, bending a little but walking unaided, comfortably crutched in brandy.

"Where's dear little Mr. Monk?" asked Aunt Dell.

Mr. Page laughed. "At the first note of music he fell asleep. I'll wake him as soon as we settle on tomorrow's hunt plans. He's had a long day. You going, Berrien? You, Angelica? Can you mount Berrien? If you can Wade says he'll stay over and ride my big Irish hunter."

Yes! Yes! Yes! I was iridescent and alluring. My heart was flying, all flags top masted as I struck up "Good Night Ladies."

Azilee roused. "How beautifully you play, Angelica. A rare treat. Stop sulking and get up from the floor, Lizora. It's six o'clock and almost dusk. Won't you ride home and take tea with us, Mr. Berrien? These folks deserve a rest."

Down came my flags to half mast.

However he behaved Beau had correct manners, as Aunt Beck had promised. Taking Azilee's big strong hand he pulled her to her feet. "Dear lady, there's nothing I'd enjoy more than taking tea with you and Miss Lizora but this morning I accepted an invitation to tea with another lady."

Standing on the recessed portico between Beau and Aunt Dell, as the horses and carriages crunched down the avenue, I stared in wonder. Was this jeweled arbor the same neglected garden I'd run through this morning? In the afterglow the dead leaves gleamed topaz; the cedars were emeralds; a few drops of moisture clinging to the shrubs were pearls; the sun, sinking into the horizon, was a sliced ruby; and the purple clouds pure amethyst rimmed with gold.

Five

There was a heavy fog and no birds singing the next morning. I was hooking my green velvet skirt to my wrist when Beau came clattering down the stairs.

"Why are you so pale?"

How could I tell him that it wasn't because of the chilly dawn but the sight of him in his scarlet coat and tight white moleskin breeches and Wellington boots with leather knee caps. His silver spurs were buckled with patent leather straps and a large gold pin held the ends of a red-striped neckcloth. I hadn't realized yesterday what very white skin he had. A sprinkling of freckles stood out strongly on it. Had he, as I, tossed and tumbled, sleepless through the night?

"Could hardly get in this coat. Must have grown since I wore it in England three years ago. Say, you look stunning."

Great Peter opened the dining room door. "Come into the fire, Miss Angel. You going to catch your death shivelling in the hall. Breakfast ready for you all."

I sat in Aunt Dell's place. Beau pulled a chair so close it squeaked as I poured him a cup of coffee. Two sleepy little Negro boys ran in and out with cold ham and hot waffles and muffins and batter cakes and syrup and peach and strawberry preserves. Neither of us ate much nor said anything beyond will you and thank you. We were too conscious of being alone together and Great Peter watching us.

The hunt gathered at the tavern before seven. Here the fog was so dense I was instantly lost in a confusion of riders and horses and boys with waiters of hot grog. Beau disappeared. Suddenly I heard Wade Hampton's booming-bear voice.

"Holy Mackerel! You scared the dickens out of me.

I suspected I was still under the influence of Mr. Page's brandy. You look like the devil's horseman for sure."

Straining my eyes in Wade Hampton's direction, I made out a scarlet coat and a tall black hat with nobody in them, mounted on nothing. Everybody else was a dark misty blur. This apparition was so weird my teeth began to chatter.

I heard Beau talking gently to Teaser. Evidently he thought the fog made him soundless as well as invisible. I pushed my mare toward his voice and touched the red coat. What if my hand closed on a skeleton arm? The running fire assured me he was there; real; and so was Teaser.

Mr. Page loomed up. "If we do go to war with the Yankees we can put Berrien on that white stallion and send them out on foggy days and moonlight nights. That sight would frighten anybody into surrender. It disturbs something deep down in me this morning. Ride off down the road, if you can find it, Berrien, and come back at a gallop. Let's see if you spook the horses as you are doing us."

No; the horses knew Teaser. They danced and frolicked around, eager to go along. Only we, the mortals, trembled at the ghostly hat and coat thundering by.

A little wind rose. The fog moved around. Day lightened. We finished our grog and for an instant recognized each other. Lizora was so fetching in a red wool outfit that I prayed for the fog to return. Mr. Monk saw me and rushed up saying boyishly, "You *must* ride with me, today. You simply must."

But Aunt Dell had put a word in Mr. Page's ear. Mr. Monk was called out with Lizora; Beau and I placed behind the whip, golden-haired, hard riding Mortimer Smith.

Excitedly belling, the hounds were brought around from their cages behind the tavern. Mortimer Smith cracked his whip; the sound of Mr. Walker's mellow horn was barely heard over the hound yelps and horse noises. We were off!

Parasol sailed over the first fence. I revelled in the exhilaration of the jump; the steaming smell of the near horses; the rocks clattering up; the couples of hounds stretched out in a line of wild sweet music; my heart going beat beat beat!

For a while the hounds whiffed around corn stalks and bushes with curious noses and ran up and down roads trying in every direction. The lead hound was running near me. He put his nose to the ground and cut silently across the road in front of Parasol. I could hear him whimpering. Then he spoke in deep full tones and the rest of the pack rushed to where he was.

"They've got a scent!" Mr. Page galloped past, a gloved hand waving us on. "Come on, old man! Speak once more. Careful don't overrun. Hie on! Hie on!"

I was pushed into a rail fence. The fog swirled thicker making the white horse and his rider invisible again. Yet I knew Beau was beside me. He had to be. It was eerie and supernatural, this not seeing him. An icy finger touched my heart. A premonition? Impulsively I reached out and caught his sleeve for reassurance.

"Look down!" Beau said. He *was* in the coat!

The fox was right at Teaser's feet. He daintily lifted a front paw and pricked his ears as if to consider whether he would be more sensible to end it now by being stepped on by the stallion or to chance it and head for the woods.

The hounds decided for him. The whole world was one exciting cry. The horn blew and blew. Tally ho! shouted Mortimer Smith.

Everybody went mad. For two miles Parasol desperately tried to catch up with Teaser but his strength of wind and power of endurance was too much greater.

I found myself riding abreast of Lizora and Mr. Monk. Content to stay back, they were laughing and talking to each other. The red outfit had caught him. Both his eyes were rolled her way. He didn't notice me as I headed cross country.

On a sharp turn I caught a glimpse of the fox pressed against a stone wall, teeth bared in a grin, the hounds almost on him. He tried to clamber over. Missed; tried again. Good, he was over, I right after him. He darted into a thicket. Far away, on the edge of a rise I saw Beau and Teaser, ahead of the hounds. Teaser was stretched out. No horse in the world could catch him. He just galloped out of sight of everybody as the fog lifted entirely.

The horn sounded Hooohoooohoohhoooh. The hounds were closing in. Mortimer Smith cracked the whip. Mr. Page hallooed. The hunt went away together for the kill. A full sun came out to celebrate the moment. The ridge was now completely clear, washed deeper blue than usual. I could see the huntsmen stark against the hills. Beau was not among them. I couldn't have missed him, he sitting a head taller than anybody. Where had he galloped?

I had trouble holding Parasol back. She loved the final run and always put what heart she had in it. Despite her plunging and trying to get the bit in her teeth I managed to turn her around and give her her head in the opposite way. As we galloped past a cedar grove Beau called my name. He and Teaser were standing close together in the dappled shadows.

It wasn't hard to stop Parasol this time. She liked Teaser. Behaving herself she trotted over to the grove.

Beau was grinning exactly as the fox had done when he was up against the wall. Teaser was throwing his head, his ears back, angry at being here and the activity somewhere else.

"Are you all right?"

"I enjoy shooting birds and spearing devil-fish and racing horses but I never was much for running down a poor little animal. I prefer running after you. Let's cut out."

"What will people say?"

"What does it matter? There's no reason for me to beat about the bush any longer. You knew from the first why I came all the way to these damned hills.

Cousin Dell admitted she was expecting me, having heard from that wretched old vulture in Charleston, who probably promised you a bridegroom and a fortune in exchange for your maidenhead. Well, here he is; or what's left of him."

Had he not looked so strained and white I would have galloped off and left him standing there. But somehow I wasn't put out at his mentioning that forbidden word. I knew I magicked him. His whole being declared it as he put his foot in the stirrup and swung lightly into the saddle, Teaser standing quietly, even bending a little to make it easy for him.

I fumbled for words. I wanted to ease him too. "Don't pay any attention to Aunt Beck or Aunt Dell. They're mischief makers. Say, you're the first person who has ever mounted Teaser without a fight. How do you manage it?"

"It was love at first sight, in the event you believe in such folly. Just as with you." He was determined to be serious. "I might as well face up. Today has been difficult for me. I've stayed as far away from you as possible in order to at least give the appearance of being a gentleman. But you kept following me; touching me; dizzying me. I never saw a woman sit a side saddle so temptingly." His voice trembled with earnestness.

My heart melted away. I was fevered with first love. "I don't want to be with other people either," I said impulsively.

We cantered slowly over a few fields, taking the short cut. He did not look over at me, just went on watching the way ahead.

"I almost lost my mind yesterday at dinner watching that Monk fellow put his hand under the table cloth. I tried to reach out with my foot and kick the devil out of him but the table was too wide. What was he doing—pinching you?" He laughed mockingly.

"What were you doing to Lizora? I saw your hand under the cloth more than upon it." I smiled, throwing discretion to the breeze.

"That was different. She expected me to pinch her."

His face had got some color back in it; his eyes glittered; his exuberance had returned.

A few miles later we were passing through an apple orchard. The lifted fog had left the bark and the branches dripping with moisture. Everything smelled fecund and full of suppressed growth.

The horses were walking together. Teaser had slowed his stride to match Parasol's more delicate steps. We had stopped talking and yet I have never felt so intimate with anyone—so close. He leaned over and put his arm around my waist. I did the same to him. He lifted my knee from the horn of my side saddle and pulled me over against him. I looked up and he kissed me. I had been kissed before but never like this. It was like a voluptuous dream of flying, winged and soaring, up and up, merging with the sky.

The horses kept on walking rhythmically, the reins slack on their necks. His lips demanded more of my mouth and more. Our souls rushed to entwine. A dazzling vista was opening when the sound of whistling made us suddenly aware of ourselves. Our lips parted. Giddily I settled back in my side saddle. Some Negroes in a cart hauling a barrel of cider nodded to us and passed on.

"Beau——"

"Don't say anything. No minister could marry us more than that kiss. I've never known anything like it. It was the drinking of a cup together. Now, I must speak to your Uncle Jim, then leave at once."

"You can't; not now."

"I almost slipped into your room last night. If I stay I will tonight. It wouldn't do."

"I know."

"After kissing you and discovering what you are——"

"What am I?" Why had I been so forward—so wanting——?

"You are my love and my treasure. What am I to you?"

We were riding locked in a clasping of hands, looking up and down on each other; I into fire-flecked brown eyes that went dreamy and went hot alternately; he into steadfast blue eyes that worshipped him.

"I have loved you from the minute I saw you. I——" words, never spoken before, came rushing out of me, I having no subtlety or talent for the game of coquetry.

He put his hand over my mouth. "Sh-h-h—Not yet. I would take you here—on the leaves—if you gave me the slightest encouragement. Shall I?"

"You can claim what you can take." Leaning forward I heeled Parasol. She responded instantly.

So did Teaser. Beau kept beside me, laughing excitedly. "I will claim what you will give. Pledge me that you will keep me as your sweetheart and no one else until the end of life and time."

"I pledge."

Parasol kept her sprint, Teaser at a mere canter beside her, until we reached The Cedars. Having heard the sound of hoofs Aunt Dell was waiting on the portico, eyes bright as mirrors in the sun.

"You two have been up to no good."

"We're going to get married!"

Jenks was sitting disconsolately on the mounting block. Not looking at me he took away the horses. Aunt Dell and I danced a few polka steps together before Beau gathered both of us into his arms.

"Tears, Cousin Dell? I thought you'd be pleased."

"She's pleased. She always acts contrary to what you expect. Let's tell Uncle Jim. He won't cry."

Aunt Dell straightened her lacy cap. "Mr. Burwell is asleep. I'll say yes for him. I'm sure he'd say yes. Yes, I'm sure. Of course I'm sure."

Beau lifted an eyebrow at me. "If I hadn't seen that rich Monk fellow, with my own eyes, mooning over you yesterday I would suspect I'd been caught in a trap." But his eyes didn't suspect. Neither did his lips as they kissed mine, lightly this time because Aunt Dell was looking. "I must be off as soon as I change my clothes but I will return on the 15th of December to marry Angelica. Please humor me and don't insist on a big wedding. My relations with my father's widow are, to put it mildly, unusual. She has passage to go abroad the end of November. I won't tell anybody my plans till she's on the high seas. Angelica needn't meet her until spring at the earliest."

You would have thought some kind of alarm would have nudged my senses but O my God I was so happy. I shut my eyes and could feel myself smiling. Such joy to give your heart freely. Anything that would happen to us together would be a wild adventure. No, I had no intuitive reaction at all.

Aunt Dell began to flutter and cluck, vowing that she'd somehow get my trousseau together if it killed her. But linens? How could she travel to Richmond and back with all the proper monogrammed sheets and table cloths and things like that?

"Don't fret, Cousin Dell. My mother had enough linens for a dozen families. Angelica won't need ball gowns. I intend to shut her up on Hilton Head and feast on her all by myself for years and years and years. . . ."

He was away within the hour. As soon as he was out of sight Aunt Dell held up a forefinger and said firmly, "Your uncle's not asleep. Never has been. Sit with him awhile. Cheer him up but don't let him talk you out of marrying Beau. You two are made for each other. And I've wanted that Beaufort house all my life. You're clever enough to handle the widow, I know you are."

I went in to Uncle Jim's bedside, hesitant and self-conscious all at once, as if I'd been caught out doing something naughty.

"Well, puss," his voice was hoarse and hard, not the voice he used to me, "old Auntie Dell pulled the rabbit out of the hat as she intended. But what about you?"

"Love at first sight I suppose. I stayed awake all night loving him. He's the first man who ever made me feel small and defenseless. I like losing my heart."

"You mean your head. His shifting moods at dinner yesterday gave him away to me. He's like that wild knight of King Arthur's—Lancelot. You'll never tame him. Hell, I don't need money that bad. The Cedars can survive without his help."

"You don't understand, Uncle Jim. I want Beau dreadfully. I intend to marry him and do anything in the world to please him."

Uncle Jim tried to sit up but his back had gone out again. He moaned and groaned for a few minutes while I rubbed his spine.

"I'm jealous, dammit. Reconsider Mr. Monk. I want you to love *me* best."

"I always will, darling, but I've definitely chosen Beau. Please let me go with your blessing."

"You'll go with or without. Nobody ever saved a Burwell from a collision course once his heart got tangled up. We've always been extravagant fools. Don't cry, honey. I can't stand that. Stop this instant. Bed with the devil himself if that will make you happy."

Six

He couldn't wait until the 15th of December.

He returned for me on November 30th. We were married in our parish church on December the second. Standing together on one of the freezing cold tombstones of a colonial ancestor that served as the floor of the chancel, our pulses racing, we said our vows exultantly not modestly.

Aunt Dell and Uncle Jim and Amun were the only witnesses. They were sitting in one of the high-backed pews with their feet on hot bricks. Naturally Aunt Dell was making a noise. It sounded as if she were humming. Uncle Jim kept blowing his nose. Amun giggled into the white ermine muff Beau had brought her for a present.

All these things touched me lightly as the snow flakes that fell on our heads as we ran to the fancy coach Beau had hired to take us all the way to Richmond to board the railway cars for Charleston.

The coachman drove us by the stable to say good-bye to Teaser.

"We'll come back for you soon," I told him. "Uncle Jim has given you to us for a wedding gift-horse."

We left him whinnying and tossing his head up and down, pawing the straw.

As soon as we were on the turnpike and the four horses stretched out, Beau turned his head away from me and looked toward the bleak mountains. "Mrs. Hazzard Berrien, *née* Elsa Czerny, should now be aboard ship bound for Hamburg, en route to a long stay at some springs near Baden-Baden. I will thoroughly acquaint you with her history before we reach Hilton Head. No questions until then. She isn't worth it. Agreed?"

I should have been shocked at my lack of curiosity but he was holding my hand and thrilling my cheek

with his lips. I was too full of bare *feeling* to be curious about anything except where he was going to
touch me next. My breast! His lovely long fingers
were inside my jacket, seeking——finding——

"This is the reason I didn't bring the boys to the
wedding," he whispered. "Edward is at Princeton. He
couldn't have come; but imagine Philip and Button
sitting across there watching me do this! And aren't
you glad I persuaded you to leave your maid behind?
Oh my love—my love—this may be the only time in
our whole lives we'll ever be alone together."

Almost at once we were in Charlottesville. I stood in
the window of our room in the inn, looking out at the
snow falling heavily. I began untying the strings of
my rose silk bonnet. "Will we be able to go on to
Richmond tomorrow?"

His white silk beaver hat touching the ceiling and
his white satin-lined black cape still hanging from his
shoulders, Beau was grinning at the unbelievably
high-puffed feather bed.

"Not if the snow continues like this. I'd hate to get
stuck and spend a night in a freezing ditch. I prefer
waiting out the storm nestled in this inviting moun-
tain of feathers. What say you, my shy wee dovelet?"

I flung my bonnet in the air. It fell on a point of
the gilded wooden chandelier carved in the shape of
a parasol. "I hope it snows forever."

A knock at the door interrupted our kiss. A red-
faced lad in a dirty apron was bringing more wood
for the fire.

"Innkeeper says ye must come down at once for supper."

"I wonder if this will bring supper and a bottle of
champagne up here to us?"

"Lor' it will indeed, master." The boy's small eyes
were as bright as the new gold piece he fondled in his
sooty fingers.

It was a simple meal of stewed rabbit and hominy.
We weren't hungry but we did drink the champagne.

Snow tapped gently against the window. The wind
had risen and banged the shutters. The fire leaped

high and the candles flickered in sudden gusty drafts. Beau sat me on his lap and fumbled with hooks and ribbons, singing the Purcell I'd played the day he first came. I unbuttoned his shirt and carefully unwound the cravat from around his throat. I pressed against him and felt his hairy chest warm against my breasts.

He put his arms around me and whispered in my ear, "Please forgive me but I must take you now. I had intended to be the teaser, knowing how fond of him you are but I can't wait—oh, I can't."

His tenderness moved me too much to say anything. I had a lump in my throat. Tears filled my eyes.

"You do want me to?"

"Yes."

He filled his mouth with champagne. Then he signed to me that he wanted to let me drink from his lips. I threw back my head and he spurted the wine into my mouth. His heart was pounding so loud it frightened me.

I swallowed the wine. "I love you, Beau—I'm ready."

He jumped up. "Well, Madame—we will now take the advice of an old Greek who advised that in the game of love advance with swiftness. May I remove your drawers? I've wanted to ever since I saw you in the pasture."

I knew I was supposed to undress behind the bed curtains and he was supposed to remain outside until I was properly in bed and covered to my chin. But that wasn't the way it happened. I helped him undress too, even buttoning up his flannel night shirt. He didn't like the way I looked in my lace nightcap and made me take it off. Then he put his ridiculous hat on and held out his arm.

"Madame, I have been trying to decide how in hell we are going to get ourselves properly into that pile of feathers. My conclusion is that we must count to three, then jump simultaneously; otherwise we'll never find each other. You'll go up and I'll go down."

"You've got to take off that hat."

"No, let it fall where it chooses. Now: One Two Three——"

The next day it had stopped snowing. The sun was shining. I could hardly bear to tear myself away from the little room at the inn. But as the horses galloped for Richmond, we were oblivious of any discomfort in the freezing clumsy coach except denied desire. At first, passing through snowy woods and frosty fields, we made an effort at small talk about things like horses and hoop skirts but when a sudden swaying lurch hurled me to the floor we grew wildly gay. Shouting with laughter at the way my bonnet looked jammed down over my nose, Beau bent to pull me up. Jolting and jostling recklessly against each other as the hard wheels plunged in and out of potholes and slid over sharp stones in the deep ruts we simply couldn't stop ourselves from making love right there! It was delightful.

Later we discovered my elbows were bleeding and his trousers torn at the knees. We stopped at a shabby inn and changed our clothes, arriving in Richmond very late but completely respectable.

We spent almost three weeks in the bridal suite at the Spotswood Hotel. The bed had a ceiling-high, solid headboard, dark and ugly as a coffin lid. There were matched red velvet Victorian love-seats in the parlor, much too small for either Beau or me to sit on comfortably. The second night we were invited to supper at the Harrisons'. Perched on the edge of one of the love-seats with the candles lit, a fire burning, we waited for the Dresden clock on the mantelpiece to strike seven. A china shepherd boy sat on top of the clock gleefully tootling a flute to a silly-faced shepherdess at the base.

I was wearing my one new ball gown, an azure gauze with long angel sleeves falling away at the shoulder leaving my throat bare. My hair was piled high with a diamond pin of my mother's holding a cluster of plumes that made me seem almost as tall as Beau. He was in full evening dress, singing a song I'd never heard before. Suddenly he stopped singing.

"Let's not go to the party."

The feathers fell first, dropping like snow around my bare throat. My breasts pushed up above my stays. The cord holding Aunt Dell's moonstones snapped and the moonstones popped all over the floor. The gauze of my dress made tissue-tearing sounds as it was frenziedly pulled up and crushed. I even helped Beau tear out my corset strings. I thought I would die as waves of rapture rose and rose to the highest peak ever and broke through us over and over.

Such ecstasy! Such complete pleasure! Such new feelings! All sharper, he cried, than if it had been easy to get to.

When we were quiet together, lying side by side on the rug in front of the now low-burning fire he said, "You are not like any other beautiful woman I've ever known. You haven't noticed that I've torn and stained your lovely ball gown. But I'll buy you a trunk full of dresses tomorrow if you'll let me finish ripping this one off and just look at you standing in the fireshine, holding a candle high so that its light licks down in little fires all over you. I've never seen skin that glows like yours; never. Oh, my darling——"

The next day we called on the Harrisons and presented our excuses, which they never believed for a moment. After that we went to a dressmaker where Beau ordered an identical blue gauze with angel sleeves and twelve other absolutely stunning costumes for all manner of occasions; then to the jeweler's where he had my moonstones restrung and bought a sapphire and diamond ring as big as a lark's egg for my finger.

Seven

I had never seen the ocean before. On the steamer from Charleston to Hilton Head I kept running from one side of the boat to the other to make sure the waves never gave out. The swells made my body feel bouncy and lighthearted. The December air was balmy, almost tropical, with a happy little west wind blowing. My heart was happy as the wind.

I can still hear Beau laughing, "One minute you're stately as an egret; the next excited and dancey as a young filly. Come, let's sit on this sheltered bench. I must tell you about my family before we reach the island."

First there were the brothers: Eddie, his favorite, exactly my age. He'd be home in a few days from Princeton for Christmas. Phillip, fifteen, the handsomest and brightest, but not the nicest. Button Gwinnett, named for a Signer grandfather, eight years old and still babyish. He had inherited his mother's gentleness and tenderness. Thank God one of them had.

"What about Elsa?" The word came out easily then curdled on the wind once I had said it, and because he didn't answer, the word "Elsa" mushroomed, like an evil genie out of a bottle, and threatened us. And I knew I could not make the genie vanish nor unsay the word "Elsa."

"What's so mysterious about Elsa? Your avoidance of her name makes me suspect there may have been something——"

"Sh-h-h." He caught my hand and pressed it against his heart. He was hurting. "Until I met you I valued Cotton Hall and my fine freedom more than anything. Not wanting to make Papa's mistakes I set out to choose a wife with my head not my heart. Papa went from one extreme to the other. Mother was too soft and giving; Elsa too hard and taking. When

52

I saw you with that damned white horse my head simply flew off. There's nothing left of me but heart. I don't care a fig for Cotton Hall or freedom any more unless you're in it."

"Oh Beau, I love you so much. Nothing that ever happened could make me love you less."

"You swear it?" He sighed and frowned then began speaking quickly and nervously in a harsh, resentful voice. "Elsa is difficult to pinpoint. First she comes on as a dove-eyed beauty, sulky and blooming. The wind blows and you see she's actually a dark-browed, ill-natured hussy, bold-spoken with brandy."

A picture of Elsa took form in my mind: Elsa the vibrant young wife of a dissolute old man, her brown hair blowing in the wind, eagerly running up to his magnificent son with a hungry smile on her wet-red gypsy mouth.

"I thought you wanted to listen and there you go, looking into the distance at nothing, exactly like your Aunt Dell."

"I am listening; with my other senses as well as my ears."

"I won't attempt to explain or understand why Elsa and Papa married each other except as a spiteful caprice to annoy her father, who was said to be a bully to his family. Felix Czerny was in the fur and real estate business with John Jacob Astor. He's rich as cream. He and Elsa were among the guests at a party on the Astor barge watching the sail boat races at Newport, Rhode Island, the summer after Mother died. A card game was got up. Papa won a small fortune from old Czerny. He was egged on by Elsa, who leant on his shoulder and claimed to have brought him his good luck.

"After he'd settled his account, Czerny vociferously let it be known that not only was he a total South-hater but hoped never again to find himself in the company of a South Carolina buffoon. If this was what Newport society had sunk to it had seen the last of the Czerny money and eligible daughters.

"Papa more vociferously informed Czerny that Newport had been founded in the last century *by*

South Carolinians. Every summer his grandfather engaged an entire transatlantic sailing ship to transport his family and household treasures and slaves and horses and vehicles from Charleston to his Newport house merely for the month of August. The Czernys were tilling the soil in Bohemia at that time, weren't they?

"Elsa said more insults were hurled. Papa refused to discuss the incident."

"Did they have a long courtship?"

"They'd never have gone through with it if they had. They eloped the week following the fatal card game. She showed her true colors when she stepped off the railway cars at Pocotaligo. The little boys and I had driven over from Beaufort and were waiting at the station to welcome her. I had recently come home after graduating from Harvard. Button was barely four years old. He'd missed mothering. When he saw Papa hand down a lovely bride-lady he took for granted she would also be a mother-lady. He ran and threw his arms around her knees. Unfortunately he'd been eating a syrup biscuit. Unfortunately, too, it being September and hot as hell, Elsa was wearing a Russian sable boa. She glared down at the sticky little face burrowing into the soft sables. 'Go away' she cried, jerking up the fur and slapping him so hard in the face with it that he fell on the oyster shells and cut his lip open.

"Papa laughed and said 'That'll teach him to keep his hands off strange women.'"

"What horrid people; both of them. What did you do?"

"The only thing possible: I picked the baby up and walked away. His blood ruined my new white linen frock coat. Eddie and Phillip followed. Back in Beaufort we went straight to our dock and headed for Cotton Hall. They've been my boys ever since. Papa forgot them and the plantations. All I had to do to get along with him was to keep money coming in.

"I want you to spoil Button a little. Maybe that will make him quit sucking his thumb. Have you ever heard of an eight-year-old boy who still sucked his thumb and won't shoot birds?"

"I'll make it a game with him to stop. I love little boys. I hope we have a dozen. Did your father and Elsa love each other?"

"I don't think any mutual affection ever existed between them. Papa had always been a petticoat-chaser but he confided that Elsa was the only beautiful woman he'd ever had who did not interest him in any way."

Beau's voice grew louder. "Everybody knew they had bouts of reckless drinking and actually fought each other like animals. The only night they ever spent at Cotton Hall they had a dreadful row. She had brought Fannie Kemble Butler's book about her life on a Georgia sea island cotton plantation. Papa tried to take the book away from her. She ran with it into the big bedroom shouting that she agreed with every word Fannie said against the South. Papa ran after her. The bedroom is a long way from the hall but we could hear them yelling at each other for hours. The house servants said that Papa did not beat Elsa that night but was beaten by her."

I was horrified. I'd never heard of such people.

"Papa beaten by a woman! How I'd have enjoyed watching it," Beau kept saying with hysterical delight. "You would too if you'd known Papa: contemptuous aristocrat, shrewd business man, cruel cruel Maussa."

Beau got up and walked up and down the deck. He took out his silver cigar case. He fingered a cigar then sat down again in a different place so that I had to turn myself all the way around to face him. He'd stopped laughing. His hand holding the cigar was trembling.

"Now," I said soothingly, "I am beginning to understand a little about Elsa. She doesn't sound formidable; just mean and unattractive."

"I guess I've been too long-winded but it's only fair for me to put all the cards on the table. Presently it is a game of hide and seek that can end in tragedy for us in May."

"Why May?"

"That's the deadline for either her or us to come up with Papa's last will."

I heard myself sigh. My new shoes had begun to pinch and the salt wind to sting my eyelids. I wanted to know about the low-lying sandy isles we were passing, the graceful green trees fringing the shores, the tantalizing vistas leading to tall houses, the shining fish that kept leaping.

Beau's face was grim, the shine gone from his eyes. "Papa's favorite pastime was setting people against each other. Between me and Elsa it was the issue of inheritance. It is the custom of the Berriens to leave their property to the oldest son, trusting him to provide fairly for the rest of the family, thus keeping the land intact.

"He got furious with me one day for wearing a blue silk cravat in the gin house, saying he'd ordered his sons to show up in red cravats so they could be easily distinguished by him in the dim light. Ergo he cut me out of his will, taunting me that he'd left all the Berrien land and holdings to Elsa. A week later he accused her of permitting Dr. Stoney to see her big toe. He had our lawyer draw up a new will naming me his sole heir. He threatened to shoot her toe off if she ever showed it to anybody again."

"What was wrong with Elsa's toe?"

"How should I know? Oh—I remember—I stepped on it in a waltz. Probably broke it. It makes no difference."

"Did you do it on purpose?"

"What a fiend you are! Of course not."

But his mouth was smiling so I knew he had. He lit his cigar and blew the fragrant smoke in my face. "I love you," he said.

"I think I'll take up smoking. I like the smell of your cigar. Do hurry and finish about Elsa. I'm tired of her. I have a million questions to ask about these islands."

"The farce of Papa's will was played out over and over. Last year, on the 20th of April, Papa came over to Cotton Hall in a rage with Elsa. He started drinking before dinner; could hardly sit at the table during the meal.

"In the middle of the afternoon he decided to go fishing. He was sitting in his canoe, throwing out the line, when a black man came splashing out of the canes into the creek and pushed Papa out of the boat. Papa struck at him and climbed back. Lots of blacks appeared around the boat and pushed Papa in again. He kept climbing and they kept pushing till by and by he didn't climb back. Liney, my Negro driver, the plantation boss man, was hidden in the canes, having followed Papa, knowing he was drunk and might tip over his boat. He saw the pushing going on but instead of helping he panicked and ran for me.

"When I got there all I could see of Papa was his hand showing in a clump of canes. A cottonmouth moccasin was twined around his arm, fanging at his wrist. Not a sign of any Negroes. Liney said they'd turned into turtles and things. He pointed out a log full of sleepy-eyed, brown-backed turtles sunning themselves, and there was a raggedy Pojo crane stalking after fishes, and a green lizard running up and down the fishing pole opening his mouth and laughing. I'll never forget that lizard. I tried to kill him but he got away. I did kill the snake."

"What did Liney mean by men turning into turtles?"

"He meant he wasn't going to reveal the identity of the men who had done it. I knew better than to ask him to. I told Elsa and the boys Papa died of snake venom. You and Liney are the only ones who know the truth.

"Our Beaufort lawyer said Papa's most recent will was, thank the Lord, in my favor. He would swear to that fact in court. But Elsa swore she and Papa had gone to Charleston *after* the date on *that* will. A young Charleston lawyer had drawn up a new one leaving everything to her: Cotton Hall, the Beaufort house, all the cotton lands, the people and the gold money."

"What had you done to aggravate him?"

"I shot a big, red-tailed hawk he was having a vendetta with."

"If nobody likes her and she hates where she lives why does she want the property? Why don't you give her a lot of money and send her away and keep the land?"

"Ah—there's the rub. Elsa would have been perfectly satisfied with just such an arrangement but Banquo's ghost returns in the form of that long-ago card game. Her father is determined to get his hands on everything Papa owned. He's already sent two teams of New York lawyers down. They've combed the courthouse records in Beaufort and Charleston. So far they haven't found anything. We have our lawyer's sworn testimony that he drew up a will in March of 1859 in my favor. There is only Elsa's word that a Charleston lawyer wrote one, favoring her, in April."

"What does the Charleston lawyer say?"

"You're not going to believe this but he was thrown from his horse and his neck broken a week before Papa died. Papa always did things in such a twisted way, insisting on complete secrecy in all his dealings, that the clerk in the lawyer's office knows nothing of what went on; only that Papa *was* in the office in April, drunk as Billybedamn.

"The New York lawyers tried to pressure the judge into deciding that Papa died intestate so Elsa could pick up at least half the estate but the judge is on my side. He has given Elsa a year to come up with the Charleston will. If she doesn't, he'll accept the word of our Beaufort lawyer that I am the sole heir. Until May I continue in control but it's maddening to even contemplate the fact that I may end up poor as Job's turkey."

He broke off abruptly and went over to the rail. He threw his cigar at a shark's fin that cut across the wake and began laughing. He clutched the rail and leant over laughing. Or was he being sick? It was terrible.

In a rush of sympathy I ran and put my arms around him.

He took another cigar from the silver case and tried

to light it but his hands were too unsteady. I struck the match, put the cigar into my mouth and got it going.

"To top it off Elsa is mortally afraid of blacks. She insists on using German servants from the North in the Beaufort house. But she *has* made an ally of my Negro housekeeper, Livia, and it's my fault.

"Elsa has a strange form of rheumatism in her hands and wrists. They are knotted and crooked up like claws. Hideous. She keeps them hidden under fancy shawls and in fur muffs but the Negroes, seeing them, are more afraid of her than she is of them.

"I send Livia over to Beaufort two or three times a week to dress Elsa's hair. Mother trained Livia beautifully. She's as competent as any French maid, but that's beside the point. Elsa must have offered Livia a handsome reward to come up with the will, for the boys and I discover her sticky fingers in all sorts of places she's no right to go into. To aggravate me even more Livia imitates Elsa's manner of speaking and walking. If I shut my eyes I can't tell which wretch is in the room.

"Livia was my wet nurse. Her own son, Pharaoh, is my number two slave. We are twins. He declares he's shorter than I because Livia always gave me the best tit. I loved her dearly once but no more. Neither do the lads."

We were near enough now to see St. Helena Island plain. Beau pointed out the tall pines and great octopus-armed live oaks dripping with silvery tatters he called Spanish moss. He said listen! you can hear the palmettos rustling. I heard nothing but the slap of the sea against the side of the steamer and lonely cries of terns and cormorants and gulls.

We watched the shore slip by. We were so close to it we could almost touch the overhanging tree branches. A flock of gaily colored birds came screaming through the woods to a salt lick to drink the salt water. They lit on the ground and it was as if someone had flung down a magic carpet patterned in glorious green, orange, yellow and blue. The boat whistle blew. Up whirled the carpet settling on a leafless silver tree, covering every twig of it. The sun shone brightly on their gay and glossy feathers.

"They have made a Christmas tree! What are they?"

"Parakeets. You can see how fond of each other they are, scratching each other's heads and necks and nestling as close as possible."

The beloved wanting enveloped us. I could feel his racing pulse starting mine.

"Oh, Angel, we're almost home."

The deck was crowded with people now. They were staring at us. We drew apart. My hands flew up, pointing to three pelicans and a dolphin playing and at a high bluff, tree crowned.

The shadows of the past hour vanished. The evil genie went back into her bottle. Beau was all happiness and excitement.

"That's it!" he cried. "See that bluff! That's my island. My house is behind that avenue of live oaks. Through their tops you can make out the cupola and some of the chimneys. And there's Myrtle Bank, the William Elliotts' house, just beyond that sea wall. Their nephew Stephen is my best friend. I hope Cousin Annie Elliott will be yours. She's a honey, full of spunk and charm. Now, we're coming to Seabrook's Landing. Goodness Gracious, Eddie's with the boys! I'll knock his head off if he's been sent down from Princeton. Follow me."

The wind from the open sea was just beginning to rock the ship. I walked down the plank, exhilarated, curious, secure and proud.

Part Two

The Homecoming

Cotton Hall Plantation, Hilton Head Island, South Carolina, December, 1860

Eight

A wide-shouldered, blue-black Negro in smart grey livery with brass buttons helped me ashore, holding my arm in much too familiar a way.

"I'm quite sure of my footing," I said sharply. He stepped back as the boys engulfed me in warm hugs. Where was Beau? I must speak to him about the man. Oh—there he was, thank goodness, lifting the front foot of a high-headed bay horse hitched along with a matching bay to a graceful barouche.

Gaily now I greeted each brother in turn; red-haired Eddie, freckled and white faced like Beau but not nearly so tall, his soft mouth curved in a smile of youth and sweetness; tall, loose-jointed Phillip, dark and broody-eyed, with a beautifully cut forehead and a jutting chin covered with fine black down; the little one, Button Gwinnett, round and brown as a nut with bird-bright black eyes. Him I loved best at once; and always.

Beau put down the hoof to embrace the slave who had discomfited me with his boldness. "Pharaoh, you old buzzard, the horses look grand."

Phillip said, "Bubba's going to explode when Eddie gives him the bad news."

"What is it, Eddie? Whisper——"

"Elsa is coming to the party. She sent word yesterday."

"I thought she was on her way to Germany?"

"She's back in Beaufort. Maybe she won't show up. She never does. I'll have to tell him the other thing, though."

"Can't it wait till we get home? I do so want him to stay happy."

"I can't, Angelica. Before he left for Virginia, Bubba invited everybody to dinner today. He likes to fit and dovetail everything so he can put on the correct face. Elsa will be as much shock as he can take in public today without exploding."

Beau said suspiciously, "What are you two talking so seriously about? Get in the barouche."

"Bubba, I've something to tell you. I tried to reach you by the telegraph but Cousin Harrison answered that you left Richmond after two nights."

Phillip said provokingly, "You really missed out by hiding."

Beau was getting nervous and tense. "Stop beating about the bush and confess what I already know: Eddie failed his examinations."

"No. I came home to enlist in the Beaufort Volunteers. I'm fed up with fighting for States Rights with my fists. You were named the delegate to the Secession Convention from Hilton Head."

"Robert Barnwell and Joe Pope are our St. Helena Parish delegates. Didn't you hear me, Angelica? Get in the barouche."

Eddie stood his ground. "Hilton Head requested permission from the governor to send a delegate of its own. The planters wanted you to cast their vote of approval. The Convention left Columbia yesterday on account of smallpox, planning to vote and sign the Ordinance of Secession today in Charleston."

"I was in Charleston this morning. I could have stayed. The devil take this party. I wanted to be at the Convention more than anything." He whirled on me. "It's your fault for insisting on staying over in Richmond another day." I stifled a giggle. He was the one who insisted! He was behaving like Teaser. I wouldn't have been surprised to see him beat the air with his cane and kick the horses in his furious frustration, but he'd never hurt me.

"It's as bad as missing out on having your signature on the Declaration of Independence."

I unbuttoned the glove on my left hand. The sapphire ring was biting into my middle finger.

"Stop looking at her like that." Not so confident as

I, Button's small hard fists struck Beau in the stomach.

"Look! Button's fighting," said Phillip. "Go to it, man."

"Why you whippersnapper!" With the tip of his cane on the little chest, Beau said, "I never thought you had it in you. Now I'll give you the *coup*."

I snatched the cane away and said coolly, "Eddie, will you hand me into the barouche?"

"Don't touch her." Beau picked me up and flung me onto the cream velvet seat, jumping in beside me.

The three boys followed quickly, troubled, silent, not knowing what to expect; certainly not what happened.

As Pharaoh reined the horses, Beau gave up and put his arm around me, laying his cheek on my head. "I am sick with disappointment, Angel."

"You aren't going to hit her?" Incredulous, Button rubbed his chest.

"If you put your feet on my new trousers again, I'll hit you. Just look at those scoundrels, Angel. Suppose they'd been sitting across from us, watching, in the coach to Richmond?" Everybody laughed, Beau the happiest.

"It's wonderful knowing Elsa's not here," Eddie leaned back, smiling sweetly.

Phillip grinned. "Instead of saying it's wonderful for Elsa to have ridden off on her broomstick, you should say: it's wonderful to have Angelica riding in style with us behind her pretty bay horses."

"Good boy, Phillip." Beau slapped him affectionately with one of his yellow kid gloves.

Button chimed in, "Will you let her stay with us forever, Bubba?"

"You ninny, why do you think I chose her out of all the gorgeous girls in the world if I didn't mean it to be forever?"

I was exuberant. I had won the first battle and three new best friends. I wished Uncle Jim could see me. I made myself go soft against Beau, nestling in the hollow of his arm. I almost said, poor Teaser.

"Do you like your carriage horses, my sweet Angel?"

"They move beautifully. How kind you are, dear Beau."

Phillip said, "Holy Mackerel."

Nine

From Seabrook's Landing we drove a winding road that, Beau explained, divided the Seabrooks' plantation from the William Elliotts' Myrtle Bank Plantation, then turned toward Port Royal Sound through the Draytons' Fish Haul Plantation.

"How exciting it must be to live on the edge of such a wide water, but it's a funny looking house."

"The Draytons have a fine house in Savannah. Everybody on the island has a fine house somewhere else. My fine house, as you know, is in Beaufort. But I'd never live away from Cotton Hall. You may think it resembles a barn but from the cupola on top you can see the whole world, and I own most of it! Look! We've crossed the boundary line—we're on my property."

"What unusual gate posts. Are they stucco?"

"Tabby," Beau said, "and in case you don't know what tabby is it is a cement-like material curious to the islands, made of oyster shells and sand and lime."

Everything was beautiful in a field and forest sort of way. The sandy road wound through endless acres dotted with Negroes hoeing and chopping dead cotton stalks into the ground and driving carts piled high with marsh mud and spreading the marsh mud over the soil to give it cohesiveness. The color of the earth interested me.

Eddie said the yellowish sand was rich beyond belief. The native Indians never cleared any of the richest land but always had great crops of corn and pompion and beans and squash. Now the silky long staple sea island cotton raised here was the finest quality of any cotton in the world and sold for the highest prices in London and Europe and Boston. As a matter of fact the prime minister of England presently sat on a cotton sack not a wool sack!

Beau said, "Enough of that, Eddie, how many women have you put to picking out seeds by hand?"

"Forty. The Eli Whitney machine you bought last spring doesn't work on sea island cotton. It's good for the upland strain but it damages our fiber. The Eaves improved steam gin is far superior. With it three slaves will be able to do the work of fifty-four next year in the seeding process. But it's complicated. It gets out of order awful easy."

"Which people have learned to opearate it?"

"Israel and Pharaoh and Phillip himself!"

Excitedly Phillip sat forward. "Israel and I took one entirely apart last week to see how it worked; we put it back together and it still worked. We can improve on it if you'll have your ironmonger in Charleston build me a few pieces."

Beau nodded indulgently, "And you, Suckathumbkin, account for your accomplishments while the master has been away on important business."

"Well, my game chickens laid twenty eggs and I shot a fox in the henhouse."

"I thought you didn't kill things," I said.

"The fox would have hurt my hens, Angelica. Besides, foxes don't fly."

Phillip laughed. "He has a dream about wings."

I said, "Do you fight your gamecocks?"

"Of course, that's the why of gamecocks."

My nose was beginning to itch but I dared not scratch. I would never understand these Berriens. "You don't make sense, Button; don't the cocks tear up each other?"

His eyes twinkling, Button said, "But gamecocks love fighting. It's natural to them. Bubba lets me keep the money I win."

"I wish fighting was more natural to you," Beau said. "You've talked your turn, now shut up. Look—Angelica—ahead——"

I saw the iron tracery of open entrance gates, with CH worked in the center of each, standing out against the blue sky and the stronger, darker tracery of forest trees. The horses' hoofs and the turning wheels ceased making sand-screaky noises, now sounding dream-soft on a pine-needled way. The soaring pines met in cathedral arches overhead. Interstitched needles patterned streaks of light into strange lines on our green-shadowed faces, giving us new expressions. Beau's features had stiffened into the exalté look I'd seen once before, his lips parted in a frozen smile.

He seemed touched with a haze, saturated with a different nimbus; and no matter how I laughed with the boys and smiled at him the aura was around him alone and appeared to be separating him, leaving us behind. There was nothing I could say that called him among us.

The gates clanged shut.

"What about the company inside?"

"What do you mean?" Beau murmured, lost in his vision.

"Why did somebody close the gates?"

"Nobody did."

"I heard them."

"Pharaoh, did you hear the gates close?"

"Ain't close, by gosh, no sir."

Stubbornly I kept insisting.

Beau said, "Run back and see, boy."

Pharaoh handed the reins to Eddie, hopped down from the box and loped off. He was back in two minutes. I saw his blue-gummed leer as he passed my side of the barouche. "Like I say, Master, wide open them gates. Hearing ghosteses, she."

"Then head on. I'm in a hurry."

My triumphancy vanished. I sat up straight, out of Beau's arm. Not noticing, he folded both hands contentedly on the silver knob of his cane, eyes darting this way that way, taking in every bush and tree and creature.

The gates *had* shut. Could it be one of Aunt Dell's fortune-telling hunches? I had heard them as plain as I now heard squirrels chattering along the branches, a pileated woodpecker cackling and the crash of an eight-pronged buck through a plum thicket in front of a circle of fluted columns gleaming white in a rise of palmettos near the road.

"Let's you and me have a picnic there tomorrow, Angelica; nobody else," Button cried, pointing to the columns. "I'll show you a wild turkey roost."

"You will practice shooting tomorrow, all day. Your burst of spirit at the landing proves you can kill if you try."

"Not live birds, Bubba?"

"You can use a target tomorrow. The next day you'll go gunning with us. I may even take Angelica along."

Button's thumb found its way into his mouth. I shook my head at him. Out came the thumb; two big tears rolled down his cheek.

Eddie handed him a handkerchief. "You can lean on my shoulder if you want to cry."

"I'm not going to cry."

Phillip said, "Our great grandfather built that little temple for a deer stand. Probably made him feel like a Caesar to stand among the columns wearing a wreath of myrtle on his head and shooting a running stag. Nobody uses it for anything now but Bubba insists on keeping it freshly painted."

"I keep everything freshly painted."

Eddie said, "Bubba smells home. He's so excited his big hooked nose is twitching."

Beau looked pleased. "Let's arrive singing at the top of our voices. I'll pitch it when we get to that big holly up there."

> We are a band of brothers
> And native to the soil
> Fighting for the property
> We gained by honest toil . . .

"I don't know that song," I said, unheard as four male voices roared together.

> And when our rights were threatened
> The cry rose near and far
> Hurrah for the bonny blue flag
> That bears a single star.

Hurrah! Hurrah!
For Southern Rights Hurrah!
Hurrah for the bonny blue flag
That bears a single star.

"Sing, Angel, the words don't matter, high as you can hit. Be our flute. And take off your left glove so everybody can see your new ring when you wave at them."

I would have given anything for Amun's sweet shrill voice among us, completing our circle. I wanted her to share my joy. How should I comport myself? Like Aunt Dell, airily waving and looking far off into space? Or should I be like Lizora—thrilled to death, squealing with delight?

Beau decided for me, rapping me on my wrist with the knob of his cane. "Sing! Shout! Pretend you've caught the fox! Hurrah! Hurrah! Here we come, Hurrah!. . . .

Ten

My heart was pounding with excitement, keeping time to the scattering oyster shells on the driveway running past a heron- and ibis-filled pond and bare fruit trees and flowering camellia bushes and pansy-bordered beds of sweet narcissus to an unbelievable white wooden house going up and out in angled directions, surrounded by unevenly spaced columns. This colonnade was filled with bonneted ladies in confetti-colored hoop skirts and wraps, and tall fine-faced gentlemen in fawn and black silk beaver hats and Prince Albert frock coats, and children dressed like grown-ups. They were singing the same song and waving blue flags.

Beau lifted me down and pushed me through a crowd of field slaves swarming the barouche. In the weirdest garments they were in restless motion, walking back and forth over the lawn, mashing each other against the tabby foundations of the house as if to push them down, every now and then jetting onto the piazza and staring through the windows at what was going on inside, then jumping back over the bannisters. I'd never seen such behavior in Virginia nor such black faces. There wasn't a mulatto or a brass ankle among them.

I still remember how fluttery I felt inside, approaching the narrow colonnade, I towering over the small, frilly women in my severely tailored navy blue traveling dress and tightly veiled derby hat. I can see the wide double flight of steps leading up to the long second-story piazza, feel Beau's powerful arms lifting me up and carrying me over the threshold into a high-ceilinged hall where two fireplaces held blazing logs.

Before the guest crowded in after us, I glimpsed several tall mahogany cases holding leather-bound books, full gun racks, portraits and mirrors in heavy gold leaf frames, massive Empire tables and too many oversized stuffed sofas and chairs in somber colors.

Button and Phillip and Eddie hovered possessively around me as Beau called out the names of relatives and friends who had come from their plantations on Hilton Head Island and St. Helena Island and Fripp Island and Daufuskie Island and Jenkins Island and Beaufort town and Bluffton on the River May, to celebrate our marriage and to learn who my grandfather on my father's side was. The older ones spoke sweetly of my mother and Aunt Dell as little girls. They had names like Elliott and Allston and Heyward and Fripp and Barnwell and Lawton and Baynard and Pope and Drayton and Coffin and Stoney and Parmenter and Pinckney and Jenkins and Davant and on and on.

From the sea of curious friendly faces one especially attracted me. Our eyes met and she came forward, a regal, white-haired lady in a black lace dress and a black lace mantilla, with a black beauty patch on her heavily powdered white cheek.

I caught the hand she held out to me as if it were a life line.

"This is Cousin Annie Elliott. Often in the winter she's our near neighbor; always my best sweetheart," Beau said.

Cousin Annie bade me welcome to the island. Her husband, old Billy over there, had taken one look at me as we drove up and declared I was the best looking girl he'd seen since my mother broke his heart nineteen years ago by marrying that wretched Virginia gentleman just because he was such a fine dancer.

Cousin Billy Elliott was a tall, gnarled, knotty man, lean and dark, with a mellow voice. He said he was relieved I had come to Hilton Head. Perhaps now Beau would relax and have a little fun out of life.

"A man without recreation is like a bow kept always taut. Call me Piscator, sweet coz, or Venator or Agricola. Today I have even heard myself named Unionist, not my favorite cognomen, but I insist the

South must stay away from the folly of Secession. We don't have the economic balance to support independent nationhood."

Cousin Annie said, "Oh do hush, Billy, Angelica looks confused enough without having to listen to your old-fashioned ideas. I'm planning a ladies' embroidery tea for Angelica, what are *you* with all your big words, going to do for her, old man?"

He took both my hands in his. "Whatever would please you most, sweet lady. Beau reports that you ride to hounds like a centauress. Alas, such sport is not practical on this sandy, briary isle. I can offer you a deer drive, or a swan shoot, or a peep at an eagle's nest, or a race in a sail boat, or a jaunt to hear and catch the elusive drum fish, or a wild cat chase, or a swim in the surf in the moonlight. I can read poetry in French to you, or, were you not of the female gender, take you on an expedition on the Sound to capture God's most fearsome creation: a devil-fish."

"None of those dreadful things, Billy. She'd like one of your nice little nature walks. You can teach her about the herbs she'll need to gather to make medicines for her people. Honey, he knows more about plants than anybody in the United States. He even writes books on them that are published in London."

But I wouldn't like a nature walk at all. "Which is the most dangerous and exciting of those fascinating options you've given me, Cousin Billy?"

"Devil-fishing, of course, but your sex excludes you."

"If Beau agrees can it be devil-fishing?"

"If Beau agrees, yes. Stop frowning at me, Annie Hutchinson Elliott. I haven't seen a woman like this since you stepped out of your fathers landau in Charleston a lifetime ago."

"Beau's going to kill you, Billy Elliott, for corrupting this sweet innocent child. Look Angelica, here's Billy's nephew Stephen and his pretty wife, Charlotte. Stephen was at Harvard with Beau, though a bit older. He plays violin and——"

"I play clarinet and he thinks I'm a fool. He's captain of the Beaufort Artillery and dotes on parading

in his fancy uniform. Say, boy, you've got your fiddle!
Are we going to have dancing? If so, I call for the
bride's second waltz."

Stephen was tall and grand looking, with beautiful
enthusiastic black eyes and soft wavy black hair. He
laughed, "The waltz shall be yours, Uncle Billy. Forgive me, but now I must summon the lady to her lord
and master. He's over by the fireplace, Angelica."

Beau was talking to a solidly built colored woman
with a high knot of oiled black hair who kept nodding
her head and waving her hands up and down like a
Meissen Chinaman on a porcelain cushion that Uncle
Jim had once given me.

Cousin Annie said, "Livia has ruled this house since
Julia died. Take care—she is your first hurdle—you
having completely captivated the boys and Beau's
friends and relations. Everybody is crazy about you.
Wait, I'll go with you."

As we made our way across the room I thought:
there's another Dinah to deal with; but a dangerous
one.

After studying me a minute, Livia bobbed down in
a jerky curtsey, eyes fixed on my kid-booted feet,
making me want to hide them under my skirt, knowing she was gloating over their longness.

"I greet you, my lady," she intoned lifelessly. "Shall
I take you to your room for a freshing before dinner?"

Cousin Annie poked me in the side. "Now is as
good as any time. Don't let her get by with anything.
I'll invite folks into the dining room. The food is on
the table. No telling how long it's been there. Let's
hope the servants have polished the silver and the
plates are clean. Make haste; we must be away before
dark."

I wanted to see my room first with Beau, not with
Livia. She opened a door directly behind where she
was standing and stepped aside for me to precede
her into a square room that held a wide central stairway; nothing else. It was like a deep well with light
at the top. Passing through two stories the polished
stairs ran up steeply to a cupola.

"There are eight bedrooms on the second floor and three just below the watch-out. The boys' and the company rooms are on the second floor. The schoolroom's on the above one, and a nursery."

It made me dizzy to look up. Someone was sitting on a step at the top of the first flight. The light was dim but I recognized Pharaoh, eating a fowl of some sort.

"Hey, Momma," he called down, "this duck everso good."

"You better not let Master catch you spilling grease on his stairs," Livia scolded. "Why you not helping your Pa? Henricuses feet ain't steady today."

"I will, in a little while. What he do? Drinked the wine?"

I resented this conversation taking place as if I were not present.

I said, "Come along, Livia," and followed her into a narrow room lined with unfinished pine tables each holding little piles of cotton seed.

"What room is this?" I asked, too loudly, nervously.

"This is the Master's office. The far door leads to an outside entrance where he can come and go secretly as he chooses; also to a stairway to the kitchen."

"Why are the seeds in here?"

"For him to select the best to use in next year's planting. No one is allowed in here but him. Never women."

I felt like a visitor being taken on a tour as I made my way between the tables and past shelves holding account books and a red volume of Thoreau and a green one by Emerson, rows of sea shells and several stuffed birds. I caressed a mounted red-tailed hawk with wings outspread. Was this the one on which our fates hung? Livia tapped her foot on the floor boards, her sharp yellowish eyes watching me intently.

"Master doesn't like his things touched."

I managed a smile which she did not return.

"What a shame it is that the Mistress is not here to make sure the party is a success. No one can compare with her when it comes to giving parties. She is much superior to these country people and she doesn't try to hide it either. She would have advised you against letting all those ladies kiss you as soon as you arrived. She would have come directly to her boudoir and seen to it that every curl was in its proper place. But who am I to give you advice? Or to tell you that your hat's on crooked and your nose needs a great deal of powder."

She pushed open a jib door in the corner of the office leading into a small room with a big, round marble bathtub, a tall mahogany washstand and an array of chamber pots on one of which I took time to sit while she kept sighing and tapping her foot irritably.

When I had gone through all the necessary retying of strings and buttoning of buttons Livia stomped down a flight of three steps to another closed door. Flinging it open she, again, rudely walked ahead of me. I had an urge to kick her undulant high bottom.

Curiosity saved my dignity as I entered a charming little boudoir looking to have been lifted straight from a French chateau. There was a pastel Aubusson carpet on the floor. In front of a lovely small marble mantel, brass andirons shaped like cupids held brightly burning logs. A tufted gold brocade sofa, deep and soft looking, was in front of the fire. Several Louis Quinze gilt chairs covered in antique *petit point* were here and there. A fragile porcelain desk painted with scenes of nymphs and satyrs held pens and writing paper. On an ormolu center table was a rose medallion Chinese jar filled with branches of perfect pink camellias.

"Mrs. Elliott sent the flowers and the jar for a wedding present to you. Don't waste time in here."

Waste time in here? This was the only pretty place I'd seen so far; a contrast to the next room, the bedroom, chill and plain, except for a soft Turkey carpet blooming with red and pink roses. A massive mahogany bed, its posts carved with a design of cotton bolls and flowers, was canopied in sky-blue silk. There was a wing chair beside the fireplace; no pictures on the walls nor any other furniture.

But what need for furniture with the French windows at the far end looking onto Port Royal Sound, sparkling like a rippling painting. A moss-draped, live oak avenue led to a grove of palmettos clustered on a high bluff that dropped through waxleaf myrtles to a landing where a clump of eight- and twelve-oared barges were moored. Coaches and carriages and saddle horses were hitched in the grove. Boatmen and coachmen and outriders were seated on the ground around a pine fire hooking rugs and scarves to keep them warm.

"Finally we come to your dressing room. The better one, of course, belongs to the Master."

My trunk was open, clothes pulled out and tossed over the floor. Two black girls with big hair, clad in garments that looked like flour sacks, were rummaging through my toilet case. One of them had pulled out my silver looking glass and was staring at herself in it.

A pulse beat dangerously in my temple. "Why have you girls opened my trunk?"

"It is customary to have the trunks of the guests unpacked," Livia said smoothly.

"Put that mirror down," I said to the girl. She glared at me, hugging the mirror to her chest. "What is your name?"

"She is one of the last shipment of slaves, direct from Africa, that the old Master purchased. Neither she nor her sister speak or understand English; they will not learn. Therefore she has no name."

"Everybody has a name. I will call her Ziporrah— the rebellious wife of Moses, in Africa, who refused to try to fit into a new life."

I fought to keep my temper. I had already been too long from the party. I leaned down and picked up my silver hair brush from the floor and pointed it at the girl who clutched the mirror. "Ziporrah! Go!" I commanded sternly, pointing to the door. "Go at once!"

She understood perfectly. Putting down the mirror, she and her sister fled.

I took my time smoothing my hair. When I had done so I forced myself to meet Livia's eyes in which was no light, except a flicker of malice.

"I will now ask your Master to come in here and see the condition of my clothes. It will interest him. Also I'll inform him that the hair of the maid you chose for me is full of lice."

"You wouldn't." Livia's voice, so low and insolent, turned shrill and the brown color darkened on her full cheeks. Her head jerked as she started picking up petticoats and dresses and slippers, running back and forth to the wardrobes and dressing table, lightfooted as a young girl.

"Livia," I heard myself saying calmly, "I don't care whether you and I make friends or not. I intend to give you every opportunity to carry on here as you have formerly done but you've deliberately gone out of your way to infuriate me this afternoon. Unless I find my clothes in order when I come back in here after the party I will inform the Master of the trick you tried to play on me. Did you think I'd be frightened of those wild blacks?"

"Oh, no, my lady," she was smoothing out a pink silk at-home gown, playing with the rose point lace ruffles. She hesitated, then spoke slowly, falsely, "I honestly thought you'd prefer maids you could train to your own liking. I know the Mistress would have preferred that. I had not told them to open the trunks. I merely——" She shrank back against the mantelpiece, effacing herself, as Beau bounded in.

"How are you two making out? Good, I see. Do you like the color I've had the bed draped in? I always think of you in blue to match your eyes. And the carpet?" He looked around happily, pleased as a little boy. "I love this room. You've done it up well, Livvy."

"I wanted to please you."

Beau went over and leant against the side window that opened toward the forest.

"If I should ever look out of this window and see a Yankee soldier riding his horse across my grass I would kill him with my bare hands."

"Suppose a whole company comes?"

"I will slay them all just as David killed Goliath. I would be superhuman. I would be a madman."

I didn't want to talk about it. I was determined my arrival at Cotton Hall should not have a cloud on it.

I said gaily, "I can't wait to see if your teapot is as handsome as the one Aunt Dell is going to leave me."

"My grandfather bought the finest tea service Paul Lamerie ever made. He outbid the King of Bohemia for it. Your pot came out of that flimsy old Hazzard house in Beaufort. Your Aunt Dell told me so herself."

"You've got a mean streak, Beau."

"Not really. I love that pink thing Livvy's holding. Put it on. I'm tired of looking at you in those dark traveling clothes."

"I can't; I have trouble with the hooks on the side. What would Queen Victoria say if I appeared at a party in such an informal costume?"

"She'd give it the nod more than at some other rules you've enjoyed breaking." He grinned so wickedly that I felt myself blushing all over, unable to stop him and Livia conspiring to get me out of the tight skirt and jacket and into the flowing trailed silk in less than two minutes.

Eleven

"Dell would approve of you in that becoming gown," Cousin Annie said as I entered the dining room. "Sit down and serve the creamed oysters. It's your turn." She handed me a long silver spoon.

I felt like Aunt Dell, frowning at the tarnish on it and the silver chafing dish; at the untidy waiters of crab cakes and venison patties and tea cakes and fruit cakes and chicken salad and olives and raisins and pecans and platters of ham and cold ducks and partridges and bowls of rice pilau and sweet potato pone and marmalade tarts scattered over a soiled *Point de Venise* lace cloth on a fat-legged Empire banquet table. What a poorly planned feast. I also frowned at Henricus, apparently the head butler, slopping eggnog over the sides of crystal cups as he ladled it from a Lowestoft punch bowl. He had a small head floundering around in a large unkempt white wig and ingratiating eyes. Noting my disapproval he was soon serving the brandy nog as deftly as Great Peter did at Cedar Grove, proving he could if he chose.

Once I caught a glimpse of myself in a pier glass across the room. The rose silk was flattering to my skin; my eyes glistened with happiness. I had become the person I had imagined in my wildest dreams. I looked around at the company, *Petite Trianon* gay, and at the enormous room that had no architectural distinction nor fineness of woodwork, cluttered with all the things that said a rich man lived here. I loved the people and the house and knew that here, among them, I wanted to spend the rest of my life, the luckiest woman in all the world. If only Amun and Aunt Dell and Uncle Jim were here to see me. Who cared about food?

Definitely not Beau. I'd hardly got the knack of

pouring sauce over the succulent oysters when I
heard him.

"Angelica, where the hell have you hidden yourself?"
He came rushing in. "Charlotte will take your place.
It's time for music. No one has touched Mother's
piano since she died but I've kept it tuned."

He was so happy he did a quick little jig as he sat
me down on a velvet cushioned stool in front of a
rosewood Chickering grand piano over nine feet long.

Standing on the side Cousin Billy was blowing a
few notes on a clarinet; Stephen was tuning his violin; Grimke Pinckney, a square-jawed girl in a ridiculous red and white striped flannel bloomer costume and a white felt boater, was tooting a thin tune
on a silver flute.

"Beau says you play all those fancy pieces like Mozart and Chopin and Beethoven. So does Stephen.
But Grimke and I would like to make some merry
music. What about 'Dixie' or 'Blue Tail Fly' to begin
with?" Cousin Billy said.

Beau said gently, "Angelica is going to play something special first."

Opening the piano lid, he whispered in my ear. I
looked at the beautiful ivory and ebony keyboard.
I'd never touched such an instrument. I riffled a few
notes. The tone of the piano was magnificent. I
wanted to play something majestic and grand, but
tenderly I found the notes he wanted and tenderly
he sang:

> This is my lady sweet and kind
> Fairer than she you ne'er will find
> I did but see her passing by
> And I will love her till I . . .

A rush of cold air plunged against the back of my
neck. I heard one door bang against the wall. Beau
stopped short before he got to the word "die." Cousin Billy blew a series of squeaky notes; Grimke
stopped flauting and Stephen fiddling; but I couldn't
control my fingers. They kept on playing faster and

faster as if my very life depended on the song continuing.

"No more, Angelica." Beau's lively melodious voice
had turned ugly and vindictive.

"What is it? What's the matter?" I asked, rising
and facing the door, remembering what Eddie had
told me at Seabrook's Landing.

No eager gypsy but the Frost Queen herself was
there, sharply limned against the brightness outside.
She was all in black velvet and white ermine. Glossy
brown curls hung down on her shoulders. Her glittery
dark eyes stabbed straight through the amazed guests
at Beau.

She had a heart-shaped face but no soft lush mouth
as I had imagined. A long, tight gash, vividly car-
mined, was opening and shutting like an oyster's
valves as she talked animatedly to a stylishly dressed
gentleman beside her. His masculine beauty was so
startling that after my first shocked glimpse of Elsa, I,
along with everybody else in the room, stared at him.

Beau had caught hold of my shoulder. He was having difficulty breathing. "It's Elsa! She must have
found the will."

"Who is that Apollo with her?" Stephen whispered.
"If he weren't so pretty I'd swear he was a military
man. He strode through that door as if he were on
the way to review his troops."

"How the hell would I know who the witch has
dragged in with her?" Beau was raging, clenching and
unclenching his fingers around my poor shoulder.

Cousin Billy put down his clarinet, "Control yourself, Beau, I'll run find Annie. She'll know what to do."

The whole room was humming with surprise like a
swarm of bees.

"We must speak to her," I said, longing for Aunt Dell
beside me, to listen, watch, decide how to avoid an
unpleasant contretemps between Beau and—her. My
heart was fibrillating absurdly. Nothing but Aunt
Dell's stern discipline where society manners were
concerned propelled me forward, forcing Beau to accompany me.

Button flew past us. I heard him running up the stairs calling desperately, "Kitty! Kitty! Kitty!"

I kept from stooping by concentrating on Elsa's escort. His handsome head held high he exuded superiority, standing with his left forefinger in the watchpocket of a grey brocade waistcoat under a deeper grey Prince Albert cutaway that showed off his manly figure. He had a finely carved forehead, cavernous topaz-colored eyes and a classic nose. There was a guarded fixity in his expression until his eyes found mine; then they became unstable. He gave a start as if he'd heard a command, bowed generally to everybody and with a quick, precise stride walked away from Elsa and stationed himself on the far side of the room in front of the big gun rack.

"Come back here!" Elsa called to him in a hoarse, harsh voice as we met each other in the center of the big room. It was like an act in a play: the audience waiting breathlessly for the opening line; the "other" leading man standing in the wings, ready to come on stage and help her destroy us.

That thought was so terrible that, without letting myself dwell on it, I felt myself smiling a bright smile, conscious I was a liar and frightened to death.

Involuntarily I turned my head toward the newcomer. He was postured gracefully in front of the guns, staring at me. I shivered as if a rabbit had run over my grave.

"May I present the Mistress of Cotton Hall," Beau said to Elsa, tossing his head in a wild way as if he was about to rear up and go after her.

So I did what Aunt Dell had trained me to do. I held out my hand to Elsa. A warning sigh swelled around me. Was everybody keening? Or was it the wind soughing in the chimney? Elsa's vivacity vanished. Incredulously she was studying my outstretched hand. Would she take it? Oh, I knew exactly what I was doing. In my desperation I was baiting her. I knew why she hid her hands in the soft white muff. I did this deliberately to give Beau a chance to quiet down.

Slowly, reluctantly Elsa removed her right hand from

the sheltering fur and stuck it into mine. It was a ball of cold rocks and spikes. Her fingernails must have been an inch long. They went in all directions. Was she going to jab me? Was I going to squeeze hard and force her to cry out for pity? I distinctly heard Livia's voice far in the back of the room.

"Poor creature; she's always in pain."

In pain or not Elsa dared me to hurt her. I resisted the temptation and drew back my hand. I'll never forget her contemptuous expression.

Pitching his voice too low for anybody but Elsa and me to hear, Beau said, "What the hell are you doing here?"

"I have come to your wedding feast, stepson. Wasn't it a bit odd that you overlooked inviting me? I don't like being overlooked."

"How could I invite you? I thought you were on the ocean sea."

"Livia tells me you planned this before I left for New York. I'd forgotten how much you resemble your father."

Cousin Annie saved the day, bursting into the hall saying she'd been rearranging the pink camellias in my boudoir and having a little rest and missed out on the excitement of Elsa's arrival.

"How in the world did you get to the island in this wind with your curls so smooth?"

"We've been here for ages. That light-skinned Negro, Robert Smalls, brought us in the McKees' steamboat. I sat a while downstairs in Hazzard's cardroom while Livia put me in order."

"Why did you change your plans about Germany?"

"Yes, Elsa, why did you?" Beau's face was as white as the pile of ermine on top of Elsa's head.

"My father changed my plans. He keeps close watch on all the South Carolina news in the *New York Herald*. He's been especially interested in this Secession movement. He said if that came about my interests would have to be protected. He sent an expert down with me to keep you from doing me out of everything. There he is by the gun rack. Poor

Frederick, accustomed to commanding thousands, standing all alone by an old gun rack! He's furious and will get even with you for it. Wouldn't you have thought Eddie or somebody would have greeted him?"

"They were waiting a signal from me," Beau said rudely.

"Behave yourself, Beau," Cousin Annie said. "Call your friend over, Elsa. What must he think of us?"

Elsa lifted her muff, both hands inside, and caught *le beau ideal's* attention.

As he marched confidently through the curious guests paying them no more attention than if they were a parting sea, Elsa laughed at Beau. "Don't look so miserable. I haven't found Hazzard's last will and testament but with the famous Frederick Pierce, who has the sharpest nose in the world for discovering strategic treasures, I'll get my hands on it, never fear. Ah, Frederick, here you are, let me introduce you to my greedy stepson, Baynard Berrien, and his bride. What did you say her name was, Beau? Oh, and Mrs. Elliott—I almost forgot."

"Angelica," Beau muttered angrily.

"I would have guessed it." Frederick was as handsome close up as he had been across the room. His voice was strong and crisp; and his bow first to Cousin Annie the ultimate in good manners.

Cousin Annie responded by saying Goodness Gracious she'd been in school in Switzerland with Prudence Pierce of Boston when she was fourteen. Frederick said she was his father's first cousin once removed, now married to Amos Peabody after her first husband, Mr. Cabot's, sailing ship was lost off the Ivory Coast of Africa.

Then Frederick Pierce took my hand, bent over and kissed it. His mahogany colored hair was worn long over his ears. It was shiny clean and perfumed. His lip were soft and silky smooth. And was that the tip of his tongue between my little finger and my ring finger?

I had sense enough not to jerk my hand away because Beau was already flaming up at the handkiss taking so long.

"Come here, Beau, old Mr. Mongin has fallen under the table," Eddie called from the dining room.

Cousin Annie suggested to Elsa that she go into my boudoir and take off her fur cape.

Frederick and I stood facing each other by ourselves. I tried to get Stephen's attention or Uncle Billy's or anybody's but, a houseboy having appeared with a silver waiter of cured sturgeon eggs on hot toast and another boy with freshly boiled crab legs, they were all gathered around eating and talking, the icy spell having been broken. No Berrien scene today, thank goodness. But it *was* getting late; almost time to start for home so dark wouldn't catch them on the way.

"Are you enjoying Beaufort, Mr. Pierce?" (Was it I or Aunt Dell speaking?)

Elegantly handling a caviar toastlet he answered, "I'm abominably bored. I'd never have taken on this business had I realized the complications."

"Are you a detective or a lawyer?"

"Neither. I'm in Government Service but on leave at the moment. Mr. Czerny is an old friend of my father's. My coming here to help Elsa is a special favor to him." He raised his dark eyebrows and looked straight into my eyes. A tiger crouched behind his.

I couldn't let him suspect my unease. "How will you help Elsa?"

He shrugged. "Supposedly I'll manage things so she will get her hands on the Berrien fortune. But seeing how you ornament Cotton Hall I just might influence Elsa to be satisfied with that magnificent Beaufort house." He leant forward and spoke so quietly I could barely make out what he was saying. "You could persuade me to do anything, Angelica."

I turned away as if I had not heard his last remark. But as soon as I turned away I felt him there, right behind me, touching the inside of my arm and I was afraid of him because I knew he was bad and I had captivated him.

Twelve

By four o'clock the guests began finding their wraps and children and maids and dahs and saying, "What a marvelous party! The surprise entrance of the two Northerners has added a certain spice to this special Secession day. Tomorrow South Carolina will probably be a whole country by itself against the world. We can hardly wait!"

Beau and Eddie and Phillip flew around outside seeing to calling up carriages and summoning boatmen, closing carriage doors, bowing over soft white hands and waving with all the graceful flourishes that had been fashioned into them since childhood.

I was saying the last goodbye when Henricus whispered that he thought I'd better step in the dining room a minute. It was the Mistress.

"Ask the Master to join me there."

Frederick was attempting to persuade Elsa that it was time for them to leave.

"No," her voice was strident and slurry, "I insist on some of old Anatole's special catfish stew and hominy grits. Did you know that's what these Southerners love better than anything? Catfish and hominy! But wait —have you brought your digestive pills? Ha! Ha! Ha!"

He turned from her and asked me where I'd studied piano. He loved music.

Unheeding, Elsa rattled on, "You should always have digestive pills along at these outlandish plantations. Don't look away from me. I didn't mean to annoy you. Oh, there's Beau! Do you know, Frederick, I can't resist the way my stepson looks at me and turns pale. It tickles me to death. But I'm terribly fond of him, yes I am. How changed you are, Beau. Every time you bend to listen to Angelica it is as though you would fall at her feet."

"What's wrong with that? Have you noticed how beautiful they are?"

"Elsa, our boatman is waiting. It's time to return to Beaufort," Frederick said coldly.

"Not yet. I've a real treat for you. Just look at that teapot on the sideboard. It needs polishing."

"What for? You won't be using it," Beau said.

She frowned and gulped the cup of brandy nog she'd been twiddling in her twisted hand and it was clearly a cup too much. "I'm ready," she snapped peevishly, putting down the cup and clutching my arm. "See, Angelica, Frederick's no longer bored since you're in the dining room. What have you done to fascinate him?"

"Nothing whatever."

"You'd better not. He's looking after me and he's a mean man. Besides, he has plans. He says the rocket is bound to go off and fizzle out and then we won't have to worry about an old will. Bring me some more of that nasty nog, Henricus. Oh! Oh! You haven't toasted the bride, Frederick! We can't leave until you properly toast the bride."

Elsa chuckled then she burst out laughing so loud that the servants rolled up their eyes.

Frederick blushed like a schoolboy. Her mad laughter embarrassed rather than annoyed him.

"What rocket, Mr. Pierce?" Beau asked smoothly.

"How should I know? She talks too much."

"Fetch me another cup, Frederick, and then I'll go. We can do our toasting later."

"You've had another cup. The boatman said he wouldn't run the boat in the darkness."

"Let Smalls wait. I'll have one more cup then two more and then I'll go."

"I am going now. You can do as you like. Mr. Berrien, will you come over to Beaufort and talk with me tomorrow?"

"If he does we must hide the good silver. Ah, I've hurt Beau's feelings. Are you angry with Elsa, Beau dear, just because your father left me everything?

This house too. I hate this house. I'll sell this house. Don't be angry with poor little Elsa."

"I'm not angry, because Papa left everything to me."

"Oh lord, I feel awful. The floor is all wavy. One more cup, Henricus, and don't spill it on my wrist this time."

Frederick turned to me, his beautiful brows almost meeting in a frown. "I suppose your husband is accustomed to scenes of this nature. I'm not, nor I would think, are you. Please come with your husband tomorrow."

Beau was leaning on the mantelpiece. He was enjoying himself. "I'm not coming tomorrow, nor the day after. Perhaps the next day."

"At your pleasure, of course. By that time I'll have had a chance to visit Charleston at least. But no tricks I promise you. Routine affair for me." Frederick was trying hard to be agreeable.

Elsa said, "Why are you looking at me, Beau Baynard Berrien? Your eyes say, Elsa you're drunk. Your eyes are full of contempt. Frederick looks at me and his eyes shine. But you must stop looking at Angelica with your shiny eyes, Frederick. I've been watching you."

Beau took my arm. "Our guests have left, Angelica. I know you are weary. Let us say good evening. Henricus, show Mr. Pierce and Mrs. Berrien out when they have finished their drinking."

Frederick drew himself together and clicked his heels. His deep set eyes blazed with anger. His hands were twitching convulsively. Had he not left his gloves in his hat I knew he might be foolish enough to strike Beau on the cheek. I realized that the whole day must have been a trial to him. This insult of Beau's was the last straw. He turned sharply on his heel and left the room.

"Oh all right, Frederick, take away the old brandy cup. It's the fourth time I've asked you." She gave a crazy little laugh then all at once she showed great excitement. "Beau, where's Frederick?"

"He's gone to find his cloak."

"Where's Angelica?"

She wasn't aware that I was right behind her.

He grinned wickedly. "Angelica went with Mr. Pierce, Elsa. Didn't you notice?"

Henricus and all the maids and serving boys lowered their eyes, trying hard to stifle their amusement at Elsa lurching from the room, waving her hideous hands, having forgotten to hide them, calling frantically, "Frederick! Wait! Wait for me!"

Thirteen

"Oh, Beau, I hear your heart." I clung to him.

He started kissing me and saying how much he loved me and murmuring my name over and over. Frederick Pierce was exorcised as Beau's kisses fired me almost as much as that first kiss. But of course nothing can ever be like that again. I put my hands on the back of his neck and kissed him too, deeply, imploringly.

"Our first at-home kiss," I whispered.

"Confound it, here come the boys. Just once more; to content me."

The boys filled up the little boudoir.

Eddie said, "Elsa really showed off today, didn't she, Bubba?"

"Making that kind of entrance was typical of her. From the first minute I ever saw her she's gone about infuriating me."

"Like knocking me down?" Button asked eagerly.

"That was one of her minor performances. Now look here, you boys, we've got to concentrate on three things: first, making Angelica happy at Cotton Hall; second, preparing ourselves to go forth to war; third, forgetting about Elsa."

Phillip said, "Not hunt the will any more?"

"Most diligently continue to search. Say, Phillip, you were outside organizing games for the young people. Didn't you see Elsa when she arrived?"

"Sure. You all had just gone into the house. She looked a sight with her fuzzy hair all flying around. I told her that Papa's card room was being used for the gentlemen's necessary and cloak room. She went in there and waited for Livia to come and fix her hair. That fellow with her was a humdinger. He is the best looking man I ever saw. Didn't you like him?"

"No."

"Why not?"

"He is the enemy. He is a Yankee."

Eddie was standing in front of a mirror smoothing his bronze pompadour. "Bubba didn't like him because he took a fancy to our Angelica."

"Didn't everybody?" Beau took my hand in his, loving it with his fingers.

"Did he, Angelica?" Button asked worriedly.

"I hope not, Button, but he *was* on the verge of challenging your big brother to a duel in the dining room."

"Hah!" Beau picked up the poker and made a few passes and lunges at an imaginary opponent. "Stand up, lads. Join arms so Angelica can gaze serenely on her four gallant musketeers; ever on the alert to save her from villains and vixens and kiss-hungry vampires. Our exploits will turn old Dumas into a pussy-cat teller of tall tales."

Each one insisted he play D'Artagnan. They drew straws. It turned out to be Button. He strutted around the room like one of his gamecocks.

I said, "I can't describe the weird way Frederick Pierce affected me. It wasn't nice."

"I liked him," Phillip continued stubbornly, grabbing Button and tickling him roughly.

"Leave Button alone, Phillip," Beau said sternly. "Go on about why you liked Mr. Pierce."

"He was eager to see everything and found favor with everything he saw. Pharaoh and I walked him down to the water. He asked dozens of questions about the channel and what size boats could come in and how high was the tide and things like that. Pharaoh showed him your secret entrance and took him up in the cupola so he could have a complete view of the sound where it meets the ocean. He said it was a finer harbor than either Charleston or Savannah. He'd sailed into both on a mission when he was a cadet at West Point. I must have spent an hour with him before the barbecue was ready for the young folks. Say—you should have seen Button playing shinny with the Stoneys. He's a peach of a runner when he wants to be."

Beau frowned and pulled at his ear, "There's something fishy about this whole business. Why didn't you alert me when Elsa turned up?"

I remembered Beau explaining the boys. Phillip isn't the nicest, he'd said. I could see now what he meant. Phillip was enjoying Beau's concern.

"Elsa was insistent on wanting to surprise you. What's wrong with that? I did send Button in when they started up the steps."

"Too late on purpose?"

I couldn't bear for anybody to quarrel tonight. I changed the subject. "Elsa won't find the will."

"How can you be so sure?" Phillip asked.

"I've got one of Aunt Dell's hunches. I'm going to find it."

"If you do, I'll be your slave forever," Beau said.

"If I don't?"

Button jumped up and down gleefully, "If you don't find it, Angelica, what will Bubba be?"

"Scoundrel, I'll still be her slave."

"I will too." The little boy hugged me and I put my arms around him. "Do you love me as much as you do Bubba?"

"More," I said, smiling.

Beau started chasing me around the center table saying now was the time for my first beating. The boys joined in, trying to head him off. We were all laughing and shrieking when I ran into the dainty porcelain desk almost knocking it over.

"The Mistress would have been very angry if her favorite desk had been broken."

Livia was in the room. Fun fled.

"Dang!" Beau said, "why didn't you knock?"

"What is *her* desk doing in here?" I asked.

"It's not her desk. It was Mother's," Eddie said. "I brought it over from the Beaufort house last week. Bubba told me to."

"Mistress is not going to like it. I'd hate to be the one to tell her."

"No one has to tell her anything." Beau sat down on the sofa, took a cushion and jammed it behind his head, lit a cigar and shouted, "Well, what do you want? Is Mrs. Hazzard Berrien still here?"

"Oh no. I came to remind you this is the time for the sing in the praise house. The people will feel mistreated if you do not bring your lady for them to greet. It is almost first dark."

"Damn the people. I don't want to."

Eddie said, "We must, Bubba."

"I'm not going. It'll smell awful," Phillip said.

"You're going. I'll break your neck if you don't. Do you mind accompanying me, Angelica? It's customary."

"I'll hurry and put on a more suitable gown."

He didn't comment, just puffed his cigar and let Button crawl up in his lap in the firelight. They started talking about invitations and plans for Christmas hunts and picnics and parties together. I thought: this is the way it will always be; this is my life, content and comfortable and exciting. Elsa will go away like a bad dream; I know she will.

The doors to the bedroom and the dressing room were open. Blue silk curtains were drawn across the windows. My dressing table was painted white with gold knobs. It was crowded with silver brushes and crystal jars and bottles and the silver looking glass. Across the foot of the bed on my grey velvet peignoir closed with gold frogs were laid silver slippers. I could hardly wait for darkness and the hour for Beau and me to open the linen sheets.

Fourteen

The five of us walked down to the bluff to see the evening star and make a wish, it being my first night at Cotton Hall. Everything smelled deliciously salt and fresh. The water made caressing, slapping sounds on the beach. Phillip tried to explain to me the why of the tide and the way the water here ran in many directions—sound, sea and creek. Parris Island was directly across; Bay Point down there at the beginning of the ocean. We'd go surf bathing there in summer. The waves went high and wonderful.

I could have stayed on the bluff for hours but Beau, restless to get this duty over, hurried us along. The barns and the work shops, even the gin house and the vegetable gardens, were inside a tabby-walled enclosure. It could have been a walled medieval town dominated by the varied rooflines of the big house looming behind. Camelot among the cotton fields!

The horses whinnied gently through their evening oats as we passed the stables. I thought: if the stables are as ill-kept as the house I'll not bring Teaser from his clean stall and expert care.

The Street, where the slaves lived, circled outside like a moat or a running snake. Through an iron gate we entered a different world, as far apart from ours as one star from another. The rows of tiny, tabby huts were tight-shut against the night, dark and forbidding. There was just enough afterglow left to make out three new wooden structures.

"The sick house, children's house and praise house! Don't say I'm not a modern master," Beau bragged, "few other plantations on the island have such advantages."

"All the big plantations in Virginia have them."

"Will you take me to Virginia sometime?" Button

turned a cartwheel in the street and went walking away on his hands.

"She's never going back there," Beau squeezed me around my waist. "Are you, Angel?"

The praise house was bright with torch lights. The people inside were shouting and singing, directed by a gaunt old woman in a white turban mitred like a bishop's hat. As we stepped inside she motioned the people to be silent. They obeyed instantly, standing immobile, waiting her next signal. She walked over and took my hand in both of her ash-dry, boney ones. Dropping a curtsey she said, "I have make you a song, Mistress. Can we have your permission to sing it, Master?"

"Go ahead, Maum Hannah, if it's a good one. If it's not you know what I'll do to you."

Maum Hannah's face wrinkled up into a toothless grin. "It a fine song, by-Jesus. I not want my back broke, for true. Will you and the little brothers set up front, Master?"

"No. We've only time for one verse."

He whispered to me, "If she gets excited she'll go on with the song all night."

"Watch, my Mistress," Maum Hannah began humming and rocking slowly from side to side. She put her hands on her hips, elbows stuck out, and began dancing kimbo and chanting:

> Watch, Mistress, watch
> Watch, I tells you, watch
> Watch, Mistress, how you step on de stair
> Your feets might slip and your crown get tear.

A white-bearded old African stood on a small raised platform at the far end of the raw-raftered building. He was swaying on his knotty stick throwing the whole power of lungs into the harsh tones of W-a-t-c-h.

"That's Livia's father. He's a mean scoundrel. Biggest thief on the island."

He couldn't have heard but with a droll look of in-

telligence toward us the old man struck out in even
harsher tones and more bewildering pronunciation
of the words.

Maum Hannah held out her hand, inviting me into the group, all moving side to side and bending
from the knees up and down, singing with their lips
closed, like a humming wind. I looked questioningly at
Beau. I didn't want to make a mistake even though
Livia wasn't present to see me.

"Go on, Maum Hannah doesn't take orders from
me or anyone. Not you, Button. Sit back down."

> Rock, Mistress, rock
> Rock, I tells you, rock

Born rhythmic, I caught step with Maum Hannah.
Shuffling and swaying she led me through the people,
who reached out to touch me, rolling up their eyes
in jubilation. I saw the girl who had looked in my
mirror. I nodded at her and smiled. She squatted
down on the floor and hid her face in her hands.
Maum Hannah's tempo increased:

> Rock, rock and play your song
> Somebody waiting to do you wrong
> Rock, Mistress, rock.

As momentum heightened, frenzy followed. Some
of the blacks jerked their heads so fast from side to
side and backwards and forwards their features
couldn't be made out; others jumped up and down
and waved their arms and shouted; some began making a barking sound.

Beau grabbed me as we shuffled around the second
time. Maum Hannah was so mesmerized she didn't
notice when I let go her hand.

> Watch, Mistress, watch . . .

The cold air struck sense back into my burning
head.

"Hysteria is contagious. I could see by your expression that you were about to catch it. Let's get out of here."

"Why was my song a watch song? I expected a welcome song."

"Who knows? They are aware of everything about us in the big house and we don't know a damned thing about them out here, beyond 'yes sir, no sir!' They say Maum Hannah can see into the future. Be thankful she's on your side. It was obvious. Next to Livia she's the most important woman on the plantation. She takes charge of the sick house and overlooks the babies while their mothers work in the fields."

"Can we go home now?"

"Tired?"

"I haven't really looked at the house yet."

"I want to show you my picture," Button said, clinging to my hand.

"Your picture indeed," Beau said.

Eddie and Phillip stopped in the barn. Dark clouds were gathering in the west. A skein of wild geese flew honking over. A flight of ducks blotted out the early stars. An owl opened like an old umbrella and flew from a down limb of a Pride of India tree to a jutting pole on a near barn, closing like an old umbrella folding into the closet of the night.

Hoo Hoo Hoo HooHooHooHoo, the owl called from the darkness. Hoo Hoo Hoo Hoo Hoo.

"Let's run," Button whispered. "Livia says owls are spirits of dead people; one might be Papa."

"Shut up."

"They say he cut off the noses of slaves that ran away and got caught. Mother was scared to death of him just like me."

"You don't remember Mother. Shut up."

"Only Elsa wasn't scared of him. She isn't scared of you either. She isn't even scared of the Boogerman. Let's run fast."

Part Three

Secession

Hilton Head Island,
December, 1860–Summer, 1861

Fifteen

"This way, Master." Pharaoh and two little black boys were placing lighted torches along the path from the barn to the house.

Henricus had got his feet and his hands steady and was waiting on the bottom step leading to the piazza, holding a torch. Tonight, as this afternoon, he was wearing the tousled white wig and scarlet coat with silver buttons. Later I learned that the Marquis de Lafayette had left both at the town house when he visited Beaufort in 1825. Henricus had found them but only wore them when he thought the occasion merited it. I had liked him in the dining room despite his sloppiness; more so now, compared with his son.

"I here to see you safe, Mistress." He walked ahead shedding light on the steps. "We has cleaned up the hall and the dining room real fine, by gosh, yes mam. I wish you and Master a good night's resting in your very big bed."

There was no parlor or library in the house. The enormous hall was used for everything. Now, without all the people, I realized its masculine attractiveness. It smelled of gun oil and books and oak logs and cigar ashes and brandy. Candles had been lit and set around in silver sticks. Beau picked up the tallest one and held it in front of the portrait of the first Berrien to come to America.

"He's like me," Button said proudly.

"We call him the little grandfather in the gold coat. His name was Pierre Berrien. This portrait was painted in Paris in 1675 when Pierre was eighteen. Before the Huguenots were forced to flee France he was close to the French king, in line for great things if he'd changed his thinking. Legend has it he was a small man but physically so powerful he was called *le petit géant*. He lived to be one hundred and twelve

years old. He'd probably still be around if he hadn't
fallen out of a fig tree on his head. The Elliotts have
a portrait of him in a shooting coat after he lost his
teeth; still fire-eyed at ninety! And holding a muzzle
loader I'd hate to have to carry."

"His hair is the same color as mine," Button said.

"Rascal, how can you tell? He has on a white wig."

"Under his wig it is brown."

"Did he suck his thumb too? Go to bed. I've shared
Angelica enough for one day. Eddie and Phillip had
enough sense to get lost. Well, love, to continue my
story: Pierre planted grapes and sugar cane and sesa-
me; his grandson, Baynard, the good looking fellow
over there in the blue coat and tricorne hat, painted
by Copley, grew long staple cotton here in 1791. That
big-nosed profile over the piano is of him too, done
in Paris by St. Memin. Baynard made our fortune.
The rest of us have had wits enough to keep it. We're
very rich, Angelica. You can have anything in the
world that attracts you."

"Suppose Elsa—"

A knocking at the front door interrupted. Button
raced Henricus to open. It was Stephen Elliott and
two Barnwells bundled up in capes and cloaks.

"Joe Pope's back from Charleston. Came on the
late steamer. He wants all the men on the island to
meet at his house. Secession has been signed and
sealed. Charleston is wild. Tell Henricus to put candles in all your windows. Every house in South Carolina is to be illuminated tonight to celebrate our glorious future. You should see our house; looks like it's
on fire. The governor has given permission for the
Beaufort Artillery to be called up at once. Where's
Eddie? Oh, I see you! Come with us, boy, I told
Pharaoh to bring up two horses."

Beau was quickly gloved and hatted and caped,
overflowing with excitement. "Dang! If I only had
Teaser I'd be the first one at Pope's place. Phillip,
call Livvy to help Henricus set out the candles immediately. Our house must be the brightest on the island.
Night-bye, Angel."

Desolately, I followed him onto the piazza and

watched him gallop away. It took us an hour to light candles in each window. Phillip and Button and I stood out on the lawn with Henricus and admired the glowing house. There were eight windows across the front on the second story, and four on the third.

Phillip said crossly, "I don't care a fig about Secession. I want to go to Princeton."

I didn't care a fig about Secession either. I'd never heard the word until the day Beau came to Cedar Grove. I wanted to say so but didn't, fearing Phillip would begin sermonizing. I begged him to have the honor of placing a candle in the top window.

"It can represent South Carolina among the original colonies."

Arms around each other, Button and I watched as the little light glowed up in the cupola. I sensed Livia beside me.

"It's scary looking, like suddenly the whole house is on fire."

She was holding a candle much too close to the wool fringe of my shawl. Why was she standing there looking at me with that smouldering expression in her eyes? I realized I was tired enough to die. My legs felt weak and I was trembling.

An owl hooted from deep in the woods, another answered and another nearer. Low in the southern sky I saw the lucid outline of the Swan flying seaward. I almost cried out Oh, do not leave me tonight. I can't sleep in that dark cold room by myself. Your wingbeats are all that make my heart go on.

A scudding cloud obscured the constellation. The wind was rising. I could hear it. But it wasn't the wind. Button clutched my hand and whispered, "Let's go inside the house quick. The people have come out. They know Bubba isn't here."

Livia said gloatingly, "They've come to see what we're celebrating. Secession! And don't fool yourself. They know what that word means. One fiery soul among them could illuminate them just like Master has done his house. Listen . . ."

I turned around. Against the starshine on the wide water, humming as a hurricane hums or a swarm of bees, were hundreds of blacks. They could sweep over us in one quick rush. Dear little Amun must never come here. Never. Only to Beaufort, and that in summertime. Only there if Elsa went away. Oh, there were so many problems all at once. I wasn't prepared for them.

Keeping my voice steady took all the strength I could muster. "I'll help you to bed, Button."

"I puts Button to bed," Livia said harshly.

"I want Angelica to do it tonight, Livia."

"Not so."

"Of course I will, darling."

Livia followed us into the house. I could feel her malevolent gaze burning my back as Button and I went upstairs. I kept remembering Maum Hannah's song:

> Watch, Mistress, how you step on de stair
> Your feets might slip and your crown get tear . . .

Halfway up Button whispered, "She's gone back down. Run!"

He said his prayers at my knee and invited me into his bed. He'd make his cats get off. All except the calico one. She'd be too lonesome. There was a stone crock of hot water in the foot which he'd share with me. "Please, Angelica. I've never slept with a lady in my whole life."

But I had to be ready when Beau returned. I'd always be ready for him.

For an hour I sat by the fire in my pretty boudoir trying to read, first a little of Emerson then a few pages of Thoreau. They were pretty but very sleepy making; I not being much of a reader. Music and sports come easily to me but my formal education was sadly overlooked.

About midnight I made myself crawl into the freezing sheets. My feet hit something rough. A stone jar of hot water! I hadn't believed Button. Gratefully I put my toes against it, knowing I'd not sleep a wink until Beau was with me.

And suddenly he was! Dawn touched the window

with a streak of light. I had slept the night through. I sat up, watching him take off all his clothes, opening the covers for him to leap in beside me and start warming his great cold feet inside my thighs. Soon the hard red sun thrust itself into the dark reaches of heaven opening it wide. Day came gloriously.

Sixteen

I was about to fall asleep, nestled in Beau's arms, when two little boys came in and built a roaring fire. As soon as they were gone Beau jumped out of bed and stood in front of the blaze warming his powerful buttocks. His grand chest covered with red hairs gleamed in the firelight like a copper shield.

"Get up and dress. It's going to be a gorgeous day. Stop staring at me. You're a witch, trying to addle my senses."

How could he be this way—so fiery and strong and eager? He'd not slept a wink.

"Was the talk at Pope's of war?" I asked drowsily.

"War and war and more war. We planned our island defense; deciding the strategic places to erect forts in case of attack. We organized a company and elected officers. Stephen and I are going to be busier than hell from now on. That means you've got to begin taking things in hand here as soon as you eat your breakfast. Never start a project without a plate of hot hominy. Rule of the house. Oh beautiful you—I always forget how slim and fragile you really are with your hair hanging down and free of all those horrible corsets and things you insist on wearing."

I started the day with Livia. She sullenly muttered she'd not been able to sleep for worrying about whether I'd tucked the eiderdown on Button's bed or left a lighted candle somewhere to burn the house down.

She was entirely unmindful of the filthy kitchen, the messy linen and the general untidiness and laziness of the housemaids and boys. She offered me the bunch of keys to the pantry, the dairy and the smokehouse. Coolly I hung them at my belt. Her mouth poked out and she said "Um Um Um" and shook her head in disbelief.

Next Eddie and Phillip took me to observe the women seeding cotton. They were sitting in a dusty loft, bare black legs outstretched with piles of soft white cotton between them, picking out cotton seeds by hand. All were coughing from the lint which clung to their noses and made their hair and eyelashes look as if they were covered with snow. I'm sure it's not good for them.

We went to the gin house where a new machine had recently been set up. Phillip and Liney and Pharaoh and another black man, named Israel, were taking turns working it vigorously. It was exciting to watch the seed come popping out like corn. Some field hands were pushing the cotton into the selectors. They were very careless and managed to jam up the process several times and had to be struck with sticks to alert them.

Beau joined us and he and I walked down the Street to greet the old ones who hadn't been at the sing last night.

It was very quiet, broken only by the raucous midday crowing of the cocks in the quarters. All of the able-bodied were away at their tasks; the children with a child-minder. The old people were mostly indoors and came shambling out when Beau beat on their doors with his cane. They made clumsy, muttery bows but didn't show any interest or pleasure at the sight of their Master or their new Mistress.

A slab-sided old man with a grizzled grey beard called from his door, "Master, me cloth ain't 'nough."

"Didn't you get six yards, Uncle Toney?"

"Yes, sir."

"That's your ration."

"Yes, sir, but that Livia cut me long tail blue so long she only left one leg to me britches."

"I can't help that."

"Ki, Master! How you like I stand in your front yard without no britches?"

Beau shrugged and told me to walk faster; from now on I must cut out the slaves' clothes. It was my duty, not Livia's.

"But I don't know how to cut out clothes. Aunt Dell never——"

A tiny withered crone hobbled out of an especially cluttery yard.

"Howdy, Master. How you do do?"

"Fine."

"How Miss Julia do do?"

"You know very well, Aunt Hecuba, that my mother has been gone a long time."

"And my sweet little Mass Eddie and naughty Mass Phillip and that new lady with kinky hair what was here one night with old Maussa?" continued the brittle old woman who, in spite of Beau's scowling face was determined to fire off her whole barrage of questions.

"I thought you were supposed to be helping Maum Hannah in the sick house."

"Yes, sir, but old Pompey gots a rotten toe."

"Cut it off."

"And little Queenie too; him have twins."

"Put them in the children's house and tell Queenie to get herself to the gin house and start picking seeds."

"Only him not got no baby clothes for two."

"That's her fault. I didn't tell her to have two babies."

"I sorry I vex you, Master, so how 'bout sending me a little nigger to pick up stick for warm old Pompey toe, by gosh?"

"That I will do."

"It's time for Miss Julia to come back to see 'bout we? Is old Maussa shut her up again?"

"You shall not talk about Miss Julia any more. This is your new Mistress."

"What she God-name?"

"Angelica."

"Lordy do, Master, you too comical for true. Where she wing at, hey?"

"They're folded up under her shawl. Don't you see how it pokes out in the back?"

If Beau heard her cackling laugh he pretended not to. I couldn't determine his feelings. Did he like them? If he didn't like them why did he continue to let them live in snug huts and feed and clothe them?

He could easily put them all together in the sick house and forget about them.

As if he read my wondering he said tersely, "That old crone is going to live forever. She's a hundred if she's a day. I should be more like my father. He believed that our plantation system was ordered by the Almighty to reap the good things of the earth by restoring a race which we saved from barbarism to their real place in the world as laborers, so that we planters could have the time to cultivate our minds and develop science and the arts and graces and apply ourselves to the duties of government. Gentlemen were created to rule and we must send our best to govern; never our second best. Blacks were created to enable us to do just that."

"Do you believe it?"

"Papa had better sense than to get stuck with no-accounts like Hecuba and Toney. Don't ask me what I believe, ask me what I *do*."

"You don't have an overseer; have you ever personally whipped a slave?"

"I yell and shake my cane at them. That scares the dickens out of them. They know if I ever did thrash one he'd be dead as a door nail. I'm very strong when I am angry."

"Did your father personally whip?"

"No, but I have a feeling Papa enjoyed watching the overseer strike the lash."

"You make him sound as if he deserved Elsa."

"He did but I don't like to admit it. Meanwhile I'm doing my best to be a good Master. Do you realize there are 400 blacks here on Cotton Hill and five whites? If I don't show strength, they will. Don't for a minute delude yourself into thinking they like to be taken care of from birth to death. I know better than that. But I intend to keep them slaves. It's the only way we, as a nation, can survive."

"You mean the South?"

"Look at those cabins. Nobody on the island has better ones."

Each one had a poultry house of rough boards behind it. It made me sick to see how they mutilated their chickens and geese and turkeys to mark their ownership. Some were deprived of a claw, others had wattles out; tails and wings suffered in weird ways. Heaps of oyster shells and broken crockery, old shoes, rags and feathers were scattered around each hut. Many of the doors were padlocked outside.

"Why do they do that?"

"The owners are at work and honesty is not a quality they have for each other. They would be cleaned out if they didn't lock their doors. They don't steal in the big house except sweets and sugar and rum, sometimes meat. Jewels and money are quite safe. Now run along to Maum Hannah in the sick house. You must doctor whoever is sick every day."

"But I don't know anything about sickness and I can't understand a word your people say."

"Just listen. You'll catch on. We call their patois Gullah because most of them came from Angola."

"Suppose I give the wrong medicine?"

"The instant I saw you in the lot with Teaser I knew you could handle anything on the plantation. Good-bye. It's nappy time for me. I'm asleep on my feet. See you at dinner."

The glossy-skinned children were well fed and happy. No problems there. I suppose Beau gives them extra rations as he would prize stock of any kind. But the sick house! Ugh!

There was a line of bare cots. Two women, breathing in a rattling way, lay covered by piles of sacks. Maum Hannah poured them some bitter black medicine from a jug. It made them cough and spit phlegm on the floor. Like the old ones they showed no interest in me. In a corner a handsome brown girl sat rubbing her big belly.

"Maybelle time come. If she go regular I pull him out. If Maybelle stall you has to help so if him dead Master not whup me."

"Master would never whip you."

"You think not? Old Master whup anybody—especially woman people. I ain't for trust ary Berrien not to whup."

"I give you my word Master won't."

"I take your word. But you can't take back the lick once it's tore the hide. My heart hears you clear. But you got to help pull if him stuck in there."

A loose walking Negro with shiny green eyes strode in, smiling and waving. Everybody brightened up, especially Maum Hannah.

"What ails you, Cudjo Manigo?"

"I gots a sore throat. Gimme some of that sweet cherry syrup on the high shelf. It cured me right off last week."

"That's for house niggers. You got to have linseed oil and molasses. Open your mouth."

"I'll bring you a possum tonight if you oblige me. Say, Maum Hannah, ain't that Maybelle over there? Hey, Maybelle, what's that you got under your apron, a watermelon?"

"If 'tis," Maybelle giggled, " 'taint off your vine."

The room rocked with laughter and hand slapping. I didn't know what I should do but I thought it was funny. I laughed too.

At this Cudjo Manigo pulled his forelock respectfully and scraped his foot, bowing low to me, "Howdy, Mistress. I do see you for the first time. I ain't aim to be impudent before you."

I found myself nodding good humoredly, even as he reached up and took a fancy bottle from a high shelf and backed quickly out of the door.

Zipporah came in. She opened her mouth and pointed to a sore tooth. Maum Hannah gave me some oil of cloves to pour on the tooth. The taste pleased the girl. She grinned at me.

"Zipporah," she said.

"Yes, you are Zipporah. I am Mistress Angelica."

"I am Mistress Angelica."

"No. You are Zipporah."

She pointed slyly at herself, "I am Mistress Angelica."

There was a commotion outside. Two of the men I'd seen at the mill brought in Israel, his forefinger gone and his thumb hanging by a shred of flesh and skin, blood spurting.

"Him get catched in cotton gin. Her eat up him hand, greedy as buckra."

Maum Hannah fetched a bucket of turpentine and plunged the poor fellow's hand in. He yelled and screamed. I jumped for a pile of rags and caught his hand. The thumb was still dangling.

"You gots to cut it off, Mistress, I too trembly handed."

Maum Hannah gave me a pair of rusty scissors. I asked for a sharp knife but there wasn't one.

Israel was different looking from the others. He was thin nosed and sharp featured and though his speech was the same it was plain that he must have come from a different part of Africa.

Through hard sobs he begged, "Please, sweet Mistress, don't take my fumb. Without a fumb I can't no more ever run the new machine. I be no more good than a 'tater digger. Please—"

My stomach was turning over. I thought I was going to faint but something inside held me up. I heard myself saying, quite calmly, "I watched you at the old machine, Israel. The main work was done by your feet pumping the treadle. One hand is enough. I'll help you train your left hand. And look—you'll have three fingers left to use. If I don't take this thumb off you'll die of blood poisoning."

"It grow back, Mistress. Aunt Hecuba work a root on me. I'll pay her everything I save all my life; even my white rooster."

"Trust me, Israel. Give me your hand."

I put my arm around his shoulder and pushed him down into a chair. "You men find him a stick to bite on."

One of the sick women screamed out "Never see a white woman touch a nigger man before. She done put a spell on Israel. He going to die dead. You wait and see."

I fixed my eyes on his. Still sobbing he held out the bloody hand. It had stopped shaking. I dipped the dull scissors in the kerosene. Fascinated, the two men hovered over Israel while I severed his thumb and bound up his hand. I sent one of the men to the house to wake up the Master and ask him to send a bottle of rum. Beau himself came with it. He began to question me loudly but I was so keyed up and hysterical by now that I ordered him to get out of the sick house. He did!

Tears ran down Maum Hannah's cheeks. She jumped around and around and patted her hands together and cried Hallelujah. The men, Israel too, kept scraping their right feet and catching their forelocks and bowing to me and saying Do Jesus and Bless your sweet spirit and You have come to us from across Jordan and things like that. Carried away with myself I gave everybody in the sick house a cup of rum, even the pregnant girl. I poured the last drops in my hand and drank with them.

They asked my God-name as Hecuba had done. I told them. They whispered together a few minutes then Maum Hannah spoke with Sunday gravity: "If Master don't denounce otherwise the people will call you Miss Angel, evenso we done Miss Julia; neverso Old Master' new Mistress."

Beau was waiting, fussing, outside. After one look at me he didn't make any comment, just grabbed my arm and hurried me back to the big house saying dinner was ready and he hoped I had inherited some of Aunt Dell's talent so far as food was concerned.

I couldn't eat the gummy rice and backbone cooked together and must have looked mighty pale. Beau insisted on opening a bottle of champagne, which recovered me from my experience in the sick house and exhilarated me. I played the piano for an hour then sat in Beau's lap in the little boudoir the rest of the afternoon and dozed while he explained the state of the Union to me.

He wasn't sure Virginia would join the nation of states. He was certain of Alabama, North Carolina, Georgia, Mississippi and Louisiana. He thought it would be wise for Amun to come here before there was any chance of a fighting war. She'd be an antidote to Elsa. The lads would be fascinated with her, as if she were a new toy to play with, leaving me entirely for him.

Seventeen

His stovepipe hat pushed back from his forehead, Beau and I were breakfasting by firelight when Livia dragged Button into the dining room the next morning. She looked heavy and coarse in a blue cotton dress and starched white apron and turban similar to the ones of the housemaids who were serving us.

"You must whip him, Master. He will listen to nothing from me."

"Stop whining, Button Gwinnett, there's no getting out of it," Beau said.

"Henricus says you have a message for me from the Mistress?" Livia said.

"Oh that. By golly, I almost forgot. Robert Smalls came down river yesterday afternoon with a letter from Mrs. Hazzard Berrien saying those damned German servants of hers read in the *Charleston Courier* about all the celebration of Secession and packed their boxes and vamoosed on the afternoon steamer. She wants you and Henricus to come at once and run the household in town. Better choose one or two maids and a few boys to go with you."

He hadn't mentioned the letter to me. I stuffed my mouth full of fried oysters so I wouldn't let it spread into a smile of thankfulness.

"What will you and the boys do without me and Henricus here?"

"Oh," he waved a waffle gaily in my direction, "Mistress can worry about that. You don't have to go unless you want to, of course, naturally."

She was more honest than I. She didn't try and hide her relieved grin. "As you say, Master. When?"

"Smalls is due back here at noon with the tide for you all in his barge. I've paid him off. No need to take any money. It won't be for long. Shut up, Button."

"I just said goody. You say goody-bye. I left off the bye. I'll say it now: goody-bye, Livia," Button said.

"Your nose needs blowing, Button," was her farewell. She quit the room without ever having looked at or spoken to me.

Beau began humming a merry little tune as he went about vigorously stirring a plateful of hot buttered hominy as though he were whipping cream.

I buttered a corn muffin and spread it with fig preserves. "If you eat this, Button, I'll go in the boat with you. We'll be a team. You will let me, won't you, dear Beau?"

"You don't want to go with me?"

"Of course I do, Mr. Berrien, but just this once with Button."

"I'd counted on showing you Skull Creek at dawn."

Phillip saved the situation, flying in saying he was freezing to death, and where the devil were his high boots?

"I'm afraid I've got them on, Phillip. Beau said—"

"A lady going gunning? I don't believe it. What will people say? Fancy my boots fitting Angelica! Can I have Eddie's, Bubba?"

"He's wearing his. Went out an hour ago to be sure the boat is ready. Sit down and eat, boy. You can have my old ones in the tack room."

"Bully—I've always wanted to use them. What ails Button? He looks like a sick cat. I thought he'd be proud for us to include him."

"He is," I said, "he's escorting me."

"I hate runny eggs." Beau cracked his tenth boiled egg and spooned it over another helping of hominy and sausage.

"What will Mrs. Seabrook think about your bringing Angelica to the breakfast? Isn't she supposed to be the one lady present and that only until the plates are served?" Phillip asked.

"She'll be shocked, of course, but not because Angelica was so foolhardy as to choose to rise at dawn and sit in a freezing wet marsh for hours as that she has on old canvas trousers, her hair in braids, a scuffy scarf tied around her pretty throat and a worn-out tweed jacket that she claims was bought in London in the reign of Queen Mary. Yet our fair Angelica insists such garb is indicative of quality."

"Only parvenus shoot in swell, brand new jackets and trousers and carry unscratched shell cases and game bags. I don't understand you South Carolinians. Why if you went into the field or on the river in Virginia diked out like an ambassador, as you are, you'd be laughed from the shoot."

"Touchy, touchy," Beau was delighted. "If I were in Virginia I would not have on this frock coat and ruffled linen shirt. I would have on a comfortable hacking jacket and some soft baggy breeches that would treat me kinder than these binding affairs. But here, on this isolated island, I am the Maussa. Maussa must never show himself to his people without his crown and coronation attire. They might be misled into considering him human."

"Nobody would ever accuse you of that," Phillip said saucily.

I got up from the table and studied my backsides in the mirror.

"No lady in the world but you could get away with those tight trousers," Phillip remarked.

Beau dropped his teaspoon in the sheer perversity of excitement. His eyes were twinkling. "Do you dare mention my bride's form? Don't you realize that is grounds for a duel? Shall it be pistols or buggy whips or swords? We can use old Baynard's duelling pair."

I had caught on that this was their exaggerated flamboyant way of talk. I tightened one of my braids.

"What put you in such a good humor this morning?" Phillip asked, beginning to eat hungrily.

"She!" he pointed his fork. "She—radiant in rags."

Then he jumped up saying good lord it was practically daydawn and *if* war came which it wasn't there'd be few perfect mornings like this with everybody out shooting.

In the west the moon was silver-setting and a few

stars still shone. A glimmer of luminosity limned the
east. The December air was fragrant and soft with
moisture. The winds had hushed. Dews lay heavy.

"Deer feed time," Pharaoh whispered, holding a
burning fat-pine knot high, lighting us toward the
bluff. Our boots made crunchy noises on the crushed
oyster shells. A family of deer on their way to a day-
time safe place jumped in front of us. The torch
caught their eyes turning them into globes of greenish flame, making them sure targets.

"Wish I had a gun, by gosh," Pharaoh muttered,
as the deer turned back and crashed away through
the pines.

A twelve-oared barge was waiting at the landing.
Unlike ones on the James, both of her sides were
hewn out of immense cypress logs and a third log
furnished the bottom and the keel. The three pieces
were artistically and deftly joined and fashioned by
a true craftsman. In the stern was a collapsible cabin
of wood with seats and a berth. The oarsmen sat
amidships. The prow was loaded with six golden
retrievers, guns and sacks and a powerful, shiny bul-
let-headed black man. This was Liney, the plantation
Driver, the head Negro, accountable only to Beau.

We set out for Skull Creek. Bearded Big May, tall
and wide shouldered, with a length of reach of arm
that would have done honor to a Roman charioteer,
and a wooden leg, was the stroke oar. He had trained
his crew of eleven like a martinet. He was the boss.
Any oar that didn't "bite" the water at the exact time
as his own received a hissed threat of what was going
to happen the next time it missed. He set the pace
and never failed to "get him." The tide was with us.
We seemed to fly over the water to Seabrook's Landing.

We moored at a little barn where some canoes were
tied up in a canal. Beau stood sniffing and cracking
his big knuckles. In the distance across the marsh you
could hear thousands of ducks waking up and talking
as if they were at a convention.

"They remind me—" Button blundered.

"Sh-h-h-h—just before daydawn the human voice carries as a trumpet. Whisper, you jackass."

"Buttons don't know nothing about ducks," Pharaoh giggled. "Poor little man."

Beau took a gun that Liney held out and handed it to me. "Familiar?"

"No. But I understand how to handle it if Button gets in trouble."

"It's a Purdey. It was mine when I was a boy." He gave Button a sack of shells. "Liney is the finest duck man on the island. He will guide you two. Eddie and I will go together; Phillip and Pharaoh. A gold piece to the winner." He picked me up and handed me to Liney, who waded in the water and sat me gently in a canoe, then fetched Button.

A wind was rustling the palmettos. Far off a rooster was crowing and close by one answered. From the dark trees bordering Skull Creek the clamor of ducks spread as light further opened the eastern sky.

Liney paddled our canoe softly down the dark tide into a smaller creek meandering through the infinite black rattling marsh and the still dim reaches of the estuary. I could hear ducks all about me now and in the air over me.

"There must be a million out here," Button's voice roared like a foghorn.

"Duck not like to hear people-talk. Just duck-talk, Buttons. Don't be nervous. I take you to them," Liney's voice was wind soft.

The golden Labrador was warm across my feet. A streak of red shot into the dramatic silver and black above the horizon. We glided along the shore through reeds, finally halting in a thick clump. A gun boomed on our left and the whole world came alive with wings.

During the rush and blast of noise, Liney said, "Here's your gun, all loaded, Buttons. When I tells you, stand up quick and shoot. You jest set light, Miss Angel, and keep warm."

The retriever alerted, knowing what was expected of him. Carefully Button stood up and found a balance. A few small ducks flew close giving shrill sweet cries. They were wood ducks, my favorites; I hoped they stayed far away.

Liney tightened the canoe against some reeds.

"Stand up high, boy; look there!"

Hundreds of mallards were rising from the water, shimmering in the lightening light. Button was overwhelmed. He must shoot. But which one? Shutting his eyes he squeezed the trigger.

"Big one!" Liney was delighted.

He lay on the water, a kingly drake, one wing high and stiff, trying to swim but going crazily around in circles.

"Drop him, Button, you've just crippled him," I said.

He took aim and hit him square in the head. Feathers flew out in a green bouquet and settled back down on the dead breast. The rest of the mallards were making a fast getaway, skimming the surface.

Liney chuckled, "They be back when they over their scary. They big juicy ones." He patted the retriever, whose wagging tail made wet thump noises on the bottom of the canoe.

It was coming dayclean. I could hear Beau and other gunners shooting up and down the creek and from all parts of the immense wild marsh. The sky was filled with flying ducks: canvasbacks, widgeons, mallards, teal, blacks. I was miserable, dreading Beau's and Phillip's scorn when Button returned with one pitiful duck. But he was he; he'd never be they. He was crying hard. What to do? I mustn't allow something like this to ruin his life.

"I'm not going to shoot any more ducks. You take the gun, Liney. I'll paddle," he sobbed.

"No. Not allow for but one slave on a plantation to have a gun. Pharaoh he on Cotton Hall. Buttons, why you got monkey on your back? Shoot. You aims fine. It's fun to shoot."

"It makes me sick inside to kill birds. Aren't you my friend?"

"I belongs to you. I'm your slave."

"If you belong to me you must do as I say, mustn't you?"

"Give me the gun." I laid my cheek against the stock as if it were a boy's cheek. I loved guns.

Liney was overcome; terrified.

"I know how to shoot, Liney. But you must never tell the Master about this."

"Oh no, Miss Angel, never will I."

"Keep close to shore; move from here; nobody can see us in these reeds. I know how the ducks fly. Be careful. Don't let the paddle rap the sides and try not to make the water curl and giggle loud. If ducks jump too sharp, swing the boat so I am in a position for a shot."

The day that had for a moment waved a red flag now showed lowery clouds. A fine clinging rain came down. The wind blew in cold from Port Royal Sound. The ducks were circling and dropping down.

"Ducks not like cold wind, either," Liney crooned happily, pulling Button up against him.

At that two canvasbacks came hurtling straight toward me flying not four feet above the water.

"They're going to knock your head off!" Button whimpered.

The ducks bore right on, flying fast. I stood steady, setting my sight between the closely coming pair and let go, bursting them to pieces so near I felt the wind from the duck's wings ruffle my hair. The drake was a bloody mass at my feet.

"I don't want to look." Button hid his head in Liney's chest.

I paid no heed. I was magicked and pulsating with excitement. I went on shooting at singles flying over and at pairs as they jumped and into the middle of heavy flocks. And every time I shot a duck fell; sometimes two; once three. Liney was the fastest loader I ever knew. He was as excited as I and never lost sight of a fallen duck, nor did our dog.

At dayclean we heard the conch blowing to start the field hands at their task of carting marsh mud to enrich the bare cotton fields.

"I t'ink," Liney grinned, "every duck on the river visiting here to greet you today, Miss Angel. You know how many you kill?"

"No."

"Fifty-t'ree."

"Enough. I bet Master didn't shoot that many. What do you plan to say to Beau, Button?"

"Look at our ducks, Bubba. How many did you get?"

"You won't tell, Liney?"

"No mam, Miss Angel. I pick up now."

We reached the little barn at about the same time as the others and laid out the ducks on the bank for the count. Eddie had forty-two; Beau and Phillip a hundred between them.

Beau looked hard at me, fixing me with his keen eyes, accusing me. Would I lie if he put the direct question? Would Button? Could I lie to him?

Over and over, unbelieving, Phillip and Eddie and Pharaoh counted the pile of ducks Button and Liney had tossed on the bank. It came out fifty-three every time. Nobody believed Button had shot the ducks. Liney? Ah—if they thought that I must quickly admit what I'd done or he'd be punished.

"Beau——"

"Your hair's come unplaited, Angelica. It's all down your back and there's a bruise on your right cheek. Did a reed hit you? Here, Button Gwinnett—Catch ——" Beau tossed a twenty dollar gold piece to Button and raised his hat to me.

He knew!

I could have knelt and worshiped him.

Eighteen

Struggling in nightmare, I was in the paddock at Cedar Grove. Someone had left the pasture gate open. The horses had thundered in and were squeezing and smothering me. I could hear their heaving breath, feel the hot foam blown from their nostrils, smell their sweat. I was trampled, mashed! I grabbed for Beau. There was no one in bed with me! I struggled awake. A black hand was holding a flaming lightwood knot at the foot bed-post. The room was full of the people. They had risen up and come to kill me. They had already taken Beau away and killed him. Tongues of fire suddenly leapt up in the fireplace. Eyeballs shone in the reflected light, green-sparked as the deer eyes had been at dawn. I screamed.

"There's nothing to be afraid of, Mrs. Berrien," Beau said firmly. He was standing in front of the fire in a trailing black velvet dressing gown and a peaked white linen nightcap. I pulled the silver silk comfort tight around my neck to hide my trembling.

Little black kinks quivered on top of Liney's big round head in a fuzzy ball. He looked twice as huge and black here in the fire-streaked bedroom as he had on the river at daydawn. Like skin-covered drums, his shiny cheekbones stood out on his face in the down glow of the torch he was holding.

"Israel most likely done dead by now," he said in his soft voice. "When I leave out the sick house, blood been squirting everywhere same like a torrench. He beseech Miss Angel to come to he and heal he."

"It's absolutely out of the question. It's almost middle-night and turning cold as hell."

A shutter banged against the window. The wind was blowing hard. It whooed down the chimney. Smoke billowed into the room.

"But, Master, Israel worth. Israel gots something in

124

his head 'sides nits and louse. He the only one understand them fancy machines in the gin house," Liney said stubbornly.

"You can ride for Dr. Stoney at first light. Tell him I say it's a real emergency. He'll come."

Another man found the courage to speak. "He sure to die if Miss Angel not come. He scared and hurted."

I can't go, I said to myself. I won't go. I wouldn't know the first thing to do. If only I were safely back at Cedar Grove with Uncle Jim. If only I'd never come to this barbaric sea island.

"Mistress is not up to such an errand. She's only been here a few days."

"Her able. I been on the river with she. I seen for myself."

"Ah, the truth about the ducks at last."

"No sir, Master. I ain't aiming to tell you no truth at all. I ain't about to tell you the truth. I promise Miss Angel not to."

"What's Maum Hannah doing? Why can't she handle things? Has she had a fit?"

"She having one. Maybelle baby stuck at the same time. Not we can stay with them, hant get we. Hant done smell all that blood and howl loud along the ditch. Maum Hannah howl with him. Where Master Eddie at?"

"He and Master Phillip and Pharaoh went to Hunting Island yesterday afternoon. I tell you what: you all go out onto the piazza and I'll come directly with a plan."

I could hear their feet scraping. "Yassuh, Master. We too regretful to disturb your rest, Master. But please, fore Gawd, send Miss Angel back with we."

The door shut quietly; I snuggled far down under the covers. Beau pulled them back. He smoothed my hair away from my forehead and lightly kissed the tip of my nose. "How delicate and young you look; all long slender neck and enormous frightened eyes. I'll help you dress."

While he was tying strings and hooking hooks on my heaviest Balmoral skirt and woolen sacque I gave him all the sensible reasons why I shouldn't be sent to my death in the middle of the night. "You are coming with me?"

"No." He held me as if I might come to pieces in his arms. "So womanly," he whispered, "and brave and fine. I would go, of course, but it's not the custom for the Master to look after the sick house. That task belongs to the Mistress. This will be the hardest thing you'll ever be called on to do. I'll give you a bottle of opium. Pour out a large spoonful for Israel as soon as you arrive. What do you know about hemorrhage?"

"I watched Jenks put a tourniquet on a horse's leg once. He'd tighten it and stop the flow for a while then loosen it. Must I go?"

"Mother would have. Elsa wouldn't. Take your choice."

"How mean you are."

"Nothing could ever harm you with Liney along."

"Suppose it were Pharaoh?"

"He's a rascal. Hurry, you're stalling. I'll escort you onto the piazza."

It was daylight when I stumbled out of the sick house door onto the small porch. Wrapped in a great cape, Beau was slouched on the waiting bench. He was carving something out of a piece of wood. I saw his proud, sweet, inquisitive look and his surprised smile as he discovered me.

"I'd given you up. You are mad to have stayed in there so long."

"But you told me to stop Israel's bleeding," I murmured wearily.

"I never mean what I say." He had risen and was holding out his arms. "What the devil happened to you in there anyway? You have a saintly aura, despite, or perhaps because of, the streaks of blood on your cheek and down your collar."

I began to cry noisily, as a child cries. "Israel's asleep and Maybelle's baby is a little girl with a harelip and a cleft palate. I simply can't stand it."

Button woke me at dinner time. "Anatole says for us to hurry before the popovers fall."

"Where is Beau?"

"You forgot? You all were supposed to spend the day in Beaufort with Elsa and the Yankee man. Bubba said to tell you he'd be home on the late afternoon steamer. I took Israel a bucket of soup from the kitchen. The doctor cut his whole hand off but he didn't bleed any more. And I saw Maybelle's baby. Golly but it's ugly."

While Button and I were eating partridges and doves cooked in a crisp pastry pie, Beau, announced by many slammings of doors and callings-out, waving a malacca cane, whirled into the dining room, followed by an erect, keen-eyed gentleman with a bristly brown beard.

Button jumped up and kissed him. "This is my godfather, Angelica. He's ever so nice."

"Angelica, meet Thomas Fenwick Drayton, our neighbor. Tom should be an army man, having graduated from West Point, but he doesn't care for soldiering. He designed the Charleston-Savannah railroad and manages it most profitably."

Beau tossed the cane onto a chair and took his place at the head of the table. "Sit by Button, Tom, so you can feast your eyes on Angelica as well as on that dainty dove leg which she nibbles."

"I'm afraid Beau is prejudiced," I told Tom Drayton cheerfully, as he took my hand.

"And why shouldn't he be?" said Tom, his voice hearty but weary. "Wasn't your mother Dell Hazzard?"

"No, the younger sister."

"The prettiest one! How stupid of me. You have her eyes. Say, come spend the night at Fish Haul Plantation with me, Button. I'll show you the butterflies I caught in the swamp last summer."

"Oh boy! May I, Bubba?"

"By all means. Stay as long as Uncle Tom will let you. You can take my horse. He and Tom's big white are still at the hitching post. I told the boys to hold them awhile."

Off Button ran.

Another game pie was brought and divided between the two men. Tom Drayton had been on the Charleston steamer Beau had boarded in Beaufort to return home. They were full of talk of Secession and its consequences.

Beau said, "The first effect it's going to have on me is to put every hand on the plantations to frantically ginning, baling and loading my 1860 cotton crop to send to Charleston so my factor can immediately weigh and ship it to England. I refuse to be caught out with nothing but paper bonds and bank notes and scrip issued by every jackass town in the Confederacy. That is if someone does lose their head and precipitate a war."

"How much do you expect your crop to bring this year?"

"At least $200,000."

"Is there a chance Secession will change the status of your father's estate as regards Elsa?"

"I'd say yes, wouldn't you?"

"Certainly no South Carolina judge would award a Yankee woman an acre, now that we've left the Union, unless she had clear title."

"She doesn't. Where will Percival stand?"

Tom looked toward the window fatalistically. "He's already renounced every tie of blood or loyalty to South Carolina. Did it publicly in Philadelphia, day before yesterday. Mother had a telegram. It put her into an instant decline."

"Who is Percival?" I asked.

Tom seemed to flinch. "He's my brother, an admiral in the United States Navy. Papa wanted us both in the services. It took with him. Could be the uniform. Gawd, but Percival's handsome! Spent much of his life on Hilton Head. Knows the waterways around here like the palm of his hand. It crushes me to imagine what could happen if he——"

Then there was Button in the door, clothes bundle in hand, smiling. Tom got up and bowed and said how charmed he was to have met me and why didn't Beau and I visit them next week in Savannah for the Cotillion?

"Be thankful you collapsed and I went to Beaufort alone." Beau stretched out his legs until his toes almost touched the fire.

We were taking tea in the hall in the late afternoon. Kneeling on the hearth, I was toasting bread on a long fork. The fire burned my cheek. Beau reached down and pulled my hair a little. I was filled with happiness.

"And speaking of alone," he continued, "do you realize this is the first time we've been in this house without the boys?"

More happiness struck me like a falling of stars. I looked up at him dazzled.

"Don't smile at me like that right now. I've got to tell you about today."

He never talked to Elsa at all. He did peep in her room. She was asleep, a half empty bottle of laudanum on the bedside table. Livia stood in the doorway with him, smirking or sneering. He didn't give a damn which. Pierce had left Beaufort within an hour after receiving a telegram from New York.

Livia couldn't say what was in the telegram, not being able to read, but it sure fired Pierce up. He was so excited he laughed out loud and beat his fists on the marble mantelpiece. The only time anyone ever heard him laugh. Pierce gave Livia all sorts of instructions and made Elsa promise not to leave Beaufort. He offered Livia cash money to stay in the house until he came back.

When?

Livia just shrugged and smiled and nodded her head up and down in the way she had of not answering.

What a disappointment to miss seeing Pierce. He had taken the malacca cane, his grandfather's, on purpose. It made a keen whip. He had thought out, during his night vigil on the sick house porch, exactly how he was going to needle Pierce into insulting him, then he was going to cane the devil out of him.

Why?

He had a bad feeling about Pierce. It was more than being jealous of the way he looked at me at the party. That was only natural. Pierce's enthusiasm over the Beaufort house was suspect. Why would a man of Pierce's type dance attendance on a woman like Elsa unless he was being excessively well paid? Unless Pierce was mixed up in something shady. That was it! Something shady. He'd wager a million on it.

No, Livia wasn't going to be brought back to Cotton Hall. I could rest easy. But Livia knew a lot about Pierce. He questioned her but, as usual, she outsmarted him and told him nothing in a great deal of talking.

"Play some Mozart for me," Beau said when he'd finished all the toast and butter and drunk most of the tea, cool with cream.

I had only got through a few bars of a gentle etude when I looked over and saw that he was sleeping sounder than little Mr. Monk had ever done; but not snoring, thank the Lord. I didn't mind. I just played softer and softer to soothe him and express the magic that was and would always be between us.

Beau and I walked out on the piazza after breakfast the next morning. The sun was touching the topmost boughs of the tall pines and glancing from the myriad glistening needles that hung motionless in the chilly air. It drank up the white frost that touched the marsh canes like a crystal blanket and the dark vapors that blurred the dim reaches of the forest.

"Look!"

Eddie and Phillip and Pharaoh were struggling up the bank from the dock carrying a deer. Dripping wild turkeys were draped around their necks.

Shivering in the cold air Eddie said they started back from Hunting Island at first light. As they passed Bay Point a wave upset the sail boat. Pharaoh couldn't swim, damn him. Eddie had to jerk out the mast and the sails so the boat could right, then rescue Pharaoh. Phillip swam after their guns. Then both of them were a long time swimming to salvage every turkey and the deer that had floated off. They'd been four hours already in wet clothes. Probably die of pneumonia.

"Done dead," moaned Pharaoh.

"Good riddance," Beau said cheerfully. "Golly, that's a fine buck. Eight prongs! Run and change clothes. I'll have a hot brandy toddy waiting for the three of you before I put you all to work."

Nineteen

Christmas was a bewilderment of putting holly behind all the portraits; stringing tinsel and clamping wax candles over a fragrant, fresh-cut cedar tree; people endlessly calling, or we boating to plantation egg-nog parties and tea parties and dinners; giving out papers of tobacco, wool hats, bright head handkerchiefs, cloth and shoes to the slaves; admiring the deer, wild turkeys, birds and waterfowl the shooters brought in; culminating in a gay, if chill, oyster roast on the beach at the Popes' plantation, on New Year's Day, following a beautiful Communion Service at Zion Chapel of Ease.

It wasn't much fun because all the men clustered together talking about the plan to construct a fort, right here where the oysters were being roasted on a big fire. Who could send how many strong slaves to cut palmetto trees and haul logs and dig fortifications? Everybody speak up!

"Does Mr. Pope mind having a fort in his front yard?" I asked Cousin Annie, who was sitting between me and her pretty youngest daughter, Harriet Gonzales.

"I suppose he figures he'll be the most protected planter on the island," Harriet said. "I'll come over to your house. We can stand in your cupola and watch all the excitement. Ambrosio, of course, will be in command."

"No, Beau will," I said, laughing, "at least he thinks he will."

"So does Ambrosio, the sweet silly. He'll give the commands in Cuban Spanish," she giggled gaily.

As I gathered up the Scotch plaid rugs and lap robes we'd wrapped ourselves in as we shivered at the long tables set up on the very edge of the Atlantic Ocean, Cousin Annie straightened the red velvet fez

studded with gold buttons she was wearing on her
white hair.

"Billy insists on spending the rest of the winter in
his experimental gardens at our Oak Lawn plantation
on Edisto to get away from all this war hysteria. The
servants packed up the silver and linen and my harp
and all the musical instruments and barged them
there yesterday. It's Billy's favorite house; mine is
Myrtle Bank, of course; the children prefer Beaufort.
I hate leaving you here, Angelica. Is Elsa really going
to stay in Beaufort this winter?"

"She's afraid Beau might find the will in that house
if she's not there. Oh, Cousin Annie, what should I do
about her? Should I try and make friends?"

"You couldn't if you tried. They say Livia and Henricus treat her like a baby. They're having a grand
time in town lording it over everybody else's servants, they going and coming as they please, so long
as they keep Elsa supplied in laudanum and warm as
toast. She perked up when that New York peacock
was there spreading his gorgeous fan and going
through the records at the Court House. Gossip says
Elsa set her cap for him, dangling the Berrien property before him as her dowry."

"He was a stagey man. He had the weirdest eyes
I ever saw," I said.

A big wind made the home trip in the barge rough.
Button snuggled in my arm. Phillip and Eddie and
Beau made a shield with their capes to shelter us.

Big May led the rowers in a song to keep them
stroking in unison.

The song was wild and elusively beautiful and un-
explainable. The way in which the chorus struck in
with curious and exotic tones between each phrase of
the melody, chanted by Big May, was very effective,
especially with the rhythm of the oarlocks for accom-
paniment.

> It's mighty cold at first cock crow.
> Blow down, you Blood Red Roses, blow down.
> You've got your order and to field must go.
> Blow down, you Blood Red Roses, blow down.

Chop that cotton in sun and rain.
Blow down, you Blood Red Roses, blow down.
The dove fly low again and again.
Ooo-o-oh! you pinks and posies.
Blow down, you Blood Red Roses, blow down.
Jedus is coming in a dark blue hat.
Blow down, you Blood Red Roses, blow down.
To lead you by the hand from where you at.
Blow down, you Blood Red Roses, blow down.

The water around us was grey and cold. The sky was grey and menacing. There were ominous vibrations traveling through the boat.

"That song frightens me."

Beau said, "That's a very ancient sea chantey. Whalers sing it on their voyage around the Horn. Nobody knows where Big May picked it up. Could have heard it in Africa as a boy."

Phillip said, "It's a hostile song. They've added a new line. I never heard the blue hat one before. I wonder——"

"What did you do wrong this time?"

"You always suspect me of something. Big May was on our landing when Pharaoh and I walked Mr. Pierce down there on the day of the party while Elsa waited for Livia."

"I think I'm going to break your neck."

"Let Phillip finish, Beau. You aren't being fair to him. He brought this up himself."

"Make it quick then. I know I'm not going to like it."

"Mr. Pierce was fascinated with the barges and the sail boats in which the guests had arrived. He wanted to know if this was the way we always got around. He questioned Big May about the channels and the different kinds of boats and how fast they went and so forth. Suddenly, for no reason, he asked Big May and Pharaoh if they'd ever seen a United States Army uniform. He took great pains describing it in detail. Particularly the snappy blue hats," Phillip said.

"Pooh! There's nothing to that. I thought you had something important to relate."

My eyes met Phillip's. He blushed and looked down. Eddie cleared his throat and said he hoped it didn't rain before we got home. None of us wanted to start an argument with Beau this afternoon. The song had unsettled all of us. Him too. We didn't want to think about it any more.

Beau stood up, calling to Big May—"You've made it in record time. Do you need the boys to help you come in?"

"No, Master," Big May yelled back. "All hand eager to row all night. That song always do heat um up."

On February 4, 1861, Jefferson Davis was elected President of the Confederacy in Montgomery, Alabama. The day the news came Beau took the steamer to Charleston from Seabrook's Landing to make arrangements with his factors, Barnwell and Son, to ship his cotton crop to England. While there he had his tailor measure him for two Confederate officer uniforms. He bought a wide-brimmed, soft grey felt hat decorated with a gold band and a sweeping ostrich plume. He wore it to supper when he returned home that night. Afterwards I played Chopin's accusing "Revolutionary Etude" while he fenced with imaginary Yankees.

He couldn't make up his mind whether to join the cavalry legion Wade Hampton was talking about organizing to be bound for Virginia, or remain in the area with the Beaufort Volunteers to defend his own vine and fig tree.

"I'll decide the day my cotton clears the harbor and is headed out into the Atlantic Ocean. In the meantime here I am on the island so all is well. The god of battle is on our side. No Lincolnite navy or army can pass my sword and pistol. I don't think this hat is as becoming as my grey beaver top hat, do you? I'll give it to Eddie."

He always spoke contemptuously of the Northern forces as Lincolnites, blaming the whole business on that gentleman, for whom I, like Uncle Jim, secretly held much admiration.

War did not seem inevitable. We became accustomed to the idea that we were a separate nation. Why should the North come after us?

Nevertheless Beau rushed around feverishly. The gins clacked from daydawn to first dark. Had it not been for the danger of fire from lanterns, Beau would have moved a cot into the gin house and kept the ginners at it constantly seven days a week. These little machines interested me more than the Grover and Baker sewing machines Cousin Annie's man had delivered to help me make clothes for the slaves and which I'd never opened.

One afternoon I was sitting on a stool in the gin house watching Israel gingerly touching the glittery new steam gin with his left hand. There were twenty of the foot-gins in the room. One was idle. Outside a drippy rain was falling from a thick sky. It was one of those winter days on which one is caught up in a foreboding that something is about to come to an untimely end. And maybe that was why not only the outline of the machines but my thoughts too seemed to come sharply into focus. I walked over to Israel.

"This steam engine is a toy. Show me how the regular foot-gin operates. I've never studied one."

Obediently he took his accustomed place. The foot-gins were about three and a half feet high and one foot wide with an iron flywheel on each side working a pair of wooden rollers that were moved by the foot like a small turning lathe.

"I suppose to feed the cotton through the rollers. Seed stay behime. I frighted to touch it."

"Put your right wrist in your pocket and tell it to stay in there."

"Cyan't use left hand."

"Talk to it."

"Miss Angel, I so bad want to be the first to prove the steam gin. Let me. I not broke it."

"It's too dangerous. Pharaoh said it almost blew up on him last night. Show me, Israel."

Wretchedly he took his stand at one end of the ped-aled foot-gin, feeding the cotton awkwardly, slowly, with his left hand, through the rollers, leaving a pile of smooth black seeds behind.

"Do it again. I'll stay and watch you."

By the end of the day he had the highest piles of seeds of any of the others. He was a whole man again. He would turn out thirty pounds of clean cotton a day. Maybe more.

"Got to keep out the best ones," he sang to the seeds. "Need a fine crop next year to honor Miss Angel."

We refused to pay attention to Pharaoh's loud bragging as he kept the fancy steam engine going at top speed, doing as much work as the twenty old-fashioned foot-gins put together.

Often I went around the barns with Beau. He showed me how the cotton, after it was ginned, was moted on frames of latticed wood, sorted according to color and length of fiber, then packed in round bags of about three hundred pounds each.

The storage warehouse was a dim forest of these bales. Sentries walked up and down guarding against rats and fire.

"This is white gold. But question not my patriotism for our new country. I plan to convert every cent I have in the banks, though not in the house, into Confederate bonds and currency. Jeff Davis is welcome to my fortune whenever he requests it."

On the 10th of March the last of the 1860 cotton was baled and the loaders began straining and toting it onto trolleys that they rolled down the bluff road to flat boats moored at our dock. That same day, in Beaufort, the cotton, billed to Barnwell and Son, was put on a steamer for Charleston at $1.00 a bale for freight.

And now, the Negroes began going into the fields to prepare the land for new planting. Some breaking of the ground was done by oxen-drawn ploughs; most by field hands hoeing. Every day the people assembled at dawn to collect hoes from Liney to turn the earth. Zipporah and her sister were among the women hoers. She turned her head away from me whenever she saw me looking at her.

The fields were laid out in squares of one-quarter acre. When the earth was ready Liney directed the hands in making rows. Precisely on the 20th day of March they made holes four inches deep in the rows about one foot apart into which the selected seeds were plentifully dropped by Liney's favorites.

Beau and I rode up and down, up and down the cotton rows over hundreds of acres. Our plantation horses could walk as fast as Parasol could trot. They were fat and round; not challenging, but comfortable enough to sit on all day with no more effort than being in a rocking chair.

In Albemarle County, Virginia, the fields were still covered with snow and frost, the weather bitter, March being our ugliest month. Here the sensuous warmth of sea island spring filled the air with its breath. Fragrant yellow jessamine and cherokee roses twined up and down branchy trees. Spicy bay blossoms, like cool greenish stars, studded the thin saplings around whose roots wild pink honeysuckle opened soft spider filaments. Tea olive trees against the house were covered in small sweet flowers. All these along with peach and apple and orange blossoms and banana shrubs and gardenias made a perfumery of out of doors.

The sea was greener. Some nights we couldn't get to sleep. We'd go out and lie in a sail boat, just drifting, looking at the wind, listening to the gulls and the terns crying and night birds singing. It was bliss, wondering if you were asleep or awake, if it were midnight or early morning; not caring about anything in the world but him and me together.

Occasionally I'd wonder if Beau would ever get tired of making love. I knew I never would. How could I when every time he looked at me or touched me it was like a skein of wild geese winging over, crying Love Me! Love Me! And he did. He said there was always a soft light lit inside of me for the moment of our shared delight. His face at those times was so burningly alive I was afraid it would consume itself.

When things began sprouting we walked together in the fields and through the gardens and in and out of the work shops. The hot sun made my skin glow but poor Beau's big freckled nose blistered three times before he gave up and called for an umbrella. A black man named Masai carried it. He was blind and dumb. He held the umbrella in one hand and kept his other on Beau's shoulder.

Masai was eight feet tall. He had been purchased in New Orleans by Beau's father on a whim, Hazzard never having encountered anyone taller than himself before. He gave the slave the name of his African tribe. He planned to dress Masai in a turban and gaudy balloon trousers and stand him at the gate of his Beaufort mansion. But Masai, powerful as he was, underestimated the power of a balky Carolina mule's heels. Blinded and his throat ruined, he instantly lost Hazzard's interest. He sat idle for years on the sick house porch until Beau returned from Harvard. Beau had a special feeling for Masai. He gave him tasks to perform like grinding corn and making pottery, both of which he performed skillfully. He was very proud. Beau said he liked Masai's hand on his shoulder. It was obvious Masai worshipped Beau. He never stopped smiling as we walked the fields.

Once a week Beau went to Beaufort to drill with the Beaufort Volunteers and play war games. He dressed up in his gold-braided Confederate uniform and Pharaoh in a bright red flannel shirt and white straw hat with long red streamers and they chuffed noisily away in Cotton Hall's fancy new combination steam and sail boat. Pharaoh was the only one who understood the engine in the center of the boat that also carried a sturdy side wheel and two sails. Its arrival in Beaufort made Pharaoh the talk of the waterfront Negroes.

Beau would sit in the bow, a tall grey linen stovepipe hat on his high red head, holding his brass sword scabbard straight up, parallel to his erect body. It would catch fire in the morning sun and flash a warning that someday he might go across the wide water and not come back at the dusking. Thinking that always undid me. I spent the whole day restlessly going back and forth from the cupola to the dock for a sight of the returning little vessel.

Maum Hannah too was reacting to the charged atmosphere. "Ain't you do hear it?" she would ask me.

"What does it sound like?"

"Like a monstrous flock of white birds wavering down on the north wind. Sometimes the wings is so loud I hides my head in my apron least they revelop me and take me away from here. I been born pontop Cotton Hall. I aims to die here."

Because of Maybelle's baby's trouble in swallowing, they lived in the sick house. Maybelle was intelligent and strong and had a fine sense of humor. We worked well together.

"Maum Hannah talking about freedom," Maybelle teased. "She think she might going to fly there on them snow-white wings."

"Nothing so," the old woman shook her head indignantly. "Any day now you going to hear it, too; you and all the people. When that flock come flying in across the sound I go continue to hide my head and let them birds go smack over me. I ain't to move. 'Bout you I ain't convince. But if you ain't wash your girl-baby Mistress going take him for cooter eitherso 'rangatan, and Mistress ain't going to let you for gone in him house get milk even."

Twenty

On the 11th of April I was sitting on the joggling-board on the front piazza in the mid-day sunshine. I was making the board go up-down! up-down! as fast as I could. We had buried Maybelle's baby a while earlier. The service had stunned me.

The people sang:

> Moonlight Starlight Oooooooh. Moonlight!
> Lay the body to the tomb
> Ooooooh John lay the body down . . .

Such a tiny body! Such a tiny box! Before the grave was filled the tide had risen. Salt water was already seeping into the hole when I ran back to the house, nobody noticing. Maum Hannah was leading the singing and moaning and calling out to Jesus to have mercy. Maybelle was screaming and pulling out her hair by the handful. Three powerful field hands held her writhing body so she wouldn't jump into the grave with her child.

Out in the sound dolphins were leaping and playing. I loved watching them. Especially a snow-white one that came often and jumped higher than any of the others. He made me think of Teaser. And that brought Aunt Dell and Uncle Jim and Amun to mind. We wrote often so I knew that Aunt Dell and Uncle Jim were planning to spend the summer at White Sulphur Springs with Cousin Anna Randolph. Amun would come to me as soon as they learned of someone else traveling this way. I needed Amun. Especially on days like today when the farawayness of Hilton Head washed over me; when Beau was somewhere else. Today he and Stephen and Francis Lee were in Savannah studying the plans for fortifications on Tybee

Island. They were due home with the tide, on the
steamer.

The boys were out in the sail boat, the breeze
being perfect, to practice handling for the summer
races in Beaufort.

The shimmering sail and the leaping dolphins made
a moving picture. The sail boat was heading in to
shore when Beau came galloping up to the front steps.
Very excited he was waving a sheet of paper and
shouting: "It's begun! We fired on Fort Sumter at 4
A.M.! But my cotton is safe away for England. Five
Lincoln gunboats are sitting just outside the bar.
They'd have snatched the whole shipment if the vessel had left a day later. Here, hold my horse so I can
kiss you. Didn't I tell you the god of battle is on my
side!"

I was dying to go to Charleston but Beau said he
was too busy. I wondered if it was because he didn't
want to run into all those girls he'd courted so sensibly!
Stephen and Charlotte went. They took dinner with
us the next week and were full of it.

"I wish you could have seen the Northern warships.
If they ever turn those big guns on the sand and tabby forts we specialize in, one blast will blow them
apart like matches."

"Why the hell didn't they help Anderson in Fort
Sumter?" Beau shattered a beautiful baked shad all
over the white damask table cloth. "You reckon it
was because he's a Southerner?"

"Could have been. Or Mr. Lincoln wanted to make
sure the world would know that *we* started the war."
Stephen helped Beau gather the fish together again.
"Whatever voices of reason dared let themselves be
heard have been stilled by the ridiculous performance
on both sides. Even Uncle Billy is breathing fire and
brimstone. I know London will be snickering when
William Howard Russell's account of the action appears in the *Times*. We met him in the Chestnut
suite at the Mills House. A wretched snob, he was.
Worse than Joe Barnwell, who said he didn't see how

he was going to fight in any army that would accept shopkeepers and boatbuilders."

Beau had the shad under control now. He was serving it without spilling too much. "I hear Barney Rhett whooped and cheered jubilantly up and down the halls of the Mills House all night long."

"Drunkenly would be more correct. You didn't give me enough roe."

Charlotte said, "General Beauregard was the lion of the hour and knew it. Stephen liked him more than I did."

"Angelica will like him. He's due here in a couple of weeks to map out the defense for the entire southeastern coast," Stephen said, passing his plate for more shad roe.

Brigadier General Pierre Gustave Toutant Beauregard was very much a poseur. He was also very short. He made me feel endlessly tall and I couldn't keep my eyes from staring down at a funny cowlick on top of his head. He didn't charm me but Beau idolized him.

Beau and Stephen and Captain Francis Lee, the Drayton nephew, of the Engineer Corps, spent every day with Beauregard riding importantly around the island discussing fortification points or boating up and down the coast from Charleston to Savannah trying to discover more strategic defense points for those cities than Hilton Head. They came to the conclusion there weren't any.

Beauregard christened the battery on Hilton Head, which was to be just below Cotton Hall on the Pope place at Coggins Point, Fort Walker, hoping that the honor would squeeze heavy artillery out of the Secretary of War. Across the harbor mouth at Bay Point, Fort Beauregard was marked out along the seashore.

The island planters sent wagonloads of slaves each morning to work on the fortifications, digging sand trenches, throwing up earthworks, chopping palmettos and constructing tabby walls.

Restless one afternoon, I decided to ride down to

Coggins Point and see Fort Walker for myself. The sun was blazing hot. Once there I regretted my impulse. I halted my fat round horse in the shade of a moss-hung live oak near where the work was going on. The slaves, bare from the waist up, glistened with sweat. They hadn't noticed me in the rustling screen of palmetto fronds. They continued singing:

> No more pint of salt for me no more no more,
> No more peck of corn for me no more no more.
> Many thousands come for me, they come for me,
> Blue hats they wear, blue hats, blue hats . . .

The verses went on and on. Some of them were particularly disturbing:

No more to nurse the Master's child, no more to nurse . . .
and
No more to heed the Mistress' call, no more to heed . . .
and
No more to bend to the Driver's lash, no more to bend . . .
and
No more to cook the Master's meat, no more to cook . . .

A hound dog chasing a rabbit discovered me and barked at my horse. The singing and the eyes lowered. Longing for swift Parasol, I cantered home as fast as possible on my rocking horse.

Beau laughed at me that evening when I told him. He said my imagination was at times delightful; other times silly. I'd do better to join the ladies of the island sewing shirts and drawers and making bullets for carbines instead of listening to African songs and making up the words.

Twenty-one

The portentous 20th of April, the day Elsa was to prove her claim, came and went and May slipped along with no summons from Elsa or the judge; nor any communications from Frederick Pierce. Beau said he suspected Pierce of being some kind of spy, using Elsa as a front to hide his secret activities. But we weren't really concerned about that, being too happy that Elsa'd not found the will and getting ready for the war being so exciting. I spent all my spare time at tea parties with the ladies making drawers and socks and sheets and things. Even the schoolboys helped dig sand at the forts when their lessons were finished at the arsenal. The academy in Beaufort had closed temporarily so the teachers could decide what company *they* were going to join.

Mail service had stopped between the North and the South. I missed *Harper's Weekly* because I was reading a serial in it called "Great Expectations," and was dying to know what Pip was going to do about his future. Beau was glad not to be bored with DeBow's radical *Review*. The *Charleston Courier* was all he needed to read, it saying exactly what he expected and wanted it to say.

The waiting, wondering, piddling period ended on the 25th of May. The *Courier's* headlines screamed that word had come by telegraph the day before that Virginia had ratified the Ordinance of Secession; and the next day that the Yankees had crossed the Potomac from Washington, confiscated and occupied General Robert E. Lee's home, Arlington, and started for Richmond!

The President of the Confederacy, reacting immediately, ordered General Beauregard to Virginia, later replacing him on the southeast coast with one of his lesser favorites, General Robert E. Lee.

Luckily Amun had left Richmond in the Heyward four horse coach on May 22nd with two elderly spinster cousins for whom the Heywards sent every year to spend the summer in Beaufort, the ladies not yet having decided whether to leave their considerable fortunes to their South Carolina kin or their Virginia relatives and each vying for the ultimate favor.

Beauregard didn't try to hide his relief. Ordnance had continued putting him off, sending down heavy guns without carriages and ammunition that didn't fit and things like that. The deer flies had never been so numerous. Every time one bit him he swelled up like a toad. He wore a handkerchief around his face as if he had the mumps and complained of everything. On several occasions he had shown himself sulky and bored. One of the Hanahans quipped: "No wonder he's nicknamed Borrey. Fits him perfectly."

The night before Beauregard was to leave the area Ephraim Baynard gave a farewell party for the planters who were packing up their silver and linen and household treasures to boat over to Beaufort for the six months of hot weather, until first frost killed the mosquitoes and risk of climate fever lessened.

Beau decided to drive, instead of boat, to Baynard's Castle on the other end of the island. He wanted to compare his stand of cotton with the other plantations' along the Atlantic Ocean, positive his was at least an inch taller and thicker. We went in his mother's elegant little two-wheeled buggy so we could be alone.

The bays trotted out smartly along Pope's Avenue that went the length of the island along the ocean. Cotton was about a foot high now, the whole island a waving sea of green: cotton, marsh, ocean, bushes, treetops. Even the white houses, sheltered in groves of cedar and pine and oak, reflected glimmery green in their heavy shadows.

I wanted to talk about the party but Beau kept coming back to things I must do with cotton in case he went to war and being lyrical about General Beauregard. I was relieved when we stopped for dinner with the Lawtons at Calibogia Plantation and I could change the subject to rice, it too a waving green sea and new to me.

At Baynard's Castle I changed into my party dress in a high-ceilinged hot room upstairs. A blonde beauty, Martha Rivers, from Charleston, hooked me up the back. She never stopped talking as her fingers flew. Her husband John was stationed at Fort Moultrie and had come to discuss a secret plan with Beauregard. All the young men in Charleston were ordering grey uniforms and buying swords and getting married. Martha's golden hair was curled in dozens of tiny ringlets tied together with a pink ribbon. She said it had been wound on kid curlers for a week. She had the widest hoop skirt I ever saw, covered in ruffled pink organdy. She rubbed some rouge over her lips. I passed my tongue over mine to make them shine.

"Your hair is too severe," she said, taking a little spit and pulling some wisps out and fashioning a curl at the nape of my neck. "And your face is too brown. It lightens the color of your eyes. You must learn to wear a hat in the island sun."

My eyes and the way my yellow India muslin dress clung to my body pleased me. A shawl of tissue silk was draped around my shoulders. Martha cleverly helped the shawl slip—this much—my neck showed startlingly white.

I could hear Beau talking loudly out in the hall, demanding to know where I had hidden myself. The door flew open and there he was. The ladies, some half dressed, shrieked and giggled, ordering him out.

I tried to appraise him coolly but it was impossible. His burnished red hair was brushed close to his head like a metal casque. His full dress coat gave a wasp-waisted effect. His face appeared to have been lifted up and set stiffly on a white winged collar starched even higher than the one he'd worn at Cedar Grove. His tight black trousers, revealing his strong thighs, were strapped under shining patent leather dancing pumps.

"We are the best looking couple here," he grinned, offering me his arm.

Some of the young men had on brand-new Confederate uniforms. The girls, smelling of flower cologne, swarmed around them, snapping their fans.

The house was silvery in candlelight, sweet and cool, with masses of running roses and lilies and gardenias in the niches and on the piano. Everybody was excited, approaching each other as if they were in a foreign country. Uniforms do that to people. Starlight poured in through the delicate ribbed fanlight over the opened front doors and in all the windows.

There was a white frosted cake on a crystal stand on the sideboard in the dining room with a big blue satin cockade in the center. It was surrounded by a wreath of magnolia leaves and open cotton bolls from last year blooming like white roses on the green leaves. On the top of the cake were fifteen smaller blue cockades representing the fifteen Confederate states.

White musicians from Savannah struck up a Strauss waltz. The whole house had been cleared for dancing, powdered wax having been sprinkled over the floors until they shone like glass. Garlands of jasmine and willow oak were draped over every mantelpiece and twined around the standing columns in the hall.

Stephen had brought his violin and was playing with the orchestra. My heart beat in 1-2-3 time. Hoop skirts swayed, a few dress swords clanked, slippers slid. And the swallow-tails of the men's full dress coats made circles as they turned and turned in the fast style of Vienna to the "Blue Danube Waltz."

At the end of that dance Beauregard cleverly made himself the center of attention, by surrounding himself with the tallest men present. There wasn't a man in the Beaufort Artillery under six feet. Beau towered over him, eating up anything he said.

Rum punch was passed around. Beauregard refused. He just wanted to stand there being the sparkling jewel in a crown of admirers, waving his hands and bowing for no particular reason as he talked.

After the punch we danced reels and polkas and more waltzes. I moved from partner to partner. By the time I had danced the Lancers with Beau I was in such a euphoric mood I was agreeable when he decided not to follow everybody into the dining room for a supper buffet.

"There's a full moon outside and I distinctly heard a whippoorwill as we skipped past the front door."

Fiddle in hand Stephen caught up with Beau at the bottom of the steps. "The General insists on either you or I accompanying him to Virginia. He flatters us; thinks we're too valuable to waste on this small island defense operation. He is convinced all the fighting is going to take place in Virginia. The Yankees will never ever get this far south. I will spare you and accept the duty, Gaston."

Beau let go my hand and bowed very low. "Oh, dear me no, Alphonse. I couldn't think of allowing you to face such hardship. I am the true warrior."

"You forget, Gaston, 'twas I who caught the twelve-foot alligator by the tail and pulled him from his hole last month, yours only measured eleven feet eleven inches."

"How will we decide between us this time?" Beau flicked his lacy handkerchief at a mosquito on his ear.

"By the first true contest, be it of wit, sport, or a business deal, that arises after the first cotton boll opens. We can't hare off and leave the mess the forts are in to Francis Lee yet. We can handle the slave labor and pressure Ordnance better than anybody else."

"There is no doubt but that I will, as usual, be the winner, Alphonse," Beau said, tucking the handkerchief back in his sleeve.

"Nor any doubt in my mind, Gaston, but that it will be I," Stephen said, running back up the steps, playing "Dixie" on his fiddle.

Light from the hall streamed down on Beau's face. He was looking up at Stephen, who had halted on the piazza and was dancing a jig as he fiddled. Beau's face had the faraway exalté expression I had noticed at Cedar Grove and then again as we neared Cotton Hall that first time.

I insisted on going into the garden, where I made a scene. "You never consult me about anything! You make up your mind and go flying off to war as if you were the only person involved, leaving me alone on this island with everybody moving to town. I'll not let you. I'll show you."

He was stunned. "You must be joking," he said. "What do you expect me to do, run and ask you if I can have a sugar titty? Why did you invite me into the garden if you intended to be rude? You seem to think I am one of those creations like your darling Mr. Monk, who can be led around by the nose and told to blow it when you choose. Well, I'm not Mr. Monk and I'm going to win any contest that comes up between Stephen and me and ride away to war as fast as my horse will gallop. Let's call up the buggy and go home. I've had enough."

We drove the long oyster shell driveway in silence except for an army of frogs and a hooting of owls until we came to the ocean. Reflected stars shattered and danced into millions of glittering shards on the breaking waves. It was a heavenly night, the air cooler here than back in the trees. Beau tied the horses to a palmetto and spread the lap robe on the sand. We stayed there for hours. We never slept. We listened to the ocean wind and the waves breaking over and over again. I said I was sorry; he declared he was at fault. We laughed, we held hands. We were happy.

From a thick of myrtles a bird called softly Peter! Peter! Peter!

"What kind of bird is that?"

"A tit," he whispered, tracing my ear with his tongue.

Dear fat full moon, dear singing wind, dear mockingbirds pouring your hearts out in the palmettos—for a short time we brimmed over with happiness.

Twenty-two

I was crabbing with Button on the creek one morning in early June when Henricus appeared on the bank waving two letters. One was from the Heywards announcing the arrival of the rich spinsters and Amun at the Combahee. They would be driving down to Beaufort in three days. They would deliver Amun at the Berrien mansion in mid-afternoon. The other note was a scrawl, barely legible: "They are poisoning me. Elsa."

Henricus looked dreadful; all skin and bones. Livia must be poisoning him too. He cried and begged me to keep him here at Cotton Hall. He'd sleep in the kitchen with Anatole and wait on me "enduring the day and far into the night." I said I'd speak to the Master.

Beau was concentrating on caterpillars. He hardly listened when I asked him what I should do if it turned out Elsa really was being poisoned.

"Tell Livia to double the dose," he said, laughing and showing the longest worm I'd ever seen. An infestation of caterpillars would drastically cut down his cotton crop.

Three days later Eddie and Pharaoh accompanied me to Beaufort. We took the twelve-oared barge so there would be room for Amun's trunks and boxes.

Beaufort was a darling little town. It was simply a small Venice with all those magnificent mansions marching at columned angles to each other along the bay and up and down a few streets. Behind the great houses were tabby carriage houses and servant houses and stables. The air smelled of sea salt and magnolia trees in heavy bloom and cape jessamine and oleanders and pomegranates. How black the enormous oak trunks were and how shiny green the

151

leaves making a constant canopy against the sun over the whole town.

Little birds, green, grey, brown and yellow, flew in and out; you know the kind of little afternoon birds that always fly singing in summer among shading trees. All so terribly attractive and different from the Virginia hunt country and from Hilton Head.

I waved at the powdered ladies I'd come to know so pleasantly, in pink and blue and lavender hoop skirts, swaying along under tiny parasols, looking as if they hadn't the strength or the inclination to lift more than a teapot; yet I knew every one of them had worked as hard as I during their winter stay on the plantations. They were laughing and gossiping, watching their husbands and sons and sweethearts racing over the bay in lively sail boats.

Colored maids in gay calico dresses and turbans followed their ladies, carrying cushions and slipper bags and vials of smelling salts. Boys, black and white together, were playing shinny and kick-the-can in the shell-strewn street. And there was Cousin Billy Elliott sitting on a long bench with a group of similar important looking gentlemen all in white linen suits and wide white panama hats, solving the problems of the world, shaking their heads and gesticulating excitedly with their cigars.

Eddie said he'd like to listen to them. He'd watch for the Heyward coach and be on the step to hand the child out. He promised.

Pharaoh stepped briskly beside me. I walked faster to get ahead of him but he kept level. "Ki, Miss Angel, you shoulda made Master Eddie come along. He'd have holped you. Momma don't take to being surprised, by gosh, no sir, she don't."

"Where are we going? I thought our house was on Bay Street."

" 'Tis; here hit."

In the high brick wall was a large iron gate for carriages. When it was opened a bell sounded, like a giant dinner bell.

"Ring it again, Granddaddy," Pharaoh shouted, as

the mean-eyed old African stepped aside for us to pass. "Have to look out for little old Momma sometimes."

Now I saw the coral and vermillion brick house through the down branches of a moss-draped live oak. It was three stories tall on an arched tabby basement. Curved white marble steps with wrought iron railings led to an Ionic-columned piazza that ran the long length of the first story. There was another piazza above this one with Corinthian columns. The gleaming white columns were countered by wooden balustrades of an airy lacy design. A railing of fragile balustrades also ran around the roof like a crown. The windows were set in impressively designed stone frames. No wonder Aunt Dell had never forgotten this house. It had a princely grandeur compared to dear shabby Cedar Grove and rambling Cotton Hall.

"We home," Pharaoh sang, reaching out for my arm. As usual he wore his grey livery with silver buttons but he'd left off his white cotton gloves. His bare hands sweated against my recoiling lace-mitted fingers. "Take care, don't slip on the stair. Momma been shining him bright. Might still be wet, him."

He banged the brass eagle that hung in the center of the wide fanlit door.

Henricus coughed as he slid the bolt and opened the heavy door. His face looked like a shrivelled prune topped with whipped cream.

"Do Lord," he bowed, "if this ain't a treat to be sure. Livvy gonna be carry off with delight when she know you is come. Step inside, Miss Angel."

Malevolent marble statues of Antigone and Orestes and various Caesars and goddesses postured on pedestals up and down the polished expanse. The afternoon sun was streaming down through a large Palladian-arched window on the landing of the double stairway. Shafted in the sunlight, Livia was descending the stairs. She was bulging out of a lace-collared, green grosgrain dress with such a wide hoop it touched both sides of the stair. She must have gained thirty pounds since December. She was as

wide as she was high. Chalk-white powder was caked
on her face. She was showing her yellow teeth in a
simpery smile.

We stood and looked at each other. It was a long
look in which we said all the things we knew we'd
never say out loud to each other.

"I have come to pay a call on Mrs. Berrien."

She shook her head, continuing to smile. "The Mistress is not receiving today. But would you care to
look around before you leave?"

I remembered how unkemptly Cotton Hall had
welcomed me. The intense tidiness of this hall and
every inch of Livia's solid body said: how immaculate
my house is!

"Yes, I'd like to see the house."

I took a deep breath and started toward the drawing room.

Livia's fat feet pattered nimbly down the steps.
"The drawing room on the other side of the hall is
more beautiful."

I walked on through a handsomely carved archway
into a formal, high-ceilinged room ornamented with
magnificently carved woodwork. The Adam mantel
had elaborate garlands and Grecian urns and a frolicky scene of mythical characters in the center.

"It smells good in here." I wrinkled up my nose.
"Someone must have been having a tea party."

"No one. It is the flowers outside that you are smelling. We ate pig's feet for dinner."

"In the dining room?"

She shrugged.

I began pulling off my damp lace mitts as I saun-
tered over to a tall window looking out on the river.
She came and stood beside me, fingering the tassels
bordering the swagged gold and blue striped satin
draperies. "This is a show place as you can see for
yourself. People often push their way into the garden
by giving my father a penny."

On the fine-stitched Aubusson carpet, patterned
with pale lilies and leaves, stood French gilt chairs in
rows, looking as if they'd never moved an inch in
their spindly lives. There were several stiff, Empire

gold-damask sofas and hard blue-damask chairs with identical backs. A harpsichord and a harp faced each other from different corners. The air felt damp and chilly. The walls of the house must be very thick. No sound of birds or hint of heat from the outside world penetrated.

Portraits of powerful, russet-colored men and patient-eyed ladies in low-cut dresses hung in carefully matched spaces around the walls. From their expressions I knew I would have liked most of them. I wondered which was the wicked Hazzard; which the gentle Julia.

"She is the sad-faced lady in the black dress with those heavy pearls. You would not have understood her."

"I might have."

"No; never, she was much too softhearted. Would you like to see the dining room? Thrown together the two rooms make a ball room."

Livia was coolly composed; not so I. I wanted to run back to the landing and sit in the barge until Amun arrived, and fly back to Hilton Head forever. But she was pushing the sliding doors. Two overpowering crimson vases that made me think they might be filled with blood stood on black marble-topped tables on each side of the doors. The dining room was painted the same pale blue as the parlor and had the same beautiful Adam woodwork and matching crystal chandelier and gilt cornices and gold leaf mirrors and swagged draperies. The Regency dining table had five pedestals and fourteen legs. I counted them while Livia kept rolling her eyes in the direction of the front window in the drawing room.

"I keep hearing horse feet," she said.

"You can't hear anything from outside in here."

But you could. The iron bell at the gate began to clang clang clang furiously.

Pharaoh trotted in from the hall. "Mistress hollering her head off upstairs and here come Mr. Heyward big large coach and a mule wagon following, pile high as the sky with trunks and boxes. Like Christmas hit."

Twenty-three

Eddie barely reached the steps ahead of the coach. He was perspiring and there were green grass stains all over the seat of his trousers. He grabbed the door handle, pulled it open, and, bowing gallantly, reached for a dainty gloved hand.

As Amun stepped out Eddie blushed to the very roots of his red head; for here was no bouncy child. My little sister had turned into an exquisite bisque-doll lady, still well under five feet tall, in a fashionable fawn linen traveling suit that curved in all the proper places. Her short hair fluttered like flaxen feathers from under a minute tan straw bowler. She was smiling adorably.

Eddie kept holding her hand, even when she was on the ground, as if she would shatter if his strength didn't bind her together. Even when I hugged her I felt his sensitive fingers curled protectively around her tiny arm.

Pharaoh broke the spell, muttering, "Will you look out there! Here come Master in my boat. No business him got in there without me."

"Ahoy the house!" Beau shouted as the noisy craft neared the landing at the bottom of the garden.

Amun picked up her trailing skirt and raced me and Eddie. My heart as always was singing at the very sight of Beau. But this time it was beating high with pride too. Israel was most capably handling the engine and expertly bringing her in.

After Beau had kissed all of us, even Eddie, he said, "I was reading the newspaper when I suddenly remembered that, at the Conversation Club last week, I accepted an invitation from Mr. Barnwell to a party at The Castle this evening. What luck! Amun can meet all the swains in Beaufort and take her choice."

"I——" Eddie opened his mouth but Beau stepped on his toe so hard he swallowed whatever he meant to say.

"Oh, shuh!" Amun giggled at Eddie's confusion. "I can't go to a party in this old thing. But I *do* have a dress I wore at the Heywards' in that bottom box."

Eddie tore into the pile of luggage like an eager bird dog. We went into the house, where Beau dared Amun to prove she could still skin the cat on his arm. She did and he caught her and tossed her high in the air making everybody laugh except Eddie, grimly standing, box on shoulder in the doorway.

I said I couldn't possibly go in the dress I had on.

Beau put his arm around me. "I fetched the first fluffy thing I could find in your wardrobe. Maybelle tossed in a few little extras. She was as excited as if it were she going to the party. It's in the boat. Run get it, Eddie."

Upstairs was a maze of bedrooms filled with heavy, dark mahogany beds and marble-topped bureaus and tables and gold leaf mirrors and cane settees and daybeds. Amun and I chose the lightest room, looking out over the busy bay. Two maids fetched kettles of hot water and made a bath in a porcelain tub for Amun while I sought Elsa's room.

It wasn't difficult to locate. I followed a petulant moaning sound through a dark hall into a dreadful-smelling, shuttered room where a pile of quilts on a sleigh-bed indicated my stepmother-in-law.

"Are you asleep, Elsa?"

"You camel And I was so hateful to you. Oh, please take me away from here. Please scratch my nose. Please tell Father to come. Livia is——" she ducked into the messy quilts, burying her head so nothing was seen but a tangled tuft of brown hair.

"Is what?" Livia was on the other side of the bed, glaring. "Mistress thinks something she is eating is disagreeing with her."

"Has a doctor been here?"

"She doesn't eat anything so there is no need for a doctor. If she'd not insist on taking so much laudanum she'd eat more. She's not sick."

"But the pain, Livia. Oh, Angelica, do something!"
Elsa's raddled head emerged. I recoiled, backing
away. Her face was drawn and a horrible yellowish-
grey color. Her glittering black eyes showed pupils
the size of pinpoints. A cold claw on the end of a
skinny arm shot out and clutched my wrist. "Take me
away," she whimpered, "I am so afraid of them."

This was too much for me. "I'll fetch Beau," I said.

"Don't do that," Livia said sharply. "Can't you tell
she's play-acting?"

I knew she wasn't. I had learned a lot in the sick
house these past months. I rushed downstairs. Beau
didn't want to see Elsa. He took his time, stopping to
comment on each statue in the hall and tell from where
and why it came and who it was. I hated all of them.

When we finally reached Elsa's room she was
asleep under a neatly arranged, clean coverlet. Livia
had hastily brushed the tangled top layer of hair. It
lay in waves about her pallid face. Had it not been
for the hoarse breathing you would have thought
she had been dead a long time.

"She looks better than usual," Beau said infuriating-
ly, "but if you insist I'll ask Dr. Ficken to come around
tomorrow."

"Do, Master," Livia purred. "Mr. Pierce made me
promise to take good care of the Mistress."

Beau clattered downstairs calling to Henricus to
bring up a bottle of Madeira. I went into the nearest
water closet and vomited.

I was dressed before Amun. I left a maid tying the
pink ribbons in her ruffled drawers. "Don't be long.
Eddie's fallen for you. Look your prettiest. I want to
keep you in the family."

"Foot!" she laughed, "he was just putting on. I bet
he won't look at me again."

Still in his grass-stained white linen, Eddie was
pacing up and down the downstairs hall, cracking his
knuckles. "Where is she? Has anything happened to
her?"

"No, silly. She'll be down in a minute."

I went into the drawing room hunting Beau. He was sitting on one of the gold sofas, dropping cigar ashes on the Aubusson carpet.

The dress he'd fetched was palest grey mull, draped on Grecian lines. To liven it, I'd put a coronelle of white egret feathers in my hair and the magic moonstones around my neck.

"I chose perfectly. Come over here and let me smell your perfume."

"No. There's no one in Beaufort who could restring my moonstones."

"I promise to be good. Say, did you see how mad Eddie got when I played with Amun?"

Eddie blissfully hovering behind her, Amun came in.

"Do you like it?" She whirled herself around in a pale green chiffon with thousands of hand-made tucks and fine lace insertions. Cousin Dell had more than done her part by Amun. This was a creation. The sleeves were flowing and to the elbow. The skirt was full and showed the tips of green satin slippers. It was ethereal, surrounding her in a cloud of loveliness. To go with it she had on a linen-colored shepherdess hat with a pale green ostrich feather. Her light green eyes looked like cologne.

"My little elf has vanished," Beau said, rising and bowing. "A beauty has entered. Why didn't you say that, Eddie?"

Eddie managed a shy smile and held his arm out to Amun. "It's only a few steps away. Can you walk?"

The Castle was an even larger house than ours. People drank punch and ate crab salad and shrimp paste and sherberts and talked about fishing and the war equally. When it began to get dark, we danced in the wide cool hall. A band of light-skinned, town Negroes made music on horns and banjos and a drum.

Cousin Billy was leaning against a window, watching the dancing. A breeze was fluttering the sheer curtains. I went up to talk to him. Charlotte joined us saying how darling Amun was. All the eligible

young men were already after her. Could she be almost sixteen? *Her* first baby had been born when *she*
was only fifteen.

I laughed at everything Charlotte said, especially
about having a baby at fifteen. Why wasn't *I* having
a baby? I fanned myself so hard I almost knocked my
front tooth out.

Beau gently pulled the thin gauze shawl up around
my neck and led me away.

"Where are we going?"

"Home, by golly. We must never spend a night
apart this whole summer. I have a duty at Fort Walker at dawn. Must get my sleep, you know."

"I can't go without seeing about Elsa. She doesn't
look right to me. If Livia gives her any more laudanum——"

"Livvy's got better sense than that for all her new
stuck-up airs."

"I'm worried about Elsa. Really worried."

"I talked to Ficken. He's going by in the morning
or the next day."

"I can't leave Amun her first night here."

"Let Eddie look after her. Stop fussing. I'm the one
who needs you. Don't you need me a little?"

Stars danced on the water. The night air smelled
sweet. As we passed our garden wall a figure slipped
back into the darkness. Did people always stand in
front of this house and look in? I held tight to Beau's
powerful arm. So long as I could, I wasn't afraid of
anything in the world.

"Beau, someone is following us."

He put his weight back on his heels. I felt his hands
go into fists.

"What are you up to, Pharaoh?"

"I doesn't like Israel in my boat, no sir, by gosh.
Please, Master, let me take you all home."

"Israel's just running it this one time. Get yourself
on over to the barge with Big May and wait for Master Eddie and Miss Angel's sister."

Pharaoh's fists were bunched in knots too. He was
breathing hard. His eyeballs glinted. "You told me
hit were my boat."

"And so it is. So it is. But dang it all, boy, you know the channel in the dark better than Big May. Sorry. Night."

Beau's voice was hard, his fists still clenched.

"I never heard you talk that way to Pharaoh before."

"Hopefully not again. You sleep, Israel?"

"No sir, Master, wide awake me." Israel's sharp Arab features and big droopy eyes showed happy in the starlight. He had the engine puffing smoke almost at once. As we moved out into the rippling incandescent river he said softly, "Ki, Miss Angel, you puts me in mind of a swan, you setting there glimmering, with all them white feathers nodding on your head."

Twenty-four

Within the week we were thrown into a stew.

Elsa died!

The doctor said from the looks of her she died of heart failure or maybe starvation, perhaps an overdose of opium. No one was to blame but herself. Certainly not Livia, who cried copiously continually.

I felt guilty and awful. I should have done something for her, lying there so pitiful and helpless and scared. Catherine Cuthbert and I made an effort to get word north to her father, even going so far as to telegraph Mr. Lincoln himself, requesting him to notify Mr. Czerny. I don't suppose he did for nothing ever came of it.

Elsa was buried in St. Helena's churchyard beside Hazzard but on the other side from Julia. A hot wind from inland riffled the wreaths of grey moss that dripped funereally from the trees, causing gnats and sandflies to swarm and chew.

The eighteenth-century church was built of brick covered with stucco. The steeple had recently been taken down so it wouldn't fall on anybody's head. It had many small-paned windows each crowned with a fanlight. The interior had elaborate gold-trimmed cornices, simple white columns and graceful balconies for the slaves. The floor was covered with flat tombstones. My feet were cooled by one in memory of a tough old Indian fighter, Tuscarora Jack Barnwell. The Barnwells had risen in the world since then, but they liked being descended from such a man.

The Berrien family connection was large so the service was well attended, even though a special sail boat race was in progress.

After the committal we stood around in the cemetery talking to everybody as if Elsa had been a dear member of the family, determined to carry everything out as indicated. There'd been enough gossip about her and Hazzard. This was the end of all our troubles.

Livia and Henricus sat in the balcony in the church but they joined us at the grave during the handshaking and curious questioning. For once I was glad of her presence. I didn't have to put on a false face and tell stories. As we started to leave the churchyard, Livia said, "Someone is calling you, Master."

It was the priest, still in his heavy vestments despite the heat. Another minister was with him. A Baptist one, so Livia said. He was very agitated. He said he had been baptizing a congregation of Negroes over on Daufuskie and had only learned of Elsa's death an hour ago. He'd got here in the middle of the service and waited until the folk dispersed.

"Mr. Berrien, this is going to come as a shock to you."

Beau was impatient to get away. He kept taking his hat off and furiously swiping it at gnats and mosquitos. "I don't need another shock today, sir. What say we postpone it until tomorrow?"

The minister said the only way he knew to explain the matter was for Beau to examine the evidence for himself immediately. It had happened one day when he was in Savannah. His assistant had done it and been sworn to secrecy.

Well then, I thought, breathing a sigh of relief, it can't be very important.

Beau walked with such long strides none of us could begin to keep up with him. Phillip fell down and tore his new white trousers. I was panting and perspiring so profusely I could hardly see for the moisture. Once inside the thin-steepled Baptist church I dropped down in a polished pew and pretended I was praying diligently, peeping around the while.

Beau's face looked like a thundercloud as he and the boys trooped from the small registry office on the left of the pulpit. He motioned me to follow them down the aisle. I knew they'd seen something scandalous. Even Phillip had a crestfallen expression.

Outside, Beau said stonily, "Elsa and Frederick Pierce were married in this church last December on the very morning they came over to Hilton Head to the party for you. It's written down in the registry book, entirely legal." He turned on Livia and snarled, "Were you aware of this?"

She and Henricus were standing respectfully by a solid pediment beside tall white columns at the church entrance. "Oh, no sir, Master. Never did I suspect that. Only——"

"Only what?"

"They might have been immoral together. I did suspect that. But nothing wicked like marriage between them."

Her damp fat cheeks never quivered nor did her eyes flicker. Henricus burst into nervous sobs and had to be patted quiet by Eddie.

Beau said, "She's no right being buried by my father and mother. To hell with getting home. I'm going back to the cemetery and have her dug up and thrown out."

It took all of us, assisted by the nice minister, to dissuade him and get him into the barge and safely away for the island. He muttered and cursed the whole way. He never wanted to see the Beaufort house again. Eddie could have it and if he didn't want it he would pass it on to Phillip, then Button; anybody but that damned Yankee, Pierce, who now was Elsa's sole inheritor!

The tide was with us. We made good time to Hilton Head. A crowd of blacks, men and women, were massed on the landing, singing and waving to us. Others were scrambling up and down the bluff.

"A great thing must have come to pass," Big May shouted to Beau, who was standing up straining to hear what was being sung about. The word "Buttons" came clear over and over.

Liney officially welcomed us. He explained that when he rang the noon bell one of the hands told him the field was crawling with caterpillars. He'd immediately put every hand to pulling them off the creamy blossoms but it was a hopeless task. Suddenly, among them was Button and the new lady, who was one of the little people and therefore magic. They saw the cotton crop being destroyed and heard the wailing of the slaves, who feared being beaten. Then, because the little person's magic was present Button flew back to the fowl yard, gathered all the flocks of turkeys, with help from Liney of course, and drove them into the big field where, in no time at all, they picked all the caterpillars off the leaves and so far as could be known not a caterpillar remained on the whole plantation!

I thanked the Lord with my whole heart for this good news that changed Beau into his delightful excited self again; that Amun looked so happy with Eddie holding her hand and leading her toward the house; most of all that Beau praised Button so highly for his brilliant handling of a desperate situation he never ever sucked his thumb again in his whole life!

Twenty-five

The Confederates won a glorious victory at Bull Run at Manassas Junction in Virginia, twenty-five miles southwest of Washington on the 21st of July. The President of the Confederacy himself rode at the head of the center column, out showing off the two heroes of the battle, Generals Beauregard and Joseph E. Johnston, in plain view of crowds of Congressmen and newspapermen and picnickers, who had come out from the city for a holiday thrill.

The marvelous news made Beau fanatically obsessed with getting into the action. He was positive the war would be won by Christmas. If he were to be cheated out of the only chance in a lifetime to exult in a battle cry he'd jump in the well and drown himself.

I could imagine Uncle Jim telling me to pipe down and be my sweet loving self. Could anyone have hindered Lancelot from questing? Certainly not Arthur! Neither Guinevere.

Not Guinevere either? I sighed and made myself as pretty as possible, even going so far as to let Maybelle make me a hideous hat that changed me into a goblin when it was tied under my chin but which would prevent my turning almost as brown as she.

For I stayed outdoors with Beau as he restlessly roamed the fields checking the hard-green fruit on the cotton for the tiniest crack showing silky white fiber. He carried on like a wild man offering a reward of a five dollar gold piece to the slave who fetched him the first open boll.

To my annoyance it was Zipporah. She came running with the fluffy white ball as if it had been an Olympic torch, snatched her prize, frowned at me and darted off.

We took tea that same evening with Stephen and

Charlotte on Parris Island. News had just arrived of
the overwhelming Confederate success at Manassas.
By first dark Beau and Stephen had worked themselves up to such a pitch of war fever that they decided to have their showdown then and there as to
which would be the first to fight in Virginia. Each
shuffled a pack of cards and handed it to me and
Charlotte.

"High card to Virginia. Don't fail me, Charlotte."
Stephen's black eyes burned with excitement.

I didn't dare look up at Beau.

"Cut the cards, Angelica," he said tersely.

I showed the ten of spades.

And Charlotte turned up the two of hearts!

The next week Beau took the train to Columbia,
accompanied by Pharaoh. He bought two thorough-
breds from the Hamptons, a black gelding for him and
a racy sorrel mare called Miss Suzy for me. Two days
after he returned he was ready to go to war.

It was so hot it felt as if the end of the world was
frying. At breakfast Beau glittered restlessly like a
man with a high fever.

A girl came in with a silver tray of watermelon
slices neatly laid on spread fig leaves.

"Put it there on the table in front of me," Beau said.
He chose the thinnest melon slice and, raising it to
his lips as if it were a harmonica, made little sucking
musical notes on it. But he didn't eat his plate of hot
buttered hominy covered with tiny little river shrimp
topped with a layer of cold clabber because, just as
I dusted it with nutmeg, Pharaoh came singing up the
avenue.

"What am I going to tell Pharaoh?"

"That you're taking Cudjo Manigo because he's a
good cook and an accomplished chicken thief."

"He won't swallow that. You tell him something."

"Not I; I wish you'd take him instead of Cudjo
Manigo. I don't like him."

"I can't. Pharaoh's too good with the boats. You and
Amun are dependent on him to get you back and
forth to town. He won't act up with Eddie here, sta-

tioned at the fort permanently; and Phillip and Button around. You're entirely safe. The people think Amun is a fairy, because of her littleness, and you're a witch because of your—"

"Don't you dare say tallness."

"Because you stopped Israel's bleeding and he didn't die."

"What must I do if Frederick Pierce turns up demanding that we divide your father's estate and give him Elsa's share and the judge says we must?"

"There's no danger of that. Not unless the North wins the war, which it may well do unless I get myself to Virginia immediately. Don't upset me on my last day." He rose, stretching himself almost to the ceiling. "I don't want any breakfast. Too hot. Well, here I go to face Pharaoh."

I never felt such a hot day. While Beau and Cudjo Manigo were getting their last things together, Amun and I sat in the milk house, I hoping to die quietly in there so I wouldn't have to take part in this wretched affair. Saying goodbye, I mean. The milk house was the only place that approached cool except the ice house, which Beau told me to keep locked, knowing the six months' supply would be our last until after the war.

"Amun, I love you for being here."

"I don't ever want to leave. Let me tell you the latest joke on Uncle Jim."

The Lord continued allowing the sun to blaze and the humid miasma to meet and merge with it.

A black and fearful looking cloud brooded over the sound seeming to descend to the waters and commingle with them. I was soaking wet, in a silly flounced pink muslin and pink kid slippers that Beau had asked me to wear, when noon came and I heard him calling my name. He was in the office, sitting at his desk.

"Come here and let me show you something."

He fiddled with some panels and opened an ingenious drawer that went down into a fat leg of the desk. He pulled out a piece of paper with the combination to his safe on it. The safe was disguised as a chest of drawers in his dressing room. You lifted the top and the door to the safe was underneath.

"Don't ever let anybody see you open this; not even the boys."

"Whoever thought of such queer ways to hide things?"

"Papa. Someday you'll find the will in just such an unlikely spot. Now—read the combination—open the door."

The safe was full of gold; small bags of gold. Beau untied one and let me finger the cool coins. "There's money enough here to pay our taxes for years and years. And remember, if any Lincolnites ever do the impossible and reach this coast, burn the cotton rather than let them have it. But never let anything happen to this house. It is my Eden."

We kissed goodbye in the hall. Against his strong tight body I felt ashamed that I was so soft, so safe, so surrounded with luxuries. My heart begged him to take me with him so that I could look after him, comfort him, delight him.

He was very gentle and said the most ordinary things: "Long staple cotton bolls open but slightly. A hand only averages 70–100 pounds a day as compared with 200 of the upland strain. Women and boys make the best pickers being lighter handed than men and less liable to damage the fiber. It should be gathered soon after it has burst the pod so the sun won't yellow it or dirt stain it."

He'd said all this before. Why didn't he notice my eyes pleading with him to say other words? But his eyes were saying them, and his fast breathing and the agitated cadence of his speaking.

I held his hand against my face to prove I wasn't crying. "Write often."

"You must write often too; tell me everything."

"We will be together for Christmas? You swear it?"

"I swear. Come now, tie my golden sash and buckle on my sword."

With Liney, heading the gathered people, Pharaoh was waiting to say goodbye to the Master. Beau's spurs jingled as he ran down the steps.

Maum Hannah was standing at the foot of the steps. Masai was beside her. Beau took Masai's hand in his. The giant black man bent over and kissed Beau's shoulder. I thought Beau was going to be the one to cry. "Don't let anybody touch my umbrella," he said softly.

Pharaoh had put his feet in a clump of phlox I had planted. He said sullenly, "This a evil day you not take me along as your man instead of that no-account Cudjo."

"You're too important for me to let a Yankee take a shot at. Hey, there's Button! Count on you to take care of Angelica, boy. You too, Phillip. You make Eddie behave, Amun."

A shower of crushed oyster shells rose from the black gelding's heels like a crystal curtain as, long in the stirrup and erect in the saddle, Beau went away at a hand gallop. Cudjo, short stirruped and bent over on his horse's neck like a monkey, was in front in a few lengths. Then, rising in his stirrup, Beau looked around at me one last time and, waving his linen stovepipe hat and giving an Indian war whoop, went into a full gallop, easily passing Cudjo, both continuing the Rebel yell so long as we could hear.

Pharaoh broke the spell. I heard him plain. He intended it that way. Maum Hannah, not by so much as a flicker of an eyelash, let on she'd heard.

"All been fine on this plantation, by golly Jedus Christ, 'twell she come here, her. Who that fixing to row me up to town? I more than ready to shake the sand of this island off my foots."

"You ain't going nowhere," Liney said. "Not 'twell I tells you, no siree. I can beat you anyday with my fists evenso my bull whip. I'm the Obshay on this place now and don't you never forget it."

The whistle of the little inter-island steamer, the *Planter*, blew as it approached Seabrook's Landing. Beau and Cudjo Manigo would make it easily.

The boys and Amun were so afraid I was going to

cry that they humored me all evening. They even went with me, in the gloaming, down to the boat landing.

"Listen," Button whispered.

A faint sound loudened. From the dark-pointed piney woods to the west it came and went, the musical travelling notes of a herd of whooping cranes bound for the tide. Nearer it came, an eerie sound that made the back of my neck crawl. Soon I could just see them, their long necks undulating, their wide wings threshing as they passed toward the sea. Now fell a deep silence. Only the whisper of the night wind in the marsh canes and the far-off slap of the tide. Not a widgeon or curlew called, and overhead pale luminous clouds drifted ceaselessly.

"Let's go in," Phillip growled, "mosquitos are eating me up."

"It feels good out here," Amun took my hand and squeezed it tight, "and the marsh smells delicious."

But what was this? A faint gurgle and chuckle from under the dock, a coldness round my feet! It was the stealthy tide, creeping like a snake, trickling through the cracks in the wood. It was time to face that big dark room and my lonely bed.

The overpowering atmosphere of the landscape of the coastal night had penetrated and strengthened me: the treacherous sand bars and swirling currents, the hidden inlets, mysterious marsh and ancient life-gnarled, moss-hung oaks casting strange shadows in the moonlight, all affected by the tide. The tide that went far out to sea but always came back in again.

Twenty-six

Amun almost died with broken bone fever as a result of my selfishly exposing her to the miasmas of that night.

For a whole week Dr. Jenkins remained at Cotton Hall shaking his head and eating rice birds and drinking Madeira while Maum Hannah cooled the fever with flax-seed tea and glasses of lemon juice sweetened with honey. Maybelle eased the poor little wracked joints by rubbing them with chloroform liniment. Maybelle's hands are long with quick brown fingers, thin as writing paper. They have healing in them.

Eddie gave up being a soldier while she lay there so white and pitiful. I never saw a gentler man. He is a rare spirit. His strength and love pulled Amun through more than anything. He returned to the fort after the two worst weeks but it was the middle of October before she recovered sufficiently to take a carriage ride with him one morning to inspect his new tent under the trees in front of the Pope house at Fort Walker and watch a dress parade on the ocean beach with a brass band from Savannah in full regalia.

Fort Walker with its seven circular transverses against enfilading fire looked formidable enough a days. Men in grey felt hats and caps walked sentry-go, muskets proudly at the shoulder. The stars and bars of the Confederacy snapped smartly on its staff in the breezes from the ocean. Bugles blew. Drums tattled.

The trouble, said Eddie, was that inside the fort nothing was ready. Of the seven ten-inch Columbiad cannons General Beauregard had requested from Ordnance to be placed in the transverses, only one had arrived, together with a few smaller navy guns. In place of the heavy guns for beach defense there

were only two light carronades without carriages or
chassis! But, worst of all, Button's godfather had pa-
triotically resigned his position as head of the railroad, having requested President Davis to give him
the command of the Provisional Forces of the Third
Military District. He and Davis had been close friends
and classmates at West Point. Davis had not only
given him the command but had made him a brigadier general.

No one was happy about this. Everybody liked
Thomas Fenwick Drayton but he couldn't seem to
grasp or carry out the coastal defense strategy Beauregard had planned. Everything that the two most
capable officers at Fort Walker, Major Arthur Huger
and Colonel Heyward, organized, he disorganized,
without meaning to.

Eddie stayed for dinner, then he and Amun went
onto the back piazza to say goodbye until tomorrow.
I had a lump in my throat as I watched them walking
out into the early afternoon sunshine. They were
sweet and shy with each other; two cooing doves; so
unlike Beau and me, wild eagles together. Eddie
looked very tall in his uniform, and boyishly slim,
nineteen years old, with soft blue eyes that shone
with idealism and love for my little sister.

"Eddie's an old worry wart," I said, trying to be a
comfort, when Amun came back in, her eyes
drenched with tears.

"You're making a mistake, Angelica, not to take
Eddie seriously."

"I do take him seriously, darling. You look so tired.
Go and lie down. Maybelle will make you an egg-nog
and sing to you. Wouldn't you like that? I'm going
outside and wait for Button."

Aflame with patriotism, like all the boys on the
island except Phillip, Button spent every morning at
the fort watching the soldiers rehearse for war, simu-
lating sea attacks and defenses, singing songs and
setting up cannons.

Cotton was being picked in the near field this October afternoon. Watching the pickers Maum Hannah

was sitting on the ground beside a clump of white ginger lilies eating her dinner gourd of rice and okra pilau.

"Go get Master Long-eye from his office," she said, "and come set with me. I eats better with company."

This was the first time I'd used Beau's telescope. The dinner wagon had arrived in the field. The slaves were grabbing gourds full of hot food from iron pots. I picked out a bright red turban. It was Zipporah. Liney was kissing her and she was wiggling her backsides. Hastily I dropped the spyglass and made myself think about something else that worried me.

"Maum Hannah, I wish I were having a baby. Do you think something is wrong with me?"

She put down her horn spoon and looked sharply all over me. "You mighty thin and delicate bone, for sho. I can easy put my hands around your waist, but that don't specify. I 'spec the field just been plough too often. Seed ain't had no chance to sprout. But sho as Gawd lemme live, you'll ketch the very first night Master home again. Nothing ail you but overjoy."

I had had only one letter from Beau so far. It was in my apron pocket. I took it out and lay down on the warm dry grass. My longing for Beau made such a shivering sensation in the pit of my stomach, I turned my head away so Maum Hannah wouldn't see my burning cheeks.

The letter was about to fall to pieces from being read over and over. But it never lost its dearness:

> September the 11th, 1861
> Richmond, Va.

My Angel,

Tomorrow I am off for western Virginia with (Robert E.) "Granny" Lee, Wade Hampton being still out of uniform on account of the wound he received at Bull Run. I don't think this action will amount to much but you will hear from me as soon as I am free to write. I am in need of much that I have not time to purchase here.

Please have a well covered travelling trunk packed with one single mattress, 1 pillow, and 4 brown linen cases, 1 dozen of the second best silver knives and forks, 1 carving knife, and ½ doz. quires of good writing paper. Send my black cape. Have my blanket lined with brown linen (you know how wool chafes my neck). Send my case of pistols also. See that the moulds are in the case. Also some extra balls for the pistols. Send the trunk immediately to Cousin Harrisons.

Last night at a party General Breckinridge remarked that a cousin of his in Philadelphia had sent a letter to Washington which had been fetched to him by an informant whose name, naturally, he did not divulge. The North is extremely critical of Mr. Lincoln's "do little" policy since Bull Run. Mr. Lincoln defends the inactivity of the Northern forces by saying the next time he sends soldiers to fight they will be better armed, better trained and more numerous than the enemy. Lincoln is considered a wily and careful man, not the bumbler I had thought. The belief is that he will not attack again until he is confident of victory. Where will that be? Richmond, of course.

This morning I saw President Davis riding down Monument Avenue between two high-headed generals. Handsomer men were never seen. Who could hope to defeat us with men like those in command?

I have been made a major in a regular cavalry unit, the name of which has not so far been disclosed.

I kiss your lips and will dream of you whether I sleep or wake because I am your adoring husband.

                                    Baynard Elliott Berrien

P.S. Someone came up the other day with a *Harper's Weekly* of August the 24th. In "Foreign News," in small print of course, it announced the recognition of the Southern Confederacy by France! You can spread the good news. Also, the Spanish having abolished slavery forever in Hayti, the war between those two countries is at an end.

And this on Slavery and The Cotton Supply: The British Parliament has been engaged in discussing the slavery and cotton culture questions. In the House of Commons, on the 25th, Sir C. Wood made some financial explanations relative to India, and asked for discretionary power to borrow £5,000,000 for railway purposes. He said the Government had evinced great anxiety to develop the resources of India as a cotton-producing country. He believed that the result would be that ultimately England would be rendered independent of America for cotton. This year the supply of cotton from India would be about 300,000 bales more than ever before.

I folded up the letter and looked out over the seemingly endless expanse of snow-white cotton.

"I'd love to be a gull and fly over the island this afternoon. I imagine it looks exactly like the North Pole in the mid of winter."

A sea breeze was blowing refreshingly. There was a crisp of autumn in the air. From the fragrant scuppernong grape arbor came a screaming of jaybirds "Pay me Pay me" as opposed to their wheedling "Take a lien Take a lien" of spring.

I remarked that the colorful orange and blue and green and purple head handkerchiefs of the pickers, men and women, appeared to be flowers blooming in a garden of snow.

Maum Hannah put down her gourd of rice and said she wished more than anything to be out there in the field picking cotton with them. One day their God, not the white Jesus the Christ, would call to them from out of a big soft white cloud. He'd call every one by his African name and then he would blow the power into them with his horn and their sacks would turn into beautiful-colored gauzy wings and they would lift them and fly straight into heaven. It had happened once already—over on Daufuskie. The Obshay had been standing there with his bull whip and hollered at them but they just kept flying off into that big soft cloud. . . . They'd leave her behind, they would, if she kept on being comfortable and old and sitting here under a shading tree with the Mistress, the breeze blowing cool around her ears.

Her soliloquy was interrupted by a jaybird-loud voice calling "Hoo-Hoooo, my lady——"

Livia was puffing up the avenue from the boat dock. She had left off her outrageous hoop and was tented in voluminous folds of black calico sprigged in tiny red flowers.

"She got a possum smile on that ugly face today, Miss Angel. Look out." Maum Hannah didn't even lift her eyes when Livia flopped down beside her on the grass and began mopping perspiration off her fat neck with the hem of her garment.

"I've found the will!"

The minute I saw the paper she held out I knew it wasn't the will but I took it and thanked her.

"Don't be surprised, my lady, at what I'm about to say," she continued pleasantly, shaking the sand out of one of her shoes and gratefully wiggling her bare toes. "I can't read, you know, of course, but if Old Master left things against Young Master I want you to tear it up."

Maum Hannah could contain herself no longer. "Undecent and no-manners as you is, *I* is surprised at that last remark even if Miss Angel ain't."

"Well, it's this way, old woman, I'm not about to swap the lion for the tiger. In other words, I choose a master I saw before he saw himself over one I learned to hate in two days on account of the way he turned Mistress against me and a few other things as well. Then, you know, I always had a soft place for Master."

It was hard for me to believe that Livia and I could feel the same way about anyone, much less two people!

"Let me see what this is. Gracious—it's just an old letter." Casually I tucked the paper in my big apron pocket. "Where did you get it?" I asked, trying not to sound excited.

"Mr. Pierce sat a lot writing at the desk in his room. Not that he ever slept there, you understand. So, just to annoy him, I hid all the writing paper, including what was written on, inside the down comfort in the blanket chest. He almost missed the Charleston steamer hunting for it."

"Why did you want to annoy him?"

"He'd made me mad with that nose-up-in-the-air

way he treated me, as if I weren't nobody, and me having full charge of the house with those German servants quit and all. I tell you I thought Pharaoh and Master knew more rough words than anybody but while he was turning the room inside out, he spoke words I don't believe even Pharaoh would know the meaning of."

"How did you get here today?"

"I came in the McKees' boat with Robert Smalls. He had something he wanted to talk out with Pharaoh. He brought me free. I need some bacon and sugar and tea and meal to feed us at the Beaufort house."

"Here, take the key to the pantry and help yourself."

"I'll keep on hunting the will." She made a pale simulacrum of a curtsey.

Shoes in hand she went trotting toward the house shaking all over like a quaking pudding.

Maum Hannah whispered angrily, "Why you been so polite to that nogood creetur?"

"This is an important paper. I must get it over to Bay Point to Mr. Stephen at once. I'll make haste while Pharaoh is busy with Smalls so Big May can take me."

As the red-shirted, straw-hatted rowers pulled our little barge down past the fort, I saw General Drayton in his plumed hat galloping along the bluff on his white horse. I waved but he was too intent on his destination to notice. It was nearly four o'clock when Big May beached the small craft in front of the old Elliotts' cottage.

Stephen and Colonel Dunavant, a charming gentleman from Edgefield, were sitting on the porch of the cottage eating boiled shrimps from a wicker basket.

After greetings and a few fashionable remarks I gave Stephen the purloined paper. "Read it out loud." I was breathless with excitement of the intrigue I was sharing.

Pushing aside a pile of coral-colored shrimp heads

and shells with his foot, Stephen stood up and, after a few choicely descriptive words of his own, read to me and the Colonel:

Memo to President Lincoln
From Frederick Pierce, Major USA

Dear Mr. President:

Port Royal is a magnificent harbor opening to a curious labyrinth of ocean creeks on the South Carolina coast midway between Charleston and Savannah. The mouth of the harbor is called Broad River and is about 2½ miles wide.

The largest man-of-war can cross the bar at high tide and anchor comfortably in the roadstead clear of the bottom.

The luxuriantly outlined south shore named Hilton Head could be an excellent base from which to operate.

Beaufort, the main town, lies ten miles up the river of the same name. It is a summer resort of the rich cotton planters where they have erected splendid mansions suitable for great uses. Shallow-draft steamers can move freely from it to either Charleston or Savannah, each less than fifty miles away. The Charleston and Savannah Railroad runs between them. If cut, all communications and transport would stop. A principal junction, Pocotaligo, is thirty miles up Broad River from the ocean and easily navigable.

In my opinion, Sir, Port Royal Sound would be a prime prize. Now if——

"Damn this fellow!" Stephen was agitated and tense. He said that in Norfolk, Virginia, a Confederate spy found a hat with a Boston newspaper jammed in the crown. The last week's paper reported the most mammoth gathering of ships that had ever assembled on this continent in Hampton Roads under the guns of Fortress Monroe: eighteen man-of-wars and thirty-eight transports carrying over eight hundred sailors and fifteen thousand soldiers! The destination was a secret but it could be anywhere along fifteen hundred miles of coastline. The Confederate spy also reported that Yankee spies had made careful studies of the Port Royal area.

Frederick Pierce! There was no doubt but he was a Yankee spy. This rough draft of a memo, though lost, had evidently been so accurately recalled that it had no delay in being read by the President.

"I knew Pierce was a military man the instant he marched through the front door last December at Cotton Hall. As for us, look around you: we won't be ready to properly defend ourselves here six months from now."

White and black men, side by side, were frantically digging sand, piling palmetto logs and working on the battery.

Colonel Dunavant excused himself to go and supervise the setting up of four cannons that had been sent over from Braddocks Point for use here on Bay Point.

When he was gone Stephen laughed a hard little laugh. "I hated to shock the Colonel any more today but I've heard additional bad news: Commander Samuel F. Du Pont is in command of the Union fleet and guess who is serving right under him?"

"I couldn't."

"Our nefarious cousin, Percival Drayton. Percival knows the waters around here like the palm of his hand. What irony—the two brothers, Tom and Percy Drayton, facing each other as enemies! Almost as ironical as that I will have a chance to prove myself in battle here at home before Beau does in Virginia. Say, has Phillip joined up yet?"

"No. He is against war in general and this one in particular. It's made a strain between him and Eddie."

"Eddie is a dear. He's far sweeter by nature than Phillip. If his conscience had been the objector I wouldn't have been surprised. Phillip never struck me as caring about anything but himself. Has Eddie tried to persuade Phillip?"

"Eddie's been over at Fort Pulaski learning how to fire a Columbiad cannon."

"I wish they hadn't assigned him that duty. Hey —the sun's going down. I'll call Big May to carry you out to the boat so you won't get your feet wet. Give Beau my love when you write."

Twenty-seven

I had two letters from Beau this morning. One had been written over six weeks ago in a haybarn in western Virginia. It was abrupt and ink stained. I could hardly make it out; except the last paragraph, which said he had procured a new horse and he had a sore throat and missed me so horribly he was seriously considering deserting and coming home.

The other, dated a little more than a week ago, was entirely different. It sparkled.

Oct. 21, 1861
Richmond, Va.

Darling,

The Confederate Government is now established in Richmond and the air is full of activity. Quite a change from the rigorous routine of the recent weeks. Society here is in buoyant spirits. The Lees and the Harrisons and the Welfords, Masons, Cabells, Walkers and others have entertained me most hospitably. I personally have eaten a large portion of the greenback ducks and the terrapins and oysters from Chesapeake Bay. I must confess that their flavor surpasses ours.

One of my favorite new friends is a rollicking fellow, General J. E. B. Stuart. He dashes up to the gate on his horse, his plumes waving. Some say he will be our Murat. Stuart loves music and sings pleasingly. We are often called on to sing ballads in duet. He is eager to meet you. It is time for you to have a frolic for I know you have been working far too hard with me not there to stop you. I choose that you frolic with me and none else. I command you to pack your most becoming gowns, especially the angelic blue gauze that is a copy of an even dearer original. I have engaged a room for us at the Exchange Hotel, which is where everything goes on. You must make arrangements to arrive in Richmond no later than the first day of December to spend a month with me or waiting to welcome me home from a fight. You can leave Charleston on the train one day and be in Richmond the next.

The ladies deck themselves in velvets and satins and jewels to cheer their heroes, political and military. Mrs. Randolph and Mrs. Ives put on regular charming private theatricals in their homes. I played the part of Mark Antony in a tableau last night. You should have seen the houri who was my Cleopatra!

My heart is already pounding at the thought of touching you——oh, my darling——

B

Houri who? What was a houri? I rushed to Mr. Webster's big dictionary that lay on a table in Beau's office. Not being accustomed to looking up words it took me a long time to find the definition. When I did I wished it had taken forever. Mr. Webster gave two meanings:

Houri—a white-skinned black-eyed woman.
Houri—a nymph of the Mohammedan paradise, supposed to be created from musk and spices and endowed with perpetually virgin youth and perfect beauty.

Which houri had been his Cleopatra? I couldn't take a chance. December 1st was over a month away.

"Amun!" I called, running through all the little rooms into my bedroom. "Honey, we're going to Richmond right away. Beau says I must come immediately. I'll send a note to Aunt Beck in Charleston. We'll spend the night before we take the train with her. What's wrong?"

Amun stamped her foot. "I wouldn't leave Eddie for anything in the whole world."

"You can't stay here without me."

"But Angelica—"

"We'll decide at tea time. I've got to find Phillip in the gin house and make plans."

Two hours later Amun and I were sitting miserably together at the tea table when Eddie came in in his fatigue uniform. I told him that Amun and I were going to have a little holiday in Richmond.

"She is but I'm not," Amun said, smiling mechanically, while I poured Eddie a cup of tea.

Eddie sat down and started buttering a piece of bread. He was very serious. He had had bad news. Yesterday, October 29th, Judah Benjamin, the Confederate Secretary of War, sent a telegram to Confederate Army Headquarters in Savannah saying he had received information which he considered entirely reliable that the massive enemy expedition was intended for Port Royal. Judah Benjamin had got permission from President Davis to send Brigadier General Robert E. Lee to take control of the South Carolina, Georgia and Florida coastal defense as soon as Lee returned from the west, which should be within the week.

"I want you girls and Button to move over to the Beaufort house, so I won't worry about you. But there's no need to rush away for Virginia, Angelica. Beau wrote me he'd invited you to come the first of December." Eddie grinned wickedly and invited a radiant Amun to take a walk down to the water and watch the first star come out so they could make a wish together.

I stayed up after everybody had gone to bed writing out instructions to Phillip to read to Maum Hannah and Anatole and Israel and Big May and Pharaoh while I was gone. It was midnight when I slipped into my bedroom. Amun's round feathery little head just showed over the grey silk coverlet. The candle on her side of the bed was still lit. She raised up when I came in.

"I'm not going away from Eddie."

"Oh Amun, I must see Beau."

"Then you of all people should understand why I don't want to leave Eddie."

"We'll come back right after Christmas. I promise."

Amun began to sob. Hard wracking sobs that shivered her whole body. I climbed in bed and held her close. She put her tiny arms around my neck and cried herself to sleep even though I promised her faithfully to think it over and maybe change my mind tomorrow.

I couldn't close my eyes. The stillness of the night was broken by a flight of geese honking over and by the chiming of hours. It's not easy for me to hurt anyone, especially Amun. One minute I felt guilty because I had made her unhappy; the next I was quivering with the anticipation of being in Beau's arms.

From the pine tree by the window the familiar owl began talking in his velvet voice, "Houri Who?" he called softly, "Houri Who?—who who who—? Houri——"

I ran to the window, slammed it down and leaned my face hard against the cold glass pane. Houri Who, indeed! Amun could move over to Cousin Annie's at Myrtle Bank. I was going to Richmond within the week.

Twenty-eight

"Let the blue gauze hang in the wardrobe until the last minute," I told Maybelle. "It must travel in a box by itself so it won't be crushed."

Amun was upstairs, lightheartedly packing for her visit with the Elliotts while I was away.

Button was sitting disconsolately on the floor in front of my bedroom fire cutting a face in a pumpkin to put on a pole with a lighted candle inside so he and Phillip could scare the people on the Street at deep dark, it being Halloween.

"What day are you going to Richmond?"

"As soon as I have an answer from Aunt Beck saying she'd love to have me spend a night with her in Charleston. Her coachman will make sure I board the right train the next day."

"What if I fall in the river and a shark eats me up while you are gone?"

Mournfully he rubbed his fingers over a soft dusty rose velvet evening gown Maybelle was expertly folding. It had a low-cut cream lace bertha that made my shoulders shine. It was one of Beau's favorites.

"Please take me with you," he begged, running over and hugging me.

I felt his little heart fluttering like a bird against my stomach. I made myself conjure up Beau's image. It shielded me from other emotions.

Cross-legged, like a skinny monk, Maum Hannah was sitting under the high bed. She'd been there since breakfast rolling bread and sugar pills. "Her ain't going nowhere, Buttons."

He took his pumpkin into the hall to show Phillip.

Maybelle leaned down and peered under the bed, "Why not, old woman? Ain't you watch me pack up about a hundred fancy clothes?"

"Not 'twell them birds flies over and off."

"And why ain't she until then, old woman?"

"Her a great lady, him, like Miss Julia; not like old Maussa' frizzy Mistress. That's why."

But when Maybelle left the room to find some red ribbon to thread in a pair of my drawers, Muam Hannah came from under the bed. "Miss Angel, can I speak out plain?"

"Yes, but not much."

"Does you really believe in a world where jest you and Master live?"

"Why do you say that?"

"Well, 'pears like you always looking into that world stead of this one."

"No, no, I like the world of Cotton Hall very much even without the Master." But I couldn't meet her accusing eyes as I said it.

On Sunday, November 3, 1861, my trunks were strapped and the hat boxes piled one on top of another in Beau's office. Maybelle was brushing my hair in front of my mirror. She brushed hair delightfully. I saw myself in the glass, soft-eyed and shining. I'd lost the deep color of summer. My skin was almost alabaster again. I was dressed for church in a stylish blue silk jacket and skirt trimmed with black braid frogs and tassels. Maybelle pulled my heavy hair into a crocheted snood and pinned a smart blue and black tasselled Zouave cap on top of my head.

"Look at them boats!"

I went over to the window. Four old tugs and a fragile river steamer named the *Savannah*, converted into warships, were chuffing along. As they passed the mouth of Fish Haul Creek someone pulled up a channel marker; farther on a buoy.

"Pharaoh says they fixing the channel so if the Yankees come they can't find their way nowhere. And dark the lighthouse been last night."

Amun called from my boudoir, "Pharaoh has the barouche waiting at the front. He's awful grumpy."

"Are Button and Phillip dressed?"

"They've ridden on ahead. Phillip said the Stoney boys have arranged a new kind of shinny game in the cemetery before the service."

When we got out of the barouche at the Zion Chapel of Ease, the clear air, the calls of friends, the rich and colorful clothes of the communicants, the gleamy marble mausoleums and grave-covers, the sounds of a band at the Muster House just down the road, the deep grey uniforms of a company marching to parade, the screak of carriage wheels, and the dark oak shade, were all full of autumn languor and pageant. The island planters, except a few of the Barnwells and Lawtons who were Baptists, were at the chapel today. Expecting something momentous to happen, they had returned to the island before first frost to hasten their cotton harvest.

As I, Amun beside me, the boys following, moved pleasantly among them, I overheard a young soldier: "That's the fabulous Baynard Berrien's wife. I understand she's packing to leave the island and not taking the boys with her."

And another: "She doesn't look the type to run scared. Who told you?"

"Robert Smalls keeps everybody on the sea islands informed about everybody else."

Because I felt shame I walked with unusual stateliness. I didn't need to be told I was up to something bad. I knew it. But I had always, before now, tried to be good. My enchantment for Beau had changed me.

I stood and exchanged small talk with people, even agreeing that Grimke Barnwell *was* outrageous, coming to Communion in *another* striped bloomer costume!

And suddenly, as the door to the chapel was flung open, I felt as if everyone knew about the trunks in the hall and was disapproving of me too. But my sin was blood-deep inside; Grimke's was merely a few yards of green and tan poplin on the outside, easily removed.

A handsome, haggard old man with silver hair and sad eyes gave Communion. I knew I should refuse the

Cup. But the wine went down smoothly as the gentle voice told me that Christ's Blood Had Been Shed For Me.

Cousin Billy poked me in the back, "Stop praying for yourself and pray for a hurricane. That's the only cannon on our side big enough to blow up the Yankee navy."

As if he'd heard, the minister, unexpectedly departing from ritual, held up his hands and intoned loudly, "The god of battle is on our side."

We all said Amen and prayed that our enemies might be trampled underfoot. And we truly believed that God was on the island with us and would grant our request.

On the way home we stopped at Fort Walker. Everybody was in high spirits. The soldiers were singing the "Palmetto Song of Battle" and cleaning weapons and swapping experiences and flirting with the pretty girls languishing in open carriages. Colonel Wagener's fifteen-year-old son, Julius, too thin for his uniform, swaggered over to Phillip, who was sitting his prancey horse beside the barouche.

After greeting me and Amun, Julius slapped Phillip on the leg with his grey cap, saying contemptuously, "I hear you joined the shinny squad instead of the artillery."

"You should have been there. We won." Phillip reined his horse and paced away.

The Wagener boy was about to make a rejoinder but Amun interrupted him. "Do you know where Eddie is?"

"He's on the way from Savannah with General Lawton and a whole company of Georgia Infantry."

"Ask him to come to Cotton Hall this evening. I'm being sent away soon." Amun lowered her eyes and suddenly sobbed like a child. How emotional she had become lately. Sometimes she talked about such spooky things it made my skin crawl.

"I thought you wanted to visit at Myrtle Bank," I said crossly, which was a mistake, making her cry even harder.

As we caught up with Phillip I had to squeeze my

hands together to keep from reaching out and slapping his face.

Button called to him, "They think you're a coward. You could at least offer to be a lookout or something."

"And you could shut your mouth."

"Phillip makes me nervous," Amun whimpered, blowing her nose.

I was nervous too. My lovely feeling of having been forgiven had entirely disappeared.

A letter waiting for me on the round claw-foot table by the door, amid hats, riding whips, gloves, and cigar cases didn't help my conscience either. It was an early October letter from Beau written before the one urging me to Richmond.

> Sewell Mountain, Western Virginia
> October 6th, 1861

Angel,

I am homesick for the sound and smell of the salt marsh in this cold clay country.

We are waiting for Rosecrans to attack. My marvellous new hero, General Robert E. Lee, has decided that a Federal advance will mean certain victory for us. Our artillery can mow down the Northern troops and we can finish off any who escape the fire. I hope to visit Cedar Grove if we ever start back to Richmond. Perhaps my friend Jenks will take over my black in return for a hardier steed, more accustomed to this cold wet climate. The rain has made the roads impossible as well as impassable. We are so cold at night that we pool our blankets and sleep as close together as spaniels by the fire.

Coast Negroes are true fire worshippers and their love for the flames that leap and the embers that glow is as great as their skill in fire-making. Tonight, as I look into the fire that rascal Cudjo Manigo somehow manages to keep going, I think of you. Those flashing eyes, that haunting low voice, that sensitive face, that quiet splendor of yours fills my heart. You made something beautiful and exhilarating of every day we spent together. That you captured my soul was not because you attempted to. It was because in addition to your

physical charm you have the integrity and the fine
feelings of a great lady.

No more tonight. Too many moths around my
damned candle and chiggers in my coat. Nighty-bye—
love—kiss

B

P.S. Say Howdy to the boys and Pharaoh.

Two babies were born in the sick house that afternoon. Maum Hannah and Maybelle and I worked
side by side until it was dark. When I started toward
the house I saw a dusky gold moon, new risen, hanging low in the east. Suddenly all the roosters along the
Street saluted the fool's gold of the moonlight in the
belief they were calling up the sun.

Aunt Hecuba hailed me from her tiny porch, "Miss
Julia! You better make haste and git inside. Old Maussa' ghost walking the world. Them roosters talking
powerful strange talk. I wonder who do throw spell
on top them? Hope 'fore Gawd I never step over
him. Hey, ain't you riz higher in your shoes?"

I called goodnight to her and ran to the house. I
averted my eyes as I passed the piled trunks and
boxes. One of the Negro babies was having difficulty
breathing. Perhaps I'd wait until Tuesday or Wednesday and make sure he was all right.

Eddie had himself rowed with the tide to Cotton
Hall for supper. Amun hovered about him like one of
the myriad little yellow butterflies that had come to
the island with October.

He was keyed up and agitated. On the ocean way
from Savannah they had sighted great sails out to
sea. There could be no mistake. It was the United
States Navy.

Were they coming here or to Savannah?

No one could guess; we must be ready to leave the
island on a minute's notice if things went against us.
The Confederate forces would be outnumbered 20
to 1 in men, ships and weapons. The tension in the
fort was different suddenly. It refracted from the in-

fantry to the artillery; from the tents to the ocean;
from Fort Walker to Fort Beauregard; turning everything into a crystallized, breath-holding waiting. No
more singing, no more bugles blowing.

At sunset he and Amun walked out in the garden
to the pool filled with herons and ibis, out of sight of
the big water. I sat on the piazza on the joggling-
board with Button and looked out over the sound.
While Button explained in detail about how his calico
cat once had six black kittens and the tom-cat found
them and killed them, I prayed. Lord, how I prayed.
And I thought about Beau and tears came to my
eyes.

Part Four

The Battle

Port Royal Sound, November, 1861

Twenty-nine

My swansdown comfort had fallen on the floor. I was bunched up in a ball to keep warm until the fireboy built up the fire. He was late this morning. I hadn't slept much, being torn between wildly wanting to rush away to Beau and knowing I should remain here until the fleet passed us by. The door into my boudoir, where Maybelle slept on a pallet by the fire, opened. Maum Hannah tiptoed in.

"You wake?"

"Yes. Is the boy baby all right?"

"Him breathe fine. I here to tell you them big birds is come for the people. Drums talk it clear. Liney done blow the horn and ain't not one hand step forward to pick up he cotton sack ner he axe ner he fish net, neither he shovel. You best rise and look thoo Master' long-eye. I sent Maybelle to take my place in the sick house. I aim's to stay right in here lest them birds put a spell on me."

She gathered the ashes containing live embers and threw fat lightwood and oakwood on them. The blaze was instant.

I flung on a flannel wrapper. Stopping to snatch up the telescope from Beau's office, I ran into the cupola and opened a window. The sky was redding over the wide world of water and marsh and islands and forests. Slowly I turned the glass seaward. A different forest had sprung up in the night. A jagged outline against the sky of tall masts and branchy sails moved through the shining morning vapors toward the entrance of Port Royal Harbor. The god of battle had put on a blue hat!

In their morning vagueness the mistily green marshes spread everywhere and the dark creeks crawled like snakes among them. Along the bluff two black men were threading their way among the pal-

195

mettos and pines. One had a drum slung over his shoulder and the other was blowing a reed pipe. They went on. Were they mine? Or the Hanahans' or the Elliotts'? Whose?

My heart went sick with fear; sick and angry. I could hear the drum distantly. It beat like blood in my ears. I thought of the five ramshackle river steamers and converted tugs, our entire defensive fleet, that had removed the channel markers yesterday and were lying in Skull Creek under the command of the flag officer on the *Savannah*, Commodore Josiah Tatnall, who had recently resigned from the United States Navy and put on a grey hat. It would be David, without his slingshot, facing Goliath.

Shortly before Beau went to Virginia we spent an afternoon in a secret place off Bay Point. He insisted on our actually putting our bodies in the ocean sea with all those sharks and dolphins. At first I was uneasy but soon delighted with the sensual feel of the waves licking and caressing my naked flesh. I laughed and jumped around.

Beau held me and taught me how to slip myself rhythmically over the rollers. Then he left me, breast deep, and swam far beyond the breakers. I was intent on his red head when I saw an enormous lucent wave rising and coming toward me. I was hypnotized with awe and wonder as it rose up and up and up to a climactic, gathering white foam on its crest. Then, gracefully curving forward, suddenly with a great roar, it exploded in my face.

I was flung down, hurled over and over in a maelstrom of sand and rushing salt water and flying sharp shells and creatures. Strangled and scratched, I was dragged and tumbled through the churning foam and left exhausted and limp on the beach.

Beau bent over me, laughing. "Why didn't you duck and let the wave go over you? Or turn your back and swim like hell with it? Why did you just stand there watching it build up?"

I was reacting in the same way I did to the big wave as I watched, transfixed and fascinated, at the power and expertise of the Yankee fleet crescending.

In mid-morning, black smoke powering from their stacks, Tatnall's little mosquito fleet emerged from Skull Creek and ran down toward the mouth of the sound. The United States gunboats opened fire on them and chased them under the safety of the guns at Fort Walker. Then a majestic warship leisurely crossed the outside bar at high tide and Tatnall scampered back up into Skull Creek.

On Tuesday, in brilliant sun and no wind, the enemy reconnaissance flotilla crossed the sound bar. It came full steam ahead and, almost directly in front of Cotton Hall, confronted several bunting and flag decorated steamers from Savannah, packed with bourbon-and-basket sightseers, who had come to watch the excitement, following Tatnall's ships.

The *Savannah* let go a ranging shot and the *Lady Davis* (they were close enough for me to read the names through my telescope) sent one back.

Gulls shrieked and wheeled, sandpipers ran up and down the beach going peep peep peep peep, turkey buzzards flopped from the tallest pines and circled heavenward, the frolicking picnic steamers turned and flew as shots ploughed the water into billows and swift white runnels of foam.

A flight of pelicans flapped between the ships. Each side took aim and began firing on them, both cheering equally when a pelican vanished in a flash of sprayed-out brown feathers.

And all along the bluff, Negroes, hidden among the myrtles, cheered too, and waved their wool hats.

The Yankees were getting bearings. Soon the recall signal was hoisted and they swung around and headed back for the bar. The wave was not ready to break.

Morbidly absorbed, I followed the warships with my telescope. I had just passed over some Confederate pickets sitting their horses under the high bluff of Fish Haul Creek mouth when a shell, fired from a Yankee ship, rocketed in a streak of orange flame right into Fort Walker.

Things were becoming too hot and dangerous. I

made up my mind to have Big May row all of us immediately up to the Beaufort house.

Amun unmade my mind, being in merry spirits, having received a note from Eddie saying he was coming to get his horse in the afternoon. She persuaded me not to go until the next day. Maybe Eddie would stay for supper.

And then it stormed on Wednesday. Button and I put on our oil cloth coats and rode over to Myrtle Bank. Everything was grey and dim. The wind whined and moaned. I prayed for a hurricane.

Surrounded by his hunting dogs, Cousin Billy was hunched by the fire in the big room looking more gnarled and knotty than usual. "This is the end of our world," he said over and over in his soft voice.

Cousin Annie was directing a nimble, lemon-colored maid and the proud white-haired butler in packing silver into a large leather trunk. "They'll never get their hands on Grandma's punch bowl."

"If they subdue the fort we'll never see Dolphin's Head again in our whole lives. We'll lose everything. Oh, my beautiful cotton."

"Do hush, Billy Elliott, how can Button and I count spoons with you continually crying 'Doom! Doom!'"

I said maybe I'd better start packing up our silver.

Cousin Billy blew his nose. "Don't overlook that exquisite Malbone miniature of Julia's mother. This whole affair is a sublime tragedy."

Cousin Annie shook a rice spoon at him. "Don't say sublime, say infamous."

"I said what I said."

It was too gloomy at Myrtle Bank. Charlotte and Harriet were in Beaufort and Button had forgotten to feed his chickens. We raced each other home and let Amun's gaiety lull us into thinking everything would be all right somehow.

Eddie rode his horse over that evening. He was very grim. Both forts were braced for the showdown, and bad luck continued: Colonel deSassaure was supposed to have landed at Seabrook's with 650 more men but so far nothing had been heard from him. General Robert E. Lee would arrive tonight in

Charleston to take command. He could get to Pocotaligo tomorrow. Suppose he were just one day too late to save us? That is if tomorrow really turned out to be the day the Lord planned to bring the Confederacy to the test. General Drayton was no help in rallying the men's morale though both of his sons were in the fort. William Edward was no older than Phillip.

"Where is Phillip?"

"He and Pharaoh are working night and day ginning the cotton we've got picked so far. It is from the choice stand," I said.

"I don't want to see Phillip. I don't think I ever want to see him again," Eddie said bitterly. "He's a thorough scoundrel."

Later when he and Amun came to my boudoir for him to say goodnight her pale radiance made me want to cry. I felt worse saying goodbye to Eddie than I had to Beau. He was sad and wistful where Beau had been crackling with excitement. But then Eddie didn't choose to be a soldier any more than Phillip did. He didn't want to fight anyone. He never had. But, to him, this war was honorable. A gentleman would never refuse to defend his home and his country.

There was a rumor that the Drayton brothers met secretly that night in Charleston and knelt in prayer, shoulder to shoulder, in St. Michael's Church. Then they separated and never saw each other again. But it couldn't have been true. The tide was against them.

Dawn found bewhiskered, wide-eyed General Drayton slouched on his big white horse on the high bluff above the fort observing the massed Federal warships and gunboats that had come all the way into the harbor during the night; and saturnine Commander Drayton standing on the deck of the *Pocahontas,* on the edge of the shoals to the south, shrewdly considering the familiar shore above the fort.

Thirty

The Lord knows where I will be tomorrow. For now I am sitting at Beau's desk in the office. One of Button's calico cats has just jumped on the table and is watching me with her yellow eyes. It is dark outside, the moon not up yet. A few minutes ago, from the cupola, I could see thousands of campfires winking like tiny stars down on the beach in front of Fort Walker. A galaxy away from here!

The stillness is sharp after the horrendous thundering noises and terrible shocks of this day. Sometimes it is muffled by the soft slap of the water on the shore and the occasional hooting of owls and a recurrent sweet note of a waking songbird among the whispering pines. All else is hushed. I keep a listen but the Street too is unusually quiet. Our people may have dared Liney's threats and gone with others to join the yelling, drunken Yankee soldiers at Fort Walker.

I'll never forget the wistful, lonely look in Amun's light eyes, accusing me of deserting her as she left the island with the Elliotts. I could see Cousin Annie's white head lifted high in defiance as her rowers headed toward Parris Island. A Yankee fired a gun in the direction of the barge. It hit just behind, geysering water all over her and Amun. One of the rowers restrained Amun from jumping into the water. Cousin Annie never dipped her head an inch. She wouldn't. She insisted on taking the trunks of silver in the barge so Cousin Billy's dogs and the butler had to go to Beaufort on Mr. Hanckel's flat-boat. Cousin Billy went with them.

Button and Liney and Israel are waiting, down at our landing, for Pharaoh to return from carrying Confederate soldiers across deep water to Daufuskie in the steamboat. As soon as he comes we will head for

Beaufort, along with Maum Hannah and Maybelle.
I don't know where Phillip is.

This morning at ten o'clock the wave of war crested
and broke over the island. Earlier the enemy warships
began crossing the bar and coming one after another
into the sound. Fifteen formed themselves into an
ellipse and began turning slowly around like a wheel
between the two forts. Commodore Du Pont had
caught the tide so he could maneuver as he wished.

We fired first! When it was definite that we *were*
their target, Major Huger fired three shots into the
lead ship, the *Wabash.* Instantly bombs came flying
up from her in a sweep through the air and fell directly into Fort Walker, exploding with a roar that
shook Cotton Hall as if it were a match box. Then came
broadsides from all the others.

Oh, that fiendish turning devil's death-wheel of flame
and destruction! It was like a world of its own whirling on its axis, throwing out flaming rockets of fire
and blue comet tails of smoke into tornados of flying
brown sand. It was a hundred thunderstorms and
ocean waves breaking and rolling and crashing and
reverberating at once.

Huddling in my boudoir staring at each other, sometimes we prayed aloud for Eddie. But how could anyone survive in that inferno? Bay Point was put out
very quickly but Fort Walker kept at it until almost
noon, when only three guns continued operable.

Young William Edward Drayton galloped up to
Cotton Hall about that time and said his father had
given up hope. The fort was a maelstrom of terror
and confusion. General Drayton was arranging to
evacuate the survivors and get them to Seabrook's
Landing and over to the mainland. William Edward
and four others were going from plantation to plantation rounding up sail boats and barges and flat cotton
boats to take the soldiers away. And begging for every wagon and carriage to be sent at once to the fort
to remove the wounded.

General Drayton wanted *me* to set up a temporary
hospital *here* at Cotton Hall where the men could be

given emergency treatment to enable them not to bleed to death on their way to Savannah and Charleston!

"What about the General?" I asked.

He was leaving at once for Bluffton. There was no more he could do here.

Phillip, who had so far refused to take any interest in anything but cotton ginning, suddenly went into action. He volunteered to ride to Honey Horn and Spanish Wells to round up boats and barges and vehicles.

I asked William about two shallow-draft Union gunboats that had been anchored at Fish Haul Creek mouth and one of the biggest warships, the *Pocohontas*, right off the shoals to the south. William said the enfilading fire from those vessels had inflicted more damage on the fort than any others because there were no guns on the bastions to answer them. The *Pocohontas* was his Uncle Percival Drayton's ship. That had done a lot to dispirit his father. It was scary, seeing him give up like that and anxious to retreat.

Riding one of the bays, Phillip called from the barn, "I don't know when I'll be back, Angelica."

I summoned Liney to blow the horn and ring the bell for men to help set up cots and make pallets on the floor of the card room downstairs and, the weather being warm, on the brick floor under the first-story piazza. The billiard table served as an operating table.

I don't think we'll ever be able to remove the blood stains. The shots that exploded in the forts simply tore the boys to pieces. I asked everyone about Eddie. Nobody saw him hit so he must have gone to Bluffton with General Drayton or be helping direct men on foot to where the flat-boats are assembled to take them to Coosawhatchie where, it seems, Beau's hero, General Robert E. Lee, has actually arrived.

So many things happened so fast that it was like the wave almost drowning me last summer.

Phillip was back at Cotton Hall by half past one.

On his way home he came on the 650 men who had landed at Seabrook's last night in the storm. Unfamiliar with the island roads they had been stumbling around all night cursing the chaney briars and sucking swamp mud!

"Why wasn't someone on hand to lead us to Fort Walker?" Colonel deSassaure was furious.

Phillip suggested that the Colonel turn back toward Ferry Point. The need for him or his men at the fort had long passed. He described how every boat on the island had converged at Seabrook's Landing and several steamers and rafts from Charleston and Beaufort and Savannah. Tatnall's ships were ferrying soldiers over deep water so they could get to General Lee. He thought Button and I had better not wait for Pharaoh to return for us. Panic was contagious. Masses of Confederate soldiers and planters' families were jamming every available raft and vessel. The planters were fleeing with some of their favorite house servants and a few possessions like jewelry and portraits and poodle dogs. One lady had put six hats one on top of another on her head. Handsome coaches and buggies and saddle horses were left standing for anybody to claim. Flight was of the essence. To stay and be captured by the Yankees or become victims of a slave insurrection would be the ultimate tragedy.

The soldiers' retreat, from the fort to Seabrook's was disorderly too, full of pain, fright and confusion. They stopped at Cotton Hall for a drink of water. Anatole and his kitchen maids cooked washpots of duck and venison soup to hand out to them. Little black boys worked steadily drawing buckets of water from the well. The soldiers were powder-grimed, half blind from being stung by sand, and deafened by explosions. They said they'd floundered through blood and sand to get out of the fort when the signal to evacuate came. Then they just took to their heels. No time for getting their knapsacks or canteens of whiskey or watches or swords or their sweethearts' pictures and letters from their tents. Julius Wagener had exposed himself to the fire to pick up the South Carolina blue flag that had been shot down. Of the Confederate flag that had snapped so lively not a single grey or red shred was left.

The last anyone had seen of Eddie he was ramming a shell into the big Dahlgren gun on the parapet. There was nobody left at the fort but Major Huger and Colonel Heyward. They were working three guns until everybody could get away. All along the road the soldiers passed cabins, tightly locked. They knocked and begged for water. The people refused to come out and help them.

The wounded began arriving around two o'clock. There were three doctors. I never learned their names. Maybelle and Maum Hannah and Israel were wonderful help. I think I was too but I cried a lot. It was all horrible and made me feel part of this awful war. The first boy was laid on the table and the doctor cut off his leg. He died during the operation and his leg was tossed into a chrysanthemum bed. One, then two, then several turkey buzzards began circling down and settling themselves on the grass and the fences. More and more wounded men were brought in wagons and buggies and carriages. We laid them in rows on the pallets, their bloody clothes red in the strong afternoon sun, their faces sandburned, their eyes like enamel. Some could walk, others were carried in shrimp nets and blankets. Liney had as many field hands helping as he could force from their cabins. They were kind and gentle to the hurt men. But Phillip was the hero. In no time he was making and putting on bandages as skillfully as the doctor. Maybelle eased their pain with her hands. Button ran around with cups of water and fanned flies.

One boy, very young, with a lost, trembling adolescent voice, tugged at my arm, "Please, mam, don't tell Mother. She didn't want me to come to war." His stomach was blown open.

Blood was everywhere. Moans and whispers sounded as loud and deadly as the cannons of the morning. This was the first direct look I ever had of torn-up flesh, pain, missing limbs, disbelieving, disenchanted young eyes. . . .

The doctors were worn out but they kept on trying until after five o'clock. We were loading the last one in a straw-filled wagon to be taken to Seabrook's Landing when three blood-covered boys came limping up the driveway, holding onto one another. They were exhausted, their skin burnt scarlet. One of the doctors signalled to Israel. He went up to them and caught the middle one. He was dead. The other two had been carrying him like a baby.

"Leave the dead one," the doctor said, "put the other two in the wagon. We'll all be captured if we don't make haste away from here."

He bowed to me and said he'd never known anyone more wonderful and my husband would be proud of me wherever he was. As the wagon rattled off he called back, "You and the little boy come with us, Mrs. Berrien."

"No. There is another brother. He was here a minute ago. Our boatman will be back here before sundown. He'll take us safely away."

Israel laid the dead boy under a chinaberry tree. A buzzard settled immediately in the top of it. From where she was standing by the well Maum Hannah lifted her voice in a gospel song. The wagon vanished.

The people had come out now from the Street, fascinated with the gory scene. They were bunched together jabbering excitedly.

A pair of beautiful thoroughbred black horses pulling the Elliotts' fanciest carriage trotted up. The carriage was filled with Negroes. On the front seat, snapping the buggy whip, sat the nimble lemon-colored maid wearing Cousin Annie's red fez and widest black lace hoop skirt.

"Come on, you all," she cried, snatching a brandy bottle from the driver, who had on Cousin Billy's silk beaver top hat and full dress coat. "Hop on. We got room."

"Get out of here," Liney yelled. "You been t'ief them horses. Don't you know Yankees planning to put which ones of you come there on a big boat and sell you to Cuba?"

Zipporah hopped up on the carriage step. The girl in

the red fez hit the horses. They whirled away at a gallop.

"Aren't you going to stop her?"

"No, Miss Angel, her ain't worth. Best let him go."

There was a forward movement of the people, a hissing between closed teeth, a rattling of knuckles.

Liney lifted his bullwhip and shouted at them. "Ary one of you whut runs while Miss Angel stay is going to get ketch by me and fetch back to Masai. Him break your neck evenso your back same like a chicken neck evenso a chicken back if I tell him to. All I gots to do is hand you over to Masai. And remember I is the Obshay and you is the slave 'twell Mr. Linkum say you is free."

I was so shattered I could not dominate any longer. I had to keep moving so I walked quickly down to the bluff. It was red as the dawn. And cool. I could feel the cold air around my eyes and on my forehead, where sweat lingered. My heart was thumping slowly, harshly. The rising wind was cold. I was damp-cold all over. I raised my hand to push some tendrils of hair back. My hands were shaking uncontrollably.

Button ran up. He looked worn out and frightened. I must pull myself together and comfort him. He said, "They are putting the boy and all those pieces of people into a big hole in the cow lot where the ground is soft enough to dig in a hurry. I couldn't watch. But look at the sound—it's full of blood too."

Wearily I explained that the redness came from the reflection of the setting sun, very beautiful, on the water. I took his hand that was as cold and fluttery as mine.

We heard them singing, their red flannel shirts the color of the afterglow, and saw them rowing: Big May in our twelve-oared barge with two of the lesser ones following and our largest cotton flat-boat.

"We'll meet them at the landing and tell them we're ready to go as soon as we find Phillip."

They came close in to shore, near enough for me to see their fixed expressions. Big May gave no sign that he heard my calling his name. But he couldn't have missed. He sang:

Moon went into the piney tree
And star went into the blood.

And the rowers bent low and answered:

Blow down, you Blood Red Roses, blow down.

We heard them singing for a long time as they kept
rowing on down to Fort Walker where they would be
free. Or so they thought.

Thirty-one

"Miss Angel-l-l-l." Liney's voice floated eerily into my consciousness as if he or I were at the bottom of a well, or was that a screech owl?

I must have fallen asleep sitting at the desk. My head was burrowed in the cat's fur. I could feel Button curled cosily like a fox around my feet.

"Wake up, Miss Angel, honey." That was Maum Hannah's voice.

The blessed oblivion turned thick and ugly. Torpor made my neck rubbery. I struggled free of sleep. "But I told him . . ." I explained to whoever was with me in my dream.

"Miss Angel, Master Eddie home."

Blessed relief poured through me. I opened my eyes. The room was full of people, some holding pine torches. I saw Phillip's tall head in the doorway. He was barely recognizable, his face blackened with soot, streaked with tears.

"Well, there you are. Is Pharaoh . . ."

The sea of blacks parted showing all of Phillip. He was carrying a grey velvet bundle. I saw plainly now. I jumped up. I went dizzy. The great wheel of fire started turning again. The world rushed into confusion. Fear prickled all over my body, from my scalp to my toes.

The bundle was soaked with scarlet. But I saw only the head. A wave of such utter anguish contracted my insides that a response I had never used before shot up from my soul. It was the response that breaks a human heart. For that beautiful classic head, so like my darling's, had fallen back in the last excruciation from its broken body. A drop of blood from a scratch on the temple was the only flaw on the chiselled blue-white marble. The eyes were squeezed together too

208

tight in the final torment. Eddie was nothing any more. Eddie was dead.

"We must bury him at once, before the Yankees get here," Phillip said stiffly.

Button had hidden his face in my soiled apron, clutching my legs. He was sobbing.

The people were swaying and moaning like an autumn wind. I fought nausea and faintness. I leant down hoping to steady myself and kissed Button.

In darkness we buried Eddie inside the ancient wrought iron fence where *le petit géant,* the little grandfather in the gold coat, and the first Baynard lay, along with their various wives and numerous children. What remained of Eddie fitted into a small red travelling trunk. Button kept on crying but Phillip and I were too shocked to weep.

Maum Hannah, looking like the gaunt high priestess who had sung a watch song to me that first night, led the slaves in rhythmic humming while the grave was dug and the pitiful little coffin lowered and the shovels of dirt went thud! thud! thud!

The bright moon was behind a spreading moss-hung live oak tree endowing it with uncanny life so that its long twisted arms, overhanging the grave, seemed reaching down to gather Eddie back into its roots.

"I am the Resurrection and the life," I began. I couldn't remember the next line so I started the Lord's Prayer. The people mumbled along with me.

As we said Amen, Maum Hannah hit the first high shrill note of their grieving song. They hoisted their voices in screaming and wailing as well as singing with their lips closed.

> Moonlight, Starlight,
> O-o-o-o-o-h Moonlight
> Believer what's the matter?
> John lay the body down!
>
> John lay the body to the tomb,
> O-o-o-h let me go!
> John lay the body to the tomb,
> John lay the body down!

Afterward, the three of us bathed ourselves in cold water and changed into fresh clothes to be ready to leave the minute Pharaoh returned with the steamboat. It was our only means of escape. There wasn't another boat left on the place, not even the canoe.

Button slept with his mother-cat on the rug by the fire in my boudoir. Phillip and I sat up all night, waiting for Pharaoh. Every now and then Phillip would climb the stairs to the cupola. The coast was lighted for miles with the flames of cotton being burnt on distant plantations to keep it from falling into the hands of the Yankees.

Phillip went out into the night and set our fields and the gin house ablaze but Liney or somebody put the fires out.

In bits and pieces Phillip told me about finding Eddie. He'd had a bad feeling about him all day. After he saw the Elliott servants in Cousin Annie's carriage he hitched the bays to the barouche, blacked his face and hands and went down to Fort Walker. On the way he picked up two pleasantly drunk Pope Negroes who effectively concealed his disguise.

The Negroes jumped down when they reached the fort and ran, hollering "Welcome, Brother," to a Yankee officer who beat them with his gun and cursed them until they melted away into a horde of blacks pouring out from the woods in every kind of garment snatched from their owners' closets, waving whiskey bottles and feather fans at their deliverers, who greeted them with cold contempt. But the blacks were too barbarically wild with jubilation and false freedom to notice. They ran around yelling and screaming but no more so than the thousands of Yankee soldiers who were in complete celebration too, drunk with whiskey and victory, brandishing swords and pistols and keepsakes they'd found in the Confederates' tents.

Phillip had no trouble making his way into the fort. It was lifeless and empty. Nobody wanted to wade shin deep through all that sand to look at bits and pieces of men flung around. Every now and then a sentry would walk past on the shot-up bastion and look down. One of them called, "What you doing in there, nigger?" And he replied, "Nuttin', bossman. Jest gloatin'."

It took him almost an hour of peering into every dead face to find his brother. Dr. Buist was leaning over him, his gold-wreathed hat still on his head. Another boy was beside him. This one was whole. Dr. Buist must have been killed instantly. He was smiling. It was the hardest thing he ever did, gathering Eddie together. He slipped back to where he'd hidden the barouche and got the grey velvet lap robe to wrap him in. If anybody had stolen the barouche it would have taken him all night to bring him home.

"Once, inside the fort, I almost dropped him. I happened to look up at the moon. A prism of red and white and blue glow circled it like a halo. It seemed like a sign that our Confederate stars and bars that had been shot to pieces were up there now telling us to keep faith. I hate myself for not fighting. Bubba is going to hate me too."

I wanted to take him in my arms as I do Button but during the year he had grown taller than I. Tonight he was a man not a boy.

He ran his hand through his dark hair. I noticed how square and hard a hand it was. The Yankees would take him prisoner if they found him here. We made a mistake in counting on Pharaoh to come back for us. He was probably in Beaufort eating supper with his mother, bragging on the number of soldiers he carried to safety.

My heart was frightened and burdened. How was I going to tell Amun, who had already this day shown herself breakable, that her first sweetheart was dead? And Beau, who had loved Eddie the most of his brothers? Nothing could atone for this. No senseless weeping, no compensation of other happinesses could ever deafen us to this deathsong of today.

Thirty-two

As soon as it was daylight Anatole fixed a good break-fast and Phillip and I set out to find a boat, any boat. We rode through fields of smouldering cotton and passed still burning store-houses and barns and three dwelling houses on the way to the Seabrooks'.

The big house was full of the people. They were sticking their heads out of windows, upstairs and down, and rocking in cane-bottomed chairs on the piazza. The front yard was strewn with smashed gold leaf mirrors and pictures and tables and Persian car-pets and mattresses. Chairs and sofas had been scat-tered over the lawn. Black women draped in lace curtains and black men in Mr. Seabrook's white linen suits and a few white men in blue uniforms were sit-ting on the chairs and sofas drinking wine out of dusty bottles. Some were lying down together on the grass laughing and singing.

Before I knew it my hands were clenched and such a feeling came into my heart that I heeled Miss Suzy and galloped right over and through them. They shook their fists and screamed threats as they rolled out of the way of Miss Suzy's sharp hoofs. I met Phillip coming up the bluff from the landing. No crafts left moored here!

We rode hard over to Squire Pope's Cotton Hope. This is one of the finest houses on the island. It had been plundered of everything. Only a spaniel bitch with a litter of puppies, in a wicker basket beside the fireplace in what had been the grand parlor, had not been molested or carried away. There was a blue and white Worcester soup bowl of fresh milk beside her basket and a half-eaten chicken wing.

"Let's head for home. I know Pharaoh has returned. He wouldn't play a trick. He loves us," Phillip said, his eyes strained and sick with seeing.

Button and Liney and Maum Hannah and Masai and some of the house maids were on the front steps.

"Did you pass um on the big road?" Liney asked.

"Who?"

"Soldiers. They done been here and took all your trunks and my best ox and wagon. I tell um Mistress still hereabouts. They say they jest going to help tote your trunks since you all packed and ready. They be back this afternoon with a bigger wagon and git the silver and china and the pretty carpet in Master's bedroom. What we going to do? Oh—bless Jesus—here come some more. Hide, Master Phillip—run——"

Phillip headed his horse for the big barn.

There were four of them. I knew the two in the lead were officers from the size of their hats and their tight fitting uniforms. The two following wore caps and bounced around in the saddle.

Uncle Jim used to say where most girls got messy and hot with violent riding I only sparkled more, became more alive. There would be such a glow on my cheeks he wanted to hug me at these times. I could feel my black hair, blown from its net, falling around my shoulders. My eyelashes were damp and seemed to reflect sunlight into my eyes. My body was limp with wet warmth and my shirtwaist clung to it revealing my breasts. I hated Frederick Pierce to see me like this.

He was controlling a snorting sorrel horse in an amazingly graceful manner. His full red lips, looking charmingly bee-stung, made a surprised mouè. "Angelical Why in God's name haven't you left this place?"

"We are waiting for Pharaoh to boat us somewhere safe."

His deep-set tawny eyes shone as they met mine. I still attracted him as I had a year ago! Oh, dearest Lord, help me hide my anger and hate. Let him help me and the boys. Amen.

He dismounted quickly, tossed his reins to a snub-nosed, yellow-haired orderly accompanying him, and was helping me down before I could protest.

"This is Commander Percival Drayton."

I refused to acknowledge the saturnine, black-bearded man in his fancy naval uniform. Button spoiled my scorn. Cradling his calico mother-cat, he called, "Uncle Percival—come and see what they did to me."

"Can this possibly be baby Button?" Percival's voice was clipped and cold.

Exhausted, confused and scared to death, I burst into tears. I was so shaken emotionally that I accepted a linen handkerchief from Frederick and blew my nose hard while he patted my shoulder and said, "There. There. Let's go inside and sit down and talk about it."

Percival Drayton said harshly, "We've no time to visit, Major. This is an embarrassing circumstance in which I do not choose to find myself. General Sherman assured me that every white inhabitant had left the island before I agreed to this assignment."

"I don't believe Angelica intended to be rude, Commander. She's overwrought. We can't leave here until we get to the bottom of why she and the boys are still on the island."

Liney and the others stood respectfully aside as Percival Drayton marched stiffly up the steps. They knew him. He was real folks.

I clutched Frederick's arm because I had gone weak and desolate and defeated inside. But I refused to faint, even though strange little stars and black spots were whirling around in front of my eyes and cold sweat bathed my forehead.

Button ran through the open door, calling back to Percival Drayton, "One of those nasty soldiers said he was going to show me what was going to happen to every Rebel in the South. Look!"

Le petit géant's throat was slashed from ear to ear!

"What else did they do?" Frederick was the stern soldier now, not the sympathetic gentleman to whom I had turned in my distress.

"They stole Grandma's little-small china picture from the table and they stuck a sword through Angelica's canopy over her bed and then they saw the trunks and hatboxes and got so excited about sending them home to their sweethearts that they took them away in Liney's favorite oxcart. You can't let them, Uncle Percival, it's *our* ox. They shouldn't steal our ox."

I dropped down on one of the fat sofas by the fire-place. I'd never regain courage enough to cope. The men looked at each other uneasily.

Percival said testily, "I intend to remain on my ship from now on. You must deal with this affair, Major Pierce. However, I strongly urge you to arrange for Mrs. Berrien and the boys . . ."

"There's just Button."

"We know Phillip is here. We saw him ride off. Go and fetch him, Button," Percival Drayton said.

"Will you promise not to take him prisoner?"

"Not if you hurry," the evil Drayton said more gently. "Tell him to sneak in the back door."

Frederick said, "We must act quickly, Angelica. The orderlies out there are no different from any other soldier, yours or ours. This situation has already piqued their curiosity. They, too, were informed that not a single plantation owner remained on the island and they were free to pick up a few little mementoes of the battle.

"Being familiar with the island, the Commander and I were sent on a scouting expedition to select suitable houses for officers' quarters. Twenty will move into Myrtle Bank this afternoon. We were too late to take over Seabrook. Pope's Cotton Hope is still a possibility."

"And Cotton Hall?"

"I have already informed headquarters that this plantation belongs to me."

My tears dried up. Faintness vanished. My wits returned.

Percival Drayton was trying to fit the neck back to the head of *le petit géant.* "It can be mended," he said casually.

"And what of my clothes?" I asked.

He shrugged, "Better them than Phillip. While you and Major Pierce resolve the ownership of Cotton

Hall I'll ride home—I mean over to Fish Haul Plantation, and see if any boats are left there. You and Button are quite safe. Phillip is the one I'm worried about."

When he had gone Frederick said pleasantly, "Did you ever find the will?"

"No. Livia brought a paper over one day she thought was the will. It was a copy of something you'd written to President Lincoln about Port Royal Sound."

"I hope I helped make up his mind. We'll occupy Beaufort in a day or two; as soon as the soldiers can be brought under control and the officers housed. I am to be stationed at Bay Point for the present with General Stevens' crack outfit, the New York Highland Guard. I don't know when I'll be able to come back here. Are you sure of Pharaoh?"

"Phillip is. What about the people who have fled to Beaufort from here?"

"I hope they have sense enough to stay in residence so the coloreds don't go crazy as they have here. Things will simmer down in a few days. We'll feed them and put them to work building barracks and a base on Coggins Point. The island has already been renamed Port Royal."

"All this since yesterday?"

"It was arranged months ago."

Phillip and Button came in. Phillip had his usual sullen expression. It made him seem boyish again.

"How are you, Phillip?"

"I'd be better if Pharaoh had gotten us away from here before you turned up."

"I assume by 'you,' you refer to the United States Army?"

Phillip laughed sarcastically.

"None of that, my boy. We are not enemies, we are friends. You, here on this island, have been conquered, taken over, as nobody in history ever has. Imagine—within a short afternoon—the whole population fled—vanished as if they'd never been—leaving every possession and cherished acre of ground they own to the conquerors. Magnificent drama!

We thought Port Royal was well fortified and expected the Confederates to put up a real battle. We only lost six or seven men. So much for that. Let's see—where were we? Oh—you—well, I'm going to help you get out of the mess you've gotten yourself into."

"And if I don't care to do as you say?"

"You are still conquered. But can't you recognize that I am your friend?" He got up and marched over to the piano and began drumming his fingers in martial tempo on the lid.

I wanted to beg Phillip not to argue. Frederick's attitude was predetermined. I was at a loss as to how to reach him. Even now I could understand my first admiration. He was physically perfect. He came and stood before Phillip. His shoulders broad, his hips narrow; his beautifully tailored uniform became him, as any garment would. His eyes alone gave him away. They were without warmth or kindness. There was no doubt but he could feel anger or concern and was a brilliant operator but his eyes revealed him. They frightened me. What could I expect from such a person?

"We appreciate your concern, Frederick," I said.

Phillip turned his head away and said nothing.

"Look what they did to my picture," Button said.

Major Pierce rubbed his hands together. His eyes that had been calm became unsteady and he talked too fast.

"Didn't you hear our men cheering from the fleet when the prismatic colors made a ring around the moon last night? They considered it a sign that the United States flag, the world's hope, is slated for a victorious epoch. Come on our side, Phillip. Last December you were definitely opposed to Secession. What changed you?"

"I saw the moon phenomenon and we buried Eddie in its light."

"A pity. Elsa was fond of Eddie. But—back to the present: it's impossible of course for me or Drayton to take you all in any sort of vessel anywhere, even over to St. Helena or Daufuskie. We'd be shot on sight. The only sensible thing is for you to come with me and put on a blue uniform and disappear, if you insist, when we go into Beaufort."

"Pharaoh will come for us today. I know he will."

"So will those looters. And they'll take you prisoner as surely as if you were a teapot they wanted. Teapot! Say—we must check the dining room."

Anatole was sitting at the table, slumped over, fast asleep, an empty bottle of Beau's best brandy in his yellow hand. The soldiers had not come in here. They were bringing the wagon back for these treasures.

Percival Drayton called from the front door, "We'd better move on, Major. There wasn't a sign of a boat at Fish Haul. But we can put twenty officers there easily. Many of the house servants have remained. I swapped my horse for Brother's big white. Much more comfortable gaits. I suggest that for the present we put a flag on the iron gates at the entrance of Cotton Hall, lock them and leave one of the orderlies stationed there with his rifle cocked."

"That's a fine idea. I'll have time to work out some sort of scheme to take care of Phillip."

"And me and Button?"

"Dear lady, your future and mine are inextricably linked. Of course I will take good care of you."

We went out onto the piazza. The men mounted quickly.

Maum Hannah raised her voice in a shrill whine, "Whuh you done with yo' brother, Master Percival? Is you killum?"

"Master Tom is a Rebel, Maum Hannah; I am an American. You should be too."

"Ain't you do love us no more?"

"Oh, stop fooling, old woman. Major, we've more important promises to keep than lingering here. Get out of the way, Button, or I'll run over you. Forward, men!"

Waving goodbye to me, Frederick cantered off.

Button advanced toward Percival's horse. "You killed my brother. And you didn't care about my picture." Button's face was furious and pinched with hate. If a child is capable of murder Button was at that moment.

Before I could call out to stop him he squatted down at the horse's heels and picked up a handful of droppings.

Percival leant forward. His horse responded, going away at a trot.

Button threw the manure at him, hard and fast, screaming as he did so, "You damn Yankee."

Liney and Maum Hannah were after him instantly but already too late. The manure had struck the yellow-haired orderly squarely on his snub nose.

"You little bastard!" The orderly raised his rifle like a whip and brought it down on Button's head.

I heard the crack and I felt the impact as if it were on my head. I stumbled down the steps and fell on my knees at Button's side.

Phillip made a leap for the orderly's horse.

A rifle jab to the stomach and more curses and Phillip went crumbling to the ground.

There was a running of people, led by Israel and Aunt Hecuba, from the Street. When they saw Button they went watchfully silent and immobile, hiding behind trees and shrubs.

Phillip struggled up, looking white and sick. Liney grunted but said nothing as he bent down and slipped his strong arms under Button, taking the little body away from me. The wound I'd been pressing with my riding skirt gushed blood all over his precious face. I heard the iron gates at the entrance clang shut.

I knew neither Frederick nor Percival Drayton was aware of what happened. They were too far ahead. I didn't blame them. But hate coursed through me with every heart beat. I, too, now, was ready to kill and kill and kill.

Part Five

Behind Enemy Lines

Port Royal, Formerly Hilton Head Island,
December, 1861–December, 1863

Thirty-three

All that night and the next day Maum Hannah and Maybelle and I hovered helplessly about the little trundle bed Liney pulled out from under the big one in my room. Phillip never left the room except when he had to: once when Israel tiptoed in and asked for help with the complicated new cotton gin; twice to eat something. He sat near the window looking out over the water. He merely sat there brooding and clenching his fists. Next to my anxiety for Button was the haunting fear of what Phillip might do if Button died.

Desperately I wanted a doctor but I could not bring myself to send to the Yankees. Deep down I was afraid of them, of making any contact with them, of involving us in the slightest measure with them.

That Button had a serious concussion was obvious. There was no way of knowing whether his skull was fractured or his brain damaged.

Lying there, unconscious, he looked small and helpless, still and cold as a stone. His breathing was barely audible and his pulse faint and irregular. Maybelle gently rubbed his arms and legs to make blood flow into them. Maum Hannah, who comprehended the spirit as well as the body, talked to him, low and easy, telling little tales her mother had brought from Africa about animals and birds which talked and acted like humans.

As shadows lengthened the next afternoon she looked over at me and said, "Buttons not hurt bad as you think, Miss Angel, for all him 'pear to be dead. Him not choose to wake up or 'spond. Them that never knowed violence finds it hard to accept and that's a fact. Po' little boy suffer from all-two things: seeing Master Eddie broke apart like a dolly, with all he

223

sawdust falling out; evenso the rifle lick pon-top he head."

"I'll never get over this, nor will he," I said bitterly.

"Why don't you go in your pretty little setting room and sleep awhile, maybe evenso say your prayers. We could use some Jesus-help."

I put down the cloth soaked in witch hazel I'd prepared to lay on the wound. "What about you? I ate breakfast. You haven't had a bite of food."

Maum Hannah laughed and kicked up her skinny feet. "I eats same like a snake; heap at a time. I'd jest finished half a rokoon when them mens comed. And I kin sleep with all-both my eye wide open, staring-wise same like a owl. Maybelle be back in a minute from supper, evenso Master Phillip."

"I'll sleep for an hour if you promise you will when I wake up."

"Sho! Sho! Now, Buttons, lemme tell you bout how-come Brer Jaguar ketch Sis Anancy spider by she sticky, t'iefing fingers pontop a tar pole he been set up in him 'nana grove . . ."

No one had made a fire in my boudoir. The air was damp and drear. If only I could weep. But my throat and eyes were dry. I was tense, strung high as a piano string.

Beside the gold sofa, on which I had sat so often in Beau's arms. I knelt. And it was Beau not God I sought for I was distraught and self-absorbed in anguished desperation. God seemed too far away. Perhaps there was no God. Beau had been here in this very room. It was I, Beau's wife, who was left behind in the midst of the enemy. It was Beau's beloved younger brother who had been killed; Beau's baby brother who had been beaten. It was Beau I needed, not God.

No prayer moved my lips. Somehow I could neither think nor ask. Only in my heart a rageful cry swelled loud enough to tear through the walls and bolt straight to wherever he was.

"Beau! Beau! What can I do?"

The room was quiet with that quiet of being shut

away from every sound. And I knelt on as the darkness at the end of the day descended and there was no flickering ray of light or comfort or hope.

And yet suddenly there was a voice in the room. And it was not my voice. And there was nobody in the room except me.

"Dang!" said the voice, and it was powerful as the beat of the whooper crane's wings going over in the night. "You'd better get yourself set for the next hurdle. There's a waterhole on the other side of the rock wall. If you aren't careful you'll land in the middle of it. Use your wits, dammit. It's the biggest jump you ever faced; but keep control of the reins. I'll be coming back to help you. Don't panic. Keep cool. Stay where you are."

I heard the words. I know I heard them. They were in the room as well as in my heart. Then vaguely I heard other voices outside in the garden. Abruptly they ceased. Silence settled down again. I opened my eyes with a start. I was still on the floor on my knees. The voice continued to vibrate in my ears.

It was a strange experience, but I understood. He wanted me to wait here at Cotton Hall for him. I rose and went into my dressing room and washed my face and, in the gloom, put my hair in order as best I could.

The real voices were coming into my boudoir now. I felt strangely peaceful and rested, not surprised to see Ephraim Baynard and Tom Elliott, in torn and scorched uniforms and muddy boots, talking with an animated Phillip, who was placing a lit lamp on the center table.

I rushed toward Tom saying he was an answer to my prayer. But had I prayed?

Phillip had told him about Button.

"Oh do come and see him," I said.

Carefully Tom examined Button. There was no movement when he tickled Button's foot. He took the inert little hand in his.

"He looks bad. How many soldiers did you say were with Percival and Pierce?"

"Three," Maum Hannah said quickly.

"Two," Button murmured weakly.

"Bless Jesus, Miss Angel, your prayers is answered. Buttons done cross safe over Jordan. I going now and take the news to the praise house. They ain't so hot on going to them blue hats after they seen what happen to us baby."

I leant down and kissed the little-small big toe.

"I'm thirsty," he whimpered.

Anatole knew Tom Elliott and Ephraim Baynard never left Cotton Hall without full stomachs. Oyster stew and venison patties and sweet potatoes and piles of hot biscuits were on the table when we went into the dim, candlelit dining room.

"It's an ill wind that blows no good," Tom Elliott said. "If that rascal Pharaoh hadn't bolted you wouldn't be here and we wouldn't have come up with this good food and the axes and men that are going to make it possible for us to sink stakes and block the mouth of the Coosaw River. Phillip, bless his soul, and Liney are collecting them."

Ephraim said, "You'd better keep your eye on Phillip, Miss Angelica. When he told us what happened to Button I thought he would go berserk right then and there. He reminded me of Beau. Thank the Lord *he* isn't here. Beau would be after the whole Yankee army if he knew. Golly, these are plump juicy oysters!"

Manners were put aside. Relaxed, we ate hungrily. I was more at ease about Button; they were safe inside a quiet house. At least for a little while. We tried to pretend it was a normal meal. But the things they told were strange and terrifying.

"How did you all escape from Bay Point?"

They were luckier over there than the soldiers at Fort Walker because Stephen, considering the possibility of defeat, had the day before the shooting arranged for his father and William Cuthbert to assemble barges at Dr. Jenkins' Landing. Only this saved the entire Beaufort Artillery from capture. When the firing ceased they spiked what guns were left, marched four miles up the beach and then on a blind path through thick woods, lagoons and marsh to where flatboats were waiting to take them over to Jenkins' Landing.

Stephen had been wounded in the leg by a shell fragment but he refused to leave until all his men were off the island.

Ephraim said, "As soon as it was dark Stephen sent James Stuart and some others over to Hilton Head to burn as much cotton as they could."

"We saw the fires. Phillip tried to burn ours but the people kept putting the flames out."

"We came to burn yours this evening. We've just finished setting fire to the big warehouse at Fish Haul and destroying what cotton gins the slaves hadn't already broken up. This is the only place on the island that's been left alone."

I explained about Frederick Pierce and his claim of ownership.

"Don't burn your cotton. String him along—until Button is able to be carried away. Accept all the protection Pierce offers. We'll come back from time to time and see about you."

"Two good spies on the island will be as much help as a regiment," Tom said.

"Phillip can continue destroying the cotton crop and Miss Angelica can keep watch from the tower on top of the house and let us know when the fleet starts for Charleston or Savannah. General Lee thinks it will be in a few days, if they're smart," Ephraim put in excitedly.

"Philip saw four gunboats going up into the Beaufort River this morning. I've been so taken up with Button I've not worried enough over Amun and Cousin Annie. Oh dear . . ."

Tom said he wasn't hungry any more. His moment of ease had vanished. I had brought him back to here and now. He twisted a big damask napkin around and around his hand.

"I slipped into town in the fog the morning after the battle. The streets and yards were jammed with coaches and chaises and wagons and riding horses.

Mother and Papa were arguing about whether to go to Flat Rock, North Carolina, or to Edisto to be sure his rose trees had been properly bedded down for the winter. He begged to take his botany books in the trunk, but she insisted on taking the silver instead."

"Did you see Amun?"

"She was sitting in my old high chair eating a soft boiled egg. When she saw me she smiled and said she was getting ready to go to the moon to be with Eddie. She'd seen the moon turn red and blue. It had been a signal to her. Eddie had decorated it for her wedding. I told her he was at Bluffton with General Drayton but she wouldn't listen."

Tom didn't know about Eddie! If I didn't tell him I wouldn't break in half. If I kept talking about other unusual things, like Amun—

"She's always lived in a sort of dream world. I shouldn't have sent her away."

"There's no need to worry about anybody Mother has charge of. Charlotte and Stephen's boys are with her too. They definitely went to our house in Flat Rock. Teddy Barnwell said when the train left Pocotaligo it was so loaded with planters and their families and favorite servants and food hampers and books that there wasn't squatting room in the aisles."

Ephraim said, "I rode through Beaufort with James Stuart that evening. The big houses had already been entered and plundered but we didn't see a single person, not even a Negro. It seemed like a city of the dead."

Tom was unwinding his napkin and then winding it again, slowly, carefully. "Teddy Barnwell made another reconnaissance into town the next morning. Everything was quiet as a cemetery. Not even a windsound in the palmettos. He went in their house on the bay. It was a shambles; books thrown all over, the draperies pulled down, mirrors smashed, the harp strings out, furniture broken. He looked out of a window on the fourth story and saw the Yankee gunboats coming . . ." Tom's voice broke. Tears streamed down his cheeks. He hit at them with his napkined fist. "If only the Yankees had gotten there before the blacks."

Ephraim said, "I don't see why you say that. They're bigger thieves than them."

"At least they would have prevented the desecrations."

I found all this hard to take in. "Why did everybody run all at once? The Yankees wouldn't have harmed women and children."

"They were terrified of being captured by the Yankees and of hordes of suddenly loosed slaves. Numbers defeated our friends and relatives, my dear, *numbers* of Yankees and blacks blowing down on them like a hurricane."

To change the painful subject Ephraim said, "I was in Coosawhatchie yesterday. I saw General Lee. No one knew who he was at first. He was still wearing his Federal uniform of the old army. He had a little grizzled moustache, close clipped, and shiny brown hair, and big wise eyes. Just seeing him had an effect on all of us. He's a big man."

The grandfather clock in the hall struck seven. Phillip came into the dining room.

"Liney has sharpened the axes and ten field hands are waiting in the kitchen. Where's your boat?"

"Hidden near the cave under the high bluff this side of the mouth of Fish Haul Creek. We saw the guard on your piazza and skulked through the bushes to the back of the house."

"What guard?" I dropped an oyster on the table cloth.

"He's sitting on your joggling-board; or was at half past five."

Phillip started toward the hall. "I'll investigate."

Tom jumped up, trailing the limp napkin. "Come back, Phillip. I don't trust you. You go, Angelica."

Taking a candle from the brass branch in the center of the table I hurried through the dark hall to the front door. I put down the candle, picked up one of Beau's riding whips from the cluttered table beside it, and slid the bolt. Outside was a bright night. The moon hadn't risen but the stars made enough light for me to recognize the snub-nosed orderly who had struck Button. My hand tightened on the whip. I raised it, then let it drop.

Keep cool. Use your wits, the Voice had commanded. Keep cool if you expect to clear the jump. There was no way of knowing whether or not the whole house was surrounded by them. They may have seen the Confederates come in. They would take us all prisoners. I *must* keep cool.

"What are you doing here?" My words spat themselves out.

The soldier jumped to his feet and snatched off his cap. His light hair stuck out in all directions. He must have many cow-licks. It gave him a terribly young look. His voice too was young, as if it were just changing into a man's.

"You scared me to death! Oh, please, mam, how is the little boy?"

"What are you doing here?" I repeated angrily, waving the whip in his face.

He shrank back against the board. "N-n-nothing."

"Are you on duty?"

"No, mam."

"How dared you come back here?"

"I can't sleep for thinking about the little boy. If I don't get back to polish the Major's boots before Tattoo they'll throw me in the provost's tent."

"Are there many guards on this plantation?"

"No. Not even at the gate any more. Only a United States flag to keep soldiers from coming in and stealing. Is he bad hurt?"

"Why do you care? You tried to kill him."

"The Lord will punish me. I've always had an awful temper. Ma says it will be the hanging of me yet. I went crazy yesterday. I never meant to hurt the little boy. Look—I brought him a present, seeing as how he was holding a cat when we got here."

Use your wits! But the Voice had said nothing about using my heart.

"He's unconscious but he'll live. He spoke a while ago. Now you get away from here and don't ever come back. Take your present. We want nothing from you."

"It's a cat. Tell him how sorry I am. I'll bring him another present soon. Tell him my name is Hans Mueller and I'm from Michigan and I have a little brother who likes cats too."

He pushed a hard cold object into my free hand and ran down the step. When I heard his horse going away down the oyster shell road I went inside. The men were standing quietly by the door.

Phillip had a pistol. "Who was it?"

"Just a young soldier who'd lost his way in the dark. He was alone," I said wearily.

"Where'd you get old Mrs. Lawton's famous Chinese cat?" Ephraim asked. "It's been at Calibogia forever. It's supposed to be hundreds of years old; Ming something."

I looked down. I was holding a white porcelain sleeping cat with yellow and black markings. A solid gold bell hung under its chin. Button would love it. I placed it carefully on the table on a pair of Beau's soft chamois gloves. Button might as well have it as a Yankee child on a farm in Michigan.

When they were gone I watched Button drink a few spoonfuls of rice gruel. Soon I left him sleeping, with Maybelle sleeping on the floor beside him, and Phillip sleeping on the foot of my bed. I climbed up into the cupola.

I knew better than to let myself think about Beau or Amun. I needed to be near the luminous sky and listen to the voices of the night. The people were singing and stamping in the praise house. The wind was blowing a chill through the pine. It made a roaring sound like a muffled cannonade. Down river, toward Coggins Point, the fleet made a black blur against the starshine on the ocean sea. The watch lights in the riggings of the ships twinkled in the distance like the lamps of a small town. I felt as if I had suddenly been carried away and set down in a foreign land. Nothing was familiar nor would be until Beau came back. And he would. The Voice had promised. We would never be separated again. Separations are too terrible to live through.

Carefully I climbed down the stairs to the third story and went into Button's own room where a fire was burning, bright and warm. The little brown fireboy was sleeping on the rug with all the cats. Not bothering to even unloose my stays I lay down on the bed and slept the deepest most dreamless sleep of my whole life.

Thirty-four

Guineas pot-racking around the well woke me from my long sleep. Guineas being chased by some little boys to catch a few for Anatole to roast for dinner. The little fireboy had disappeared. Only the purring cats remained stretched out on the rug in the warmth.

When I leant down to peer in Button's mirror I saw my own familiar face, not the haggard mask of the past two days.

I ran lightly down the stairs. I was kissing Button gently on his wrist when I heard Frederick calling from my boudoir.

"Open the door, Maybelle," I said reluctantly.

Frederick strode in, agitated and annoyed. He handed me a bunch of single red camellias tied with the wreath of gold leaves from his hat. "You shouldn't allow people to walk into your private sitting room unannounced. It's not safe, I tell you. Where are the housemaids? Have they run away?"

If I would ever like him it would be for this little bouquet of flowers he had picked himself.

He didn't give me a chance to thank him.

"The boy who took my horse says Button has been hurt. How?"

"He fell out of the hayloft." I don't know why I continued protecting Hans Mueller.

Frederick forced one of Button's eyes open then rode immediately back to headquarters for a doctor.

While he was gone I bathed and put on an old violet wool at-home thing that had not been good enough to pack for Richmond but which became me.

It was a strange, strange day. Terrible lead-colored clouds scudded across the sky. The wind was up. It pulled at the trees and pulled at the water. The only soothing thing was the memory of the Voice. As

I sat beside Button hoping and praying for another response from him, remembering the words of the Voice strengthened me. I was quite calm when Frederick returned with the doctor.

He was a tall thin Jew with beaming black eyes and a narrow head full of glistening black hair. He exuded knowledge and skill. After a few minutes he decided Button had a fractured skull and the kind of concussion that could give him a lot of trouble later on if I made any attempt to move him until the injury was entirely healed.

"You and the Major leave me alone with him for a bit," he said. "I want to study his breathing and test him for one or two things that might change my diagnosis."

Anatole sent in tea which Frederick and I took in the hall by the fire.

"You've had the pot polished!" Frederick exclaimed, admiringly touching the finial with a carefully manicured finger. "Do let me pour."

He was in a talkative mood.

"On November 9th, which was yesterday—"

How could it be only two days since the battle? Two years! That's more like it.

"Like what?" he asked.

"Oh, I was just wondering something aloud to myself."

"What do you keep staring at up in the chandelier?"

"A rat," I giggled, realizing I must look exactly like Aunt Dell at this minute. Particularly in the ancient violet tea gown which had been hers to begin with.

Frederick reprimanded me for being frivolous at such a distressing time. The trip to Beaufort in the gunboat had been dreadful; like going into an empty, elaborate theatre devoid of actors, completely set up for a play to begin.

"Or end," I murmured sadly, passing him a plate of cold duck legs with a peach sauce to dip them in.

"I said begin," he emphasized firmly. "General Isaac Stevens was fascinated by the town and plans to preserve it for his headquarters. While Stevens went about giving orders to soldiers to clear out the Negroes who were looting and destroying everything in sight in the houses and the gardens, I went around to our house." He whispered the "our" intimately, touching my cheek with the same manicured forefinger. It was as if I had been stabbed with an icicle but I managed a false simpery smile.

The front door of "our" house was locked; the wooden shutters closed on all the windows. He beat and called. Livia, after peeping through the glass at the side of the front door, let him in.

She must have gained fifty pounds, resembling a brown toad wrapped in a white lace curtain. And the stench! Nothing but death could smell as the inside of the house did. Henricus was lying in the center of the hall on a long marble-topped table. Livia said he died of an attack during the big gun shoot. The old white wig partially obscured his face but his lips were pulled up from his teeth in a snarl. Two black boy babies, naked, were laid out on marble tables too.

Livia said that on the day after the big gun shoot all the good-smart Negroes left Beaufort with their owners. Then the blackest and worst field hands and bush Negroes came yelling from the deserted plantations into the town to steal and smash the front windows of "her" house and surged in. But she knew how to handle that kind!

She told them that this was a funeral parlor. She was the boss lady. She turned dead people into statues. "Look," she shouted, "at all the ones I've turned, standing on stools, up and down this hall!"

If they touched anything in this house they would die instantly. Their hearts and haslets and livers would become stones. She'd stand them up on marble pedestals too, in all sorts of positions. See! She was turning her own husband right now. Touch him——

One man did and fell in a fit, frothing and writhing. She opened the front door and they ran all over each other getting out.

What a windbag Frederick was! I was growing tense and upset. Why was the doctor taking so long with Button?

I started to jump up and run from the room. Something inside me warned me not to. Then I had a sudden inspiration.

"What are your immediate plans, Frederick?"

My interest pleased him. He poured another cup of tea and leaned toward me: he was in total agreement with General Stevens, who strongly urged General Thomas Sherman and Commodore Du Pont, the ones in overall command of the action to move inland while the Confederate forces were demoralized and scattered. Stevens proposed to attack the railroad in brigade strength and destroy every bridge on it for thirty miles. Then he would countermarch to Beaufort, or embark on transports from Hilton Head, and, reinforced by every man possible from General Sherman's command, strike at Charleston by the inland waterways of the North Edisto, the Wadmalaw and Stono, coming up behind the heavy harbor and sea defenses that guard the city.

"And then take Savannah?"

"Exactly. Stevens fought with General Lee in Mexico. He's confident that once Lee takes hold, the odds, which now are all in our favor, will change. Unlike Sherman and Du Pont he knows Lee's ability to pull rabbits out of empty hats."

"Will Sherman and Du Pont take *your* General's advice?"

"I doubt it. They think all victories down here are going to be as easy as the Battle of Hilton Head."

The door opened and the doctor came out. "The boy's life signs are all satisfactory," he said, unwinding his hands as if he had been praying. "I can't imagine that particular fracture resulting from a fall. Are you sure that's the way it occurred?"

"What difference does it make so long as he's going to recover." Frederick was ready to leave. "Take a look at some of the pictures, doctor. Good, eh?"

"What happened to that lovely old French portrait?" The doctor's sensitive fingers traced the sword slash.

"Your soldiers frightened Button by cutting his grandfather's throat." My voice broke. I couldn't speak another word.

Frederick put his arm around my shoulder. It was a strong arm. I was embarrassed but I let him. He said that there was a clever young artist at the headquarters who was sketching the Battle of Port Royal for *Harper's Weekly*. He'd send him to mend the picture. His work was excellent.

"That will please Button." I was so grateful that I said I'd be happy for him to bring General Stevens and the doctor to dinner tomorrow.

"We'll be here at two o'clock." Frederick swung up into his polished saddle. His foot in the shiny pointed-toed boot touched the groin of the sorrel gelding he rode. He gathered up the reins and with a possessive smile, trotted off ahead of the nice doctor.

Phillip came in raging and accused me of flirting with the Yankee peacock.

"I'm using my wits for a change. We need Frederick Pierce's help for Button's sake. I hope you'll take care he doesn't get wind of what *you* are doing, burning houses and cotton and all."

We were walking along the bluff watching a school of dolphins leaping in the rough water.

"Or that *you* are planning to betray his confidences to the Confederates."

I thought I would fly to pieces at his ugly tone of voice.

He apologized and we tried to laugh; but the strain that had fallen between us remained. I never felt close to him after that.

A few days later Stephen sent word for me to meet him down on our dock at moonrise. I stood on the cold Belgian stones of the steps waiting and listening. A boat came near. It had an engine. The whistle on it went toot-toot. Was it he or Pharaoh?

The boat travelled on down water. It was Pharaoh. I climbed the steps, went back in the house, lay on my sofa and cried.

Later in the evening Stephen came, looking cold and grey and tired as his uniform. He had been sitting in the dark cold marsh for hours. Pharaoh kept circling and coming back by our landing.

Stephen had regrouped the Beaufort Artillery at Garden's Corner. From Coosawhatchie General Lee was planning to defend the bridges where the Charleston-Savannah Railroad crossed the rivers. He would not attempt to string out a defense all along the railroad. He would mount a guerilla attack. From the bluffs and bridges Confederate cannon could disable any Yankee ships that came up the rivers. He, Stephen, was in charge of harassing the enemy on the sea islands and keeping up the guerilla war from the creeks and marshes whenever the Yankees ventured away from Coggins Point.

He had come to see about me and Button before he wrote to Beau. "General Lee has agreed to enclose a note to Wade Hampton requesting that Beau be transferred from Virginia to fight here. We need his special skills dreadfully. He's always been a guerilla at heart. Have you got any information out of Pierce?"

I told him everything.

"Ah," he sighed with relief, "then Beaufort will be saved; what's left of it. General Stevens is a gentleman. Come, let's go up in the cupola. I'll explain the things I want you to watch out for. But as soon as Button can be moved I'm going to take you away from here. I don't trust Pierce's good will toward you."

Thirty-five

A month has passed and still Beau hasn't come. His letters, which appear mysteriously on my desk after a raid by the Confederates, are short and tell nothing. He has no idea of the horrible situation here. He is broken-hearted about Eddie but thankful the rest of us are safe at Cotton Hall. He is counting the hours until he can be transferred. Until then, which he prays will be soon, riding with big Wade Hampton continues swift and exciting as a fox hunt.

Button was slow recovering. He had terrible headaches and spells of nausea. He still has them.

Israel came in yesterday. He begged me to visit the gin house more often. Nobody was doing a full day's task. They purposely break the rollers and scatter the seeds. The steam machine was out of order. He couldn't find Master Phillip to fix it.

Phillip was in Beau's office reading a Latin book. I sat across the table from him and asked why he wasn't where he was supposed to be.

"And where is that?"

"In the gin house. Liney and I can't be everywhere," I snapped.

He put down his book and studied me closely. At that moment the change in him from boy to man was startlingly apparent. I'd never fully appreciated how sharply cut his chin was. It jutted out like a spade. He should grow a beard to soften it. All this merely emphasized the change; it wasn't the cause of it.

"If you'd spend a little time reading those *Harper's Weekly's* your Yankee friend fetches you'd know why I don't bother." He picked a paper up from the table and shook it at me.

I opened my mouth to say something sharp, but changed my mind. His dark broody eyes were too cloudy. He said, "Mr. Chase, who, in case you don't know, is the Secretary of the United States Treasury, has decided that his department needs our 1861 cotton crop to help finance the war against us. He is sending rascals he names Cotton Agents down here to ship it north. Ours will be the first to go, it being probably the only one properly ginned."

"Nonsense," I said impatiently.

"They call us fiends in human form. We must be wiped from the face of the earth. I prefer reading Ovid to ginning cotton for them."

"If I pay my taxes they can't take our cotton."

"Wait and see. To make things worse a Benevolent Society called the New England Freedmen's Aid Society in Boston and similar groups in New York and Philadelphia are recruiting Abolitionist preachers and long-nosed female missionaries and radical students from Harvard and Yale to come down here and supervise education of what they call 'contrabands' —what a ridiculous term—why can't they call them 'people' like we do? and and prove that Negroes can grow cotton for pay without being subjected to the driver's lash or the vicious greed of the human monsters who own them. It's all there in cold hard print. Read it. You'd better. And we'd better get away from here as soon as possible."

"You certainly are more in the know than I." I spoke slowly because I was confused.

"I know that by remaining out of uniform, I'm a coward."

With a bang I hit the table with my fist. "No! No! Never that. You're caught in an unusual trap. We both are. But as long as we are you *must* help run the plantation. I know too little about it. Liney says it will be time to begin planting the new crop soon. Suppose I give up and just sit here waiting for somebody to ride up and carry me off?"

Phillip rose and went over to the window and stared out into the grey December sky. Rain was pouring down. When he turned, his chin was trembling. "Oh, all right, I'll fix the damn machine and gin all of our special long staple cotton for some Yankee mill to turn into lovely gauze for some Yankee girl's ball gown. But one day it's going to stick in my craw so bad that I'll disappear. You and Button will have to make out as best you can, waiting here for Bubba to give up joy-riding on his grand new horse and sneak back down here to save you. He's always had everything his way. I've always been the one left behind."

I flinched. "Well, go on with your reading," I said coldly, and stood up.

Whereupon Phillip abruptly left the room.

A while later when I'd calmed down I put on my oil cloth coat and sloshed through the mud to the gin house. The noise was very loud. Over in the corner Phillip and Israel were laughing happily as the complicated steam gin whirred along.

I quickly withdrew and made my way back to the house and told Anatole to fix a crusty pudding with meat and dumplings for dinner.

"That's Master Phillip's favorite." His fat yellow cheeks creased with smiling. "Mine too!" he smacked.

That same night Stephen sent a messenger to ask Phillip to meet him at the Stuart mansion when it was dark. By midnight from that direction flames were shooting so high it looked as if the battle of Port Royal had begun all over again.

For a while every day was just like every other until the day Frederick suprised me overlooking the milk-girls in the dairy. He was in a great gloom. Worse than Phillip.

I put down the cream skimmer, but he quickly said, "I like watching your hands do that. It quiets me. This infernal inaction and boredom is driving me crazy. General Stevens wants to take a quick dash across the Coosaw, make several adroit moves with well-trained troops, capture General Lee and push inland. If we only had William Tecumseh instead of Thomas West Sherman as our general in command we would have already occupied Beaufort and taken

Charleston and Savannah. I made a reconnaissance last week. There's not a single gun mounted in Savannah."

His blue hat was on sideways. He acted like a puppet on a tight string who could not stop his talking. If he stopped he would drop to pieces.

I thought: he's caught *la grippe,* he's feverish.

"Let's go in the hall where it's warm."

"I'm perfectly all right." But his mouth twitched as he followed me into the house. He sat close to the fire and seemed to get hold of himself, laughing shakily.

"There are many problems in addition to the sluggishness of the top brass. Mainly what to do with the Negroes. They are slaves without masters, in a slave land, in the possession of us, the conquerors, who say we do not believe in slavery. But we refuse to acknowledge them as fellow Americans. In India the British work side by side with Hindus and elephants but here not a Union soldier will work along with a black. As a consequence of overwork five thousand of our troops are on the sick list. They're more afraid of the blacks than you Rebels were."

"Are the slaves happy?"

"I don't think so. They sing and shuffle around a lot and eat a lot but some of the loyal ones are bitter that their masters left them behind. All are bewildered, and wonder when and whether their former masters will return."

"Why don't you send the people back to the plantations they came from and pay them and put them to work?"

He didn't answer that question, continuing his monologue. "We're feeding the contrabands and building shelter for them and don't permit them to lift a finger to help themselves."

"Then why don't you put them in soldiers' uniforms and give them guns? That would make them equal to be shot at anyway."

"It's my thinking exactly. General Sherman won't listen to me."

I heard no more from him for a few days but then on Christmas Day a carriage and a horseman trotted up. It was an icy day, cold and clear. My heart stopped as it does every time an unexpected horse clatters up to the block.

The door flew open. "Is Mrs. Berrien at home?"

As when he'd appeared at Cotton Hall the day after the battle I was unable to believe the effect of Frederick's beauty. Standing in the doorway, his arms full of ribboned packages, his amber eyes glistening with anticipation, he could have been the model for any one of the symmetrically perfect statues I'd seen pictures of: Narcissus, Antinous—especially Apollo because, despite his erect way of holding himself and his military walk, there was something rounded and soft about his comeliness.

"Can an uninvited stepfather share your Christmas dinner?" his excited voice rang like a bell.

In another time and another place, naturally another life, I could imagine myself holding my breath with admiration, wanting to be friends with such a man. I really could. And this mortified me.

"Merry Christmas, Frederick."

Phillip, who had been piling logs on the fire, excused himself and went into the stairhall. He didn't want anything to do with Frederick any more.

Frederick's shining expression turned cruel. He said, "Pharaoh often brings me news of Cotton Hall, Angelica. Did you know he was still in the area? Phillip must watch his step. I can catch him at something anytime I choose. If he continues to behave in this manner I might be tempted. I abhor rudeness. And you," his voice lowered to a whisper, "must not stand on your landing dock in the darkness any more. The bluff is full of lurkers and watchers who love to peddle information."

Frederick's attention moved on to Button. I lowered my eyes so Frederick wouldn't suspect my resentment, nor my fear.

"You seem improved, boy."

"Yes sir," Button lifted his hand weakly. He was

propped on a pile of pillows on the sofa nearest the fire where Maybelle had laid him to watch the Christmas tree. "I wish you'd brought your orderly."

Frederick put down his armful of presents and called for Hans, who came grinning with a cage containing a big green and yellow parrot! Button laughed for the first time since his hurt.

For me Frederick had bolts of fine fabrics to compensate for the loss of my winter clothes. I couldn't resist. I just had to let my fingers touch. As I was exclaiming over a particularly soft length of red velvet, he tossed a sable cape around my shoulders.

"This was Elsa's."

The fur was lush and exotic feeling around my neck and shoulders. I snuggled my chin into its luxurious softness.

"It looks pretty on you, Angelica," Button murmured, tickling the parrot's back with his forefinger.

"I can't wear this." I was appalled at myself.

"Why not?" Frederick clenched his fist and shouted so he made the candles on the tree tremble.

I closed the silk frog that held the fur at my throat. Be careful, the Voice had said; keep cool. I stroked the fur. "There was no sense in my letting a qualm of conscience upset you, Frederick. It is a beautiful wrap and so deliciously warm."

He put his hand to his forehead. "I didn't mean to raise my voice at you. Phillip put me off balance for a minute."

Thankfully Anatole sent our deftest serving boy, neat in grey livery, to say that dinner was ready. I opened the door into the stairhall. Phillip hadn't gone far. He was leaning on the newel post, looking miserable.

"It's your house," I said gently, "I want you to carve the turkey. Don't let Frederick do it."

He came but his hand shook so on his spoon that he never finished the crab soup and he had a time with the turkey. Throughout the meal he was silent and ill at ease.

Frederick ate and drank much wine, enjoyably, and never ceased talking and laughing at his own wit. He reminded me of one of Uncle Jim's pet bores, "always Meum with him, never Tuum" he would groan.

I tried but failed several times to draw Phillip into the conversation but Frederick tossed anything Phillip said aside like an empty shell thrown up out of a wave. As if there was something stupid or wrong in it and his handsome eyes, when they turned full on Phillip, blazed resentfully.

Button and Hans had a lovely time talking about game chickens over their little table in the hall by the fire. To Button's delight Frederick stayed a long time. Too long. I was absolutely exhausted when they finally said "good evening." And Frederick's precise and mirthless laughter stung my ears long after the carriage rolled out of the driveway.

Thirty-six

General Lee left Pocotaligo for Virginia on March 2nd at the request of President Davis, to take over the command of the entire Confederate Army. Lee had drawn up long-range plans for Stephen to continue the guerrilla tactics that were driving General Sherman and Commodore Du Pont at each other's throats, causing them to delay advancing thus giving the Confederates time to strengthen their defense.

I was in the cotton field watching the hands drop cotton seeds into holes when Phillip brought the news that the first group of dogooders had arrived at Hilton Head on the steamer *Atlantic* from New York. He and two of our fishermen had been in the town selling a wagon load of fresh-caught shadfish. There were 64 of the newcomers. He'd counted as they disembarked.

Frederick Pierce had noticed him and forced him to guide two of them to the Widow Stoney's house. One was a thin-haired preacher, the Reverend Thomas Howard of Boston, who talked constantly to our fishermen about the dignity of man and how he was going to teach every black in the islands to read and write; the other, a former New York City policeman, had been sent to superintend cotton farming on the island.

"I thought some Pennsylvania officers were living at Fairfield," I said.

"They were glad to see the policeman. Negroes stole all their boots and watches recently. I said I bet it was some of their own soldiers. They didn't like that. Oh—we stopped on the way home and picked some blackberries. Have you brought in any clotted cream today?"

The berries were sweet and juicy. Phillip made an effort to be cheerful. After we finished he said he'd select some books for me to read to pass the long evenings if I'd teach him to play the piano.

His voice was strangely subdued. "It will be a favor to me."

I choked up. I wondered what had brought this mood on. "All right," I managed a smile, "If you'll choose Beau's favorite books for me."

"No. You must read things that mean something to you. Not romances. You're too romantic as it is. I know: *Lady Montague's Journal!* It's fact and you'll be able to identify with her. For amusement—let's see— Samuel Pepy's *Diary!* What fun you're going to have. Now sit down and start me on the road to fame. I already know the scales."

"My music was in one of the trunks the Yankees stole. I wonder if any of your mother's is in the piano stool?"

I'd never opened the padded silk stool before. I'd not thought of it. Music was there, neatly piled. On top of the music was an envelope addressed in a heavy scrawl to Beau.

"That's Papa's handwriting! Listen:

> If the will you long to see
> Play Mozart's Minuet in G

There must be a trick inside the piano strings. Hurry —Play——"

That was an easy number. I knew it by heart. I played fast then I played slow while Phillip lifted the lid and watched the keys and the strings.

Nothing happened. Nothing was in there. I closed my eyes, exhausted and disappointed. Phillip's forced lightheartedness was breaking me down. I felt ill. I had been with him, alone in the house with him, so much that I could sense his moods. I knew he was fighting with himself. To leave here? Or to stay? Which was the braver?

"That's typical of Papa." He lowered the piano lid, went over to the book shelves and fumbled among the books. Finally he found what he wanted. "Mary Wortley herself! I tell you what—let's you and I each begin keeping a diary. Ten years from now—when we are at peace again—we can read them out loud and laugh at ourselves."

"No more music lessons this afternoon?"

"No. I've a rendezvous over at Honey Horn. Read Mary's feelings for an hour then write down your inner feelings for an hour. I'm a stern schoolmaster."

I watched him as he made his way to the stables. Thinking himself unobserved he let his wide thin young shoulders droop dejectedly. He huddled his neck down into the shabby old workman's jacket he was wearing and pulled a black knit fisherman's cap down over his ears.

There was an unusual number of terns and gulls flying. They wailed and swooped and cried like broken hearts. When it was dark, flames from the direction of Honey Horn lit up the whole sky like a winter sunset.

The next morning I read over the first entry in my diary: There are always two women in me: one woman desperate and heartsick for Beau who feels she is drying up; another who is ready to leap into any plantation happening as in a play, hide her real feelings because they are despair and longing and helplessness, and present to the boys and the people, in the house and in the fields, smiling encouragement and the will to *do*.

But always I am dreaming of Beau, reliving my life with him. This keeps me sane, able to greet Frederick and his fellow officers who come for musical evenings and morning fishing, with interest and enthusiasm. My Beau-dream makes it possible; assures me that magic is still somewhere in the world for me. Were it not for this my rhythm would falter to a thin whine.

On certain days I have frantic energy and plan gigantic crops and harvests and dramatic escapes and victories. I have days of such utter despair that I can sit at the piano for hours and not a sound of music flows from within me into the keys. Those days I count jars in the pantry or sort feathers for pillows or spend long hours in the sick house or the gin house. But in the very act of doing these things I feel as if I had died and am living another woman's life.

Sometimes my imagination goes crazy. One afternoon I saw Beau suddenly, striding toward me through the greening marsh, his vitality bursting out of his shirt ruffle which was open with his throat showing; and his proud eager look and his surprised smile as he discovered me. Another time I watched Beau walking naked along the beach. His powerful buttocks, his white, white skin, his wide manly shoulders set me shivering. I saw us sitting together, our toes in the salt water—then all of us lying in the shallow waves, our bare bodies touching everywhere.

The thought of leaving the plantation discomposes me. It is as if I am under a spell. I dread Frederick's visits. He might upset me and cause me to say something dangerous like where the cave is in which Stephen has a cache of guns and ammunition, or that Phillip burnt the Stuart house down, or when the Confederates plan to steal across Skull Creek and attack the new fort near Ferry Point. If Frederick ever suspected me of collusion he would not hesitate to send me away to prison as a spy. For all his courting and concern, I have better sense than to underrate his restive eyes and his ruthless nature. And then here at Cotton Hall I am where Beau will come for me some day.

And whenever Stephen brings a letter from Beau —as I open it I think—does anyone in the world know the meaning of ecstasy but me?

Thirty-seven

I began writing important happenings in my diary as well as my thoughts and feelings to share with Beau. Surely it would be soon. It had to be. I couldn't live much longer without him.

"On April 11th the Yankees easily took Tybee Island and, to quote Commodore Du Pont, 'corked up Savannah like a bottle.' The next night the whippoorwills started singing all night in the trees near the house and reechoing from the distant woods until you wanted to wring every neck of them. Quinine is $15 an ounce at public outcry. Half the soldiers at the town they call Port Royal are cramped up with dysentery and river cholera. Our cotton is coming up, lush and green."

In May something happened to which I paid scant attention, being taken up with worry over what to do with all that cotton stored in our warehouse. I would have scoffed if anyone had attempted to tell me that Robert Smalls' theft of the river and island steamer, the *Planter*, would mean life or death to me someday. Smalls was Pharaoh's Beaufort crony. He worked in Charleston as a pilot for the owner of the *Planter*.

On May 13th he slipped his wife and children on board, put the captain's cap on his head, pulled his coat collar up around in his ears, imitated Captain Relyea's voice, easily cleared Charleston harbor and delivered the fast little craft to the fleet at Hilton Head as a war offering. In return he was given a fancy new blue cap and uniform and made a pilot in the United States Navy!

The huge wharves at Coggins Point were finished, a customs house erected and the port opened to foreign trade. Supply ships from the North arrived every day and returned full of cotton and confiscated harps, furniture, paintings, silver, carpets, children's toys, private libraries and fine carriages along with the cotton.

A dreadful man named Nobles had been given a contract by the United States government to confiscate and sell cotton and property and anything else that took his eye on a straight 5 percent commission.

I think our cotton was the first he stole. I had been fishing with Button in the tight little canoe one of our carpenters had made from a cypress log. We meandered along the creek enjoying the life of it. Writhing water snakes hung from the trees on the bank like colored streamers; glistening gold-hearted lilies, stitched over by thousands of dragonflies, starred the black water; purple gallinules darted and flitted among the reeds; ibis and egrets flapped and stalked.

Around eleven o'clock I noticed Button drooping. The sun had tired him. I paddled back fast and could have screamed when I saw a group of flat-boats tied up at our dock.

Union soldiers were straining and pushing and grunting and gasping as they lifted and rolled heavy cotton bales down the bluff. Negroes lined the avenue, rolling their eyes, giggling and squealing at the unbelievably beautiful sight of white men toting cotton.

Liney helped me from the canoe. "Miss Angel, this a terrible thing; but worse—Mr. Cotton Agent Nobles in the house fixing to move out Miss Julia's piano."

"He dare not."

"Heap of them in there. I beg and plead hard, same like Israel beg and plead about the cotton. They threaten to knock me in the head. Maum Hannah set herself pontop the piano but one of the men's push her on the floor and hurt her bad. Maybe dead, she."

I pulled up my skirt, not caring who saw my long swift legs, and rushed up the avenue and into the big hall. Maum Hannah was lying on the floor sobbing. Maybelle was crouched beside her, wailing.

There must have been twenty soldiers bunched in a knot in the middle of the room. One of them had his foot up on a motley linen sofa and, as I entered, spat a big glob of tobacco juice on the carpet.

"The old woman's bluffing. I didn't hit her hardly atall," he was explaining to a tall, warty-nosed man in a cheap black slouch hat and a black claw-hammer-tailed coat.

I knelt down by Maum Hannah and put my hand on her pulse.

"Come closeter," she whispered.

I laid my head on her chest. Her heart was steady as a clock.

"Git Masai. I is fooling but that there man with the ugly nose ain't no more to fool with than a moccasin. He aim to empty this house for sho."

"Run, Maybelle. I'll stay here." I rose and glared at the civilian. "I think her ribs are broken and she's bleeding inside. By what authority, sir, are you in my house?"

I didn't scare him. He came over and punched Maum Hannah with his toe. "I think, Madame, you are quite aware of my position as cotton agent. Major Pierce knows we are here."

"Does he know you are trying to steal my piano?"

"Well now—as to that—I'll have to enquire. Did he know, Corporal Clyde?"

Corporal Clyde was the one who had spat on the best rug. He reddened, swallowed the tobacco and began carrying on as if he were choking.

Led by Maybelle, Masai entered the hall during the commotion. I guided him over to the piano.

"If anybody touches this piano, Masai, break his back," I said loudly.

Maum Hannah let out a piteous screech. "They done kilt me, Masai. Revenge me with the jawbone of a ass; break them in half. Ooo-h-h—Jesus——"

Mr. Nobles looked level at me and he looked down at Maum Hannah and he looked up at the eight-foot giant advancing toward him, his enormous fists raised almost to the ceiling and his soundless mouth opened

in a silent war cry. Mr. Nobles' claw-hammer tails
flew out straight behind. He was first through the front
door followed by all the soliders except one fat,
pudgy little man. Masai caught him by the shoulders
and snapped him back and forth so hard his head almost fell off.

"T'row him offen the piazza," Maum Hannah was
sitting up laughing. "T'row him far as you can."

He hit the oyster shells with a clomp. I went onto
the piazza and stood beside Masai. He put his hand
gently, protectively, on my shoulder. We stood there
together—I and the giant. If only he could have
seen the men, led by Nobles, haring down the bluff,
two of them dragging the injured soldier like a sack
of potatoes.

Liney and Button were under an orange tree,
watching curiously. One of the soldiers ran back
and threw a lit pine torch toward the warehouse.
But Liney and the people quickly stamped the
fire out.

All night, drum beats, fiddle scrapes and the thump
thump of dancing feet accompanied the celebration
in the praise house. This had been the finest day of
the people's lives. No sore backs tonight from toting
all that heavy cotton. White backs were sore tonight.
Their backs were limber and fresh as foxes.

The fact that the entire 1861 cotton crop had been
stolen didn't specify. It always went away on flat-
boats the same as it did this afternoon. No money
ever crossed their palms. All was as it had been for
the past hundred years. Nothing had changed for
them. Not yet anyway. Only for the Berriens.

Phillip blamed me. If I'd permitted him to burn
our warehouses this couldn't have happened.

"Stephen advised me to carry on here as always."

"Bubba told you to burn the cotton rather than let
it fall into the hands of the Yankees. You're the boss-
iest woman I ever heard of."

We both said things we shouldn't. He left the house
before sunup. All day I fretted and waited and

watched for him but he never returned. I sent Liney, riding a mule, into the town to look for him the day after.

Frederick rode back with Liney. He was in a very superior humor. Didn't I recall his explaining quite clearly about the cotton agents? Nobles was only doing the job he had been sent down here to perform by the United States government. The piano? Pooh —Nobles said the soldiers had come in the house to get out of the heat. Unwise of them, of course. But what can you expect of hirelings?

"That's no longer important to me. Phillip is."

"I saw him twice yesterday," Frederick said. He was sitting beside me on the joggling-board puffing contentedly on a meerschaum pipe. "He was standing on the wharf where a dinghy was moored, waiting to take some English sailors back aboard a ship sailing for Liverpool loaded with cotton. Probably yours."

"Did you speak to him—he was dreadfully put out with me about——"

"What?"

"Not burning the cotton rather than losing it to—to—you all."

Frederick's soft, moist red lips curved up at the corners like Cupid's. "He's too hot-headed. Bound to get in trouble. It's just as well——"

"What is just as well?" He was teasing me. I was wriggling and squirming, mouse-like; he purring, playing. "When else did you see him?" I asked desperately.

That was what he had been waiting for. His claws tightened. "He was *in* the dinghy, headed for the ship. I suppose he signed on as a crew or cabin boy. Now, don't look like that. Actually, you owe me a debt of gratitude. I had made up my mind it was my duty to turn him in for destroying government property. We know he burnt the Stuart place. He would have been sent to a prison camp up north. You forget how old he is. And *he's* probably in love with you, too."

I burst into tears, which was the worst thing in the

world I could have done. My tears acted as a fuse to set Frederick on fire. He grabbed me, roughly, powerfully, sinuously and began saying the most outrageous things.

"Your luminous eyes drenched with tears are magnificent—thrilling. Knowing you are suffering so beautifully makes me want to tear you apart like a rose. When this war is over we can shut ourselves up in our grand houses and never open the doors to anybody—not anybody——"

It felt as if a thousand cold serpents were writhing around my body. I hit him with my fists. That seemed to frenzy him more.

"You are adorable—gorgeous——"

Finally I stopped struggling and his hug relaxed. As he reached for a handkerchief I tore myself away and dashed into the house slamming the doors. Maybelle was sewing by the window in my boudoir. She put her healing arms around me and made me lie down on the sofa.

"Hush, hush, sweet Missy. It all right now. Listen, there go his horse-hoofs clompering off."

"Look out of the window. Be sure it is Major Pierce."

She put her head far out. "Him it. And singing pontop him voice. Happy him. What make this thing?"

As I described his behavior it seemed unreal, unbelievable. He had always been so formal, so correct in his movements, so strict about doing the proper thing.

Maybelle said, sadly, "I been watch him a long time. That a bad man. Keep far off from him. You remember the poor little baby I borned all broke up in she face? Pharaoh been catch me one night outside the hen house and do that to me. The more I fought and begged the higher Pharaoh laughed and the more he done. I been scared of mens ever since."

Thirty-eight

Hans came with a basket and a formal note on thick white paper the following morning. Frederick's letter expressed regret over a breach of etiquette, but, stated he, fascination must be named the culprit. To redeem himself in my favor he was diligently working on Phillip's disappearance. He would not swerve until the mystery was unravelled.

"Look in the basket," Button cried. "I think it's candy!"

We hadn't had anything sweet except cane syrup lately, our sugar barrels having vanished with Nobles' men.

"Put it down. Hans will take it straight back where it came from."

"Oh, Angelica—it's bonbons and chocolates!"

To see Button lively and wanting something again dwindled my pride if not my anger and curiosity.

"All right, but don't offer me any. What's in the other package?"

It was six pairs of elegant white French glacé kid gloves. All of mine had gone with the trunks. The gloves felt smooth and rich to my fingers. "Here, Maybelle, you can have these." I handed the package to her and hurried out onto the piazza, refusing to be tempted.

The white dolphin was leaping and playing among a school of dark ones. My heart lifted. The dolphin's coming today was a sign that this lonely exile would soon be over.

On June 7th the axe fell. Congress passed the necessary legislation whereby all occupied land was placed under direct tax. If the tax was not paid all lands and property thereto were forfeit to the United States government.

President Lincoln himself stipulated that the forfeiture was only to last the Secession owner's natural lifetime, to return to his heirs. The catch was, that though a proper notice was published in the *Beaufort Gazette*, any Secession owner who crossed the enemy line to pay would, of course, be captured.

Stephen and the curly-haired Kirk brothers brought me a copy of the *Beaufort Gazette* in which this notice appeared.

"I hate losing my Parris Island place most of all," Stephen said bitterly.

"You speak as though we've lost the war," I said, surprised at him who was usually so consumed with plans for getting at the enemy and doing him in.

"Not at all. I stepped in a mudhole yesterday and didn't change my shoes. I think I'm catching a summer cold. Very depressing—a summer cold."

"Can Angelica pay Beau's taxes?" Rollins Kirk wondered.

"She can try. Presumably she's still a property owner, Cousin Hazzard's will not having been found; and then, the Berrien property *may* belong to a Lincolnite. They'll take her money and put her in jail later. Women have all the rights in our society.

"For the present, thank the Lord, she can continue as our rendezvous. If the will *is* found, and Pierce *has* inherited from Elsa, we will take our good Angel and Button away at once whether she chooses or not."

They teased me about being Penelope. Luckily I knew that story.

"Ulysses *did* return," I laughed, "and they lived happily ever after."

Though the sheer loneliness of my days was sometimes crushing, most days were over-full of activity and, if not happy, I *was* content in my waiting. I was Beau's wife. I lived in his house.

Did I know Phillip's whereabouts I'd be perfectly content.

Frederick's next letter was brought to me weeks later, in the empty warehouse where I was fussing with two women about scattering precious cotton seeds in the middle of the floor. Israel was awkwardly trying to oil the steam gin.

"Go and help Israel, Maybelle."

"No, Miss Angel, I helping Masai find he foot."

Liney insisted on Masai and Maybelle accompanying me whenever I went among the people now. He said that Pharaoh slipped up and down the Street at odd times creating bad feelings and wants inside them; always when he was sure Liney was away in the fields or in the woods.

Hans and Button found us there in the warehouse. I read the one sentence of the letter and sent them to tell a stable boy to bring up Miss Suzy immediately.

"Keep Israel company, Maybelle. I must make haste to the town. I can manage my hair and my riding dress without you."

"Stay, gal," Israel's intelligent eyes twinkled. "I likes your company."

When Israel had been near death, Maybelle had handled him tenderly as if he were a baby. But now —a well man——? She swallowed hard and hung her head.

"Oh foot, Maybelle, can't you see he needs you?" I said, laughing.

She looked up at him. Her large, expressive brown-velvet eyes had tears in them but her lips widened in a tremulous smile. "Might's well," she shrugged indifferently, "t'wont hurt nothing."

"If you'll hold the oil, I can manage the rag easier," he said softly, as if to a fluttery bird.

"It makes no never-mind," she moved close to him. I could almost hear her heart thumping.

I turned away so neither he nor she could detect the matchmaking gleam in my eyes. I ran so fast to the house Masai had to take long steps to keep his hand safely on my shoulder.

Fortunately my best summer riding habit was still folded in tissue paper in the bottom wardrobe drawer. It was a blue linen, cut in high style. The trailed skirt was exaggeratedly long to loop gracefully over my wrist. The little cropped jacket was fashioned tight over my bosom with smoked pearl buttons. I hadn't dressed up lately, it having been so hot, and I had never been down to the town. As a matter of fact I hadn't left the plantation since November 8th, 1861, and here it was July 15th, 1862!

Deciding it was best to pretend that the incident on the joggling-board had never occurred, I pinned a sassy little white straw boater with black ribbon streamers at a tilt on my head and whirled around in front of the mirror admiring my blue-heron silhouette.

In heat, Miss Suzy was in a cantankerous humor. Had I known I would have taken one of the fat walking horses. Hans had a great deal of trouble controlling the big-footed plough horse he was riding. We ghosted and skittered the whole way, through weevily, weed-filled cotton fields, on the white sand and crushed oyster shell road that glistened blindingly.

"The Major's letter says he has news of Button's brother. Button has missed him."

"Button is a family person, like I am, mam."

"You've been kind, helping with Button's game chickens. I appreciate it. Come to see him often."

"I will, mam. I had chickens like that back home." Hans' horse gave a mean buck. "Ride on ahead, mam. I'll run this cuss over that cotton field and take some of the orneryness out of him. I'll catch you by the time you hit town."

I leant forward. What fun to let the mare all out! I'd missed the fox chases—the glorious gallopings —the wind in my face.

Soon though, as if by magic, I was forced to slow down in a bewilderment of tents; acres and acres of tents, covering the whole Smith place. When they finally gave out I noticed, to the west, four long narrow buildings, facing each other, with smaller houses in the between area. Blacks were lounging and playing and sleeping on the ground; women, children, men, scantily clad, some almost naked.

Beyond was the town I had glimpsed shadowly across the trees from my cupola. Hans was nowhere in sight but Frederick wouldn't be hard to find, I knowing the exact location of the Pope house.

I'd always been fascinated with tales of the '49 gold rush; the frontier towns that had mushroomed in weeks. Suddenly I was in one teeming with 50,000 people foreign to the island.

Yankee tradesmen, their trousers tucked in high boots, scrawny necks circled by string ties, narrow heads covered with slouch hats, were pushing and hailing soldiers and sailors and cotton agents. Red-cheeked sailors in blue bell-bottomed trousers, their caps stuffed high with snuff and chewing tobacco, stood in queues in front of an open, thatch-roofed tattoo artist's stand. Soldiers swaggered in and out of English boot shops, Beard's photograph parlor, dry goods emporiums, bars, drug stores, food markets, bakeries and two hotels: the Palmetto House and the Sea Island Hotel. Plain-bonneted female missionaries in long black skirts trailed worriedly along. They pulled their skirts aside as tipsy soldiers bumped into them; they pulled them even farther aside when they noticed me on my shining sorrel. Negro hucksters sang, "Eh, swimp—fresh swimp—huckleberry!"

This noisy bustling street was called Robbers Row on the east side and Sutlers Row on the west; both signs pointing the same way.

But where was the Pope house? I hesitated accosting any of the sharp-eyed tobacco chewing tradesmen and soldiers who were looking at me as if I had just come from the moon or from one of those houses people whisper about.

Though I didn't want to see the bristling fort where Eddie had died, I knew it was in front of the Pope house. I guided my uneasy mare shoreward through a maze of sprawling warehouses and big caliber artillery pieces. A switchback engine, whistling merrily, chooed by. Straining mule teams hauled stacks of ordnance from the wharves. Oh those wharves! I never saw such vast expanses in my life. And the

noise! Men were thumping creosoted logs in place
for an enormous boat basin. Sawmills whined. Bosses
shouted. Whistles shrilled. Wheels turned.

Tugs were busy carrying supplies from the wharves
to the merchant vessels, and barnacle and salt-en-
crusted old ships used for blockading, and ships of
the line, riding at anchor offshore. Overhead gulls
laughed and shrieked derisively at the rackety hul-
labaloo on the beach where a year ago soft-voiced
folks and singing servitors had gathered in the winter
for oyster roasts and in the summer for sail-boat races
and devil-fishing expeditions.

I reined Miss Suzy left along low barracks with officers rocking on the verandahs and fresh painted
houses with lines of washing and cook fires in the
back yards.

These residences ended near a dusty square on
which were Adam's Express Office, the United States
Post Office, and on the corner, facing the water, a
rambling four-story hotel—the Port Royal House. A
sign in front advertised it as "rivalling the hostelries
of Newport, serving fine meals and French wines and
Cuban seegars." The porch was filled with fanning
ladies wearing sequins in their yellow hair laughing
with droop-mustached civilians in black stovepipe
hats. I recognized the evil Nobles among them.

But where could the familiar Pope residence have
hidden itself? Disgusted at being stared at more than
staring, whistled at and beckoned to, I rode behind
the quartermaster's depot and back around the officers' quarters. Ah—here it was, in front of an extensive quadrangle of stables!

The big old house was surrounded by armed
guards and soldiers on horseback coming and going
like ants. Built on an arcaded tabby basement like
ours, the wide front steps climbed up to the second
story. Officers in gold sashes and wide gauntlets, despite the heat, ran up and down the steps, their silver Mexican spurs jingling gaily. I should have waited
for Hans. Someday my lack of patience was going to
be my Waterloo.

Frederick must have been watching from a front window. He appeared at the head of the steps, barked an order to one of the soldiers to take my mount, another to guide me to his office, turned sharply on his heel and marched inside.

How short the steps had seemed on that New Year's Day at the oyster roast when Beau had dared me to race him to the top; how steep and wearisome today.

Everything had been removed from the pretty parlor Mrs. Pope had been so proud of. Soldiers were rustling papers at plank tables and rosewood desks. A painting of two Pope deer hounds still hung over the mantlepiece but someone had cut off one of the tails, leaving an ugly hole in the canvas.

Frederick's office was in what had been old Squire Pope's gun room. The racks and cases of antique and modern rifles and shotguns and pistols Pope had inherited and purchased all over Europe were the only things in the house that appeared to have been left alone.

Frederick rose from behind a large plain desk neatly stacked with papers. He clicked his heels, bowed stiffly from the waist, saluted the officer who had showed us in, and motioned him to leave.

He didn't say anything for a few minutes. The strange fixity I'd noticed the first time I saw him was in his eyes.

I spoke first. "I can't wait to hear about Phillip."

He ran his tongue over his lips. "Where have you been? My orderly reported in an hour ago, saying you had managed to lose him in a cotton field."

"It wasn't Hans' fault. Nor mine. Miss Suzy was hard to handle. She ran too fast. Suddenly I lost my way among the tents."

"And then—suddenly, you decided to take a tour of the town and inspect the artillery and the ordnance and the position of the ships?"

"The town was such a marvel to my eyes."

"And you will remember every detail to tell your night visitors? Your Rebel friends——"

Prickles of fear crept hand over hand up my spine

from my stomach and tightened the back of my neck. Please, voice-box, I begged, don't crack and tremble. Please stay calm sounding. That's the only way to handle Frederick.

"You haven't been at Cotton Hall lately," I said aloofly, pretending to overlook his insinuations.

Frederick stretched out his smooth carefully tended hands. "A recent fiasco on James Island, six miles from Charleston, has occupied me entirely."

"Oh? Tell me about it."

Keeping his tone low he grew talkative and effusive. Robert Smalls and Pharaoh had guided the expedition up the Stono River. He and General Stevens, Colonel Benham, and Colonel Leasure were in command of various units. They had been overconfident of surprising the Confederates.

The Charleston Battalion came whooping out of the woods at them as they waded ashore and scrambled up the steep bluff fixing their bayonets. Oh well —no more of that except I might be interested that of 685 casualties, 529 had come from his own beloved Highlanders. The defeat had broken General Stevens' heart. His brigade left Beaufort yesterday and was here on Hilton Head ready to embark aboard the *Vanderbilt* tomorrow for Newport News. General Saxton, who was replacing Stevens, would not take the loving interest in the treasures of Beaufort as had Stevens.

"You are going with him?"

"I am taking Colonel Benham, under arrest, to Washington. He behaved badly at James Island. But before I leave I must discover who could have been at a vantage point to notice the departure of the ships from Port Royal Sound? You've known all along I am in Army Intelligence. Don't pretend innocence."

He was baiting a trap. A rock was in my chest. Woody Barnwell, in his grey uniform, had stood with me in the cupola on June 2. With his powerful telescope he had caught the movement of the ships. It had been easy, from the number of them, to guess their destination. His horse had been waiting on the other side of Skull Creek.

"Was it you, Angelica?" The deep-set, tiger-eyes glittered into mine.

I didn't move a muscle. "No. It was not I."

"You swear?"

"I do."

"On Beau's life?"

Well, I hadn't actually carried the information. "Yes."

"So much for that. I forgive you. Now for the good news: Phillip is safe in Liverpool. The *Athena* arrived from England, empty, this morning to load up with cotton. Phillip, having learned its destination, cleverly sent me a message by the captain to give to you. He is all right and will remain in England."

"Doing what?"

"Working in the Cotton Exchange. He knows cotton, doesn't he?" Frederick laughed, but his laugh didn't sound nice.

"I'm glad," I said, finding a handkerchief and dabbing at the perspiration on my upper lip.

Then Frederick pushed back his chair and leant over and opened a low drawer of the desk. He took out a long envelope. He handed it to me and went on talking about how he'd always thought Phillip the brightest of the brothers while I unfolded an already opened telegram addressed to Captain Stephen Elliott, Gardens Corner, S.C.

I regret to inform you that Major Baynard Berrien is . . .

My eyes refused to see the next line. I looked at the windows. A sea breeze was playing with the scrim curtains.

"The Army of the Potomac has been pounding away at Richmond for seven beastly days." Frederick's words sounded far away as if they were floating like stars out there; entirely cut off from my universe.

In Chickahominy swamp . . . I regret to inform you. I regret to . . . I . . .

Nausea was strong in me. The floor rushed up to meet my face.

When I opened my eyes Frederick was bending over me. He had stopped talking. He pulled me back in the chair and straightened my hat.

"I didn't think you'd take it like that. Didn't you hear what I was saying when I handed you the telegram? Beau is alive. He's been taken prisoner." He looked at me with amused distaste. "I can't stand that hat on you."

The clammy chill on my forehead began to warm. I fought hard to get hold of myself. It had been a joke. Beau wasn't dead at all. I laughed shakily and said how silly of me. I had never fainted before. Aunt Dell used to say when she heard impossible news she either fainted or fanned frantically until someone else accepted it.

Frederick handed me a china cup of water. I managed a forlorn little smile as I drank a few sips. "No prison can hold Beau."

Frederick went back behind his desk and sat down. He leaned forward. His hands were pressed so flat and hard on the top that they looked almost fat. "Unlike the problem of Phillip there is nothing I can do about Beau. So don't ask any more favors. But should it become known to the War Department that his wife was or is a spy in United States territory it will go hard with him. He may even face a firing squad. Do you understand?"

"Oh—you are not human—" I cried, suddenly anguished beyond caring what I said. "You sit there and torture me. You don't even have human eyes. You are a beast. I hate every Yankee on this earth. Especially you. There is nothing I wouldn't do to——"

Frederick was beside me, pressing his hand which had seemed soft a minute ago, like a steel clamp over my mouth.

I must have shouted. He pointed with his other hand to the door. I could hear what was going on in the next room. Had they heard me? Evidently not, for no one came to investigate. He kept his hand there a long time looking strangely down at me as though considering which role he would play next.

"Do you feel strong enough to walk up into the signal tower and see the activity that goes on there?" He smiled, cheerfully.

I closed my eyes, worn out. The quick changes in his mood and tone of voice, in addition to the shock of hearing that Beau was a prisoner, were making me break down. On top of it, though smiling, Frederick exuded a controlled restlessness that made me ill. I knew I must do anything he suggested. He would be gone tomorrow.

"I'm quite all right now."

Watch, Miss Angel, how you step on the stair—
Your foots might slip——

Why did I think of that silly song now? Frederick was curtly answering a young officer's question. Behind me two officers whispered together. I gave no indication, but I heard them clearly.

"Pretty Pierce has caught him a good looker this time."

"How tall she is."

"I never saw such blue eyes."

In the signal tower a soldier was wigwagging a message to a ship out in the sound. The tall-masted ships looked like a forest of dead trees on the silk-stretched water. I could see, from one of the tallest, a wigwagging answering.

"We won't waste time here. I merely wanted to point out something I think you missed on your peregrination earlier." Looking left I saw our cupola lifting above the pine trees; toward Port Royal Sound were the commissary buildings and officers' quarters and on the right was the long dock.

"I saw those this morning."

"Now look oceanward."

Fort Walker—I mean Fort Welles—was in the center distance.

Frederick took me by the shoulders and turned me farther right. "You missed that huge quadrangle out on the Point where the waves are breaking so high, didn't you?"

I nodded.

His eyes narrowed into two shining slits—"That's a combination hospital and prison. The Gulf Stream breeze sweeps through the hospital with cooling, cleansing force. It's always full. The prison, when it is completed, say in a few weeks, will be always full too—of captured Confederates."

"They would be the fortunate ones."

He laughed. "What a joke if dear Beau lands here! Many will die from dysentery on the cornbread and pickle diet that is ordered for them. Are you ready for lunch now?"

Thirty-nine

We made our way across crowded Union Square. Frederick stopped in the newspaper shop on the corner and introduced me to Mr. Sears, formerly of the *New York Times* newspaper, now publishing his own paper, the *New South*, every Saturday.

"How can he make any money here?" I asked dully.

"He's planning to make it in real estate, not paper," Frederick answered, "which brings me to a most confidential matter. Best discussed as we make our way over to the Port Royal Restaurant, where eavesdroppers are always gathered."

In his wordy way, his eyes going right and left to be sure no one passed too near us, he said, "I am being sent on a vital mission into the border states. I have no idea how long I'll be away. In the meantime the taxes must be paid on Cotton Hall and the Beaufort house. It is of the essence, the plans of the War Department being what they are. I gave Livia the exact amount for the Beaufort house and my signed statement of ownership. It's wisest for you to pay the Cotton Hall tax. Do you have any United States money?"

"Yes."

"Good. I have arranged for a young captain, in whom I have complete confidence, to escort you up to Beaufort when the due date is announced. You will not fail?"

Me fail to secure Beau's beloved Cotton Hall? I was about to make a scornful reply but caught myself. "I want to do it," I said earnestly.

"Another thing: General Hunter, who is different from slothful Sherman, doesn't look kindly on your remaining, even under guard, on the island. I don't mean to permit you to choose your destination hence either. Don't argue with him if he comes to see you as soon as I sail. He's an ass."

"What do you mean 'under guard'?"

"Since the James Island affair the entire coastline along the sound is to be patrolled. You'll be the safer with soldiers on Cotton Hall."

We had reached the restaurant. It was a low raw building with a palmetto thatch roof. Thinking how mortified Aunt Dell would be if she could see me in this situation, I said shakily, "I am really ill, Frederick. You must believe me."

Evidently he did for he sent a soldier on the double to the stables to have Miss Suzy brought up.

"You must be very careful when you go to Beaufort to pay the tax to say nothing about the will."

"Of course not," I murmured, settling myself as comfortably as possible in the side saddle, with Frederick continuing to hold onto my right hand.

"And no more meetings with Rebels. Your every move will be watched."

"Certainly not." I was dying to strike him with my little whip and dash away from this nightmare.

He kissed my hand, looking up into my face. "What's happened now? You are pale as death again."

"I told you I was ill," I gasped, withdrawing my freezing fingers.

"Remember to miss me a little," he called.

Using the last drop of inner restraint I possessed, I lifted my head high and heeled Miss Suzy into a slow trot toward the endless acres of enemy tents.

Forty

We were sitting on a pile of pinestraw in the little temple in the woods. It needed painting. Pine pollen had badly stained the columns, making it almost invisible among the straight dark trunks.

A flock of wild turkeys were gobbling softly at each other a ways off and a family of partridges were running around in the underbrush going tick-tick-tick-tick-oil-oil-oil.

Stephen sighed, "From the sound of things you could almost imagine nothing had changed here."

"How in the world did Wade Hampton get so mixed up about Beau?"

Stephen laughed, "That Cudjo Manigo saw Beau's riderless horse in Chickahominy swamp and went running to headquarters yelling 'Loose horse; dead master!'"

"I wonder why Frederick told me he was a prisoner?"

"He was—for twenty-four hours. Lanneau Dubois was one of the wounded lucky enough to be put on the train to Florence last week. I happened to be at the hospital in Charleston when he was brought in."

"You hop around like a cricket, don't you?"

"I'm ordered to take charge at Fort Sumter in the spring. I'll be too still then."

"Spring is a long time off, thank goodness. Do you suppose Beau will ever get leave to come home?"

"The situation in Virginia is desperate at the moment. And you know how hotheaded he is. We keep writing him how well you are getting along. If he knew about your people going and that you're virtually a prisoner, nobody could prevent his deserting. Then he'd have to be shot. Have you written the letter I told you—all about the cotton and the flower garden and the birds?"

"Here it is. I did my best, but oh, Stephen, it's so hard."

"Tell me about Hunter—I understand that even the Yankees think he's a fool."

I described General Hunter in his cockaded hat, slouching in his saddle, followed by a soldier on foot, carrying a United States flag, and another beating a drum and a dozen more soldiers, going up and down our Street announcing that Congress had passed a law freeing all slaves. General Hunter had personally issued an emancipation proclamation! Every able-bodied man must come to headquarters and join the army. They would be given a pair of beautiful red breeches and a gun as well as folding money. If they didn't come willingly, Union soldiers would drag them in.

"What about picking my cotton?" I asked him when he finally rode around to the front of the house and confronted me.

"That's Mr. Howard's province, not yours. He's in charge of all the cotton on the island."

Then he said his wife was not a horsewoman, though a fine pistol shot. Major Pierce had told him of my comfortable barouche and matched bays. I, now being forbidden to leave the plantation because of being under suspicion of spying, would have no more use of them. Nor of any of the other horses, nor the little buggy. And he needed a few milch cows. . . .

When Liney blew the horn the next morning not a single hand came out. On the roll call Sunday night, a few old ones like Hecuba and Pompey and of course Maybelle and Israel and Maum Hannah and Masai and, oddly, Anatole, were the only ones to answer.

"When did the guards come on duty?" Stephen brushed a circle of yellow butterflies away from his head.

"That same afternoon General Hunter was here. Their tents are pitched near Fish Haul Creek mouth. They are anywhere and everywhere, day and night. Button is enjoying their company. He brings out his gamecocks and they make bets. They're homesick and bored." A butterfly lit on my knee, its wings palpitating delicately.

Stephen sighed, "The whole war gets so damnably boring at times. I wonder how Percival Drayton has survived sitting in his cabin out there aboard the *Pocohontas* for almost a year. I'd go mad, shut up like that, staring at my home shore, remembering my cool gracious house. They say he never puts his foot beyond headquarters. He didn't even attend his mother's funeral."

"He would have been taken prisoner."

"I doubt it. Family loyalty makes people blind at such times."

"Not Percival."

"He's a black sheep. His blue uniform killed his mother. Her dying words were 'Tom shot at Percy. Percy shot at Tom.' Aunt Tee was there. She'd seen Aunt Annie in North Carolina. She said Aunt Annie had withered and grown bitter."

"I can't imagine her that way."

"Nor could she imagine us as we are this very minute," Stephen laughed.

"Will you mail a letter to Aunt Beck in Charleston from me?"

"Ephraim Baynard's going there soon. He'll take it to her. Say, did Liney join Hunter's South Carolina Volunteers?"

"No. He says only President Lincoln can set him free 'not no t'iefing, fancy-hat General.' He looks out over the unworked cotton fields and seems depressed and confused."

"So long as he remains no harm can come to you."

"I know."

"I feel sorry for little Button. I wish he'd gone to North Carolina with my boys."

"I'd be lost without him. I'm teaching him to play the piano. He's inherited his mother's talent. We read a lot and play games and run races. He seems happy."

"Now that Cotton Hall is so strictly guarded and that new Union encampment, Fort Mitchel, hampers our Skull Creek assaults, I've moved our rendezvous to Dolphin's Head, near Myrtle Bank. The Yankee officers staying in the house rarely go near the water; not even to watch the sharks or the devil-fish. When you get back to the house send Button over on his pony. I'll show the cave to him. He shall be our messenger boy. The soldiers will never suspect him. You must be above reproach from now on."

I wondered what Charlotte would think if she could see her elegant handsome husband with an unkempt black beard covering his face, a battered wool hat on his uncombed hair, thick dusty brogans, the kind we issued to the field hands, baggy, patched linsey-woolsey trousers, his hands calloused and cracked, and one of his side teeth missing. No wonder the soldiers at the gate hadn't questioned him.

And what would Beau think of me in a faded green and red calico sacque and skirt, my hair in a plait down my back, the hideous goblin hat tied under my chin? Ah, but this was the way he'd seen me the first time!

"I hope you get your wish and are transferred to Virginia soon, so Beau can come home," I whispered, as Stephen climbed in an oxcart loaded with manure.

He squeezed my hand. "You miss Beau as much as I do Charlotte, don't you?"

The clumsy, wooden-wheeled cart rumbled slowly down the sandy road. I closed my eyes and begged the Lord to send Beau quickly.

I am on fire with wanting him.

Forty-one

The only planter besides me in the courthouse was a Mr. Pritchard, who cautiously explained that he lived on Hunting Island near Bay Point and, like me, had been left behind when the Confederates retreated. We stood in line along with a lot of colored people.

Mr. Pritchard lifted his wide panama, bowed and insisted "Ladies first!" when we reached the table at which sat a jolly-faced, fat soldier with bushy eyebrows and big teeth.

"Keep your proper place, lady." The fat soldier pointed a stubby pencil at me. "Don't push. Step up, sir."

He picked up a paper and began reading in a loud monotone.

"What in the hell are you reading?" Mr. Pritchard turned beet red to the tip of his thick nose.

"The Oath of Allegiance to the United States. Either you take it or your plantation will be confiscated and you will be declared a prisoner of war. Next."

"Even if I pay my tax?"

"You're either a Secessionist or you ain't."

Mr. Pritchard paid and took the oath in a mumbling voice. When he left he didn't look at me.

"Step up, lady. And don't give me any of your no-good paper money." I tightened myself against his rudeness. I told him my name and the location of Cotton Hall, clearly and quietly, refusing to be bothered by amazed mumbles and titters in the room.

He thumbed through a book, looked curiously at me, stated the amount I owed and leant back.

I untied my reticule and handed him a small sack of gold coins containing the sum he had named.

"Gold!" He poured the coins on the table top in

front of him. He touched them lovingly. "Where did you say Cotton Hall is?"

"Just give me a receipt," I said coldly.

I don't know what would have happened next if the captain who was accompanying me hadn't stepped up and held out his arm. He intended to make sure I had no complaints of rude treatment by him to write to Major Pierce. He, among others, had seen how quickly General Hunter had been relieved of his command and replaced by General Ormsby Mitchel after Major Pierce went to Washington. And, from his conversation on the island steamer en route, he was enjoying his assignment on the easy island of Hilton Head. Particularly the waterfowl and deer shooting and fishing. He loved to fish.

While the captain visited General Saxton in his Beaufort headquarters I walked down Bay Street. Soldiers and blacks stood in the gardens and rocked on the verandahs of the tall houses; a parade was going on. The band was big and brassy. The soldiers were wearing blue uniforms, the red-breeched ones having been disbanded and the recruits returned to the cotton fields when General Mitchel took over in August.

I lingered in the unclipped garden of the Berrien house, making up my mind whether or not to pay a visit to Livia. She made it up for me, having noticed me from the front parlor window. A thin little black boy in the best Berrien livery came running out to invite me in.

Why not? I could make a long interesting letter of this to Beau without telling him a word of the scene in the courthouse.

The little boy had left the front door open. I noticed several bright-tignoned heads peeping over the top railing of the stairs. The pretty tan and cafe-au-lait young faces under the tignons vanished into the darkness at the top of the stairs as I entered the hall.

Where had the statues gone? Not a single god or goddess remained on its proper pedestal.

"Announce Mrs. Berrien, Bray-boy," Livia shouted.

Four people were taking tea in the blue parlor: two whey-faced white ladies in black taffeta dresses, the mean-eyed old African who was Livia's father, in a frock coat that hung to his ankles and a pair of Beau's trousers that wrinkled down around his bare feet like an accordion, and Livia herself, serenely pouring tea from an exquisite gold and white French porcelain pot. She had gained another fifty pounds since the first fifty Frederick had described. Her glossy brown face looked like a bag pudding. The oiled knot on top of her head stood up like an exclamation mark. Her eyes were barely visible in the pouches that hung under them. But bright they were and sharp as ever. She was shaking with laughter.

"Come in, my lady, and meet these schoolteachers. Sit down, Daddy, and stop spilling cake on my good rug."

The lilies on the Aubusson carpet peeped shyly through his wide toes; cake icing made a halo around his flat heels.

The ladies held out lace-mittened fingers. They were frigidly polite.

"Will you have a cup of tea, my lady?"

I took the fragile cup Livia handed me and sat down on the edge of one of the little gilt chairs that had at last moved from its appointed place. One of the legs was about to drop off so I sat lightly, trying to make conversation with the two schoolteachers who, it appeared, were working with Miss Laura Towne on St. Helena Island at the Penn School. There were forty teachers in the Beaufort area now, they said, and two thousand pupils between the ages of eight and twelve. All black. It was a challenge. If they could only understand what the children were saying! It was a foreign language to them.

"But nobody has learned to read as fast as Mrs. Berrien here," they agreed.

I raised my eyebrows at Livia. She nodded. "That's always been my name," she said pleasantly.

The old African began to cackle. "I name Mr. Bones. I always did hanker after Mr. Bones in the minstrel show."

"Well, now, Mr. Bones, you be nice to these teachers while my lady and I go in the dining room and have a little conversation."

The teachers rose at once, as if they'd rather die than be left alone with Mr. Bones. Livia waddled to the front door with them. When she returned she told her father to get out, she'd had enough of him for one day.

I said there was a band out in the street. He scampered away, lively as a goat.

Settling herself in a blue damask *bergère*, the only chair in the room ample enough to hold her, Livia said, "Those teachers are a sight. But they showed me how to read, easy as pie. I humor them along in everything. Just before you came in one of them described a fly fan in Mr. Coffin's dining room. They think it was a whipping post and pulley for stretching and whipping his slaves while Mr. Coffin and his family ate their trifle and ambrosia."

"As if sweet old Mr. Coffin ever would have." I had to laugh, imagining the outraged account of Southern bestiality they had sent back to the Freedmen's Bureau in Boston.

"What's happened to the portraits and the harpsichord?"

"The day after General Stevens left, General Saxton came and had the portraits and all the books in the library and the harpsichord carried away. It wasn't my house then, of course, naturally. But I was curious. I asked questions. He said he was sending them to Washington to a Smith and son place."

"The Smithsonian museum?"

"It sounded like that, Smithsonian! I like the way that name sounds. I think I'll change mine to Mrs. Livia Smithsonian. Why should I want the name Berrien? You keep it."

I told her I thought she'd made a marvellous decision. She nodded wisely like a great soft Buddha.

"Where are those handsome red vases that stood on each side of the door leading into the dining room?"

"They were smashed the night Henricus died. That was before the soldiers came."

"Everything is awful—terrible. I hate this war."

Livia giggled an agreeing giggle, and said archly, "You like my house, my lady?"

Tolerance departed. I put down my mother-in-law's delicate cup.

"What house?"

Not responding to that, she said she wanted me to know that the reason she had been rude to me when I first came to Cotton Hall was because it had been her house for so long. She loved fine houses. Now she had one of her own there wasn't any reason for her to be rude to me any more. As a matter of fact she respected me. How could I stay over there on the island all by myself? She'd be scared to death.

I asked her to explain about her house. Where was it?

The whole town of Beaufort was to be sold at auction in February, 1863. General Saxton had allowed her to buy this house before the sale, since the taxes on it hadn't been paid. He knew she would take care of it.

"I thought Major Pierce gave you money to pay the taxes on this house and a proper testimony?"

"But it wasn't his house!"

Livia laughed so hard the various rounds of her face shook with laughing. "It's easier for you to move around than it is for me. See that brass box where the harpsichord used to be? It's full of music."

I knelt down on the floor and opened the box. Mozart's Minuet in G was on the top of the pile. Written in black India ink, in bold script, the will was between the two sheets. Beyond the legal preamble it was very short:

"To my wife, Elsa Czerny, because she hates it, I leave all my property on Hilton Head Island together with the dwelling house. But none of the carriages nor the piano.

"To my oldest son, Baynard, because I am his father, I leave the Beaufort house and all my various properties on the other sea islands and in Mississippi and along the River May, together with every painting and piece of silver and article of furniture and creature that walks on two or three or four legs that I have bought and paid for."

It was dated later in April than the one Beau had. It was the true and valid will.

"Get up, my lady. Don't look sad. Sit down close to me."

All that flesh had softened her inside as well as outside. Her expression showed genuine concern and sweetness.

"This will kill the Master," I murmured.

"I know it, my lady, but if I hadn't bought this house somebody else would have. I paid two hundred dollars for it. Money I've saved since I was a girl. Nobody but you and me knows about the will. Nobody has to know. Mr. Pierce's money's safe in the bag he handed me. He'll get it back."

"He'll get you too."

"Not hardly. Now as to Master—I wake up in the night sometimes and remember his sweet little white face and that silky red head pressed against my breast. He was the beautifullest baby you ever saw. And love me! Um! Um! Um!"

Her face was full of joy. I felt myself smiling. If only I had a little red-headed baby to nourish at my breast.

She poured herself some lukewarm tea.

"Forget what I just said, my lady. Favoring Master over my own child made for trouble. Pharaoh was always jealous of everything Master did and had. He's so tickled that this is our house now you'd think he was Jesus Christ. I'm glad he isn't here today. Nothing of Master's is safe around him any more, not you—not Button. I didn't nurse the other boys. I guess that's why I never cared much for them, though when I heard about Master Eddie I was sorry. I admired Miss Julia. She's the one made a lady out of me."

"I thought you were crazy about your last Mistress."

"For a while I thought she was the world's wonder, handling old Master like she did. But after Mr. Pierce came along she wasn't ever any good to anybody. Least of all herself. I lost respect for her."

"I've paid the taxes on Cotton Hall but it belongs to Major Pierce. How tragic for all of us," I said.

Livia crossed her fat little feet and leant forward.

"Didn't you hear me say nobody but you and me know about the will? Nobody must ever know. Not Pharaoh—not Master—not Mr. Pierce. Take it home and tear it up. Throw it in the fire. You've got to protect your man. And Master *is* a man. Old Master was the meanest creature ever lived."

As I was leaving I looked up the stairs to see if the girls were peeping at me.

"You saw some of my girls when you came in?"

"Yes. Why did they hide?"

"They thought you were one of those prissy schoolteachers."

"Who are they?"

Livia was too fat to shrug her shoulders but she shook them a trifle. "Oh," she said airily, "just girls, out to keep soldier boys from being too lonesome. This house has heaps of rooms."

An autumn storm was gathering. The wind blew chill all the way down the choppy river to the big dock on the Point whence I would be escorted home and left until tax-time next year. I was completely downcast. Today I had no hope of the war ever ending or we winning. We passed Seabrook's Landing and rounded the bend from Skull Creek into the sound. I looked over at Myrtle Bank, glowering glumly in the leaden light. A school of sharks cut between the steamer and the Cotton Hall landing. Cousin Annie's house showed dark and gloomy in the darker trees.

"You are cold, Mrs. Berrien. Here—take my cape."

"Not cold, just thinking sad thoughts."

"I realize returning to Beaufort was hard on you. I'd hate it if it was Montpelier, Vermont."

"Not so hard as knowing I am going to be twenty years old tomorrow and feel as if I were already ninety."

"You! Ninety!"

It was good to be able to laugh, even with a Yankee.

Button was so glad to see me I made him a pair of velvet covers for his best gamecock's spurs. When he ran to the chicken house to see if they fit I carefully hid the will where Beau can never find it. Nobody can. It is sewed inside the stuffed hawk! The blazing fire begged me to toss it in. But destroy a legal will? I'm not quite ready to do anything that sinful. Maybe tomorrow. Certainly if the need arises.

Forty-two

General Mitchel died of climate fever four months
after he took over from General Hunter. Twice he
visited Cotton Hall. He was sympathetic and concerned about me and Button. Things would have
turned out differently had he lived. But to my misfortune General Hunter was returned to his former
command and I was closer confined than ever. I mean
watched and guarded.

During December of 1862 Liney cut and piled
enough wood to last us the rest of our lives; nailed
heavy wooden brackets on each side of the outside
doors; fitted oak poles across them so nobody could
'broke in,' fenced and ploughed a plot of land for a
vegetable garden near the house, and carefully explained to Button about the piles of seed on the long
table in Beau's office and when to plant them.

Maybelle, Maum Hannah, Button and I picked every boll of cotton on a special section and, the steam
gin having gone out of order, picked all the seeds
out by hand. It seemed to take forever and ruined
my fingernails.

On Christmas a wind like a carving knife cut in
from the sound and we had a wedding. Button gave
the bride away. Maybelle and Israel stood up together in the dining room, I reading the marriage
service from the Prayer Book. Anatole, in his tall
starched white chef's hat, presided over a bowl of
egg-nog. The few old people left on the Street were
the wedding guests. We toasted first Maybelle, giggling in a ruffled white organdy dress made from the
fanciest summer counterpane; then Israel, quietly
proud, in one of Phillip's black broadcloth Sunday
suits; then their future.

That was when I realized Liney was going to leave
Cotton Hall. It was the way he kept looking out of

the window and sighing, rather as if someone had died.

On the last day of the year he brought three croker sacks full of cotton seeds and put them in my wardrobe. "These the only fine long staple cotton seeds left on Hilton Head," he explained. "Them Yankees done sent the whole 1862 crop north to be gin. Ain't select a single seed for next year's planting. Don't nohow let them get they fingers on these. Them ours."

"Happy New Year, Liney." The icy wind was blowing against the windows. The pines were roaring in their tops like an ocean sea.

Liney pulled his forelock, scraped his foot, and said gravely, "Miss Angel, I is so pulled in half I is 'bout to bust. I begs you all to go off with Mr. Stephen next time he come. January 1st been what Mr. Linkum say is 'fore God Free Day."

I wanted to plead with him not to desert me. But his eyes! They were too wonderful.

"Well," I managed brightly, "you'll make a fine soldier."

"Oh, no Miss Angel. Never me shoot a gun at Master. You didn't thought I'd fight against Master?" He was about to cry.

"Where are you going?"

"Take the steamer over to Beaufort then heading up the road. I feels powerful bad leaving you and little Master Buttons but the feeling of being free is too much bigger than ary feeling I ever felt. Could be I'll travel west. Just think, Miss Angel, Liney can go anywhere Liney wants! I can't hardly believe it. Anywhere I wanted!"

Forty-three

February 25, 1863.

Tom Elliott slipped in one night last week and slept on the sofa in my boudoir until it was light enough for him to check the fleet with his telescope. He wants me to do this every day, sending Button with information of the slightest sign of activity on their part.

He had sad news: Cousin Billy died in Flat Rock, N.C., on February 3rd, the day after some mean person told him about the Yankees digging up his rose trees and destroying his experimental gardens on Edisto and burning all his wonderful books. Cousin Annie heard from Aunt Dell after the funeral. She sent me word about Amun. She has retreated entirely into a child's dream world. Dinah nurses her devotedly. Aunt Dell and Uncle Jim are spending the winter with Cousin Randolph on the James River, their house being so much warmer than Cedar Grove.

Warm! Will I ever be warm again? I seem to be always carrying wood and making fires. At night the fires go out. We freeze and snuggle into our beds as soon as it is dark. Since Liney left, I keep all the shutters along the piazza closed and the doors locked. A hammer on the table, between my big bed and Button's trundle, keeps us company.

I hope I can sleep tonight. Last night the wind moaned and I gloomed and trembled and heard locks being broken and windows being raised and footsteps padding up and down the stairs—all the chimeras of loneliness. By midnight the whole world had turned into a murderer.

The United States has sold at auction the entire town of Beaufort. Many of the finest houses have been bought by Negroes for as little as $90. Button has planted turnips and lettuce and cabbages and onions. He has learned two Bach fugues in a simple arrangement I found among his mother's music. Maybelle is going to have a baby! O, I am so envious!

While I write in my diary she is sitting beside me, sewing the sinful red velvet into a dress from a pattern Aunt Dell must have tucked in my shoe box, bless her. It has a tight waist with a high, Chinese neck and a flowing skirt that dips train-like in the back. I will hold it up when I dance. It reminds me of Mrs. Merriweather. I hope Maybelle can arrange my hair on top of my head and wisp the little curls on my neck. But when will I wear it? I vow not until the night Beau comes home.

April, 1863.

The plantations on Hilton Head have been sold for taxes, at auction, to the United States and to Yankee land speculators, and teachers and former overseers and African "heads of families" for $1 an acre! That included the dwelling houses and farm buildings and everything in them, rather what has not been shipped north. O poor beautiful lost houses! The owners and heirs will now be forced to buy them back when they return to the island. I wonder if Mr. Lincoln knows about this?

One of the dreadful land agents came here, insisting on selling Cotton Hall to a group of our former slaves who banded together to buy sections of twenty and fifty acres. Luckily Button was in the barn helping a cow which was having difficulty calving. I ripped open the stuffed hawk, showed the old thief the will proving it was owned by a Yankee. As soon as he went away I sewed the poor bird up again with the dreadful document inside. I have become shameless but *they* are corrupt and dishonest even with each other.

Often in the dark of night, lines of marsh tackeys pass through Cotton Hall. Cargoes stolen from the customs house are stowed on their backs, tightly covered with tarpaulin. The ponies originally broken to hunting are accustomed to traveling by night and don't shy or whinny when alligators grunt or bats whizz over their heads or owls hoot. The soldiers who patrol the bluff look the other way as the smugglers pass with their loads of opium and quinine and loaf sugar and ham and silks and corsets and Paris bonnets.

One night Israel followed them to Skull Creek where flat-boats were waiting. They headed along Skull Creek for Calibogue Sound and hid in the marsh. The next night they poled and rowed into Confederate lines on the Savannah River where the cargo was probably sold at enormous prices.

Israel and Button and Masai have finished ploughing. Maybelle tied Israel's right wrist to the plough handle and put the lines around his neck. Masai grasped the handles of his plough and Button led the mule. What a picture! Every now and then Masai let go the handles and raised his arms heavenward and his lips moved as if he were singing a praise-song to the sun. We planted about ten acres of corn but only six in cotton; that mainly to perpetuate our finest seeds.

Hans brings news from the town. Rear Admiral John A. Dahlgren has replaced Du Pont as commander of the fleet. I suppose that's why now I see squadrons of navy ships steaming from their anchorage and going up the coast to bombard Charleston. Button takes word of this to the hide out.

When they return, those squadrons, some of them are limping badly. Hooray for Stephen in Fort Sumter and the Confederacy!

Small gunboats make regular circuits of the island looking for Confederates and to prove they are still formidable.

Last week one of their gunboats, the *George Washington,* lingered overnight in the Coosaw River and a Confederate battery shot it to pieces in one blast. Most aboard were killed. The rest wallowed through the sucking mud and marsh to safety helped by the pilot, who was the last man overboard—a huge wooden-legged Negro. I'm sure it was Big May.

Last night, evening rather, I sat for a long time on the piazza in the thinnish half-light and the doves kept calling sadly down in the swamp and suddenly a great drowning wave of desolation washed over me and I thought my whole life has been a tangle of ecstasy and longing. I can't think of facing ten or twenty years more sitting alone on this piazza hearing the doves crying. I thought other thoughts one mustn't think, so I came quickly inside and began such engrossing and real things as measuring some medicine for Aunt Hecuba's stomach and weighing peaches for preserves. And then I found a letter from Beau that had appeared mysteriously on my writing desk (brought by my little messenger boy!) It was a blessing and a balm. I lay down and slept sweet and sound until almost now. But oh—the doves have begun mourning again—and the day looms long—long——

August 20

Button and Hans have gone on a camping trip down to Calibogia Plantation to gather rice-birds. These are the only kind of birds Button can be counted on to collect. I can never fathom his aberration in refusing to shoot game but willing to snare, trap or catch it; always delighted to eat it. He explains he can't squeeze a trigger at a living thing. It makes no sense. They plan to sell them to the restaurant in the town for $1 a dozen. Button explained that the bobolinks settle in the rice fields and grow round and too fat to fly. They roost along the cross-ditches. He and Hans will go after them in a boat Hans knows about. Button will pick them off the grass stems; Hans will pinch their necks and drop them into bottles.

We need the money to buy medicine and red thread and shoes. I dare not show a gold piece again. We would be murdered by robbers.

Beau has been away for two whole years! Here I am chained to my rock while gadflies eat out my heart. (I hate the word—liver.) The heat is terrible.

What wouldn't I give for just one long cool look at the Blue Ridge Mountains, with Amun dancing beside me, and Beau galloping along the ridge on Teaser! There—I've written away half of my bad humor. I hear Israel outside calling to Maybelle to stop bending over that washpot. Her baby is due next month. She is about to burst with happiness.

As will I when I see Beau. Tom Elliott says Stephen is preparing to go to Virginia and Beau to come to South Carolina.

Pray God it be soon!

The marsh is alive with birds, redwing blackbirds, rails, marsh hawks and curlews. The air is filled with swallows migrating. I have never seen so many bluebirds flocking, as if they are on their way to a family reunion. The mockingbird still sings, but faintly. The whippoorwill only near the dawning. Tonight there will be a full moon.

Full moon of August—I name you Lonesome Moon.

September 2

I've had a letter from Aunt Beck in Charleston! Ephraim slipped into the town one night recently and went to her house to borrow my great-grandfather's medicine box with silver scales for weighing opium, someone having stolen Dr. Jenkins' scales at Pocotaligo and morphine so scarce a days that every titrate counts.

Aunt Beck apologized to me for all the bad things she had said and heard about me and hoped I'd forgive her. Ephraim got very wrought up when she repeated some of them to him. He assured her that I was the greatest heroine the Low Country had ever produced, recounting my acts that have proved invaluable to the Cause. She will give a tea party immediately so that she can pass on this good news to the family connections thus clearing my good name in Charleston, which is where it counts.

What an old hypocrite. I never met Aunt Beck. I hope I never do but I must pretend gratitude and affection so she will continue to send me news of Uncle Jim and Aunt Dell and Amun.

She included some in that letter: for now they remain at Cousin Randolph's on the James River mainly because of Amun, who has lost her mind entirely. Fortunately "a former slave named Dinah cares for the little lunatic." (Those were Aunt Beck's exact words. I could have killed her.) Some nights Amun has to be restrained from running away and throwing herself into the river because she sees the moon reflected in it. Only the foolish Burwell sentimentality keeps her from the asylum in Richmond where she belongs. Uncle Jim has had a stroke but Aunt Dell is fine. A pity it was Uncle Jim's leg that was paralyzed not his tongue. This news made me cry.

October 14

I am twenty-one. On my birthday, a blue, dazzly day, Button and I had a picnic in the temple in the woods. We walked, each carrying a basket, through high broom grass. We saw a fox, very long, with his grey brush stretched, which had been barking, for the sun was hot; he leapt lightly over a rail fence and entered the grass. It made me homesick for Cedar Grove. Though grey, not rufus colored, it brought back the fox of three years ago—the day of that heavenly kiss.

Button has changed; grown tall. His round boyish limbs have lengthened out; his face is losing its merry childish round, is hollowing slightly under the cheek bones. But he is still playful as a puppy and his voice a sweet soprano. I could never have remained in this lonely situation without him.

Outwardly I delighted in watching him bait a turkey trap. Inwardly I raged at the fate that has cut me off from everybody except an eleven-year-old boy. I don't want this exile, this isolation. But then I asked myself whether, given the chance, I would leave here, abandoning Beau's beloved Cotton Hall to the Yankees? Could I face the Savannah and the Charleston and the Beaufort relatives? From Tom's hints many of them speak bitterly of me; hinting at collusion. How, without Beau beside me, could I reply to *J'accuse?*

Soon a gobbler entered the little glade and went straight to the trench and began picking up grain greedily. Sunlight flashed from his gleaming breast as from planished bronze. His iridescent plumage showed all the tints of autumn leaves and, as he stooped to feed, his long beard touched the ground.

I sneezed. He gave a squawk, ran a little way and shot through the pine trunks.

As I think back on the past two years I find myself making a great effort to consider them as an adventure which, while begun like any other, has enriched and simplified my life. In Flat Rock or back at Cedar Grove I would have been without Beau the same as here.

And I have learned so much. Small things have become totally important: the coolness of the swamp, haunted by birds and creatures, the sweet whistle of quail at dawn. I have learned to read the poets and the historians. After galloping through Lady Montague and Pepys I went on to Gibbons and Macaulay and Lord Byron and Keats and Scott. Beau and I will have so much to talk about. We won't have any friends on the islands. Ramon Rivas, who bought Honey Horn for $90, would scarcely be a suitable dinner guest; nor the bald-headed preacher who bought Fairfield nor all those old maid teachers who are pretending to be ladies in Mr. Coffin's house.

Maybelle's baby is a little boy. I love to sit and rock him. He is good and beautiful. He has her big brown velvet eyes and Israel's Arabic nose and soft straight hair. He is named Billy Boy.

The Confederates have won a costly victory at Chicamauga and Beau is a hero. He has been cited over and over for bravery on the field of battle. Tom came last night. "Stephen is in Virginia."

"Can that mean Beau is coming to this area?"

"I'm sure it does," says Tom.

I wear my goblin hat and cotton gloves religiously

so I will be soft and pale and alluring for my beloved.

December First

What irony! Frederick has returned! He is a colonel and looks as though he spent the year in an
Olympian atmosphere, resembling a Greek statue
more than ever. He has asked to bring three of his
fellow officers for Christmas dinner. I did my best to
detect signs of sensitivity in his handsome eyes but
all I saw was sensuality and power. But O, as he left
he called back, "I'll go to Beaufort after New Year's
to see if Livia has found the will." I rashly said: "Do
you trust her?" "No," he replied, "I wouldn't be surprised if she hadn't even paid my tax."

Part Six

The
Competitors

*Cotton Hall Plantation,
December, 1863–September, 1864*

Forty-four

I think Frederick realizes now that there is no ordinary way to have my company. But rather than not have it he accepts the way it has to be. He is friendly. He is courteous and, quite firmly, not to be denied.

I, too, accept the inevitable and am bland as he. We are acquaintances, not intimates, who meet at a concert, rustling in our politeness, smooth and wary. But, too, we are aware.

Last week Button disarmed us. It was a gorgeous winter afternoon—crisp and clear. The bored guards were going to take part in a race. Button was to be master of ceremonies.

Frederick and I following, Button led us to the avenue going down the bluff.

"Once down and up," he cried excitedly. "Everyone has to run when I say so. Come on now."

Two by two the blue-uniformed boys rushed down to the landing and panted up. Hans and a lad from Kentucky tied for first place. The prize was a hatful of fresh game hen eggs.

"Come on, Angelica, you and Frederick next."

"No." I laughed, "I am the only girl."

"I will, if you will," Frederick challenged.

I had always been swift enough to beat most boys in Virginia but I was running against Mercury in Frederick. I ran faster than I ever did with a fury that in the end defeated me.

I was determined to humiliate Frederick in front of the marveling soldier boys. Instead he won easily, going along with me till we started uphill then slipping easily past me to the top. Had he been a more human person I would have known he mocked me.

Anatole came from the house with a bowl of tea punch and a plate of molasses and benne seed cakes

and put them on a table near the front steps as Button skipped down the steps with the prize, holding
it proudly aloft—a pair of Beau's riding gauntlets
from the table by the front door.

We were resting on a bench after the race. Frederick jumped up. His eyes found mine then they
looked houseward where the guards had gathered
around the punch bowl talking. They hadn't noticed
the gauntlets. Frederick looked at Button and me.
His eyes were shining but impersonal. Carelessly he
took the gloves and slapped them against his thigh
while I held my breath, not knowing what to expect.
Then he did the unexpected; tossed them back to
Button.

"I won and enjoyed winning but you keep the
prize. Only take these back inside the house until the
owner returns for them. Or did he recently wear
them here? They are unusually soft and pliant."

Button looked anxiously at me. Had he done something to hurt Bubba?

"Take Beau's gauntlets back into the house, darling," I said gently. "Frederick knows he hasn't been
here."

"I know everything that goes on here," Frederick
said. "If I didn't I might suspect you."

He kissed my hand and thanked me for a pleasant
time, reminding me of my promise to entertain his
friends on Christmas Day. He was entirely formal but
a seed of suspicion had been planted. I know because
the next morning another guard joined the four who
lounged lazily around the house day in and day out.

As Frederick marched around the house to the
mounting block I suddenly remembered to make a
face at his back. It was a casual not an unpleasant
gesture. It was as though to remind myself that no
matter how much I might actually have enjoyed running the race I did not wish to have enjoyed it.

Forty-five

Woven wicker hampers of delicacies and baskets of ribboned packages began arriving from Frederick the week before Christmas. Each day brought a new marvel. Anatole was out of his mind over having real sugar and sherry and vanilla and coffee and black pepper and white flour and soda and baking powder and lemons and oranges and raisins and nutmeg and cloves again.

Maum Hannah muttered disapprovingly, shaking her head as Anatole gloatingly unpacked each hamper, until a whole bunch of bananas, carefully cradled in straw, was lifted from an ox-cart on Christmas Eve and hung in the pantry.

Now I am the only one discomfited by the almost forgotten odors wafting through the house, making an even spicier smell than the feathery green cypress tree Button brought from the swamp this morning and is decorating with coconut balls and gingermen and strings of red berries.

On this morning of Christmas, Maybelle persuaded me to try on my new dress, the other two choices being the ethereal blue gauze still hanging, unironed, in its cotton bag in the wardrobe, or a mitch-match green and blue woolen skirt and shabby challis shirtwaist.

"But I promised myself not to wear this until Master comes home," I said, caressing the luscious apple-red velvet.

We were in my little sitting room. Sitting on a stool Maum Hannah was holding Maybelle's baby close to the fire, he having had croup the night before.

"Please keep it on, Miss Angel. It revives my spirit to see you looking like this," Maybelle said.

Maum Hannah sucked her teeth, poked out her

297

mouth and commented drily, "Um Um, weuns gots to put us best foots forward not backward this day so as not to rile Mr. Yankeeman and his guesteses. A culloo been fall down my chimbley last night and 'cortch him wing and make great confushun bringing news. Him and me gone in a cohoot fuh hold you safe this Jesus' born-day. Keep on the red dress. You pleasures my eyes."

Aunt Dell used to say that vanity was my cloven hoof. I can remember, as a child, dreading to take off my shoes and stockings after such a judgment, positive I would discover I had only two toes and a real horn-hoof.

"Please, Miss Angel, you looks like Christmas. Set and let me get to work on your hair," Maybelle said excitedly.

A delicate little ruche of rare old lace I'd come on in a lacquer box of Julia's letters softened the high neck of the dress. The ruche surrounded my chin making my face appear to be held up on a stalk.

The guests were due at one o'clock. At half past twelve Maybelle had my hair piled high and careful little wisps of curls carelessly straggling down. When I turned my head and saw them in the mirror the memory of the way Beau loved to open them and put his lips on the nape of my neck made my lips part and my cheeks flame.

Maum Hannah was "quizzing" me with a wicked expression. She knew! She always knows what I am feeling. The baby had been fussing for the past half hour. She held him up. "Come here, you Maybelle, open your buzzum and gie this chuckwilluh a titty. Ain't ever seen such a wide open mouth on no cullud chile before."

Maum Hannah followed me out into the hall. She had something on her mind but was going to make me ask what.

"What news was the curlew bringing?" I asked politely.

"I ain't yerry too plain. Rokoon been walk pontop the path side my door when culloo been squawking and 'splaining, then them chock-tongue houn'dogs lift up and one of them sojers start chooting. But I yerry enough fuh axe you to be careful when you crack your teet at dinner. Don't say nuttin shawt ner shaa'p. Refend yourself with mealy words and stay close 'side Buttons."

"I will, Maum Hannah, you're so dear to me."

"And t'ank you," she dropped a quick curtsey, "berry much for them warm shawl and shoes and special for gimme Miss Julia music box. I been covet that ever since she comeyuh as a fold-wing dove of a bride. But never did I t'ink hit blan to me. Well, I going t'ief a 'nana now. Um—Um—You looks lak Wenus, fuh true."

Israel had learned to serve smoothly with his left hand, keeping his right arm akimbo, wrist against his spine.

Seated at the long damask-covered table were two exceedingly New England colonels who were living in Beaufort with their stiff, stylish wives, a bemedalled commander from the fleet who had brought his pet monkey, now happily attached to Button's shoulder, and Frederick, preening himself with pride at having furnished such a Yule feast, expertly carving his town-turkey.

I was at the end of the table, my back to the door, facing the pier glass mirror. I couldn't help comparing this charade with the first one I'd seen mirrored there—the gay laughing ladies, the courtly gentlemen, the compliments, the fans, the merry little serving boys darting through the crowd like silver fish.

When Frederick had finished with the turkey, and everybody's plates were heaped with rice and oysters and cornbread and pecan stuffing and candied sweet potatoes and creamed onions and turnips and pickled peaches, Israel filled the ruby Bohemian crystal wine glasses. At Frederick's invitation the commander rose to say grace. It wasn't our kind of blessing but a long windy exhortation to the Lord.

I closed my eyes, sending Christmas wishes to everybody I loved. Amun was the first one to come into my mind, poor dear little Amun.

"And let not the infidel protrude himself among us this holy day and also Lord——"

I sat up with a start. My stomach tightened in a knot. Something was about to happen today—tonight—this very hour. The presentiment was so strong I went weak all over. My hands trembled violently on my napkin. My pulse was fluttering in spasms like a dying bird's wing. I was ill—I was dying——

"And Merry Christmas to all of us so far away from home!" The commander lifted his glass to toast.

"Look!" Button's hand flew up, hitting the commander's wrist. His glass fell, spilling red wine over the white cloth.

"Look! Look in the door! It's Bubba!"

For a fleeting second I saw Beau in the mirror.

Everyone turned. The open door showed the empty hall, bright in fire and sunlight.

The great fence the Voice had warned me of was in front of me. I had to clear it or die under merciless hooves. "Nonsense," I cried, "how you startled everyone, especially me, with your ghosts. Fetch the Commander another wine glass, Israel."

Frederick had thrown down his napkin. He was striding along the table. I put my hand on his arm as he passed me. "This sort of thing has gone on ever since Button's head injury. He saw Phillip in the chicken house yesterday."

Frederick hesitated as Button took the cue. "Maybe it was Bubba's ghost. Maybe he's dead. Yes, that was it. I saw a ghost. It was a grey one."

"Eat your rice, Button." How could my voice come out so calm when my insides were churning to pulp?

Frederick sat down but he was watching me, his eyes steadier than usual. A muscle in his jaw twitched uncontrollably. I knew he wasn't satisfied. I looked down at my plate lest my fear and my wild excitement show.

Frederick couldn't stand the strain. He got up so abruptly his chair turned over. "We'll settle this quickly. If Button really did see a Confederate soldier who reminded him of his brother you would doubtless like to wish him a Merry Christmas; if it is an intruder, I shall see to it that he is taken immediately to the prison."

"Frederick," as I spoke I could see my face in the mirror, my white, white face and agitated eyes giving me an arch coquettish look I was far from feeling, "please sit down and let's finish dinner. This is the first time I've had such charming company in so long. I wanted——" I hesitated, and then rushed on—"to sing some Christmas songs with you after dinner."

As he hesitated the stiff ladies' tongues loosened. They hastened to my aid, gushing about how *they* would have jumped up and screamed with joy if *their* husbands had peeped in the door after two and a half years. The vision couldn't have been Baynard Berrien! The commander put in a few pithy comments on his wife's headaches. Even the majors took a turn at teasing Frederick about letting a child's exuberance spoil a good dinner. He'd probably been sipping wine while we were concentrating on oysters.

I thanked the ladies with my eyes, especially the one with a towering pompadour of red-gold hair. I'll never forget either of them for what they meant to me that day. Their rushing conversation gave me a chance to steady myself enough to carry on, to mask my terror and leaping exultation with an Aunt Dell vagueness.

Frederick never took his eyes off me, trying to fluster me. Once I dropped my fork on the plate. As if the clatter were a signal, he excused himself to have a word with the soldier on the front piazza.

He was soon back, nodding at the majors, relaxing them, if not me. I expected a soldier to burst in with Beau at gunpoint or, worse, hear a gunshot outside.

The oranges and grated coconut in the ambrosia stuck in my throat, still I went through the motions of being gay. Or rather that dead lady's face in the mirror, grimacing like a skull, was being gay.

When the soldier finally came he reported crisply, "Nothing."

He and the other soldiers had searched the empty cabins on the Street and all the outbuildings. Should he send a detachment to look again, just in case? No one in a boat or on a horse or on foot could have gotten on the place or in the house in broad daylight without being seen. Guards had been posted at every entrance since yesterday.

"Were you expecting someone?" I asked, staring at nothing in the chandelier.

Frederick said, "Christmas is a homing time."

I thought they'd never stop cracking pecans and eating raisins and drinking champagne. Then I played the piano forever. We sang every Christmas song I ever heard of.

Frederick had a beautiful voice and so did the commander. One of the ladies had a rich contralto. Button's true soprano was heartbreakingly sweet. When I thought I was not observed my eyes sought the windows, still clear in the afternoon sunlight, and I listened for sounds beyond the songs. But what if suddenly I heard *his* voice singing "I Know A Lady Sweet and Kind"? Tears stung my eyelids. I missed a chord.

Luckily the monkey took that instant to break loose and jump, chattering shrilly, up on the mantelpiece, knocking over a white biscuit eagle, ending the musicale.

We saw them off from the piazza, Button and I, arms around each other.

Both ladies hugged me asking if they could come to call and would I take tea with them some afternoon.

Frederick kissed my hand in such a way as to announce to his peers that he was my suitor. I did not pull my hand away. I even smiled.

We watched the horses and the carriages disappear around the ibis pond. When we couldn't see so much as a speck of them through the piney woods, Button and I went silently into the house. From the windows we saw the guards patrolling the garden and the bluff. We dared not talk. One might be hidden in the house, listening.

Maybelle came to us in my boudoir. She whispered that soldiers had questioned her and Anatole in the kitchen. She dared not leave Anatole alone with them, knowing Anatole. The soldiers stayed in the kitchen the whole time we were singing. They ate all of the turkey and fruit cake that was left. She and Israel and Anatole and Maum Hannah had to cook some corn pone and pork chops. She thought the soldiers went out but they might have slipped into the stairhall. She wasn't sure.

Button and I, still not talking, spent two hours looking in all the rooms, every closet, under beds and in the woodboxes until dark, when we went to our miserable beds. What could we say to each other? What could we do?

Forty-six

I couldn't sleep. Had it been Beau? Had my being constantly haunted with longing made that fleeting image in Beau's likeness? One's mind can play as many tricks as one's heart. If it had been Beau where had he gone?

Button slept soundly on his cot by the banked fire. Around midnight I heard a noise. I lay rigid trying to hear it again and identify it. There it was! A sharp sound and the snap of something thrown through the open window hitting on the floor.

I went down on my hands and knees and felt all over the floor but could find nothing. I looked out of the window. An old half-moon was resting, belly up, on top of a pointed pine. When I never did, why had I left the window open?

At first I saw only blackness, gradually the side garden, the far trees and farther the moon-tracked water and the dark blur of ships upon it. I strained my eyes for a figure in the garden. But there was no one on the dead grass. The guards must be gathered in one of the outbuildings against the cold night.

I was shivering and frightened. If Beau had come home, why would he be hiding outside? He knew all the secret ways to get in. What was out there that was terrifying? Who else was out there? Frederick? At the thought I clutched my woolen kimono over my thrusting breasts and drew back into the inside dark. As I moved, my bare toes touched something hard and sharp. I picked it up. It was a big oyster shell. A string held a piece of a handkerchief that was crumpled in its hollow.

Something dreadful was going on. Whoever had thrown the shell was afraid to show himself. I dared not draw a match and light a candle in here. I tried to read by the low coals in the fireplace. I couldn't make out the words. Not stopping to put on my slippers I ran into my water closet, shut the door and lit a candle.

"Open the front door silently," was scrawled in pencil on the scrap of linen.

My feet were freezing. I took time to pull on some heavy stockings and soft slippers and ran, feeling my way, through Beau's office into the cavernous seeming hall, keeping away from the streaks of moonlight in case anyone was looking through a window. When I was safely at the double front doors I had to give all my strength to lifting the heavy board Liney had put there to keep the people out.

The big brass key in the lock moved soundlessly but when I turned the china knob a sharp grating I'd never heard before exploded on the stillness like a cannon. My teeth chattered so loud I knocked my head against the door panel trying to listen if someone was breathing on the other side. There was no movement or noise on the piazza. Slowly I gave the right-hand door a pull and shrank back behind it.

Between the jamb and the door a long shadow flitted and was gone. Then I thought I saw it again. A crouching form detached itself from the side of the house. As from a draft of wind the door pushed against me and closed again so quietly I knew the key had not been turned in the lock. Someone had come in. He was breathing hoarsely. A smothered scream started in my throat, an involuntary instinctual sound. I jumped from behind the door. A hand clamped itself over my mouth, a powerful arm pinioned me.

I was dying, I was drowning. My heart was throbbing so hard I went limp against the strength of that arm.

"It's Beau," he whispered; but oh so softly, a breath, barely heard in my ear. I wanted to melt into his arms, say his name. But he continued to hold me tight, his hand over my mouth, letting his little finger outline my upper lip, light as a butterfly wing. We stood together, pressing ourselves together, staring into each other's eyes, listening desperately.

Footsteps on the piazza, furtive ones. A sudden light

swept the piazza, torches flared in the driveway, up and down the steps, along the bluff. A lantern was held against the glass sidelight of the door. It searched the hall. The beams of light could not find us where we were huddled against the panel of the door. But what if the lantern bearer turned the door knob and the door swung inward?

He did not. Footsteps no longer stealthy tramped down the steps. Torchlights flared jerkily down the avenue to the bluff.

In the stairhall that was like a black tunnel, where no sound came or went, Beau whispered, "Did you know the place is swarming with soldiers?"

"No."

But I should have known. Frederick had not taken Button's startled outcry lightly. His suspicion had been fiercely aroused and, whatever else, he was a professional detective as well as a soldier.

We held our breath, tense, clutching each other's hands, waiting, listening, to know if they were going to come in the house.

Was Beau wondering why I had been entertaining Yankees at his dinner table? O, there was so much explaining to do. "Beau——" I began.

"Sh-h-h- not tonight. All I want is to be in my bed again with my love in my arms."

"Button is asleep in our room."

"Dang! I'll break his back. Is anyone in the company room upstairs?"

Was he being sarcastic?

"No."

He let go my hand, hesitated and then said, quite simply, "I've hardly slept since I left Virginia, being so hellbent on getting home. No one must know I'm here except you. Come."

Be still my heart. Please, God, don't let this be the stair Maum Hannah warned me to watch about climbing. My foot mustn't slip nor my crown be damaged this night. Not this one.

Like thieves or intruders we slipped into the great cold company room and climbed into the mammoth poster bed, arctic in linen sheets. Neither of us could talk. We dared not unloose torrents that might carry us away from the verity—the bliss of being back in a world by ourselves.

We approached each other timidly at first; reverently as if we were votives nearing a holy altar. I felt the paradise of his naked skin on mine. Our lips met, tremblingly. But love quickly unfolded his wings and we were one wing; raised, pointed, soaring, up and up and up, breaking through whirling clouds into a seventh heaven of shooting stars and overflowing fountains over and over, then fluttering, lower-lower-lower into a downy nest of oblivion.

"Beau, darling——" I wanted to tell him that this loving was the same essence as our first kiss. But he had fallen asleep. I curled deliciously against him, remembering Maum Hannah saying that primitive people call this sudden deep sleep after loving the "little death" believing that, at the magic moment, a woman steals the man's soul away from his body.

All night I couldn't tell whether I was asleep or awake, only that we were together. I just lay there with my arms around him and knew that things were never going to be the same. He hadn't been made for this changed life style. I was sad because I could feel what he must have felt skulking into Cotton Hall, his home, his world, as if he were not the master but the slave. Because I loved him so desperately, I ached for him and there was nothing I could do about it.

As the first glimmer of daydawn touched the window he whispered, not opening his eyes, "My horse is tethered in the old temple. He needs to be fed and watered. If possible, hide him in a stable."

I slipped downstairs, poked up the embers in my bedroom fire and threw on some lightwood then three oak logs so Button would be warm when he woke. I put on heavy dark clothes and went out into the mist. No one was about. Not even a rooster had crowed. I hurried down the sandy road, through the broom grass to the pine woods. I just could make out the temple through the black trunks when a first ray of

sun struck one of the columns. I ran closer. The sun
ray thrust inside the temple revealing a snow-white
god-horse, head thrown high, new-moon ears sharply curved, left back foot gracefully crooked; pale
blue eyes rolling; whickering softly.

"Old horse!" I cried, silently to myself, moving
slowly so as not to frighten him in case he didn't remember me. "You wonderful funny old horse!"

Teaser was safe in one of the back stalls munching
corn and fodder when the first blue-coat made a
marching circle of the house. I know he was the first
because he was yawning and he tipped his cap politely as I stood on the kitchen porch calling Anatole.

Maum Hannah was sitting on the bottom step of
the stairs when I came with a covered tray holding a
plate of hominy and sausage and butter and a
china bowl of ten soft-boiled eggs.

"What are you doing here?" I asked crossly.

"What you?"

"I'm going to eat my breakfast in peace in the
schoolroom."

She burst out laughing. "Ain't you the heading one!
Has I ever sung you the song my old momma used
to sing? Goes like this:

        Tremblin' woman and a tremblin' man
        God gwine hold them in a tremblin' hand."

"How did you know?"

"Culloo been name Cudjo Manigo name that night.
Name one rascal other close behime."

"Don't tell anybody. Not even Button."

"Never will I. But this make a nice place to set.
You go long bout yo' business, once you done et up
there."

Forty-seven

Beau slept most of the day. I sent everybody, including Anatole, to tasks in the fields or on the Street, excusing myself, saying I had a sick headache which the afterglow of passion darkening my eyes and softening my mouth denied. Maum Hannah must stay inside and take care of me. By mid-day most of the soldiers went back to the town but a few still ambled boredly around.

About half past four I went into Beau's office to find his copy of Rasselas to read aloud to him as a surprise, when he woke. He was sitting at his desk. He must have come down while Button and I were taking an early tea in the dining room.

He was washed and shaved. He had on his long black velvet dressing gown and the exaggeratedly high, white silk beaver top hat he'd worn at our wedding. He looked like a grand duke preparing to meet the emperor. Rather, the emperor waiting for his empress.

When he saw me he smiled. My heart rushed out to snatch the tenderness his smile held for me. But now I saw how he had changed. The dark red hair, showing under the hat, was silver-streaked. His whole expression had altered. His strong hawk-like features were even more definitely graven. Deep lines gashed beside the corners of his mouth. There was a grimness about him but no hint of disillusionment. The dream lingered but the glitter had dimmed.

"Maum Hannah and Israel have made me respectable again," he said. "I can revel in fresh linen and silk for, let me see, it gets dark early, probably another hour."

"How long have you been awake?"

"A couple of hours. While Maum Hannah was arranging for my bath I went up in the cupola. I started to jump down from there and end it all after scanning the desolate reaches of my once carefully tended fields and forests. It will take years to put it back in perfect shape. Not an ox-cart, not a black, not a farm animal was in sight; no marsh mud nor manure was being spread. Then I looked toward Coggins Point and saw all those ships and wharves and buildings. I thought of the risks you've taken and how brave you are. And I thought of Eddie and false Phillip——" He couldn't continue. He hid his face in his hands.

Wild words gushed out of me, and tears. "It's been awful. So awful. And having to put up with Frederick. You don't know how he makes me feel."

"Don't tell me things like that. What right have you to complain to me who has been through more hell than you could ever dream of? And now having to hide like a thief in my own home!" He flung his arms out as if crucified.

I ran and put my head on his chest. His arms came down slowly and circled me and we stood holding to each other, rocking back and forth, grieving and loving.

All of a sudden he laughed. "What a baby I am. No more of that. Stand back and let me look at you closely. I've been so taken up with touching I haven't given my eyes a chance. Your hands are rough. There's a hole in your shoe and, turn around, your hips are even slimmer. Usually I prefer a woman with big soft round——."

"Fool! If you'll stay another night I promise a whole flock of whooper cranes will fly."

"Dammit, don't weaken me. Your contented purring kept me awake until daydawn."

"Just one more night?"

"Summon Anatole, if he's still around. You're scheming to starve me into submission."

"We don't entirely trust Anatole. I'll fix you something after he goes down on the Street."

"By golly he won't betray me after I describe what I'll do to him if he opens his mouth. He remembers

Papa. And, while you're out, find Button. The two of you can stay with me while I eat in here."

"I love you."

"You're an evil woman but fortunate in that Stephen took great pains to prepare me for your Yankee connection. Otherwise I might have rushed in and killed you all at table."

Button was on his way to the house from the stables when I went outside to call him. His eyes were big with wonder. "Guess what's in Miss Suzy's stall?"

I put my finger to my lips. We looked around but saw no one.

"A giant white rabbit," he said loudly.

As Beau wolfed down freshly broiled oysters, and warmed-over wild ducks and rice and sweet potatoes and cold venison he told us things we didn't want to believe.

The South had paid dearly for the victory at Chickamauga. Too many lives had been lost, too many soldiers had been wounded and had deserted. The Confederacy had too little ammunition, too few new pairs of shoes, no factories. For every thin grey line, there were waves and waves of blue ones rising up, well armed and shod, rested and fresh. Poor Stephen, he'd missed the morning glory of the war; now the afternoon with its lengthening shadows could bring but one final dark answer.

"You don't mean what you are saying."

"Forget it. My part now is to harass the Union fleet and undermine the confidence of the men who've been marooned on this easy island. And Button-boy, you're going to help me."

"Beau, I don't think you should put too much on Button. He had a terrible accident. His head—"

"My head is fine. Don't be mean, Angelica."

"We are the last two Berrien musketeers, Angel. He can be a great help, now that he's stopped sucking his thumb. Make a check on the guards outside, Button."

Maum Hannah led Masai into the room. Beau stood

up at once to greet the giant, who gently ran his enormous, sensitive hands from the top of Beau's silk hat all over his face, down his neck, across his chest then cradled him in his arms. His mouth was working. Tears covered his cheeks.

Maum Hannah loosened his arms. "Le' he go now, Masai. Him and Miss Angel gots private business."

Masai stood back, bowed respectfully and obediently put his hand on Maum Hannah's shoulder.

"Master," she said as they left, "'fore God, take care of yourself. I hates to bring you bad news but Pharaoh been on the Street last night. Him seen the white horse. I feared him took the word to the town."

"Oh, don't worry about Pharaoh." Beau airily blew a cloud of cigar smoke in my direction. "I've always been able to outsmart him. Even when we were babies."

Button reported that the guards were sitting on the bluff throwing oyster shells into the water. They appeared to be settled there until sunset.

"Then you must create a diversionary action." Beau was all excitement and keenness. "This will be our first mission together. While you keep the soldiers' attention away from the bluff I'll sneak down to the beach and make my way to the cave. You're positive it's in the same old place?"

"Right under Dolphin Head. The entrance is covered with myrtles. A trail of red berries goes across them. I'll ride over on my pony. But what about that white horse?"

"I'll return for him after dark. Tom is to meet me near the mouth of Crooked Creek with a flat-boat and take us over the deep water. I'm due at Pocotaligo tomorrow."

"I can't imagine Teaser standing still in a boat."

"He's been in shakier standing places than that. He's never let me down."

"Suppose Tom isn't at Crooked Creek, will you come back here?"

"I'll hide in the marsh overnight. Button can ride

along the creek tomorrow with some food, just in case."

"Let me."

"No. You must carry on here as you always do. Get on with your diversion, Button."

I helped Beau take off his robe and put back on his worn uniform. We talked in whispers, though no one could possibly hear us in our bedroom. Not with all that pistol shooting going on outside.

"Send a note every day by Button to the cave. Pick Pierce for news. Play up to him, keep his confidence. But if he ever lays a finger on you I'll kill him."

I knew better than to tell the truth. "He would like to," I said coquettishly.

Relieved, Beau laughed. "Thank the Lord nobody ever found Papa's will. Wouldn't it be horrible if the Lincolnites *did* win the war and old Pierce *did* have a legal claim on Cotton Hall!"

"Organizing a shooting contest was clever of you, Button."

"The soldiers were glad for anything to pass the time."

"Did you take part?"

"I won."

"What did you offer for a prize this time?"

"Well, as I was going out of Bubba's office I saw that ugly hawk of Papa's ..."

My fingers crumpled the page I was turning. "But you won. Where is the hawk?"

"Nowhere. After I won the target practice I told one of the men to throw it up and I'd hit it flying. It's already dead, you know."

"And the stuffing?"

"What stuffing?"

I wanted to scream: stop turning the screw! "The insides," I said impatiently.

"Oh those! I pretended the hawk was Papa. That's why I shot so well. I hit it the first time the soldier threw it and blew it to smithereens. The scraps of paper and the feathers just blew away in the wind."

Cotton Hall was safe! That thought plus the memory of last night made me feel wonderful all over.

As soon as it was quite dark we went to bed, Button and I, knowing Beau was somewhere out there waiting for a chance to slip Teaser out of the stable and steal away. He insisted on our following our usual routine. We didn't know whether there were extra guards or not that night. Did Beau leave while the lamps still burned, or later when we slept? We did not hear him. The stall was empty when Button went out to feed his chickens. Only my singing heart was proof that Beau had been here at all.

Forty-eight

Frederick's possessiveness increased. He could not leave me alone. He wangled permission from General Hunter to bring me to the theatre in the town. His enthusiasm was dashed when I refused to go with him to see *The Spectre Bridegroom* in the new theatre.

He procured Miss Suzy back from General Hunter, whose wife had been bucked off on her first ride. He planned gallops for us around the island together. I told him we didn't have enough feed for a thoroughbred.

Then came precious oats and hay, which I accepted gladly to treat my precious Teaser when he came, unexpectedly. Miss Suzy could do with corn and fodder. She wouldn't buck so much.

Frederick picked up some field hands who had been rejected by the officers recruiting 5,000 Negroes for General Saxton's South Carolina Volunteers. "All you need do is pay them the going U.S. wage of $1 an acre for the crop they cultivate."

At that time I think he really cared. Or he was so enraged with Livia's having tricked him and bought the Beaufort house he wanted to make sure Cotton Hall didn't continue so neglected. Because after the war——

I refuse to think things like that.

If he did care, with me it was the opposite. I was afraid of him; he gave me the shivers. But I could not refuse his offerings nor his help, not with Beau heading the list of "most wanted Confederate officers" to be shot on sight, not taken prisoner.

So I opened, in his presence, the bolts of silk and organdie and cards of fine lace and thanked him. As soon as he left I tossed them in the corner of one of the downstairs water closets.

I puzzled Maum Hannah and Maybelle and Button, being in such high spirits. I sang all the time. I couldn't help it. I was so in love that nothing else seemed important. Certainly not Frederick Pierce nor his foolish gifts.

Every time I noticed his horse at the hitching post, or that Button warned me he was walking up the bluff from the dock, I would make a face and stamp my foot, then invite him to take a cup of tea with far too many airs.

That Button insisted on staying in the room with us annoyed Frederick but it did not lessen his visits. He would rattle his teacup and act sullen. Sometimes it took me the whole tea time to get a smile out of him and a bit of information that might interest Beau. He tried all sorts of ways to get rid of Button. Once, knowing his concern for animals, he did manage to lure him outside, by asking him to pick a painful stone out of his horse's hoof. That night when Maybelle unbuttoned my camisole she saw an ugly red mark on the white of my breast. She scolded Button for leaving me, telling him that Frederick pinched my shoulder and hurt me.

After that I made a point of wearing my shabbiest clothes and messing up my hair, but even then Maybelle said I'd never looked prettier nor livelier. But it was as though I was so overflowing with happiness I didn't care who it splashed on, the squawking parrot or Frederick. What difference?

The change in me evidently made Frederick more suspicious or else he misunderstood me. Hans told Button that often Frederick would say goodbye and pretend to leave then steal back and stand in the shadows, smoking his pipe, watching the house, until the candle expired in my room.

One morning in mid-February I jumped out of bed as usual then had to lie back down quickly. The room was flying around. I was deathly nauseated. Button flew for Maum Hannah. By the time she arrived I was feeling all right. After a few crisp questions and answers, we joined hands and skipped around. I was carrying Beau's baby! I was the most blessed woman in the world. Nothing in heaven or on earth could dim my joy. Or so I thought that morning.

After dinner Frederick came with an ostrich-feather fan on exquisite mother-of-pearl sticks from Tiffany and Co. in New York. Giggling, I was fanning myself when I heard him reminding me of my promise to accompany him to the ball in Beaufort on February 24th in honor of General Saxton's fine new entertainment hall.

"She can't go to a ball with anybody but her husband," Button said.

Frederick glared at him. I was feeling squeamish. I asked Button to hurry Anatole with the tea. Reluctantly he went out. Frederick quizzed me curiously.

"You must," he said quietly, but with an undertone of violence. "I have permission from General Hunter for you to leave the plantation in my care."

I was horrified even though I knew he thought he was giving me a pleasure.

"Beau is old-fashioned," I answered, "he might divorce me."

"Ahh," his beautiful mouth curved up at the corners. "Then I'd abandon my hunt for him. I'll call for you about four that afternoon in a carriage. We'll go up to Beaufort in the *Courier*. Many officers and their wives will be along. Don't worry, we won't be alone."

Button fetched the tea tray himself and poured the tea. I kept fanning, the queasiness continuing. It was all I could do to nod and get a few sips down.

Soon after Frederick left I sent Button to the cave with a note to Beau. I wrote URGENT on the envelope.

Two days later Button fetched an answer:

A—
By all means go the ball, you can pick up vital information. We will attack the pickets at several points

during the affair. Take a hatpin along. Use it if necessary. By the way, what is *your* 'special news'? Mine is that I adore you.

B

"Did you see anybody in the cave?"

"Ephraim and five others. They are going after the battery on Pinckney Island tonight."

"Only six men?"

"There are lots more hiding in Crooked Creek. Ephraim said Bubba has put new life into them, gotten them all pepped up."

He saddled Miss Suzy and his pony. We made our way up and down the creek. We saw nothing but bald eagles soaring and snakebirds and herons in the marsh.

The guards spoke rudely to me when we returned. "Where have you been?"

"Did you think I'd escaped?" I asked coldly.

"We'd get it in the neck if you had."

Why had I done such a foolish thing? Now they would be more vigilant than ever.

Forty-nine

Frederick announced his arrival, beating with his fist on the front door. Maum Hannah let him in. Grumbling she told me to take my time, she didn't like the way he was behaving; no-manners and short-patience. Couldn't I plead a chill or a fever?

"The Master thinks I should go to the ball, so go I will."

"Master ain't no know-all."

I was wearing the red velvet. Maybelle had fixed my hair as unbecomingly as possible, drawn skin-tight away from my forehead and wound into a severe knot on the back of my head.

"Your Greek coiffure exhibits your profile to perfection!" Frederick's eyes shone as he bowed and clicked his heels. "Wear the sable coat. The wind on the water will be cold at midnight."

"You and Masai sit here in the hall with the lamps burning until I get back," I commanded a frowning Maum Hannah.

Frederick drove a skittish mare to a little one-seated buggy much too fast over the sandy road. I kept falling over against him. Thank heavens officers and schoolteachers who lived at Pope's and Seabrook's and Myrtle Bank and Honey Horn were waiting on the dock for the island steamer to come from the town to pick them up.

Frederick kept me apart from them, enjoying their stares and their low-voiced comments. "It's the Southern lady who stayed behind on the island when all her kind ran away. Nobody knows why for sure. They say . . ."

The steamer was almost full of party-goers from the town when we crowded aboard. They stood around the deck, those high-ranking, gold-epauletted and medalled majors and colonels and brigadier-generals and admirals and commanders with their hoop-skirted wives and daughters, who knew Frederick, waiting for his reaction to their raised eyebrows. He laughed. They laughed. I tried to laugh. But I knew what they were thinking. Their slyly exchanged nudges and those eyebrows betrayed them.

I was stiff with embarrassment. Frederick smoked constantly but talked very little. As we entered the hall he said, "Remember, don't tell anyone your husband is in the Rebel army. I didn't realize you would create so much curiosity. But I might have known. Your beauty puts out everyone else in the room. All the women hate you."

Regulations permitted only a very few women in the Beaufort area but tonight was special. Officers had brought their guests in all available carriages and in canvas-topped field ambulances and, from the islands, in barges. Thank heavens I wouldn't have to squeeze in one of those with Frederick going home.

The hall was so brand-new it smelled as if it had just come from the sawmill. It was decorated with United States flags and bunting and garlands of smilax and cedar. In front of the boxes, where generals and admirals nodded and clapped white-gloved hands, a Zouave unit in full colorful regalia stood at attention with bayonetted rifles.

The boxes were furnished with handsome high-backed mahogany dining room chairs from Dr. Fuller's house on the bay. Ponderous satin and velvet and horsehair-covered sofas from plundered parlors lined the flag-draped walls. A pair of matched crystal gas chandeliers from the Elliott house illuminated the center; hanging oil lamps went the rest of the way up and down the red, white and blue ceiling.

It had been so long since I'd been at a ball my feet began involuntarily tapping time as the band played reels and polkas, schottisches, lancers and waltzes. The officers, stiff at the waist with their gold sword sashes, bowed to their partners and led them to the floor, highly polished with powdered wax. The women wore low-cut gowns, their hair either in layers on top of their head with little corkscrew curls at their temples, or swept back into hanging snoods held in place with plumes and flowers. Imitating pictures of Southern ladies they danced with their fashionable heads tilted. They even fanned themselves flirtatiously between numbers.

My Yankee lady friend of Christmas, the one with the high, coppery pompadour, came up and took my hand in hers. She led me up and down in front of the boxes, introducing me as her friend. That allayed some of the chill I felt toward me in the atmosphere.

"Would you like to go somewhere and sit down? You look like death . . ."

"No. I'm all right." The morning sickness had overtaken me here, of all places.

"Why haven't you danced?" her husband asked.

Frederick said, "She's going to right now. Bully— it's a waltz." Away we swept, dipping, swaying, turning. I kept smiling desperately and he kept turning, as if he knew I was suffering and was getting an enormous thrill out of it.

The band played on and on, and the couples turned and postured and marched and skipped and I was a red velvet puppet with a smile painted on my face and the figure who was pulling my strings was a puppet too.

Several young officers asked to be presented to me but Frederick refused to share me with anybody. His white-gloved hand burned on my white-gloved hand but his face was cold and expressionless, except for his eyes, which saw something challenging ahead that reflected wickedly in their amber depths.

Shortly after supper, General Gillmore left his box; soon after him, General Saxton. The younger officers noticed and spoke in low voices of a rumor brought by Robert Smalls from Hilton Head that the Union army had suffered a bad defeat at Olustee, Florida.

General Saxton returned. He was pale and grim. He walked to the center of the hall and raised his gloved hand. We were dancing a rapid lancers. It took a minute for the band to hush and the last couple to stand still. Then he announced that the transport *Cosmopolitan* had just come upriver from Port

Royal Sound with 250 wounded aboard bringing them into hospital here. All conveyances were requisitioned. People would have to walk home or to their various docks. The ball was over.

Frederick had all sorts of threatening comments to make about Livia as we made our way in company with several other couples down to the main dock. I tried not to listen to him for now I *was* hearing things. Olustee, Florida, had been where the fight had taken place. The damned Rebels had won. Some of the fleet would go after them at daylight.

The tide was with us going back to Seabrook's Landing. It didn't take long. Frederick kept standing too close to me, pressing his arm in my side, upsetting me terribly.

It was midnight when we said goodbye to the ones who disembarked with us. I stiffened against any advances from him but I needn't have. He gave the mare such a cut with the buggy whip she bolted.

I've never witnessed such a fight between a man and a horse. She was strong and infuriated. He was strong and excited, enjoying cruelly tearing her mouth and jerking her head up and back until I was sure her neck was going to snap. When we reached Cotton Hall, she was so lathered and trembling she could hardly stand. Her head drooped, foam fell from her mouth, her sides heaved as if she were about to burst.

"And now, Madame . . ." He reached out his gloved hand to me. I panicked and started running up the stairsteps to the piazza. My foot caught in the hem of my dress. I tried to pitch forward but I stepped back into my train falling backward, straight into Frederick's arms. A scream rose in my throat, stifled by his soft sucking lips on mine.

I had seen how strong he was when he bested the mare. My cape fell off as he dragged me into the arcade under the piazza, I kicking and beating at him with my fists.

"I adore you. I will have you." His hand was under my chin pushing it up so hard I couldn't open my mouth. With one arm he prisoned both of mine behind me, mashing me against a tabby pillar of an arch. His body all the way against mine, he held me while he took off his right glove and began fumbling with the buttons of his trousers. I tried to lift my knee but his legs had mine powerless. We were the same height which made it all the easier for him.

He kept working with the flap of his trousers until it burst open. Then he began jerking up my dress and tearing at my drawers. I was fighting and struggling.

"Curse all these clothes," he hissed, pressing me harder. I couldn't move. The tabby column was crushing my back and shoulders, my thighs were paralyzed. I let myself go limp, sagging down onto the brick floor. He was on top of me in an instant. I was even more powerless against his brutality than I had been against the ocean wave. I was sobbing, moaning helplessly. I thought of the stallion approaching Bonnie Bet, his snorting breath, his wild eyes, his reared power.

As then, a voice snatched me to safety. A light blazed around us. "Colonel Pierce, Colonel Pierce. Where are you, Colonel Pierce?"

The brutal lust my struggling had intensified, shrivelled. The terrible mouth left mine. He scrambled up, pulling me with him.

"Don't scream. Stand in front of me. Pull down your skirt. I can't find my flap buttons."

Torches and surprised leering faces surrounded us.

"Colonel Pierce, we were sent here to tell you to return to headquarters immediately. A shipful of wounded has landed—oh, excuse us, sir, we'll wait for you on the other side of the house."

"The lady is ill. I was trying to pick her up. Don't you see she is ill?" His voice rasped hatefully. He mopped at my neck with a handkerchief. It came away all red. "She fell against the steps. Can't you see she is ill?"

"Quite obvious the lady is in distress, sir," the leader said sarcastically. "Here comes help for her."

I must have been in complete shock for I just

stood there blinking at their torches, hearing Maum Hannah telling Masai to pick me up and put me over his shoulder with one hand and take her shoulder with the other.

Frederick patted my head as Masai lifted me easily as if I had been a wounded fawn. "Poor Angelica," he whispered, "don't stop loving me."

I managed to whimper through bruised lips, "Don't you ever come near me again."

Maybelle and Maum Hannah put something that burned dreadfully on the bite on my throat and the scrapes and scratches on my shoulders. Tenderly Maybelle rubbed soothing ointments into my aching breasts and sore cheeks.

Maum Hannah undressed me like a baby. When she saw my torn drawers she got very quiet but after a little investigation she began to chuckle. "Ain't no harm been done to you, Miss Angel. Your crown ain't tear atall."

"I could have told you that." My words floated dreamily.

"We all gwine be berry careful neber tell Master." I'd die if Beau knew. He or Button.

Unaware of Button crying over by the fire I said, "Maybelle, my nose is beginning to feel funny. Is it broken?"

Maybelle was rubbing my aching back. "No. It's the opium. Just lie loose and give it a chance to take away all the pain and the remembrance of the ugly thing that went on. Just lie loose and easy, Miss Angel—loose and easy."

Part Seven

The Vision

September, 1864

Fifty

Today Button came in with a branch of purple berries and a burst pomegranate and I realized that autumn is here.

The baby will soon be born. Everybody watches me apprehensively. I am the only one who isn't concerned about not being able to summon a doctor in case of trouble. How could there be any trouble? I am too well and happy and the child so vigorous he fairly leaps with joy.

The past months have been full of joys, snatched but sweet. Beau has come often but since May we've had to be very watchful.

During the winter we grew careless. The sergeant who had saved me after the ball reported the incident to General Hunter, who sent a complaint to Washington about Frederick. Hunter and Frederick have been as vindictive toward each other as Hunter and Du Pont. The happening at Cotton Hall was a coup for Hunter.

Frederick went to Washington to defend himself and denounce Hunter and hasn't returned. I pray he never does.

As soon as Frederick left, General Hunter sent for Miss Suzy, his wife having learned to post, and he removed the guards Frederick had stationed around the house. That didn't mean we weren't under surveillance or that I could leave the plantation. The whole shoreline was picketed and patrolled from the town of Port Royal around to Ferry Point where Fort Mitchel has been appreciably strengthened, Confederate surprise attacks and batteries having become the usual, not the exceptional, occurrence.

Well, to go back to May and being careful: it was the night the wild swans swam on the ibis pond. Button had moved back upstairs to his old room with his cats. I took a hot bath and curled up in bed to read but it was no use.

I was too excited. Button had brought a letter from the cave telling me to leave the secret door to Beau's office unlocked that night. The wind from the sea was very loud. The tall pines swept the sky like brooms in a giant's hands. I looked at the clock and it said midnight. When I looked again it was nearly four so I lit a candle and waited for dawn, watching flecks of light and shadow beneath the live oaks.

I put on one of Beau's soft flannel night shirts and opened the shutters and sat down on the window seat and looked out over the sound. The silver water was lighter than the sky. I saw a pronged buck outlined. He was still as stone.

A sail boat was putting out. The sail caught the wind and the boat went away fast. The buck shot out like an arrow from a bow and went in flying leaps down the bluff. Then the first gull and more and more. At five-thirty I heard the sound of hoofs on the oyster shells. I ran to the washstand and splashed cold water on my face, put on my goblin hat and flew down into the garden. Beau was there—with Teaser standing quietly, both lathered with sweat and flecks of foam among the flowers. Such roses! Such lilies!

"I can't stay," he said, "but I had to see you today; to touch you. What is that under my hand? It feels like a little fish fluttering."

"He started moving last week."

"For God's sake take off that awful hat so I can kiss you properly."

"Can't you come in at all?"

"No. We are like the sun and the moon, meeting briefly only at dawn."

The sail boat was tacking in to shore fast.

"I'm afraid Pharaoh saw me as I emerged from the woods and rode along the beach. I don't dare stay. Go back to bed. You must keep my little fish safe."

"I love you!" As he vanished into the pine woods

I heard my voice trailing after him, lonely as a gull's cry. There had been something unusual about him. It worried me all morning.

In the middle of Button's music lesson I realized what it had been. He wasn't wearing a Confederate uniform! He had on one of his white linen suits and a black tophat. So that's why he dared cross Skull Creek in a flat-boat in daylight! He could have been any Yankee land speculator sniffing out a deserted plantation. Only Pharaoh would have recognized him; been a danger to him.

Soon after this, Maum Hannah reported that tales were going around among the Negroes about a phantom horseman who rode through cotton fields in the hot summer nights, dropping spell-dust for them to step in the next day. The old ones on our Street were convinced it was Old Master Hazzard's evil spirit. I suppose those on other plantations named it *their* "Old Master's" ghost.

Weeds began choking the crop all over the island, except for our pitiful little five acres, which Button and Israel and Maybelle, but not old Pompey and Toney, chopped. The wage hands Frederick had sent to me returned to Mitchelville, which was a real black town now, through which no tall white ghost on a tall white horse rode at owl-hoot time.

As summer heightened Beau began taking more foolish chances. One cruelly hot day in August he was sitting on the joggling-board smoking a cigar when General Hunter himself came to call. Beau jumped through an open window into the hall by the time the untidy general panted to the top step. I continued joggling placidly. When he noticed my condition his face grew very red. He knocked over a vase of gingerlilies on a little table, throwing his dusty, cockaded hat in the middle of it.

Flustering and blustering, he sat down in a split oak rocker. I offered him a glass of sangria from a silver pitcher by the bruised gingerlilies. He gulped it down and picked out the fruit with his stubby fingers.

"Do you know anything about somebody scaring the hell out of the cotton pickers on the island?"

"I have none. There could be no way of my knowing."

"When have you heard from Colonel—I mean—General Pierce?"

"When was he made a general?"

"Sometime this summer. I understand he's coming back here on his way to Atlanta where he will be attached to General William Tecumseh Sherman's staff. You are sure you haven't heard from him?"

I shook my head, smiling happily as the little fish gave a mighty kick and turned a somersault.

What was he saying? General Pierce outranked him now. His wife was enjoying Miss Suzy. She'd taught her to stand while they practiced pistol shooting on the beach. He hoped General Pierce wouldn't be as surprised to see me as he——

He thought I was pregnant by Frederick! How hateful of him.

I can't abide vulgar men. I rose, asked him to excuse me and swept, waddled rather, into the hall.

Beau and I peeped through the window to make sure he left. General Hunter said something to his orderly as he mounted, then rode away shaking with laughter. I prayed the little fish would be safely born and I slim as a willow when Frederick *did* return.

That was a whole month ago. Apparently Frederick decided not to put himself through the torture of a Hilton Head September and is somewhere in the north of Georgia. This has been a strange day for the end of September. Perhaps we are going to have a hurricane. If we do I hope Beau is marooned at Cotton Hall. He's sent word to leave the secret door unlocked. Maum Hannah says weather can bring a baby as well as the full moon. There are only two guards today. They are sitting under the palmettos on the bluff hoping a sea breeze will blow.

But it won't. Not today. It's a hazy day. The haze is so dense that I can look at the sun as easily as I can look at the moon. The sun appears a pale green, approaching blue, color. His edge is perfectly defined and his rays cast no sensible shadows. Maum Hannah calls it a devil-day because on days when he can't cast a shadow to trip him up the devil walks abroad.

Suddenly, I craved the luscious seed of the ripe pomegranate Button brought in earlier. I must eat it at once. It was on the silver waiter on the big sideboard in the dining room.

Button was in the office cleaning Beau's 12-gauge shotgun and his rifle. He tried so hard to be a man. Sometimes he looked blotchy and had dark circles under his eyes after a day picking cotton in the hot sun. He was too young to work as hard as he did.

"Button! Come and share the pomegranate with me."

"I don't like pomegranates. I'll run out and pick some figs for us when I finish this gun. That late tree that has those big purple ones is full," he called back.

Pomegranates aren't easy to eat. I was picking out the lucent little coral-colored seeds and popping them into my mouth when I heard the front door open and shut. Button must have gone for the figs. As soon as I finished the pomegranate I'd fetch some fresh cream from the dairy to pour over the figs.

"Are you in the dining room, Angelica?"

I'd prayed every night to dear God never to hear that voice again.

"Angelica, is that you over by the sideboard?"

I shrank back in horror. Instead of the cool polished wood, I felt those cold bricks against me, heard the beast panting, saw his face.

I shook my head. "No," I gasped. "No."

He held out his hand and touched my arm. "Oh, come now. Surely you've forgiven me. I swear to you . . ." He paused, his hand still touching my sleeve. His fingers tightened on my arm. He pulled me away from the sideboard. "I can't believe it." He bent toward me, his beautiful cruel face close, his animal eyes questioning mine.

My arm was numb from the pressure of his fingers.

His lips were drawing back from his teeth. There were red patches on his cheeks.

I had to get away from him. I had to get out of this dark, deserted room. With the windows closed and the blinds fastened I could hear nothing outside. Nobody could hear me. Button at the fig tree would never hear me.

Frederick was smiling now. His smile was an unnatural smile, more like a snarl.

I knew I should humor him; not force him into sudden violence. I kept swallowing and digging my nails into my hands. "Let's go into the hall. I'll fix us some tea." My voice sounded shrill and false. Somebody else's voice.

As though I hadn't spoken he continued standing there staring at me.

Like a bird looking at a snake I couldn't take my eyes away from his eyes. How shining they were in that perfect face of his, how evil, how full of hate. I gave my arm a jerk. It was a mistake.

"Whore!" he screamed. "Strumpet! I'll kill you and it!" His hands closed around my throat. The little fish began struggling frantically to get out. Or was that me? I was choking, my head was pounding with blood: my eyes were bursting. For a wild instant I thought I saw Button standing in the door pointing Beau's rifle. And then my head exploded and Frederick Pierce pitched forward against me and fell in his blood at my feet.

Fifty-one

Blood was soaking through my sewn-on, pink linen slippers and oozing between my toes. The back of Frederick's head was gone. I gently pulled my feet from under his face and stumbled out of the room, past Button in the doorway with the rifle still pointed. I didn't speak or ask any questions. I hardly noticed his open mouth and surprised eyes. Bumping into sofas and chairs I reached the piano and felt my way along it, trying to get to the door leading into Beau's office. I would be safe in Beau's office. I could shut the door and hide in there from the hideousness of Frederick.

I got as far as the long seed table when the first grinding pain caught me, twisting me into an unloosable knot. Moaning, I clutched the table and bent over it laying my face on the cool pine surface.

Then, suddenly, as though a candle had been blown, the fiery pain went out of me. I straightened up and turned to see Button.

"He's dead. All dead. He can't ever hurt you again. I killed him."

I don't think I really heard what he was saying but comprehension of what had happened was trickling into my mind. And with it came weakness and terror. Everything was too loud and bright. Outside a loud wind was blowing from the sound, and the sky was a bright dazzle and the garden all flying green and gold. Little yellow butterflies were flittering everywhere. The pines were making such a soughing nothing could be heard above them. Had the shot been heard out there? Was Hans out there? I must act immediately to deliver us all from evil. But I could only moan as the iron agony caught me again.

"You aren't mad at me, are you, Angelica?"

Button was patting my hand. His cheek was

333

pressed against my bare arm. An overpowering sense of gratitude swept through me, bringing a temporary ease.

"Mad at you? Mad at my darling brave precious Button? You've saved my life and the baby's life. You are the bravest boy in the whole world."

"Oh, I didn't mind shooting him at all. You're squeezing my hand too tight though."

"Darling, can you keep on being a man till Bubba gets here?"

"The first thing we've got to do is get rid of him."

Button spoke as coolly as though he had just killed a rattlesnake, not a living human being. I was the one who had panicked. Now I must think clearly before another deeper contraction came.

"We can't move him by ourselves. Where is Hans?"

"He's down on the dock crabbing. He'll help. He hates Frederick."

"We can't put him in that position. First, get your pony and lead Frederick's horse to the big road. Hit him hard and head him toward his stable."

I made my way into my boudoir. Maybelle was mending a petticoat. She took one look at me, ran to the open window and yelled, "Go to the sick house for your things, Maum Hannah. Leave the baby for Aunt Hecuba to mind. Miss Angel got's blood all over she foots."

"It's not my blood."

I was breathing rapidly, almost panting. It seemed to make the pain go away faster. I told Maybelle what had happened. I told her to get Israel and Masai to bring—him—into the office so we could hide him. Thank the Lord Anatole was picking peas in the garden and hadn't heard.

"Masai and Israel gone in the ox-cart after that old sow what they think done had pigs in the broom sedge."

"Then we'll have to do it ourselves. Find a rope and something to wrap his head in so he won't bleed all over the hall."

At first Maybelle wouldn't let me help. By the time Button returned from loosing the horse I couldn't

help. It was all I could do to grope my way back
to the office, get a bottle of ink and pour it over
the blood stains on the dining room rug. At least it
would confuse Anatole. I tried not to watch as Maybelle and Button dragged Frederick into the office,
pulling and pushing and bumping against things with
thuds that sounded like explosions. Surely Hans
could hear them and Maybelle's grunts down at the
dock even with the wild September wind in his
ears.

Every now and then Button cried out as the rope cut
into his flesh. Maybelle kept calling on Jesus to help.
Finally the thing that had been Frederick was on the
floor behind Beau's desk and the door locked into
the hall. The pains were coming too fast. The little
fish was in a frenzy to get out. Soon I was going to
be forced to scream.

"Tell Hans that Frederick's horse is gone, then go
quickly to the cave and send whoever is there for
Beau. Tell him I'm dying. O-oh Oooh—"

"What if nobody is there?"

"Wait till somebody comes——"

"What if it gets to be night?"

Button's manhood was ebbing. A very frightened little boy was standing beside me.

Maybelle said softly, "Jesus take the care of you,
Buttons. Can't you see Miss Angel getting ready to
born us baby? You best make big haste."

His eyes lighted up with excitement. "Really?
Gosh, I'll get rid of Hans in no time and hurry to
the cave. Oh, Angel—make it a girl. I'll be awful
jealous if it's a boy."

Fifty-two

Have mercy on me, Lord, I moaned, listening to myself mewing like a cat.

Night had come warm and starry. I was sitting in the wicker birthing chair by an open window in my bedroom. Why didn't Beau come? Was Frederick still in the office? Had Button lost his way?

Open me, Lord. Let the whirlwind out. It is killing me.

"Here, Miss Angel, puff on my pipe awhile," Maum Hannah said soothingly. "You needs it more than me."

"I don't like tobacco." I turned my face away so she wouldn't see my tears.

" 'Tain't baccy. 'Twill ease you to go outside yourself and watch awhile. You is borning too hard and too swift."

Maum Hannah was sitting beside me holding my hand. Maybelle was on the floor with kettles and basins and rags waiting to help me when the time came.

I clamped my teeth on the reed stem of the corncob pipe and drew in a mouthful of pungent smoke. The taste was heavy and rich. After a few puffs the smoke mellowed pleasantly. I tried to smile but I could feel my upper lip twist into something that must resemble a growl. I hated myself. Why did I have to be doomed to struggle forever and ever. Why?

I knew I must get hold of myself; help myself. I made an effort. "What is in the pipe?"

"Hemp, Liney called it. I calls it grass. It grows on the ditch bank back of the sick house. Old Master planted it for a 'speriment. I found it one day out hunting some Life Everlasting, which is the color of silber but has a kind of 'baccy flavor. I couldn't find no Life Everlasting but this had the same little dried-up blade what crumbles good so I done a 'speriment my own self. I likes it. It do help."

I finished one pipe and frantically began another. Beau hadn't come but I wasn't worried any more. Everything was going to be all right. *All* right—right —right.

Long before the child was born I saw him with a ring of light aureoling his flame-colored head. So beautiful he was, my little love. Playfully I blew smoke in his direction and tried to tell him that I forgave him for hurting me so terribly.

All through the final agony I held on to my vision, that is, until I heard quick footsteps which my heart recognized before I did. The footsteps came to a stop. The slam of the door softened my scream and the Voice I craved to hear above any sound in the world called my name.

The vision was kneeling down beside me kissing my cheek, taking the pipe from my clutching fingers, cradling me in his arms.

"Push, Miss Angel," Maybelle said loudly. "Push hard."

"Gimme the pipe, Master. You sho you wants to stay in here, Master?"

"Of course I'll stay, old woman."

I kept trying to tell Beau that I'd already had the baby. I'd seen him. He was perfect. I was terribly excited and wanted to share the vision that was so overwhelming the whole room was filled with it. I tried to speak but a tornado was inside of me rushing me into a hellish black tunnel where I felt my whole life pulled out of me in a gush, taking the pain and torment with it, leaving me bathed in a blissful pool of peace.

Someone picked me up in strong arms and carried me to the bed. Smiling I nestled down in the feathery softness and closed my eyes to sleep. I was so very tired.

But they wouldn't let me sleep. "Angelica! Angelical!" Beau was standing by the bed holding a bundle of white flannel in his arms. A candle burned brightly on the bedside table. Everything was unusually clear and distinct. I could see the deep lines gashed down the sides of Beau's mouth, the tears on his cheeks, his proud eyes. His hair was not as fiery as usual. It had too much silver streaked in it. His voice was too tender to bear.

"It's time for you to welcome our son, darling." He bent down, to show me what was in the bundle. I saw a tiny round head covered with wet black hair, a gaping little mouth and a tight red fist beating the air and I knew I loved him but——

Startled, I sat up, crying out, "This isn't the baby I saw. He had red hair. He shone——"

"That were Master you seen," Maum Hannah laughed, wiping my face with a cloth soaked in eau de cologne. "All the time you been talking so wild about your vision you was looking right straight in Master's eye."

I laughed hoarsely, reaching out for the wriggling, warm little bundle. As my hand came in contact with Beau's bare wrist the familiar fire shot through me and I felt madly intoxicated and full and rich and foolish.

"Wonder what Teaser will think of him?" I croaked, feasting my eyes on the baby who seemed made of red velvet, lusciously soft. His face was all wrinkled with a big nose and tight-shut eyes. I hoped they would be goldy-brown like Beau's.

I couldn't believe the look on Beau's face. It was so full of sweetness and sorrow and pride.

"I had no idea," he said humbly, "the baby would affect me as he has. I thought I was accustomed to boy babies being born at Cotton Hall. But this one —Oh Angelica—Edward is our true climax."

"But the child in my dream was named Baynard."

"This one is Edward. Please, Angelica."

At that moment I loved Beau so much I wanted to shout and dance and throw roses up into the air. I was consumed with fulfillment and ecstasy.

A timid knock and the door slowly opened.

"Buttons," called Maybelle, "look what us got."

"Ah, D'Artagnan!" Beau put his arm around Button, "Say howdy to our littlest musketeer. What do you make of him?"

Button was trying hard not to be jealous.

The baby made a dreadful face.

"He looks like me," Button said gallantly.

"How do you know, silly?"

"When he opens his eyes they will be just like mine and *le petit géant's.*"

Beau turned to Maum Hannah. "Are you sure Miss Angel is all right. What was in that pipe? She seems——"

"Sho. Sho. Hit was the pipe help her out. She's full of dreams but I got a bucket of cobwebs here to use if she bleed much again. She were a big boy him and come too quick."

A screech owl quavered shrilly in a near pine.

"Go, Master," Maum Hannah was shifting herself from foot to foot in time with the screeches. "Dat been a deat' owl, him."

Far in the night I woke. All the happenings had gone back in their proper places. Lying on my side in the big bed, the room dark except for a candle flickering over by the window, I heard Maum Hannah crooning to the baby in the cradle.

I waited, my crazy heart thumping unevenly. Beau was in my boudoir talking to Israel. He had gotten rid of Frederick forever. "Maum Hannah, bring Edward to me."

I was suckling the little fish, serene as a clear sky after a heavy thunderstorm when Beau came in to me.

His fingers caressed my sore throat. They were trembling. I looked up. His magnificent face in the upglow of the flame was exalté as though he were touching the true grail. I hoped I wasn't going to cry. "Beau, darling——" I reached up my hand to touch his face.

He pressed my fingers to his lips. "Gawd," he said shakily, "look at that boy go! Just six hours old and already drinking like Billybedamn."

After that there fell a very deep silence. Beau took off his shabby grey shirt and hung it in the window, then he said I looked better. He sat down on the bed and told me about what had happened with Frederick.

They wrapped him in a canvas sail Israel found in the boot room. Button keeping watch, they carried him down the bluff to the dock where Israel had moored the dugout canoe. Once as they slipped and slid down the steps, the body seemed to turn itself in their hands. It was as though he were alive, not dead, and he imagined Frederick's cruel fingers on my throat.

Ah, that was why I was so hoarse and croaky! Not from screaming; I hoped I hadn't screamed, except at the last, in front of Maum Hannah and Maybelle.

When Beau and Israel reached the landing the tide was still running in so they put Frederick down and crouched in the shadows. A good thing, for soon a patrol passed along the bluff. The patrol cast their flares down toward the landing, saw the empty canoe and went on their way.

As they were loading Frederick in the canoe, Israel's wrist gave way and they dropped him. The water pulled him down, swirling him under the dock. It made a hideous sound as he thumped against the piling. Beau jumped in, swam around under the dock until he found him. Israel tipped the canoe so he could roll Frederick in.

Just as they shoved off the patrol came by again.

"Get down, Master, I gots a big fish sack I'll throw over you."

"I lay there by that cold dead body and I was scared as hell, not of him, but of the danged patrol. They yelled down when they sighted the canoe. Israel stood up and yelled back. 'It's just Israel—trawling.' They told him to go ahead. Golly, but he rowed the hell out of that canoe with one hand and a stump."

Beau went over to the mantelpiece, found a cigar and paced up and down beside the bed, puffing jerkily.

As soon as it was safe he crawled out from under the smelly sack. They rowed to the middle of the sound. When they felt the tide turning they threw Frederick in. The tide started rushing out fast. Plenty of sharks were around. It was quite luminous with star-glow. Suddenly about 110 yards off a huge black shape rose from the water and sailed over 300 feet toward them. They could see its horns and its big pop eyes as it came down with a splash that almost submerged the canoe. Israel fell down in the bottom of the canoe, positive the devil himself had come for Frederick.

"What was it?"

"A devil-fish, a giant ray. I hope it didn't frighten away the sharks. I'm banking on them destroying the evidence."

My face was burning.

"Master!" Maum Hannah beckoned to Beau. He followed her out of the room. When he returned he bent over the bed and kissed me lightly, saying he must be gone before the sun caught him and burned his breeches. Maum Hannah wanted me to sleep. She was afraid I was getting feverish.

I wasn't, but I knew better than to urge him to stay until the dawning. "When will you be back?"

"In a few days at the most. It looks as if the Yankee fleet is on its way for another attack on Charleston. I have an appointment to waylay and harass them with 600 men near Edisto tomorrow."

"I'd forgotten about the war."

"It's just as well. We're in the dickens of a fix. Sherman has defeated Hood and occupied Atlanta; Memphis is captured; and General Sheridan has beaten the hell out of us in the Shenandoah Valley. Even the *Charleston Mercury* admits that four of our generals were killed there, three thousand of our soldiers taken prisoner and God knows how many dead. Stephen lost his right arm."

I cuddled Edward and pretended to shut my eyes, peeping at Beau through my lashes. He was fingering the fringe of the blue silk canopy.

"I shall hate leaving this pretty bed behind. It's been in the family over a hundred years."

My eyes flew open. "What do you mean?"

"As soon as I've finished on Edisto I will bring a barge big enough to carry you and Button and Maum Hannah and Maybelle and Israel and the babies over to where I'm headquartered."

"You don't mean for me to leave Cotton Hall after staying here this long?"

Beau began to button his shirt, his face grave, in an expression of deepest sadness. "Whether they find Pierce's body or don't find his body suspicion of his disappearance will fall on you and Button. Pierce's orderly knows he was here. When will my lady be able to rise, Maum Hannah?"

Maum Hannah limited herself to remarking that Miss Angel was no ordinary lady who must lie in bed for a month after borning a baby. Miss Angel could be up in three days. But the sooner the barge came the better. She had one of her bad feelings. It had started when the screech owl talked so ugly earlier in the night.

Beau sighed. He was completely exhausted. Maum Hannah stood watching him with a nervous air and finally said, "Make haste, Master, grass done start growing."

Fifty-three

What appeared from the window to be a whole battalion of blue cavalry dashed up to the front steps the next morning.

"Has General Pierce been here?"

"Yes, sir," Button replied smartly.

Maum Hannah and I were hiding behind the curtains of one of the open hall windows, listening, our hearts in our throats. But Button was nimbly explaining that the general had come and gone yesterday morning, not even informing his orderly.

Maum Hannah was even wiser. "Miss Angel, lemme put a tight dress on you. Saunter out there on the piazza and let um see your figure. That the soldier been ketch and save you last winter after the party."

Though unsteady on my legs I managed to walk out on the piazza. After a few good mornings I said, "General Pierce came but I was ill, so I didn't see him."

There was much head shaking and talking among the soldiers. The lieutenant in command motioned to them to spread out and ride everywhere—over my cosmos and Michaelmas daisies, through the broom sedge, around the ibis pond, down to the marsh, into the piney woods. Around mid-day they galloped off, leaving guards stationed by the front door.

Two afternoons later when we sighted more Yankees coming up our oyster-shell driveway we were better prepared for them. I was feigning broken bone fever. Maybelle had taken the cradle into my big water closet.

"Don't let him cry."

"Nome," she smiled, "I still gots plenty of milk."

The slatted shutters of my bedroom were closed

and a wet cloth soaked in camphor water on my fore-head when the same lieutenant and a captain insisted on coming in.

"Hit's ketching," Maum Hannah nodded pleasantly, "runs from one to anurra easy as skeeter bites."

The lieutenant's concern for me showed through his stiff politeness but the captain was suspicious and unfriendly. He had bushy blond hair and big round green eyes that bulged out. The island summer sun had not treated him kindly. There were red splotches across his handsome nose. He watched me closely while he asked many questions. To all of which I replied: "He was here but I was ill so he went away. That's all I know. That's all anybody here knows."

"How long did he remain in this house?"

"Button said he left at once when he couldn't see me. He didn't come back, did he, Maum Hannah?"

"Hanh? Who that come back?"

The glossy green eyes dismissed her scornfully. "Are you positive, Mrs. Berrien, that he didn't insist on visiting you in your bedroom and somebody stopped him?"

"Who could have stopped him? The boy? Maum Hannah?"

It was hard to hide the fear that was smothering me. My icy fingers were tearing the Mechlin lace on the sheet I was clutching at my throat. What was he going to ask next?

To my surprise he smiled sardonically and shrugged. "You don't object if we look over the house?"

"Certainly not."

He was curtly ordering the lieutenant to search the house when Edward started crying but hushed immediately.

"What is that?"

"Hit Button's she-cat having kittens up the stairs," Maum Hannah said quickly. "I show him to you."

The lieutenant left with her at once. The captain hoped I would be feeling better tomorrow, bowed and went into Beau's office. There must have been a dozen soldiers waiting in there. I could hear them opening closet doors, then going out and tramping around as they poked in rooms and closets and cabinets. Finally they left, carrying with them every bottle of wine that Anatole had not drunk from the cool room, and anything else they fancied. One had the branched candlestick that stood on the piano, another a basket of silver forks and spoons, others had tureens and waiters and crystal decanters and Dresden vases.

Had they not been on horseback they would probably have taken some of the pictures and furniture. It was sickening, not only because I hated to see Beau's lovely family treasures in their hands and know they would go up north and become heirlooms that would never be precious for them as for us, but also because I realized that they would not dare have done this without permission from higher up; ironically, too, that only Frederick had saved us from this these past three years.

They spread their loot on the grass before combing the grounds around the house. When they went swarming down the bluff toward the dock, Button put his arms around me and buried his face in my swollen breast, I not daring to go to my baby for ease. He nuzzled his head a little. I felt his tears soak through my cambric nightgown and I suffered for him. He was too young for this, far too young.

None of us could find the heart to talk. Maum Hannah sucked her teeth and shook her head while a shrill fretful little chant sifted eerily through her closed lips.

The sun was striking scarlet from west to north when the captain and his soldiers trudged back up the avenue. The captain knocked on my door and entered. I must have looked really ill, for he said quickly, "There is nothing wrong here," and went away at once taking all the soldiers, even the guards, with him.

"You should have accused him of stealing our things," Button fumed, after he'd assured himself *le petit géant* still hung, though askew, in the hall. "You should have fussed at him."

As if I dared! I must concentrate on restful sleep with my sweet baby at my breast, and pray that tomorrow Beau would bring a barge and take us safely away from here.

A week went by. I was beginning to feel almost as strong as usual. I forced myself not to sit on thorns. Maum Hannah made bundles of the most necessary things for the baby and me. Button wrapped the portrait of *le petit géant* in a quilt to take along with his calico mother-cat and a hat full of game chicken eggs. Maybelle and Israel and Billy Boy moved upstairs in the room next to Button so we could leave at a minute's notice.

One of Beau's scouts slipped in on the eighth evening bringing word that Beau would come in two nights.

"We will be ready," I said, flooded with relief and happiness.

Later that same night I had another visitor. Edward had finished his midnight supper and was back in his cradle, Maum Hannah snoring loudly on her pallet beside him.

It was a moonless night, very dark. I heard the door knob turn and the merest whisper of my name. The door was locked but whoever was on the other side did not want to knock and wake anyone but me. It must be Beau! I jumped out of bed and, not putting on my kimono, ran across the room and shot the bolt. The door opened and a man stepped in; a slender, snub-nosed, light-haired man.

"You shouldn't open your door like that."

I turned to run but he grabbed my arm and said softly, "It's Hans, Mrs. Berrien. I'm not going to hurt you but if you make a racket the guards will hear and come to investigate and find me and shoot me."

"Wait—I'll light a candle."

"No, don't make a light. I'm warning you so you'll know what to say when they come."

"Tell me quickly. What is it?"

"They've found General Pierce."

So this was the end. It had been bound to end

like this. I dropped down in a chair and the memory I had been trying to evade rushed back to me with so terrible a force that the whole room was filled with the hateful presence of Frederick.

"A Negro pilot named Pharaoh found his body washed up near the mouth of Fish Haul Creek. He must have drifted into the marsh. He was all tangled in a fish net and jammed under the prow of a boat. Pharaoh brought him to headquarters. He had been shot in the back of his head. They made me look at him. It was a dreadful sight."

Hans began to sob. Hard dry sobs. "He was a bad man. He used to beat me and steal my letters from home."

Somewhere out there in the night a dog began to howl—a prolonged wavery sad, sad, sad howl. I felt cold, so cold that I knew I should wrap something around myself. But I had not the strength to make the slightest movement. I just huddled in the chair with my arms crossed folded tight against my breast. My head was aching from the pounding of my heart or the terror and the dread of Frederick.

"You were brave to come here."

"You have been good to me, Mrs. Berrien. I'll never forgive myself for hurting Button. General Hunter says you are a spy and have killed a Union officer and that he will hang you, maybe even little Button. I came to beg you to go away; far away . . ."

"But Hans—"

"You think the house is unguarded but it isn't. Soldiers are everywhere out there."

"Will you be safe from them?"

"Mrs. Berrien, I am one of them."

He turned suddenly, pulled the door open and disappeared into the dark. I was startled by his quickness. I ran after him but he was already halfway across the hall.

"Thank you," I whispered as loud as I dared, but the dog's howl caught the sound up and I don't think Hans heard.

I went upstairs to Button at once. I was so weak I knelt down by the bed. He was sleeping in a tight ball with his mother-cat curled in the back of his neck. He waked easily, alert at once. He slid off the bed and squatted on the floor beside me.

"Has Bubba come?"

"No, Hans was here. Pharaoh found Frederick. They're saying I killed him. We've got to leave here immediately."

Button was quiet a minute, patting my shoulder as if I were his mother-cat. Then he began to pull his trousers over his nightshirt. "I'll go straight to the cave and see who is there. Maybe they've got a boat. It's our only hope."

"Don't take any chances. I'm frightened."

"Israel will come with me. You wake the others and be ready when we come back."

Israel must have been sleeping in his clothes. By the time I was at the foot of the steps he and Button were right behind me. "Guards are everywhere outside," I called softly to them as they slipped out of the secret door in Beau's office.

Now that they were gone I felt how still was the night with the first chill of autumn in the damp air. I made sure the blinds were drawn and pulled the curtains so no light would show. Then I lit a candle and sat down in front of my mirror with the dampness and cold clinging to me and the menacing darkness outside of the house closing in like a prison around me. My eyes were deep dark pools of fear and my face white as a spirit.

I felt Maybelle's soothing hands, cool and light, loosing my heavy braid of hair. She began brushing it and arranging it securely in a net. Then she helped me dress and holding hands we sat together on the rug in front of a new-lit fire, waiting for Button and Israel to return.

The day was warm with fog on the water and in the woods. Around mid-day General Hunter himself arrived, followed by a platoon of soldiers and our empty barouche, drawn by *my* matched bays. To complete the ugly picture, Pharaoh, in a splendid blue uniform, was perched on the driver's seat. His blue gums showed under his wide lips, lifted in an enormous gloating grin. I was on the piazza anxiously scanning the bluff for Button. He had been gone almost twelve hours.

I knew they had come for me. Beau was too late to save me, but I thanked the Lord for not letting Button be at home and Hans for warning me.

The freezing formalities over, I requested permission to be allowed to change into more suitable attire in which to ride to town. I took time to feed the baby. It might be late in the afternoon when I returned. Maybelle must nurse him in the meantime. If the soldiers came inside she must hide him.

Weeping and trembling so she could hardly fasten the closings, Maybelle helped me into the trim traveling suit and the severe bowler and veil I'd worn here as a bride.

I was strangely calm and almost relaxed. For I hadn't killed Frederick. So long as I kept to my story that he had left Cotton Hall by himself on horseback they could interrogate me and try to confuse me but they had no proof against me. Even so it took several flick-ups with my left foot behind on the trailing skirt and much concentration on how Aunt Dell would comport herself in a tumbril to face the blue horde restlessly waiting at the foot of the steps.

I might have carried the charade off had not Button galloped up on his pony just as General Hunter himself handed me into the barouche.

"Where are you going?" He was scratched and dirty, his pony almost foundered.

"Hah! a witness!" General Hunter straightened his cockaded hat over his unruly hair and motioned to his orderly to hold his horse. He put his hand in a fatherly way on Button's shoulder. "Well, my good man, you're just in time to tell your sister goodbye."

"You can't take her away, sir. She didn't do anything. I shot Frederick Pierce. He was trying to choke her. I——"

"Button—hush——" I sank back against the soiled cream velvet seat and closed my eyes as the world crashed down on me. My story had been fool-proof, but not Button-proof.

". . . in the dining room. You can see the blood stains under the ink stains we poured over it. I did it. You've got to leave her here with the baby. You've got to."

Dear Button; brave courageous foolish Button. He had destroyed me. I drooped, my head fell forward, too heavy for my neck.

Pharaoh was laughing so the bays began bucking and dancing. There was no use for me to say anything more. No use at all.

"Go in the house with the boy, Captain Prescott. Bring the baby to its mother. I'll arrange for it to be sent to a suitable home at once. Its father, the General, probably deserved to be shot but that's not the issue. Hurry, Captain, this is the best luck we've had in the case."

Unaware of what he'd done to me Button was talking rapidly to the green-eyed Captain Prescott as they ran up the steps. Unexpectedly the sun came out. I watched wisps of fog settle down on the water and listened to the flit and wail of killdeer plover and from the Street the untrue notes of a feeble flute.

Captain Prescott came back with nothing in his arms. I could breathe again! His spurs made jingle-jangles as impersonal as cathedral bells as he ran gracefully down the long steps and saluted General Hunter.

"Sir, the only baby in the house is a little nigger about a year old. He's sitting in a high chair banging away with a silver cup. Would that be the one, sir?"

"Hell no, Captain. I meant an infant."

The soldiers laughed and poked each other.

"Is the nigger one hers too?" one of them guffawed.

"Put that soldier under arrest," General Hunter barked. "Are you sure there is not a white baby in there?"

I leaned down and managed to gasp through clenched teeth, "General, the baby died."

That suited him just fine. One less item to bother with.

"Forward!" He lifted his gloved hand and went away fast, we bumping after them. He was a grand horseman. I don't think I ever saw a finer. I concentrated on watching the way he went up, down; up, down, in the rapid trot.

Near the ibis pond, seeming to rise up from the oyster shells, Maum Hannah and Masai were standing in the middle of the road. General Hunter jerked his horse to a stop. From the look on her face Maum Hannah intended to stand there and let him run over the two of them. It would give me a chance to jump out of the barouche and head for the woods. At least that's what I think was in her mind.

"Get out of the way, old woman." General Hunter was pointing his big shiny pistol at Masai, not at her. "I'll blow the head off that giant in one trigger pull. He might be able to lick me but he can't get away from having his head blown off by this. Move——"

She pulled Masai aside, shaking her fist and jumping around like a dervish as we passed by.

Button was running along beside the wheels.

"Angelica! Angelica! They won't believe I shot him. And Bubba said——"

He had seen Beau! A cloud of the October yellow butterflies flickered in front of my eyes. Through them I saw that Button had stopped in his tracks, his hand over his mouth, looking anxiously around. But apparently none of the soldiers had been paying attention to him. The word "Bubba" meant nothing to them. But it did to Pharaoh. And it made me alive again.

Pharaoh turned around. His face was impassive, his eyes hooded. He said, "Best set. I aims to keep closet to the General." He cut the bays with the whip.

Bracing myself I leaned forward to lessen the bounding jerk of the barouche as we passed the little temple in the woods, funereally draped in wet tatters of grey moss, desolate and forlorn, the great-armed live oaks dripping sadly over it. The sun hadn't penetrated here.

But wait . . . something was unsymmetric about the temple. Or had the flickering butterflies agitated my vision? There was one too many columns! I turned my eyes sideways without moving my head. It was not a distortion of vision. Beau was standing there —himself a tall grey column, motionless in the foggy forest scene. Strength poured back into me, pulling me up arrow-straight. I tossed my head arrogantly, waving my handkerchief in his direction as if I were chasing butterflies.

Fifty-four

The two stubby amazons, combination schoolteachers and nurses, my keepers, were garbed for the occasion in heavy black skirts and black taffeta shirtwaists, high in the neck, not a cheerful sight. They were waiting restlessly just outside my half-open door, talking loudly, unheeding the wounded men calling for water and mercy up and down the long hot hospital ward.

"So many have died in here lately that the death march isn't even played any more when they are taken to the cemetery. I wonder what the band will play today?"

"Maybe 'Dixie'," one giggled.

"The best bands are already in formation on Union Square in front of the gallows."

"Can you believe that thin blue dress she's wearing? If I had one like it I sure wouldn't get it messy at a hanging. I bet she'll flirt with the hangman and he'll forget to tighten the rope." More giggles.

"General Hunter was so spruced up when he gave Captain Prescott his final orders you'd of thought he was fixing for President Lincoln instead of just *her*."

"He was furious at that crowd standing around the hospital to watch her start off. He yelled at them to disperse but they didn't pay him any attention."

"It beats me how she can just sit there, like as if she was dressed up for a social, sort of smiling, looking at all them ugly seabirds flying."

"Southerners are different from us, like Chinamen. They don't have human feelings. Look how they treated the poor blacks all those years. Don't you remember what the Freedmen's Bureau told us about Southerners before we left Boston?"

"I can't wait to hear those bands playing. Imagine us being picked to ride in the carriage with her and the Captain! I just wish my mother could see me. She never believed I'd get this high in life."

Yesterday, after the kangaroo court where everybody except Admiral Dahlgren voted to hang me as a spy and a murderer, the guards walked me here through the prison, which is next door to the hospital. General Hunter ordered them to do this.

All that was raw and bare in the long double row of prison barracks beside the extensive, white-painted hospital quadrangle, was softened into picturesqueness in the misty light of late afternoon. Gulls and terns still wheeled and the ocean crashed foamily against the shore.

The guards were courteous and kindly as they walked me the length of one of the bare log buildings containing small windowless cells on each side no wider nor higher than I am tall, into which they said they locked 8 or 9 officers from dusk to dawn. The Johnnie Rebs slept together out on the naked floor. There wasn't a chair or a table, not even a wisp of straw for bedding.

"How do the prisoners keep warm?" I asked. "It was so cold last winter water froze the minute it was spilled on the floor."

"We felt sorry for them but what could we do? They kept themselves alive by running up and down all night to keep their circulation going. You could hear their pounding feet a long way off. We'll cross over to the other buildings now, then we'll get on to the hospital. You'll be taken care of there."

Postponing it as long as possible I dragged my feet between the prison buildings where men in filthy rags were squatting on the sand beside little holes in which scanty fires smoked. They were cooking their daily ration of one cup of cornmeal into a hoe cake to eat with a half a cup of onion pickles. Around one particular fire, six haggard-eyed ragged creatures hovered anxiously over a pair of wharf rats roasting on spitted sticks. They paid no attention to me, starved as they were for meat. The mean-eyed amazons were waiting to receive me at the hospital.

"Don't leave me here," I begged the guards whom I now considered my best friends.

"We must obey our orders, mam." Each took one of my hands as if I were a little child and led me into a long building full of dreadful smells.

"They'll take care of you, mam. They'd better."

"Who are you to tell us what to do?" my jailers shouted, jerking me away from the uneasy guards.

They were heavy and plump looking like pillows with their meager hair screwed up in straggly knots on top of their big heads. Their soiled white shirt-waists showed dark brown circles under their muscular arms.

They pulled me into a tiny bare cubicle holding a cot and a washstand. It had a little window, which was open to the ocean. I gulped in the sweet salt air.

They pointed at a blood stain on my shirt and shook their heads. I shook mine too. I was determined not to say the first word.

"We'll wait while you undress and wash yourself. There's water in the bucket."

"No," I said angrily.

"Then we'll do it for you."

They advanced simultaneously in quickstep. I undressed and forced myself to use the dirty lye soap and filthy rag that was beside the pail of cold sea water.

They watched, stared rather, with unfriendly mutterings, commenting on my long legs and slim hips. They touched my swollen breasts and laughed coarsely.

Naked and shivering, hating them, I stood before them while they laughed and looked. I suppose I would have been kept like that all night if a Negro woman hadn't come in with a voluminous white cotton sack with three holes cut in it.

"Your supper's ready," she said carelessly to the women, throwing the cool clean garment over my head and gently helping my arms find their way out.

"They got cow-meat and potatoes." Her eyes met mine flashing the message to me that she knew those two were up to no good.

"Beef! Let's hurry before it's all gone. Keep your eye on her, Cindy. She's a bad one." Their heavy footsteps running past the wounded in the room sounded iron hard.

Cindy closed the door. I stood by the window looking at the sunset and the red afterglow thinking tomorrow wouldn't be a good day for hunting and how sad Uncle Jim and Aunt Dell would be when they heard what had happened to me. I remembered one Christmas when I was six; I was leading my pony and he began running away. My thumb got caught in the rope and almost pulled off. It had hurt horribly.

"Not as much as if it had been your neck," a crowd of cormorants squawked as they flew past.

Later Cindy came softly with a bowl of milk and biscuits and sat on the floor and told me how her man had been whipped to death once over on Bull Island by the Obshay for killing a thoroughbred horse colt in the dark, mistaking its eyes for a deer's eyes. The deer wasn't to be for her and the children. Her man had been sent by the Obshay to kill the deer because the Obshay's wife wanted to make a liver pudding.

When Cindy left me she said kindly she was sure Jesus the Christ would forgive me for my sins and take me into heaven where I could sit with his mother, Mary, on the right hand because I was a real lady and would not be offensive like those common women who had the charge of me here. Woman Obshays, both of them.

I wanted to thank Cindy and I couldn't. I lay down on the cot and pulled my knees up close to my stomach. The darkness seemed to pulsate around me with the ocean waves that beat on the shore under the open window like my frightened heart. At times even the flimsy building seemed to shake to those beating pulsations. Thus I could almost hear the night passing. Now and then, in the ward, a wounded soldier screamed in pain.

Once, on the sand outside the open window, I heard

hoofbeats. And five shots in rapid succession. Pistol shots close by. Ought I go to the window and scream to Beau that this was an ambush? General Hunter knew, as surely as I did, that he would attempt to find me. He probably had soldiers hidden in the sea oats all along the beach. When Beau approached the hospital they would fire. Or—worse——they would capture him and hang him along with me.

I made an effort to rise, listening not only with my ears but with my whole body. There were no more shots. The ocean's pulse was regular and strong. There was only one thing to do. Pray. I began "Please take care of my little fish and poor dear Amun," whispering, as if it were into God's own ear; "and let me see Beau once more, just once more." I was careful not to ask the impossible: that I might be saved from death. That was too much to ask after what had happened. That was why I did not waste God's time with that. But if only I could see Beau again.

I must have babbled myself to sleep. For all at once it was daylight and outside my window a flock of ponderous pelicans were winging by.

How long did I sit by the window after breakfast waiting, praying, suffering? Three hours? Four? I lost all notion of time. It might be noon but also it might be nearly sunset. It was a warm overcast day so the sun could not tell me. And the waves had started booming louder and nearer. The tide must be high again. I heard an excited voice outside my door.

"Mrs. Berrien!"

Hans' voice! I started and walked on air, reaching the door just as it opened.

It was indeed Hans with a big cotton bag in his arms. I sensed his agitation and excitement as the stubby females said give them the bag and he said that the male nurse over by the bed in the corner asked him to send them over to help him.

Irritably they trotted off. Hans stepped quickly in and closed the door.

"There's a note for you pinned inside the sleeves.

Hurry, read it and hand it back to me to destroy."

We both snatched at the draw-string and tore the bag open.

The note was pinned inside one of the blue gauze angel sleeves:

When you walk out of the hospital door look around until you spot me. Sergeant Mueller has told me the plan. We must accomplish ours before you start for the Square. Give no sign until I am very close to you, then run to me like the devil. The red velvet dress makes my flesh crawl. This is your only other dress I could find that would leave you free to run and jump.

Half stupefied I returned the note to Hans. "How did they happen to send you?"

"General Hunter is smart enough to know that your servants are familiar with me and would let me in. They say he felt bad when you left the courtroom and he saw your skirt." Hans gesticulated to me to be quiet, never taking his eyes away from the door as footsteps came pattering. Abruptly Hans changed tone, "If what your servants sent is not suitable, Madame, you must take the matter up with General Hunter, not me. It's not my fault."

Fifty-five

I saw his proud aristocratic face the instant I stepped through the doorway onto the low-roofed walkway that went all around the hospital. Beau was directly across the white sand with the ominous, slick ocean undulating behind him.

He was wearing a white frock coat and loose white trousers strapped under black patent leather boots. A sky-blue cravat circled his high pointed collar and his tallest stovepipe hat was on his head. Teaser was making slow loping circles like a circus horse, plod-plump plod-plump, in figure eights in and out among the massed sensation seekers, on horseback and in buggies and standing in awed groups, waiting for the female spy-murderer to come out. Though the army and navy brass had filled up Union Square, the curious would have the first look and then they would follow the procession to the gallows.

Green-eyed Captain Prescott was waiting with a detachment of smartly groomed soldiers at the foot of the two steps from the porch to the sand. I listened carefully to the Captain's instructions, approving them with a nod.

"She's gone out of her mind. She's completely crazy," one of the amazons said to the other amazon. The scent of grease on her tight hair was drawing gnats and mosquitos. She let go my arm to slap at them.

And Beau kept cantering Teaser in and out among the horses and carriages and nearer and nearer until nobody noticed him any more than they did the pesky flying things accentuated by the humid atmosphere.

I was tensed to move the instant he gave me a sign. I was so exhilarated and excited my cheeks burned and my eyes sparkled.

"What's holding things up?" my left-side keeper snapped.

"The prisoners have set fire to the barracks. Can't you hear them yelling and screaming? They've just found out who she is and what's going to take place."

Captain Prescott lifted his hat to me. He looked very sad, not unfriendly at all. Just sad. "I must investigate the disturbance, Madame. Would you like to go back inside and sit down?"

"No. The fresh air is welcome."

He mounted, ordered the nice lieutenant who seemed to be his understudy to take charge here until he came back, and with four soldiers trotted away to put out the ragged wisps of frail smoke and silence the feeble banging of fire wood against the stockade wall.

Still keeping the same hypnotizing lazy lope, the next big circle brought Teaser right up to the hospital. Beau's left stirrup hung empty. His bright hawk eyes met mine. I jerked my left arm from the fat careless grasp, jumped down onto the sand, got my foot in the stirrup. Beau's arm was around me pulling me up behind him.

"Hold tight!"

Teaser was away like the wind. Everybody was shouting and screaming and wheeling their horses and getting-up their buggies to come after us.

"Put down your rifles," I heard the lieutenant yell. I looked back. He was waving his hat at me! I hope he saw me smile at him.

I buried my face in Beau's back and hugged him to keep from falling off as we galloped diagonally through the acres of tents, a path no one could follow through Mitchelville where drums began beating furiously to tell the pursuers we were going that way.

"Look back. Are they behind us?"

"Not yet."

"They will be in a minute. We've got to make a fast run on the main road."

I could see them now—a dark blue cloud rising up in the wet sandy road.

We turned abruptly into a dense growth of palmetto and tangled vines, stopped behind a massive moss-curtained live oak, and were instantly invisible.

"Don't make a sound."

Teaser's heavy breathing was lost in the wave of thundering hoofs passing.

"They're headed for Cotton Hall."

"Aren't we?" Now that my arms were around Beau I was wild to hold my baby too.

"No. We're going along the creek bank. Keep your face against me so thorns won't scratch your eyes out."

As we stumbled and slushed through muck and marsh canes a bull alligator roared, blue jays quarreled and a copper snake slithered between Teaser's back feet. Darkness was coming fast as it does this time of year. Fog fingers blew in and out of the trees and marsh as we ascended the bluff where going was easier.

"Where are we?"

"We're right at the old Drayton cotton landing. Look down."

A burning pine torch stuck in the mud showed a small barge. In it Maybelle was sitting with my baby. Button was holding Billy Boy and his mother-cat. Israel was talking to a wiry colored man in a ragged Confederate uniform who reached up for me.

Cudjo Manigo said he had been standing there for hours, his ears and eyes straining up the bluff, where shadow and light mingled but where he would know that it was Master there in the gloom and no one else, and whether it was safe or not, or whether he must shoot to kill.

I was so joyed at touching Edward and kissing Button and hugging Maybelle that I barely remember Beau telling Cudjo Manigo to take Teaser and ride like hell to Crooked Creek and hide until a flat-boat came to ferry them over to the mainland.

"Where is Maum Hannah?" I looked around the wet clearing expecting to see her emerge, grumbling at the mud, from behind a tree.

"Climb in, Angelica," Beau had taken time to light a cigar. He was untying the rope that bound the barge to the splintery landing.

"Not without Maum Hannah."

"Maum Hannah's doing something very important for me."

Maybelle pulled me down and threw an oil cloth square around my shoulders. "Maum Hannah doing things her way, Miss Angel. She say she ain't never set foot off Cotton Hall and she don't intent to start now. She tell me to say you and Masai been the all-two people she ever loveded bestest in the whole world and she sent you her charm to keep safe. Take it."

It was a funny wizened piece of root that resembled a human figure.

"It came from Africa with her mammy as a little girl."

Leave Maum Hannah? Well, I'd come back when the war was over and we'd all live happily ever after. Edward was soothing my aching breast but my heart was hurting with love and the hate and the sorrow that was in it.

Beau shoved us off and then climbed aboard. He and Israel secured their oars in the locks and we moved steadily and quietly up a wandering arm of Fish Haul Creek. As we neared the mouth of the creek there was a shout from the high bluff. I thought we were seen but no shot followed, no torch flared down toward us. As we approached the sound the mist on the water deepened. We could hardly see, or be seen, but we heard a familiar chuff-chuff-chuff.

"Dang! Not a soul knows about this piece of the creek and that old landing but me and Pharaoh. He must have found out we aren't at Cotton Hall."

"Master!" Pharaoh's voice floated through the mist. "He's spotted us."

The fog instead of thickening, suddenly lifted and we could see the little side wheel steamboat and, massed in the sound, gunboats and tugs bristling with guns.

"Pull into the marsh, Israel, Pharaoh's trying to swamp us."

They gave a mighty pull. We swept close in to shore as a battery above us sent a cannon ball whizzing down over our heads and an angry broadside from an alert small gunboat raked the water in front of us sending spray salt all over us and silhouetting us plainly against the canes.

The little steamer was in the creek, bearing down toward us, to run us down and drown us. Beau managed to turn the barge and the steamer passed so close we could see Pharaoh's eyeballs and big bared teeth shining. "I come to holp you, Master. Ketch this line I throwing out."

"Everybody get down," Beau shouted as Pharaoh's pistol exploded in our ears. Israel cried out in pain, and dropped his oar. Still holding the baby I leant forward and caught the oar before it was lost.

Beau rested his oar reaching for his pistol from a holster at his feet. The boat spun around, caught in a sudden eddy of current.

"Kill him for me, Master," Israel moaned.

The noise had brought more flares carried by men searching for us on foot and on horseback along the bluff. We were being shot at from all directions. We didn't have a chance now. Pharaoh was approaching us again, hollering and yelling, "I got you now. I got you now."

But he misjudged the distance. He passed by so close the oar I was holding made a rataplan against the rim of the side wheel.

Now he was caught in such a narrow place in the creek arm he was going to have to go a long way up to turn around. "He'll run aground in a minute," Beau said grimly. "I thought he had better sense than to come into this creek on the ebb tide. He can't swim. We're free of him until the tide turns."

"He want to kill you so bad, Master, sense don't specify," Maybelle said. She was holding her apron against Israel's head. "Gimme the baby, Miss Angel. Israel nick in he forehead. You best keep he oar. Blood blind he eye. But not bad hurt him."

Beau was struggling to get control of the barge. The tide was strong against us, running seaward. I could row better than Israel. Soon we were out in the sound but darkness had come so we were safe—until Pharaoh returned.

Button saw the first flames like devils' tongues leap from the watch tower on top of Cotton Hall, then, almost at once from all the chimneys, sparks came shooting as from giant Roman candles.

I heard Beau gasp, saw his features tighten and his face draw into a tragic mask. Button screamed. "Our house is on fire!" It was with a sense of shock that my mind cleared enough to hear what he was saying: "Poor house. Poor house. Poor house."

Beau said stoically, "I knew I could count on Maum Hannah."

"How could she—in such a hurry?"

"I poured kerosene and piled pitchpine all over the house last night. Button helped."

"You poor darling."

"Hush," he stormed, pulling hard on his oar. "Never let me hear you say that again. I am rich. I am happy. I am blessed." He threw his head back and gulped in a lungful of wet night air.

"What about all that gold in your desk?"

"Last night Cudjo and Israel and I dug holes and hid the gold and the best silver, especially the teapot."

"Where?"

"By the east column of the little temple in the forest. We scattered loam and pine straw so carefully the first rain will obliterate any trace we might have left. Don't worry. It'll be safe. If I die you and Button will know where to find it."

I fought off desolation and despair for him and for me. I willed the tears not to come, and my pity for him to stop and all my thoughts to vanish. I willed strength to come to my body so that I could pull harder, pull us away from that flaming pyre that was no longer our home, and from our island paradise, that was no longer paradise.

"For God's sake, Angelica, get in time with me. Let's sing—Blow down, you Blood Red Roses . . ."

"Not that, I hate that."

"All you pinks and posies . . ." Israel's voice was weak but true. "Up the river in wind and fog——"

"Blow down, you Blood Red Roses, blow down," Beau sang.

And now fate grew kind, lifting up from the water a fog, thick and low. It came down on us like a soft blanket of invisibility filling the boat like a bowl of warm milk. Yet Beau's high head was above it. He said he could see the stars and the shooting flames of Cotton Hall. If the rest of us kept low we couldn't be seen. He was a bodyless head, floating on the fog. He'd scare the bejesus out of anybody who saw him.

The western sky was illuminated by the fire and even the fog radiated droplets of pink and orange. The sound was full of craft. We could hear them. We mustn't sing any more because Pharaoh had got loose despite the tide and turned around and was pursuing us over the water. Listen to the little steam engine!

The fog thickened. Even the illumination of the fire vanished. We could see nothing, nor could anything see us. Once our oars scraped a tug that had run aground in the entrance to Broad River or Beaufort River, I couldn't tell which. Beau knew the water so well that even blinded by the fog he got across the confluence of the Broad and the Beaufort rivers and managed to hold to the bank of the Broad, which came clear at times. Once I dipped my blistered hand in the water to cool it.

"Don't do that," Beau snapped, "a shark is swimming beside the boat. He smells Israel's blood."

"I've got to rest a minute, Beau." It was my blood the shark was after. I was sitting in a pool of it.

Beau guided the boat over to the dark tree-tangled river bank and tied a rope to a low branch. I nursed the baby while he slept, waiting for the tide to turn.

The baby continued to fuss. He was hungry. I didn't have any milk. Maybelle unbuttoned her dress and gave him Billy Boy's supper. Button handed Billy

Boy a chicken leg he'd fetched in a flour sack of food. When he woke Beau ate some chicken and biscuits and drank a lot of rum out of a crock. I drank the rum but I couldn't swallow any food. I was too exhausted to keep it down.

When Beau and I settled ourselves to row again I discovered I had lost my oar. I must have loosened it from the lock when I reached for the baby. Beau tried paddling with one oar as if the barge were a canoe but we went around not forward. There was nothing to do but keep our direction with the oar and let the tide take us up river.

Would the night ever end? Would the fog ever lift? The water became rougher and swifter. We were knocked and buffeted about. Everybody was numb and the fog helped our numbness as a bright starlit night would not have done. We would just drift on and drift on and when day came and the tide turned again and took us back down stream we would face the Yankee fleet and it would be the end.

Beau couldn't decide whether in the fog we were drifting over toward Parris Island where a Yankee battery waited to blow us out of the water or, in our turning around, were we drifting toward the safe bank of the Broad River; or suppose we hit shore on St. Helena? We could be anywhere. Beau and I crouched side by side there in the fog blanket, sometimes holding hands, sometimes just touching each other, with thankfulness that we were together, and that the fog continued. Button and Billy Boy and the cat were asleep on the floor of the boat. Maybelle, holding Edward, and the wounded Israel clung silently to each other in the stern.

Once Beau muttered, "Why have you stopped singing? I wish you'd keep it up and get my thoughts off Cotton Hall and Frederick and those damned Yankees."

I started, low and trembly . . . "I know a lady sweet and kind." Beau commenced to hum the tune. Suddenly, not three feet away a voice challenged,

"What the devil? Are you deliberately trying to get that gunboat's attention?"

I hushed as though the devil himself had clamped my lips together.

"Who is it?" Beau's voice was hoarse. He was frightened too.

There was no reply. The heavy silence tortured and choked my throat. The only sound was the chuckling water rippling against the rocking boat.

"Who is it?" I called, my voice scarcely human in my terror.

"A lady, by gosh!"

"The dickens it is!"

Beau stood up. "It's Colonel Baynard Berrien and his family."

"Hold out an oar."

The flat-boat was right beside us. A shadowy figure reached out and caught Beau's oar, pulling us over.

"Dang! Tom, you old goat!" Beau shouted, as we touched the flat-boat for a minute. Then like a chimera of the fog it slipped past us and disappeared. But Tom Elliott's voice floated back, crisp and clear.

"We're poling around to throw a rope to you and pull you into shore. Sit very still and keep quiet. The river is full of sharks and Yankees."

Cudjo Manigo and Teaser were standing on the river bank when we came in.

"How the hell did you get here, you old scoundrel?" Beau grabbed Cudjo Manigo and they hugged each other while Teaser whinnied crossly.

"Us git tired waiting in them bushes and decide to swim across."

"It's a wonder the sharks didn't bite your legs off."

"Tried, but me and Teaser kept kicking them in the head. I mighty proud to see you safe, Master."

I hadn't the strength to stand.

Beau carried me in his arms up the magnolia-lined avenue to a pretty, wide white house at the end. It was morning. The fog had lifted up here and the light was bright. Three smiling gentlewomen were in the kitchen stirring a pot of hominy grits and peeling shrimp and beating eggs. When one of them said "You poor dear" to me I suddenly realized that this was the first Southern white lady's voice I'd heard in almost four years. And I began to cry uncontrollably and go to pieces.

Fifty-six

Now even Beau is convinced I will get well. I am lying in a hammock on the wide piazza of the Misses Lynah's house soaking up the October sunshine, feeling strength pouring back into me. Since my hemorrhage I have drunk so much beef tea and eaten so much hominy, with butter and blood squeezed from beef whipped up in it, that it's a wonder I haven't turned red all over.

Maybelle says the paleness becomes me more than the sunburn of summer did. She is wonderful. She has nursed Edward as if he were her very own. He has thrived on it. He smiles and coos and holds up his silky black head and wrinkles up his big nose and looks around at the world with bird-bright eyes like Button's.

It is my birthday. There is a lot of going-on inside the house. The Lynah girls are making a surprise for me. Beau is on the way here from Pocotaligo for the occasion, bringing General Wade Hampton, who has come from Virginia to fight in his home state now that General William Tecumseh Sherman has left Atlanta and started marching through Georgia to burn South Carolina. Button is sitting in a rocking chair beside me, his purring mother-cat stretched across his legs.

Lazily I make a great effort and say, "I remember your bringing your cat and your chicken eggs from Cotton Hall but where is *le petit géant?*"

Stifling a yawn Button says, "Hasn't Bubba told you that a lot of Confederates are going to Brazil if the Yankees win the war? Israel made me bring the sack of cotton seed Liney hid in your closet instead of the grandfather in the gold coat. Israel said those fine seeds would start us getting so rich after the war that

369

I can have my picture painted in a whole gold suit. Little Edward won't ever know the difference."

"Um!"

"There are millions of little yellow butterflies in Brazil. We can pretend some of them flew ahead of us from the island to make us feel at home there for the rest of our lives."

"Oh!"

"Angelica! You aren't listening and your eyes are looking away—way off. Why?"

Ah, dear Button, because I hear only the thunder of hoofs and see nothing but the sun-god color of Beau's flying hair as he comes galloping across the fields to me on the blue-eyed silver horse.

ABOUT THE AUTHOR

ELIZABETH BOATWRIGHT COKER was born in Darlington, South Carolina. Her marriage to James Coker in 1930 joined two of the oldest and most aristocratic families in the South. Mrs. Coker is the author of seven bestselling novels, including *Daughter of Strangers, India Allan, La Belle* and her most recent, *Blood Red Roses,* which are all set in the South of the Civil War. Her books were book club selections and have been translated into half a dozen foreign languages. She now lives in Hartsville, South Carolina, the seat of Coker College, established by her husband's grandfather.

Turn the page for an exciting
Special Preview of another book.

A Special Preview of
the opening pages of another sweeping novel
of the South by the author of
BLOOD RED ROSES

LA BELLE

by
Elizabeth Boatwright Coker

A ravishing beauty is torn
by divided loyalties and
consumed by passion as
the South plunges into war.

PART ONE

Newberry, South Carolina

1846-1849

The mother of the too famous beauty, Boozer, . . .
has been married three times, and yet by all showing
she did not begin to marry soon enough. Witness the
existence of Boozer.

Mary Boykin Chestnut,
A Diary from Dixie

1

As the clock struck half past eight, Mr. David Boozer of Newberry, visiting lecturer in practical medicine at the South Carolina
College, had abruptly concluded a discourse on the most
efficient manner to deliver a difficult calf from a pure bred
heifer as opposed to delivering a difficult calf from a heifer of
the common herd. The young gentlemen had just clattered
away, when two youths from Newberry, students at the college, burst into the classroom.

"Thank the Lord, Mr. Big Dave," they gasped, "you're here!"

"What the devil," Big Dave sputtered, "are you young
scoundrels up to?"

"There's a girl barely sixteen years old having a baby in our boardinghouse and we can't find a doctor anywhere. Come quickly."

"Not on your life. I dismissed my class so I could go and hear Governor Johnson bid farewell to the Palmetto Legion before they take off for Mexico. Wish I was young enough to go along. Yes, just wish I was."

One of the students grabbed him by the shoulder. "Oh do! Mr. Dave, hurry for the Lord's sake, hurry. The old people who own our boardinghouse have gone to Charleston for a visit. We're all by ourselves. Just us boys and her—"

"Can't you leave me alone?" Big Dave shouted testily.

"Her—hollering like a sick cow—ooooh—aaaah—ooow!"

"She's got shiny black hair and bright black eyes and a mouth shaped like a heart and the whitest, creamiest skin you ever saw."

"She swears the baby is coming two months early."

"She's a widow woman and poor as a church mouse but mighty pretty and young and going ooooh—aaaah—"

"Oh, rest your rattling." Big Dave jammed his bell-crowned beaver hat uncomfortably upon his enormous Swiss head and turned his back on the excited boys, but he knew where he was headed. "Well, now why don't the boardinghouse lady just send for a midwife? Whole thing sounds sordid and none of my affair." He opened a bag on the desk in front of him and checked the contents, then, his old fashioned claw-hammer tailed coat flying out behind, rushed into the hallway, the boys following.

Sancho Cooper, the African infidel, who waited on the boys at the college was ready with Big Dave's buggy when he came running down the stairs into the bitter night.

"My Lord," Big Dave shouted, looking down at the boys, "you thought I was a soft-hearted old fool and would swallow your mad tale! But I have no intention of missing Governor Johnson's speech. Pierce Butler is from near Newberry and my good friend. I couldn't miss it." He picked up the reins then called back to the boys, "You say the girl is all alone and already at the screaming stage?"

The clock in the Town Hall was striking four. Weary and The horse galloped all the way to the boardinghouse.

elated, Big Dave sat in front of the wide kitchen fireplace staring down at the miracle of flesh he held in his hands. She was pink and perfect and, rather than premature, had probably been cradled an extra month in her mother's womb. Would she be brunette or blonde? The tuft of hair that showed was bold. The eyes were shut but the very long thick eyelashes were light. No, she would not be dark like her mother. A pretty nose—not the usual baby button. He leaned over and kissed it lightly. And the mouth was exquisite. As if she realized Big Dave's adoration, the infant yawned and stretched herself and her dainty toes pushed strongly against Big Dave's thick tender fingers.

"You ack like you witched, Mister Big Dave," the Negro midwife spoke from the head of the narrow cot where she was sponging Amelia's face with a rag wrung out in half-wine half-water.

"No, not that," he said softly.

"You sho' pult that young'un out quick at the last. Wonder this'un's still here but blue as she turnt, her pulsk is hitting back sho' as shooting."

"Foot-first delivery is usually fatal to one or the other," Big Dave said, wrapping a shawl around the enchanting little creature's girl-nakedness. He rose from the stool and, holding the infant close against his rumpled shirt front, went over and looked closely at Amelia.

"Did you have to be so brutal?" she asked hoarsely.

"To save the baby, yes. Would you like a little laudanum?"

Amelia gulped down the potion the midwife fixed and turned her face away from Big Dave. "You might have killed me," she said hatefully.

"Is there anyone you would like me to notify?"

"There is no one."

"Who is going to take care of you? The midwife will leave as soon as she gets you cleaned up unless you can pay her to stay."

"There is no one," Amelia repeated, closing her eyes, "no one."

"Can you look after yourself and this child?"

Amelia's black eyes slithered open and, with a shock, comprehended the sincere pity that Big Dave betrayed with all his being. "I don't know, sir," she whispered weakly, schemingly.

"You're nothing but a child yourself," he said tenderly.

Amelia managed to agree with a pathetic sort of sob.

The midwife made a sound halfway between a snort and a giggle.

Big Dave held the baby girl closer. "Would you like to come home with me to Newberry?" he cried from the depths of his kindly heart.

The laudanum was easing Amelia. Home! How long since the word had had any meaning. Why, home meant a wide feather bed, servants, petticoats that rustled, wine with your dinner, polished card tables, fiddles and flutes and dances with tall, thin, fine-faced soldiers!

"Is he rich?" she whispered to the Negro woman.

The midwife leaned over Amelia and this time she giggled lewdly, "Big old farm, big old house, lotsa big old country niggers, all the big old widderwomen in the Up-country trying to ketch um. Looks lak you gonna land on yo' foots too, gal. Same like that pretty little baby there did. You better grab Mr. Dave quick cause you is mighty tore up inside; you go have trouble when you gits older."

"How will we get to your home?" Amelia was truly drowsy now. She held out her thin arms and Big Dave handed her the baby, grinning fatuously as a new father. "I have no money."

"I'll drive you and the baby there in a coach piled with feather cushions as soon as you are able."

Amelia whimpered a little, nodding. The child felt good against her swelling breast. A good child. A good omen. She would keep the child fast and never let her get away. Already the child had proved she was an extraordinary female.

"Mary. I'll name you Mary," she whispered to the goldy head, "and if you *are* as beautiful as that foolish old man declares, our fortune is made!"

And the infant opened her rosy mouth and began to cry lustily and hungrily.

She shall from henceforth be known and recognized
by the name Mary Sarah Amelia Boozer. . . .
Chancellor Job Johnstone,
November 21, 1848

2

Big Dave was not rich but he was moderately wealthy. He
owned Birdfield's Hotel in Newberry, several lots in the town,
hundreds of acres of cotton, tobacco, corn and pinelands and
plenty of Negroes to work his fields. His plantation dwelling was
similar to an English basement house.

The first story was of brick finished with stucco and the two
upper stories and attic were of clapboards. The interior woodwork, rather finely carved, had been done by a Mr. Schoppert
of Newberry. Big Dave's slaves had made the brick, and all
the lumber for the house had been cut from his acres. The
lime for mortaring and plastering had been imported and
brought from Charleston in wagons. There wasn't much of a
flower garden, since no woman had lived at Aveliegh in so
long, but there was a handsome English sundial between the
house and the long brick kitchen.

Big Dave was a godly, churchgoing man who never drank,
danced, or gambled at cards. He was a well-known figure
throughout the Upcountry with no reputation for wenching,
though a widower for many years. He went about dressed in
plain, sober clothes; his beard was usually cut in time; and
in the country he wore a broad-brimmed Panama hat
pulled square on his coarse white hair. He had, in 1827, married
Elizabeth Wallace, of the district, and sired two sons, but they
were all dead now and when he wed the Yankee woman and
brought her and her baby into his home there was a small war
of tattling tongues.

Big Dave doted on the child who insisted on calling herself,
not Mary, but Marie. As she emerged from babyhood with
laughing eyes, red cheeks and dancing feet, he spoiled her

outrageously. He bought her china dolls, stuffed her with sweets, threw her in the air till she shrieked with joy, and showed off her accomplishments to every visitor.

Marie loved to follow the shadow around the sundial and Big Dave would say her hair was the true sun and that big yellow ball up in the sky just an imitation of it.

Newberry often heard more of the battles between the parents over the rearing of Marie than it did of the glorious exploits of their own sons fighting a war with Mexico. When the beautiful Pierce Butler was killed, leading the Palmetto Regiment at Churubusco, and his flag-draped body came home to Edgefield, it was of secondary importance to the fact that Mary A. P. Burton had petitioned her "next friend, David Boozer, she being an infant, born in Columbia, and since the intermarriage of her mother and the said friend it is now desirable to both the petitioner's mother and her stepfather that her present name Mary Adele Peter Burton should be altered to that of Mary Sarah Amelia Boozer—".

As soon as the adoption was made legal, Amelia constantly nagged Big Dave about bringing his will up to date. So in March 1849 Big Dave had his friend, Judge Belton O'Neall, draw up a completely new will:

THE STATE OF SOUTH CAROLINA,
Newberry District.

I, David Boozer, make the following disposition of my estate to take effect at my death as my last will and testament.

First. I direct all my just debts to be paid. . . .

Second. I desire my Executors to enclose a graveyard at Aveliegh Church from 45 to 50 yards square with a wall of split rock from $4\frac{1}{2}$ to 5 feet high, so as to include the grave of my first wife as well as my own with sufficient space also for the grave of my present wife; and to erect over the area included by the wall a covered wooden building of the most lasting material, to be finished and painted in appropriate style and in the most endurable manner. And I appropriate $1000 out of my estate to these purposes.

Third. . . . My wife Amelia is to have during her life the free use and the right to dispose of the clear profits of the estate, charged with the maintenance and education of her daughter, Mary S. A. Boozer (formerly called Mary Burton). . . .

Fourth. I authorize my Executors to sell. . . .

Fifth. When the said Mary S. A. Boozer shall come of age or marry, my Executors will give off to her to be settled to her sole and separate use my negro man Stobo and his wife Hannah. . . .

Sixth. After the death of my wife I give my whole estate to the said Mary S. A. Boozer to be settled to her sole and separate use not subject to the control nor liable for the debts of any husband she may ever have.

Seventh. If I should have any child or children born after the making of this will I wish such child and each one of such children to have equal enjoyment and benefit from and share of my estate with the said Mary S. A. . . .

Eighth. If the said Mary S. A. should die leaving no issue then living all the property given to her by this will shall return to my estate and go to my next of kin . . .

Ninth. I appoint my friends the Hon. John Belton O'Neall and George Gallman executors of this my last will and testament.

In witness whereof I have hereunto set my hand and seal this 23rd day of March 1849.

/s/ David Boozer (Seal)

Signed and published by the said David Boozer as and for his last Will and testament in the presence of us who have at his request and in his presence subscribed our names as witnesses thereto also in the presence of each other.

/s/ John S. Carwile
/s/ John B. Carwile
/s/ Thomas H. Pope

As time passed, Amelia and Big Dave quarreled; Marie and Big Dave never. In the three years they were together, Marie and Big Dave never said any but loving words. Amelia went often into the town. The family were seldom together, except at teatime. While they ate a hearty meal, Amelia shuffled and clicked a deck of cards. If the child or Big Dave tried to talk to her, Amelia would put a red queen on a black king and say, "How stupid you two are. Hush, can't you, I've wagered something special on this game of solitaire."

Marie didn't understand until many years later that Amelia was staking this or that decision on whether *she* or the cards won the game!

One afternoon in May, 1849, Amelia took Marie into town in the carriage, black Stobo driving. Amelia ordered Stobo to stop at Birdfield's Hotel "just a minute to get the child some candy." They went into the parlor where three men in tall beaver hats and long, tight, fawn-colored pants and black frock coats were sitting at a round table. They called Marie "Sugar" and smelled of the wine Amelia so often drank at teatime.

Marie smiled at the men, especially a tall one Amelia called "Hugh Huger." He had wonderful sensitive hands and Marie liked the way they felt on her hair. He said to Amelia, "What a pretty child. What a dear, darling, little thing."

"You Santa Claus?" Marie asked pleasantly.

"No. I am a doctor."

"I don't wike doctors. I go find Stobo now."

Amelia leaned down and pinched Marie's cheek. She said in an excited way, "You'll like this one, Mistress Mary, this is my very best friend, Dr. Hugh Huger Toland. I bet his pocket is full of sugar plums."

Dr. Toland bowed gravely and Marie allowed him to pick her up and sit her on his knee.

There was always lots of money on the table and after each card game Amelia would laugh and pick up the money and stuff it into her reticule.

After a while, Marie heard Big Dave calling out her name.

"I is here, Big Dave," she shouted, "come see me quick. I is ate a whole cone full of candy."

He ran in followed by Stobo and the minister of the Aveliegh Presbyterian Church. Big Dave snatched Marie off Dr. Toland's lap and hugged her tight, and Amelia screamed, "How dare you follow me?" to Big Dave, and "You damned nigger!" to Stobo, and terrible mean things to the preacher. And the preacher who was very young and horrified said, "Woman, I'll put you out of the church."

Amelia laughed and ran her eyes all over the young preacher's body and flicked her cigar ash onto the preacher's tie and he wiped it off as if it were pure fire and then Big Dave said apologetically to the preacher, "Mrs. Boozer is just a child herself. Don't put her out of the church."

Amelia was wearing a necklace of silver ornaments set in black marble, wrought by the Indians. Big Dave had turned it up in a ploughed field one day. The heavy necklace rattled as her shoulders shook with her vehement laughing. Big Dave handed Marie to Stobo and took Amelia by the arm and jerked her up from the chair. Two of the card players had disappeared. Dr. Toland said, "I would like to explain this to you, Mr. Boozer."

Big Dave said, "We've nothing to say to each other. Stop laughing, Mrs. Boozer."

Amelia said, "How sick I am of you! I can't bear the sight of you."

The preacher said to Big Dave, "Do you want me to go home with you, Mr. Boozer?"

"No. I can manage my wife," Big Dave said sadly.

"Well, I'll come to the farm tomorrow. And let me tell you I am mighty surprised to have found you in such company, Dr. Toland. Mighty surprised."

From that day dark tales sifted from the Boozer farm into the town. The Dutch Fork people were superstitious folk and firmly believed in witches. They were positive that evil forces were at work to destroy the lovable, foolish man. It was told and retold, first by Stobo and black Hannah, then by the country people and the townfolk, that one June afternoon Amelia was sitting at a table playing solitaire on the piazza and all the while nagging at Big Dave about moving into the town. Marie was playing hopscotch at the foot of the steps and Big Dave heavy as an ox was hopping with her.

"Not ever into the town," he bellowed up to Amelia, "not ever—ever—ever! Not even *if* Hell freezes over."

Marie laughed at Big Dave's clumsy feet mashing down a clump of toadstools. Amelia slapped down a deuce of clubs, saying contemptuously,"Oh, fiddle foot!" and flashed her black eyes toward a beautiful stand of piney woods.

That night a raging fire consumed every one of the virgin monarchs.

On a morning in late summer Amelia was buying a jug of corn whiskey from one of the covered wagons that came down regularly from North Carolina peddling the stuff through the upper part of South Carolina. Big Dave was leading Marie on his big horse up and down in front of the coach house and he called to the wagoner to get the devil off his farm and never come back or he'd give him a hiding with his buggy whip.

Amelia coolly counted out the money from her reticule, told the North Carolinian to be sure and come by next time, picked out a jug and, shrugging her pretty shoulders, walked back to the house by way of a large field, golden green with sweet, ripe tobacco. A hawk swooped wide and Amelia watched it until it disappeared. Even after it was lost in the horizon she stood there in the hot sun staring away at nothing over and beyond the fragrant plants.

During the night, worms stripped every valuable leaf off the tall green stalks.

This was told too and people came to see, and it was a true thing that had happened.

Then in the autumn, on a windy afternoon, Amelia drove herself in the one-seated buggy to a tavern in the town. She was brazenly wearing a red dress cut so low over the bosom that wagers were made in the courthouse as to whether a man could see the whole business while standing on the street or whether he had to be passing her on horseback and looking down.

The next Sunday the preacher turned Amelia publicly out of the Aveliegh Presbyterian Church for wearing unseemly clothes on the street and for gambling at cards with strangers in a tavern.

Big Dave began to waste away. His thick white hair thinned and his round blue eyes seemed covered with a film.

In November, Stobo drove Amelia in the carriage to Columbia to sell Big Dave's cotton. Big Dave wasn't feeling well enough to go himself.

Instead of finishing the business in a few days Amelia was gone two whole weeks and during that time drove all the way to Charleston. It also happened that Dr. Hugh Huger Toland was doing some special surgery in Charleston that November. But Big Dave never knew about that. Unless Stobo told him, which was not likely. However, he suspected something for Amelia returned with a whole trunkful of beautiful new frocks and bonnets.

"Where did you get the money to buy those clothes?" Big Dave asked her when she came out on a Sunday to go to town in an expensive white silk and lace dress ornamented with solid gold buttons and a white silk and lace bonnet.

"From the cotton money."

"Thats' a lie. The factor has sent me every penny of the cotton money. You are carrying on with Dr. Toland. I've heard things. I won't have my name or this child's name soiled by you."

In December, on Marie's third birthday, Stobo drove him and the child to town to the bank. Marie stayed in the carriage while Big Dave went in the bank and transferred his whole cash account of $25,000 into Marie's name. Then he went to confer with Judge O'Neall in his law office. Marie remembered a little about this later, but only that the leather on the chair scratched her leg and that the Judge's whiskers tickled when he kissed her cheek. She didn't remember Judge O'Neall urging Big Dave, for his personal safety, to rewrite his will. Nor did she remember Big Dave saying, well, yes, but he'd try and reason once more with Amelia.

Amelia was not yet twenty, Big Dave said wearily, maybe later she would behave more decorously. Maybe being a Philadelphian, she was just bored with Southern country life; maybe he should try living in the town; maybe that would satisfy her. The child was such a gay sunny little thing that he spent his entire time playing with her. Maybe he should take Amelia to some parties where she could play at dropping the glove, or grinding the bottle, or brother I am bob'd, or throwing long bullets. Maybe if he took her to watch some wrestling or jumping or running races or let her shoot for a hanging beef on Saturdays she would mend her wild ways. When she chose she was a mighty attractive female, but that was seldom. And he hoped there was nothing too serious between her and Hugh

Toland. Hugh's wife was just sickly—that was why he enjoyed being with a woman so strong as Amelia.

Judge O'Neall listened to Big Dave and then he put his hand on his friend's shoulder and said, gravely, "Don't fool yourself, David."

"Why not, Judge?"

"There are too many 'maybes' and, actually, not a soul in Newberry would play at games with Amelia. Those who aren't convinced she's having an affair with Hugh Toland are convinced she is a witch. Come on now, let's rewrite your will. If Amelia knew you'd not hesitate to turn her out penniless and she had no hold on your property, she'd change her ways. She's a handsome woman, I'll grant you, but there's nothing kind about her. Try being cruel and you'll see her come to hand mighty quick. I have an idea that being poor is all in this world Amelia Boozer is afraid of; that money is the one thing she craves or respects."

"I know you're right, Judge, and I'll surely come back in tomorrow and tend to it. But Mary can't sit still any longer now can you, sugar-pie? Say good-by to Judge O'Neall, Mary Sarah."

Having been born with a flair for charming the men, Marie ran and held her face up for the Judge to tie her bonnet ribbons. Big Dave had sent to New Orleans for the lace bonnet that set off her face like a halo. "Why this child has sky-colored eyes! Real spirit-eyes!" Judge O'Neall made a one-sided bow. "I've never been flattered with such a come-hither look in one so young."

"Where have you been?" Amelia asked Marie when they returned.

"Out," Marie answered, starting to greet fat, shaky, jovial black Hannah and give her a paper cone of peppermints she'd fetched her from the town.

"Who did you see in the town?" Amelia knelt down and her sharp eyes bored into Marie's soft ones.

"Nobody."

"Yes—you *did*, you naughty girl. Tell me or I'll shake it out of you."

"Man. Man wikes Big Dave. Man hates you and I hate you."

Marie ran away to Hannah who petted her and began greedily sucking a peppermint.

Amelia went onto the piazza. Stobo was passing the steps. Stobo was a smallish, glossy Negro with sharp Jewish features and straight black hair. Big Dave had sent him to the Low-country to one of the big plantations when he was a boy to be trained as a coachman and butler. Consequently, Stobo felt and acted superior to all the other Negroes and most of the white people here in the Upcountry. He was a very lone-some man.

"Where is Mr. Dave?" Amelia asked.

"Out in the coach house, mending the door handle."

"Where'd you all go in the town?"

"See the judge."

"Oh—Judge O'Neall?"

"That's the one."

Stobo watched Amelia run, lithe and swift, to the coach house and go in and close the door. He heard her talking, loud and ugly. He heard Big Dave curse her. Then he walked away. Such things were not unusual here on this plantation. Mr. Dave should have married better. Someone from the Low-country where his mother had been raised. This was one mean Yankee woman.

Stobo was grooming the horses, the cook was chopping kindling wood, Hannah and Marie were upstairs, the field hands were ploughing under cotton stalks and singing very loud, when the shotgun went off. For a while they all got quiet and listened, then, hearing nothing further, went on about their ways.

Pretty soon two of Big Dave's nephews came by to see their uncle about some hound dog puppies. Amelia called to them from over by the well to take her into town if they were going that way. She put on a green shawl and a green bonnet and drove off with them in their carriage laughing and talking.

At the dusking Amelia returned, called to Stobo who was setting the supper table, told him to put on two extra plates for the boys and asked had his master come in and if not when had he last been seen?

"You the last one seen him in the coach house," Stobo said insolently. Then his shiny brown face turned ashy gray, his hooked nose flattened and his dry thin hands grew cold and moist as Amelia fixed her eyes on his, paralyzing his will, shattering his nerve, draining his blood, softening his bones.

"I did *not* see him in the coach house. You go this minute and find out if he's still there. The boys want to talk to him."

Big Dave was still there. The upper half of his head had been blown off and a double-barreled shotgun was clutched in his stiffening hands.

At the funeral the relatives and the friends of the much loved David Boozer drew away from the widow brazenly wearing the white silk and fancy lace dress with the gold buttons, as if by the merest contact with her they would wither away as the sensitive briar will do when a hand touches it. For Big Dave couldn't have shot himself with that double-barreled gun he was holding when Stobo found him. His arms weren't long enough.

Amelia could not be shaken from her story that she'd been to the town that afternoon and never been near the coach house so there was no inquest. But there was a church trial in the Aveliegh Presbyterian Church in Newberry immediately after the funeral and Amelia was accused by the minister of murdering her husband. But due to the testimony of the two young nephews who had driven Amelia to town that afternoon; and to the fact that Dr. Hugh Huger Toland came from Columbia and defended her, saying he had been playing cards with her in the hotel during the time Big Dave must have shot himself, she was cleared of the murder. And Stobo never opened up his lips to say one word against him.

At Amelia's request, the executor sold Birdfield's Hotel in the town for a nice sum. Then, taking her daughter, the Boozer carriage and the two slaves who belonged to Marie, Hannah, the nurse, and Stobo, the coachman, Amelia moved away from the open hate and hostility of the people of Newberry, back to Columbia where Judge O'Neall, for the child's sake, used his influence and enabled Amelia to engage rooms in a good boardinghouse.

In the meantime public opinion in Columbia became so bitter against Dr. Toland that he packed up his sad, but forgiving, young family and moved West to San Francisco where he was appointed chief surgeon at the Marine Hospital and where he spent the remainder of his useful, famous life.

As for Amelia, in 1853 she met Jacob Feaster of Fairfield, a healthy, young gentleman of property and fine family, who had a room in the exclusive establishment. Jacob had heard the gossip about Amelia and Hugh Toland, but her black eyes captivated him and he began to ask her to go driving with him in the evenings. Suddenly one warm evening he proposed to her. He worried all night and then decided he was up to his ears in love with her. And they were married at once. . .

Follow the fortunes of Amelia and her beautiful but spoiled daughter, Marie, who grows up to become the scandal of Charleston, South Carolina.

Read the complete Bantam Book, now available wherever paperbacks are sold.

RELAX!
SIT DOWN
and Catch Up On Your Reading!

☐	10077	**TRINITY** by Leon Uris	$2.75
☐	2300	**THE MONEYCHANGERS** by Arthur Hailey	$1.95
☐	11266	**THE MEDITERRANEAN CAPER** by Clive Cussler	$1.95
☐	2500	**THE EAGLE HAS LANDED** by Jack Higgins	$1.95
☐	2600	**RAGTIME** by E. L. Doctorow	$2.25
☐	10360	**CONFLICT OF INTEREST** by Les Whitten	$1.95
☐	10888	**RAISE THE TITANIC!** by Clive Cussler	$2.25
☐	11966	**THE ODESSA FILE** by Frederick Forsyth	$2.25
☐	11770	**ONCE IS NOT ENOUGH** by Jacqueline Susann	$2.25
☐	11708	**JAWS 2** by Hank Searls	$2.25
☐	8844	**TINKER, TAILOR, SOLDIER, SPY** by John Le Carre	$1.95
☐	11929	**THE DOGS OF WAR** by Frederick Forsyth	$2.25
☐	10090	**THE R DOCUMENT** by Irving Wallace	$2.25
☐	10526	**INDIA ALLEN** by Elizabeth B. Coker	$1.95
☐	10357	**THE HARRAD EXPERIMENT** by Robert Rimmer	$1.95
☐	10422	**THE DEEP** by Peter Benchley	$2.25
☐	10500	**DOLORES** by Jacqueline Susann	$1.95
☐	11601	**THE LOVE MACHINE** by Jacqueline Susann	$2.25
☐	10600	**BURR** by Gore Vidal	$2.25
☐	10857	**THE DAY OF THE JACKAL** by Frederick Forsyth	$1.95
☐	11952	**DRAGONARD** by Rupert Gilchrist	$1.95
☐	2491	**ASPEN** by Burt Hirschfeld	$1.95
☐	11330	**THE BEGGARS ARE COMING** by Mary Loos	$1.95

Bantam Book Catalog

Here's your up-to-the-minute listing of every book currently available from Bantam.

This easy-to-use catalog is divided into categories and contains over 1400 titles by your favorite authors.

So don't delay—take advantage of this special opportunity to increase your reading pleasure.

Just send us your name and address and 25¢ (to help defray postage and handling costs).